ALSO BY KAITLYN DAVIS

A Dance of Dragons

The Shadow Soul ~ The Spirit Heir ~ The Phoenix Born

Leena's Story (The Novellas)

~

Once Upon a Curse

Gathering Frost ~ Withering Rose ~ Chasing Midnight

Parting Worlds ~ Granting Wishes

~

Midnight Fire

Ignite ~ Simmer ~ Blaze ~ Scorch ~ Burn

~

Midnight Ice

Frost ~ Freeze ~ Fracture ~ Shatter

THE

RAVE

AND THE

DOV

The
Raven
And The
Dove

KAITLYN DAVIS

THE
RAVEN
AND THE
DOVE

THE
RAVEN
AND THE
DOVE

KAITLYN DAVIS

To my family for their unconditional love,
my friends for their overwhelming support,
and my fans for their incredible enthusiasm.
Thank you from the bottom of my heart.

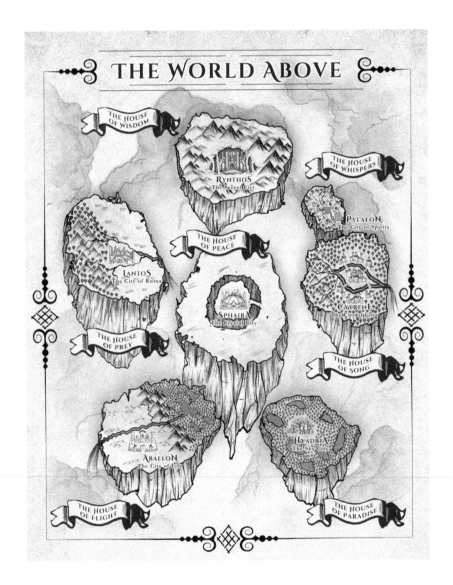

THE WORLD ABOVE

THE HOUSE OF WISDOM

THE HOUSE OF WHISPERS

RYNTHOS
The Secret City

PYLAEON
The City of Spirits

THE HOUSE OF PEACE

LANTOS
The City of Ruins

SPHAIRA
The Crystal City

CYRENE
The City of Love

THE HOUSE OF PREY

THE HOUSE OF SONG

ABAELON
The City of Life

HYADRIA
The Sky City

THE HOUSE OF FLIGHT

THE HOUSE OF PARADISE

THE
RAVEN
AND THE
DOVE

PROLOGUE

The king had never known the warm kiss of the sun. Still, he stood at the edge of his ship, forearms resting on the damp wooden rail, face lifted toward the sky. Those golden rays were the stuff of songs.

His world was gray—the vapors swirling off the dark surface of the sea, the mist against his cheeks, the endless fog. True, he often found himself searching the gloomy expanse for one small crack, one tear in the cloudy folds, one glimpse of the sky. But it wasn't in search of the sun.

It was in search of salvation.

In search of her.

The stomping of boots pulled him from his reverie. The king spun. His first mate crested the steps to the quarterdeck and dipped his head in greeting. With a sigh, the king stepped away from the rail, away from his thoughts, and opened his mouth—

An invisible pulse of energy whipped through the air. The blast struck the king in the chest, and he stumbled back, slamming into the rail. Sparks of silver and gold danced across his vision.

He blinked, and blinked again, trying to clear his sight, trying not to hope, but the dazzling gleam wouldn't fade. Across the effervescence, his first mate's eyes were wide with disbelief.

"My Liege—"

"Silence," the king ordered as he turned and studied the fog. Spirit magic simmered in the air, flecks of stardust and sunlight, glimmering majestically against the impenetrable haze. The king lifted his palm and released his *aethi'kine* power, shooting a golden arc over the sea. His magic merged with the aura descending from the sky, one and the same.

"She's here," he whispered, the softest confession.

Across the deck, his first mate gasped.

"She's here!" the king shouted, as though the authority in his tone could invest the words with undeniable truth, since he believed in them with all his soul. He'd only ever felt power like this once before in his life—on the day the prince was born. And he'd been anchored in these deep waters ever since, in this very spot, waiting to feel that pulse of magic again. "Wake everyone! Prepare the ship for battle. The day has come!"

His first mate sprinted away without another word. The king kept his eyes on the surface of the water, waiting for the inevitable.

Waiting.

Waiting.

Waiting.

Not three minutes later, he saw the telltale glow in the dark. The ocean began to bubble and steam. Black-as-night liquid turned midnight blue, then warm aqua, then fiery orange, as though the world had flipped and the sun was no longer hiding behind a layer of fog, but was somewhere deep beneath the sea, surging toward the surface.

And then the beast emerged.

Its long screech was loud enough to make the king step back. The dragon pumped its wings, once, twice, roaring into the sky. Droplets of boiling water fell like rain. The king closed his eyes against the burn, waiting for the wave of steam to dissipate, and reached blindly with his magic. The dragon's spirit was an inferno, too searing to grip, too potent to control, and even with all his power unleashed, the king wouldn't be able to hold on for very long. Still, he sent the command through the golden energy pulsing from his palm.

Stay.

Do not move.

Do not fly.

Stay.

"Bring it down!" he screamed for all his soldiers to hear and opened his eyes. The dragon hovered in the fog, but the king's magic was losing strength, losing vigor. The beast was the biggest he'd ever seen, ever battled. Already, his insides burned as the dragon fought back, a silent war, shooting fire and fury through the spirit connection the king had no choice but to maintain. "Bring it down!"

Magic flared in the air around him.

Blue sparks dipped beneath the sea and swirling water rose, splashing against the beast, dousing its flames. But the fire returned in moments, churning from a volcanic core no *hydro'kine* power could touch.

Yellow streaks cut across the sky, twisting into a windy vortex, *aero'kine* magic. The dragon was pulled into the storm, confused and swept away, wings flapping against the invisible currents, unable to fly free.

Dark swirls ensnared the beast's head, the work of his shadow mage. Blinding ivory beams burrowed through thick scales, pure burning energy from his light mage. As the king dropped to his knees, the scorching beneath his skin too much to handle, a metal arrow pierced the dragon's heart, leaving a trail of deep emerald *ferro'kine* magic in its wake.

The beast wailed.

But still it fought, wings pumping, spirit fuming. Boils erupted on the king's arm. His breath came fast. His pulse pounded faster. He blinked the spots from his vision, pushed the pain from his mind, and held on with all his power.

"Bring it down!"

Another metal arrow sliced through the fog and landed true.

Then another.

And another.

Until finally, the dragon dropped and crashed into the water, suspended for a moment on the surface with its wings spread as steam erupted from every fiery scale that kissed the sea. Tail first, it sank, disappearing within the dark, liquid folds.

The king landed with a *thud* against the deck of his ship. Shadows hovered at the edge of consciousness, closing in. Hands gripped his shoulders. Muddled voices whispered. Reality slipped further and further away, but he couldn't go. Not yet. Not until...

"Bring me the boy," he rasped to whoever was listening.

Something cold was pressed to his forehead.

Something hot burned his chest.

Energy exploded beneath his skin, both foreign and familiar, popping and sizzling and crackling—frantically wielded, he knew, by the young prince who now said, "Stay with me."

The boy's voice was one breath from a cry.

Stay with me, the magic whispered, not letting the king sink away, not letting him die, not yet. Youth and vigor and life flooded his veins, a river of gold, a rush of pure potent might.

The king blinked, opened his eyes, and found the deep blue gaze of his son—not by blood, but by something more important. Magic. Fate. Destiny.

"Your queen is here," he murmured through wheezing breaths. The prince shook his head as though he didn't care. The king snatched the boy's cheeks and held them tightly, using the last of his remaining energy to force the prince to listen, to hear, to understand. "You must find her, Malek, whatever it takes. You must always remember who you are, who she is, and what the two of you mean. No matter how hard it is, you must find her."

"I will," the prince promised. "I will."

It was all the king needed to hear.

He closed his eyes.

He let death take him.

And in that split second before thought faded completely, he wondered if maybe, after all these years, his spirit would finally see the sky. The sun. The stars. The moon. Yes. But most of all, the isles floating high above the fog, the winged people who lived there, and the queen of prophecy, who together with his son, would one day save them all.

18 YEARS LATER…

1

LYANA

"I feel you hovering."

"I'm not—" Lyana stopped and rolled her eyes as she stared down at her best friend, releasing a heavy sigh. Because, of course, she was hovering. Standing at the end of Cassi's bed, bouncing from one foot to another, biting her lip, staring—all right, hovering. Although, technically...

Lyana snapped her wings, freeing them from their snug position against her back, and stretched them to their full ivory glory. She pumped them once, twice, three times to float above the bed. "Now I'm hovering."

Cassi rolled dramatically onto her back, a black-and-white speckled wing falling over the edge of her bed as she moved, and offered Lyana a sleepy, though still effective, glare. "What could you possibly want so early in the morning?"

Lyana shifted her head to the left, staring through the crystal wall of the palace at a sky tinged lavender by the rising dawn, then turned back to her friend. "Come on," she grumbled. "Don't tell me you forgot what day it is."

"How could I possibly forget when it's all I've been hearing about for weeks?" Cassi paused for effect. "But waking me up with the sun won't make the day come any faster."

At that, Lyana put her hands on her hips, unperturbed, and smiled—a wicked sort of smile her best friend undoubtedly recognized. "It will if we sneak out to the sky bridge."

Cassi blinked twice, expression not changing. "Are you serious?"

"Am I ever not serious?" Lyana asked innocently. Cassi opened her mouth to respond but was cut off. "On second thought, don't answer that. I mean it. I can't sit here and twiddle my thumbs all day while the other houses make their way to the palace. I'll go crazy. Crazier. And you have to come with me. You have to. Even if just to keep me out of trouble... Well, more trouble."

Shaking her head, Cassi winced. "I should have seen this coming."

Lyana nodded. "Yes, you should have."

"Ana..." her friend whined.

But the use of her nickname would not change Lyana's mind, not today of all days. "Just get up, all right? I brought our furs and our hunting gear. Nothing will happen. But Elias is only on his shift for another thirty minutes, so we have to go now, or we'll miss our chance."

"Elias? Really?" Cassi snorted, shaking her head. But she

eased to a seated position and flexed her wings, awakening her tired muscles.

"He's my friend," Lyana said with a shrug, tossing the extra furs onto the mattress before slipping her own around her wing joints and tying the openings at her shoulders.

"He doesn't know how to say no to his princess is more like it," Cassi huffed, but grabbed the clothes and started changing.

Lyana watched her, smirking. "Few people do."

Cassi snorted again as she pulled on her pants and laced her boots. "Let's go before I change my mind. I'm already beginning to overheat in all these layers."

Not needing to hear any more, Lyana turned and marched toward the door, the bottom tips of her wings barely grazing the floor. The air in the palace was always warm and slightly humid, but in clothes meant for the frigid tundra outside, she found the temperature oppressive, heavy in a way that made her feathers itch. She slid one of the double doors open an inch, peeking through the crack toward the curving hall outside and the atrium beyond. The palace was a tall, ovular dome, with the rooms corkscrewing up along the outer perimeter, leaving a hollow central core for easy flight. The exterior walls were made from translucent crystal stones, allowing the sun to shine through and trapping the heat inside. But in order to maintain a proper seal, there were only two ways in and out of her home—and both were located at the very bottom of the structure. In a few hours, the palace core would be bustling with movement. Right now it was, for the most part, empty.

Perfect, Lyana thought, biting back a grin.

Turning, she found Cassi over her shoulder, eerily silent as usual even in movement, and whispered, "Let's go."

Her friend nodded, somewhat reluctantly. It was still a nod.

Lyana pulled the door fully open and sprinted into the hallway, then dove over the railing and tossed her wings wide in one quick motion. The air whistled as it whooshed through her feathers, her dove wings not nearly as stealthy as the owl wings following behind her, but still doing the trick. The breeze created by her body whipped her clothes as she plummeted to the floor. Luckily, she had bundled her tightly braided hair into a knot atop her head earlier that morning, so it was no bother. In fact, there was nothing she loved more than the stinging kiss of the wind against her cheeks.

Cassi flew past her as easily as she always did.

Lyana tried to hold back a frown when her friend threw a goading look over her shoulder, but failed. Cassi's owl wings were predatory, made for a quick attack and nearly vertical as she dropped in a straight line toward the ground. Lyana's wings were meant for maneuverability and agility, not for hunting. So, although she soared as quickly as she could, keeping the flapping to a minimum, there was no way she could beat Cassi in a rapid descent. And Cassi knew it.

"What took you so long?" her friend teased from the shadows as she waited with crossed arms on the mosaic floor at the base of the palace.

The colorful stones seemed dull in the early morning haze, but in a few hours they would sparkle. The floor had been designed to mirror the sky above. At midday, when bright rays spilled through the apex of the dome, the crystal palace became radiant with the power of the sun.

Lyana ignored her friend and spun toward the discreet door nestled on the northwestern side of the room. It was the only discreet door there. The other four, positioned at north, south, east, and west, all towered at least thirty feet high and were impossible to open without alerting the entire palace. Though, of course, that was the whole purpose. One led to the banquet room, one to the sacred nest, one to the arena, and one to the official entryway, where an indoor market was held every day to sell goods and create a sense of community. But Lyana didn't want official, she wanted secret, so she ran her fingers along the wall, searching for the telltale groove of the hidden back door. And...

Got it, she thought as she pressed, hearing a *click*.

The door swung open, revealing a narrow, dark passage, built from limestone like the interior walls instead of lucent crystal. The hidden route was courtesy of a former king with a paranoid streak unnecessary in a land that had been at peace for hundreds of years—but Lyana wasn't complaining, when it made sneaking out of the palace for a few hours that much easier.

"This place always makes me feel claustrophobic," Cassi muttered.

Lyana grabbed her friend's hand because, to be honest, she'd always felt the same way. The ceiling was barely two feet above her head, the walls weren't wide enough to spread her wings, and though a handful of oil lanterns lit the space, everything felt cramped, especially to bodies made for open air.

"We'll be outside soon," she said. An undeniable excitement pulsed through the words. As much as Lyana loved her home and understood the need to remain indoors in such a hostile, cold environment, she'd choose the wintry bite of open air over the palace walls any time.

"Are you sure about that?" Cassi couldn't help but wonder.

Lyana frowned, shaking her head. "We're back to this?"

"Well," her friend drawled, "I just remembered that I ran into Elias with your brother last night, right before bed. Exactly how many cups of hummingbird nectar did you have to plug into him before he agreed to this little plan of yours? Five? Ten? He was flying in zigzags when we left him."

Lyana shrugged. "I don't know. A few?"

"That's what I thought. I'm not sure how hospitable he'll be feeling after all."

"Just come on."

With a roll of her eyes, Lyana pulled on Cassi's arm, urging her friend to move a little faster. They reached the end of the passage after a few rushed minutes, but before Lyana could pull the door open, a deep voice stopped her.

"Don't even think about it."

Lyana paused with a heavy sigh. But it was just an unexpected setback, a little delay, nothing more. She forced a wide smile onto her lips and opened the door. "Morning, Luka."

Her brother stared back with his arms crossed and his ashy wings outstretched, blocking the door to the outside. The atrium was made of crystals, meant to blend with the surrounding town, and it was lit brightly enough to reveal the disapproving lines etched in his dark skin. Two years older, and he never let her forget it. To his left, Elias stood with drooping shoulders, his tan wings folded and his face remorseful.

Lyana wrinkled her nose at him. *Traitor.*

"It's not Elias's fault," Luka cut in, aware of every thought racing through her mind. "Did you really think I wouldn't know you'd pull a stunt like this? I didn't even realize Elias was on duty until I got here this morning to wait with him."

Lyana spared Elias an apologetic look before concentrating on her brother. "Luka, come on. We'll only be out for a few hours. I'll be back before Mother and Father even realize I'm gone."

He raised disbelieving eyebrows. "When have I heard that before?"

Valid...

"I mean it," Lyana insisted. "I just want to watch the first house arrive. I just want to get rid of my nerves. I need some fresh air, or I'll go crazy. Don't you, of all people, understand?"

"I do, Ana." His hard gaze softened. Before she could press the advantage, however, his brows scrunched together. "But this week, of all weeks, we need to be on our best behavior."

Her wings drooped. "Why?"

"You know why. We're representing our family, sure, but we're also representing the House of Peace, all our people, all the doves. And most importantly, we're representing Aethios, god of the sun and the skies. We can't dishonor that."

"I wasn't going to," Lyana said softly. She stopped short when Cassi bit her lip to keep from commenting. "It's just, Luka, that's not all we're doing. And you know it."

He sighed but remained silent with his jaw clenched.

Because she had a point.

Yes, they were the prince and princess of the House of Peace, but they were also a boy and a girl about to be paired off with a mate for the rest of their lives in a political partnership, instead of the love match all their friends would someday make.

The heirs from each royal house were currently on their way to her home for the courtship trials—their most honored tradition, during which all the royal matches would be arranged. They were held once in a generation, usually as soon as all the second-born children came of age, though occasionally exceptions were made, as they had been made now. Lyana was a month shy of her eighteenth birthday, but the other families had grown impatient to see their children mated and hadn't wanted to wait a full year for the next summer solstice.

So tonight, after months of planning, the ceremony was set to begin with the parade of offerings. Tomorrow the tournament would commence, giving each heir a chance to display his or her skills and win the top choice of mate. And in four days' time, the matches would be determined. While Luka, the firstborn and crown prince, would welcome his new mate into the crystal city, Lyana would be leaving everything and everyone she'd ever known to follow her mate to his lands, as was tradition.

Part of her was excited.

Part of her was scared.

All of her was out of kilter.

If she could just see one prince from another house—not all of them, just one—maybe the nerves that had been fluttering in her stomach for the past month like a flock of wild fledglings would finally go away.

Lyana stepped closer to her sibling, widening her eyes, silently pleading. Her wings lifted and shifted just enough to make her appear small and fragile, like the innocent little sister he still saw her as, despite the evidence to the contrary. A slight wobbling of her lower lip puffed it into a pout. She didn't have to turn to see her best friend roll her eyes—she just felt it without looking.

Her brother's icy exterior began to melt. Deep in his honey irises, she could see the shell cracking. He closed his eyes tightly and released a loud, frustrated breath as his body slackened with defeat.

"Every time," he muttered.

Elias offered him a consoling slap on the back. Cassi shook her head.

Lyana jumped forward and pressed a quick kiss to his cheek, wings rippling in anticipation of the endless sky. "Thank you. Thank you. Thank you!"

"Yeah, yeah." He folded his wings, revealing the door to the outside, but didn't fully step aside. "You'll be back before noon?"

"I promise."

"You won't let anyone see you?"

"I promise."

"You won't do anything idiotic?"

"I promise."

Luka scoffed and turned to Cassi. "You won't let her do anything idiotic?"

"I'll do my best," Lyana's friend replied solemnly.

Luka sighed. "If you get caught by Mother and Father, Elias and I were never here."

"My lips are sealed," Lyana promised.

Luka looked at Elias, giving his friend room to stop him from making a decision he shouldn't, and moved out of the way. Before her brother had time to reconsider, Lyana pushed through the door, sucking in sharply as the frigid air brought an instant tingle to her skin and nearly stole the breath from her lungs. Behind her, Cassi hissed at the cold. But to Lyana, the bite was one of liberation.

She spread her wings and pumped them, muscles awakening and warming her body as she took to the sky, unable to stop herself from sneaking one quick glance behind. There was nothing in the world quite like the flare of the rising sun reflected off the crystal buildings she called home. But in a few days, she'd be leaving. And her destiny was waiting at the sky bridge—in her hollow bones she knew it. She turned her gaze to the horizon, letting her wings and her eager heart carry her toward the unknown.

2

LYANA

They sped across the barren, arctic land, keeping low to the ground. Without the cover of trees or vegetation, Lyana's warm umber skin and tan furs stood out too much, no matter how well her snowy wings blended into the landscape. And she'd promised her brother she'd keep out of sight...for the most part.

"I see the edge," Cassi called from Lyana's right. Her owl vision was superior at far distances, especially in this still-soft morning light, a fact she rarely let Lyana forget. But she didn't mind. Because to read even the simplest note, Cassi had to wear glasses—a fact Lyana never let her friend forget.

"Do you see the sky bridge?"

"Yup," Cassi called.

"Anyone there?"

Cassi paused for a moment and shifted her focus, before shouting back, "Not yet."

Good, Lyana thought. It meant they had time to get to their favorite hiding place before anyone could spot them, exactly as she'd planned. One house. That was it. That was all. She hadn't been lying to her brother. She just wanted to see one house arrive, then she'd fly back, play the good little princess, and do her part.

One house.

She swallowed a tight gulp, but the sound of whistling winds pulled her attention from the future and back to the present. They'd nearly reached the edge. A few feet before the ice and rock gave way to nothing, Lyana flapped her wings, easing her speed for an easy landing. Cassi, on the other hand, preferred to land at a run, shifting her feathers down to slow herself beforehand. Two different wings, two different styles.

What other styles are there? Lyana wondered, gaze shifting to the crystal bridge a few hundred feet to her left. It nearly blended in with the sky as it connected the inner and outer rings of her homeland. Theirs was the House of Peace, and as a sign of peace, no other houses would enter their inner island through flight. Instead, they walked over the bridge, vulnerable and submissive, with their wings tucked against their backs.

She wished she could see them fly, though, all the different houses, because she longed for something new. Sure, the doves had visitors from time to time, but most of the traders didn't venture inland. Instead, they exchanged their goods at the outposts and towns scattered around the outer loop of her isle, avoiding the hassle of the sky bridge at all costs. Cassi was the only other bird she'd spent a lot of time with, but after so many years, she hardly even registered her friend was an owl and not a dove. They'd been a duo for as long as she could remember, ever since the day the guards had found Cassi abandoned on the ice and brought her back to the palace. Lyana had begged her parents to let the owl stay, too curious by half about this mysterious orphan discovered in the tundra. They searched for her parents and sent letters to the House of Wisdom, but no one claimed Cassi. Before long, she'd become part of the family.

Now she was old news.

Not exciting, not anymore.

Not like all the flocks flying toward her home at this very moment.

Patience, Lyana thought, hearing the voice of her mother in the back of her mind. *Patience.*

The lesson her parents always tried to teach—the one she had never bothered to learn. Because she wanted to see it all. She wanted to see everything. The libraries the owls kept. The great plains the eagles scoured. The tree villages the songbirds built. The paradise the hummingbirds cultivated. And more, so much more.

Lyana shifted her gaze from the two icy landscapes and the bridge connecting them to the blue sky that arched above and curved below. Then she looked farther down, and even farther, curiosity leading her eyes to the hazy white fog thousands of feet below.

The Sea of Mist.

According to legend, their floating isles had once been part of the land hidden beneath the fog. They'd been slaves to cruel masters who used magic to keep them weak and subservient. But their people had prayed to the gods to save them, to give them a home where they could finally live free from tyranny, and the gods had listened. Aethios, her patron god, master of the sun and sky, along with six others, surrendered their material forms and used their divine power to rip the isles from the ground, lift them into the sky, and gift their faithful servants with wings. But Vesevios, god of fire, refused to sacrifice his strength and remained below, where a raging sea rushed to fill the void, drowning him and all his power as a punishment for his greed.

Lyana tried to picture the world as it had once been, endless blue from sky to sea and back to sky. They said the waves were once as tall as mountains. That even from the height of her isle, nearly fifteen thousand feet in the air, she could have seen them crash and splash and rage. But the god of fire never forgot how he'd been bested by the other gods, and his anger bubbled under the surface, growing and growing with each year, until eventually the waters turned so hot, they began to boil and steam. And now, no one knew what existed beneath the fog. Water? Barren, rocky land? Molten fire? Nothing? And no one wanted to find out.

No one, it seemed, except her.

Lyana was dying to see beneath the Sea of Mist. To fly through the impenetrable white and discover what lay beyond.

But that wasn't her future, no matter how she wished it could be.

Her future was here. Now. Waiting across that bridge.

"I think I see movement," Cassi hissed under her breath.

Lyana blinked, tearing her eyes away from dreams that could never be and focusing on the present. "Let's get in position."

Cassi nodded.

Together, they jumped off the edge, wings bearing them aloft and flapping in the strong gusts whipping through the channel. They couldn't speak over the loud, blistering winds, but they didn't have to. They'd spent their entire lives sneaking out of the palace to explore what little bit of land they had access to, and they knew it better than anyone else. Just like they knew each other better than anyone else. They didn't need words as they drifted below the edge, moving as one toward the cave below the sky bridge, hidden under a large outcropping of rough stone. The entrance was masked by shadow, and it was far enough to the side to make it nearly impossible to find, yet it provided a mostly unhindered view of the translucent stones overhead. It had taken the two of them years to discover it, but only a second to claim it as their own.

Lyana soared through the opening, finding a perch before tucking her wings as tightly into her back as possible. Down here, surrounded by rock and shadow, her furs and skin acted as cover, should anyone think to glance down.

Cassi took the empty spot by her side.

"Can you see who it is?" Lyana whispered, hoping her voice wouldn't carry.

Cassi shook her head. "Not from this angle, not quite."

They waited, watching silently in absolute concentration.

It wasn't long before Lyana began to bounce on her heels, excitement getting the best of her. "You don't see anything?"

"Shush. I think—"

They spotted the two blurry figures at the same time. Men, most likely. Old or young, Lyana couldn't tell, but it wasn't their faces or bodies that had grabbed her attention as they stepped to the foot of the bridge, getting close enough for her to see them standing at the edge. It was their wings. Their deep ebony wings. Even with her dove eyes, and even from this distance, the black iridescent feathers that somehow both reflected and absorbed the sunlight were unmistakable.

"The House of Whispers." Cassi all but breathed the words. A moment later, her arm shot out, anticipating Lyana's itch to lunge forward for a better view. Cassi forced them both deeper into the cave, out of sight.

But the image of those wings was crystal clear in Lyana's mind. She grinned. "The ravens."

3

RAFE

"So, this is the infamous sky bridge?" Rafe asked, crossing his arms. "I have to admit, I expected more."

"Expected more?" Xander snorted, shaking his head. His brother's gaze shifted to the far side of the bridge, the open channel below, then back to Rafe. "Expected more than a bridge made of clear stones that spans a distance of nearly three hundred feet? You expected more than that?"

Rafe shrugged. "I don't know, we've been hearing about this place since we were kids. I expected something...larger? Grander? I don't know..." He gestured with his hands. "More."

Xander laughed. "You've always been difficult to please."

"Me?" Rafe touched his heart in feigned denial. "Maybe I just have high standards. There's nothing wrong with that."

"Maybe you're just too stubborn for your own good,"

Xander mumbled, his voice barely audible above the blistering winds.

But Rafe heard him.

He heard everything his brother said, whether he wanted to or not, because he'd spent his life learning how to pay attention—to his brother, to his people, to anything and everything that might affect his place in the House of Whispers. That was what the bastard son of a dead king needed to do to earn his keep—love his crown prince unconditionally and leave no room for anyone to ever question his loyalty.

Yet even surrounded by nothing but air and ice, he had no snappy response for his brother. He couldn't deny that he was stubborn. He also knew why Xander had brought him to the sky bridge so early in the morning, twenty minutes before the rest of their people planned to show up.

"I'm not going to do it," Rafe murmured.

Xander sighed loudly, but without surprise—with something more akin to frustration. "You have to."

"I don't. And I won't."

"Rafe, now is not the time—"

"It's the perfect time, Xander. It's the only time."

The crown prince's midnight feathers bristled, but he took a deep breath, ever the calm, collected brother, and continued with his plan undeterred. Rafe, on the other hand, stepped forward, nostrils flaring as he turned to face his sibling, wings stretching wide even as he tried to rein them in.

"Xander," he protested.

Patience and unrelenting persistence were Xander's own

brand of stubbornness, and he ignored Rafe, pulling free the chain he always wore around his neck to reveal a large ring previously hidden beneath his leather overcoat.

"You have to take it," Xander said in an unflinching tone.

Rafe preferred to think of this as his brother's *royal* voice, because it was a royal pain in his ass. Still, he glanced down at the silver band resting in his brother's open palm. The polished obsidian stone faced out, mocking him with the royal seal. Rafe had spent his entire life convincing the ravens he had no desire to steal his brother's throne. And yet, here he was, being asked to do that very thing during the most important week of their young lives.

He lifted his gaze back to his brother's. They'd been born four months apart, from two different mothers, but they might as well have been twins except for the color of their eyes —Xander's the soft lavender of the royal line, and Rafe's the vibrant blue of a bastard born of the sky.

"Don't ask this of me, brother," he whispered. "Anything but this."

Xander's gaze was harder than its soft color seemed to allow, full of compassion yet unwavering. The gaze of a king. "I discussed it with the advisors before we came, and we all agreed. The House of Whispers might accept me for what I am, love me for what I am, but we need to show strength before the other houses."

"You're strong," Rafe argued.

"With my words, yes. With my actions, yes. With my conviction and my love for our people, yes." Xander finished softly, "But for the requirements of the courtship trials, we both know that's not the case."

Rafe tried to hold his brother's gaze, to keep it steady and uplifted and proud. But instead, Xander dropped his eyes. And Rafe's followed, landing where they had been led, on the empty space where his brother's right hand should have been.

"The trials will test our physical abilities," Xander said, finally looking up. Any other person would have been fooled by the calculated emptiness of his eyes, but Rafe knew his brother too well. He could see the hurt, the shame, and the pain his brother's disability caused. None of it was warranted, but it was there all the same. "Before the other houses, during the trials, you have to take my place. You have to pretend to be me, so our people can finally have the mate match they deserve."

Rafe knew what people gossiped about in the dark halls of their castle. How the ravens had lost favor with the other gods, how their patron god was weakening, how they'd been cursed. The House of Whispers had found a mate match in only one of the past five courtship trials. The royal families of all seven houses had been cursed with too few males to females, or too few females to males, and while love matches could be of the same sex, the matches of the monarchy must produce blood heirs.

For four generations, the ravens had been the odd house out, returning home from the trials empty handed, forced to find a mate within their own house instead of in another royal family—until the last ritual. Xander's mother, the crown princess at the time, had been matched with a second son—a falcon from the House of Prey. But he had possessed a wandering eye in lieu of a sharp one. The king consort, meant to prove the gods had once more blessed the ravens, instead committed their most egregious crime. And Rafe, the evidence of that crime, understood how much pressure his brother felt to erase the ill omens of the past.

"Do you really think this is how Taetanos would want his favor won?" Rafe asked, eyes slipping toward the sky bridge and the snow-covered tundra on the other side. It stretched into the horizon, hiding the House of Peace within its folds.

"He's not just the god of death, brother," Xander pointed out, still looking at Rafe. "He's the god of fate and fortune. He's the god that gave us the same father and nearly the same face. The god that dealt me my hand and you yours. He's the god that gave us these roles and these cards to play."

A chill crept along Rafe's spine as his brother muttered those undeniable words. For the first time, he felt the bite of this frigid, foreign land.

"And what does the queen say?" Rafe asked, trying a different approach. Xander's mother hated him and everything he represented, as did many of his people. There was no way she would agree to this insane plan, no way she would ever admit he was better equipped than her son for any challenge. Truth be told, Rafe thought she was right in that belief.

"She understands the necessity."

It was all Rafe could do not to snap his wings wide open and fly away. Not to retreat. Not to run from this role he'd never wanted, not even in his imagination. "So that's it? It's settled, whether I want it to be or not?"

"You'll don the royal seal until the final day of the trials, when the matches are revealed, and then we'll switch places. Tradition dictates you'll be wearing a mask, anyway, and I'll stay out of sight. No one will even suspect anything. My face will be the one they remember in the end, so you have nothing to fear."

Rafe frowned. "Easy for you to say."

"True." His brother grinned.

The frown only deepened. "What will you be doing during all of this?"

Xander shrugged, bright lavender sparks flashing in the corners of his eyes. "I'll be playing you, of course. The loyal, quiet, subservient second to the prince, who does everything his older brother commands."

Rafe arched a single brow in his brother's direction.

Xander continued jovially, "Who does everything his older, and *wiser*, brother commands."

Rafe sighed.

He'd give in.

He'd known he would. He'd known it before they'd even left home. And now, looking into his brother's confident, kind, and silently pleading face, he knew there was no way he could say no. Not when Xander was the only reason Rafe even had a place and a people to call home. Not when Xander was the one who had begged the queen to let him stay after their father died. Not when Xander had risked so much.

Who am I kidding? he thought, his heart warming despite the chilly air. *I love him too much to ever say no.*

"I'll take the seal after we get to the House of Peace," Rafe conceded. "You should enter as our crown prince and rightful heir, not me."

Xander pounced on his moment of victory, offering Rafe the ring. "Take it now, before you have a chance to change your mind. And before any of the other houses have a chance to see..." He trailed off, his gaze again dropping to the rounded end of his right arm.

Rafe jumped back. The edge of his boot scuffed against the crystal as he stepped onto the bridge. "Later."

"Now."

"Later."

"Would you just listen to me for once?" Xander half laughed, half sighed the words.

Rafe grunted but lifted his hand. Xander dropped the ring into his open palm. As he positioned the chain around his neck, he felt the weight of the obsidian stone all the way to his core. Nothing had ever felt so heavy. Yet for his brother, he could do this. He would.

"It looks good on you," Xander whispered, his tone almost vulnerable.

Rafe shoved the ring beneath his shirt. "It looks better on you."

The edge of Xander's lip twitched with amusement. "Obviously."

Before Rafe could respond in kind, a thunderous roar cut across the sky. His wings unleashed instinctively, standing to attention as he turned with his brother, their movements in unison as they tried to locate the source of the sound. They'd heard it only once before, but that deadly snarl was impossible to forget, as were the memories that came with it.

"It can't be," Rafe muttered.

"Not here," Xander agreed.

As their gazes dropped to the open air beneath their feet, they both realized they were wrong. A body of angry orange-and-red flames emerged from the mist, leathery wings smooth as they cut through the fog, vapors swirling in its wake.

The fire god had sent his fury.

A dragon was headed straight for them.

4

RAFE

"Get back," Rafe shouted, shoving Xander's chest and pushing him away.

He pumped his wings and launched himself into the air over the sky bridge, shifting into fight mode as the beast approached. It left a trail of dark smoke, stark against the expanse of bright gray. A change in the air behind Rafe caught his attention, and he turned to find his brother flying a few feet away, hand searching for the knife at his hip.

"Get out of here," Rafe ordered. "Go get the others. They can't be far."

"I'm not leaving you." Xander shook his head and tightened his grip on the only weapon he'd ever bothered to learn how to use, a single throwing dagger.

Rafe wouldn't have it. He dropped into Xander's space and grabbed the front of his jacket, holding his brother in place and forcing him to listen. "You are the crown prince of the House of Whispers, the sole heir to the throne, and your life is too important to risk. So, go. Get the others, right now. This isn't an argument. If the dragon attacks, I'll keep it distracted until you return with backup."

Xander pursed his lips, biting his tongue.

Rafe refused to back down.

The two brothers stared at each other, their eyes flickering with the memories of that long-ago night, the night that had made Rafe an orphan and Xander a king far, far too soon.

"Go," Rafe murmured, his voice deep.

For once, Xander relented. He held Rafe's gaze for one more moment, a violet streak of pain across his irises, before racing away.

Rafe watched until his brother was nothing more than a dot on the horizon. Then he turned to face his target, pulling his twin swords from the X-shaped scabbard resting in the hollow between his wings and drawing strength from the way the steel sang as it slid free. The dragon circled, a lazy hunter on the prowl, flying higher and higher, snout lifted as though following a scent in the air.

At the sound of Rafe's blade, it looked up.

Something sparked like metal on flint.

Hatred lit those blood-red eyes, a reflection of the loathing in Rafe's gut. Always there. Always churning. A living, breathing beast no different from the one flying toward him now. Fire erupted from the dragon's slick scales, sizzling with heat. The burnt, acrid flavor of smoke filled the air—a taste Rafe would never forget. When the beast released another roar, the wind seemed to shudder, as though the entire world answered to the thunder within that call.

Lightning traveled down his spine.

Rafe tried to blink away the images, but he couldn't. They came too fast to slow down, a flood rush from a broken dam, too overpowering to fight. Just like that, he was five years old —wings hardly more than fluff as he sat with his mother and father, late in the night, the only time they spent together. The weather had been particularly lovely that evening. Rafe could still envision his mother mentioning the beauty of the night, her blue eyes shifting toward the stars as they twinkled across the clear sky. His father, upon hearing the words, had rolled from the bed, walked to the balcony, and flung the curtains wide open to let the cool breeze in.

Even now, Rafe could almost feel the brush of wind against his cheek. It had been crisp yet not cold, perfectly balanced against the hot fire crackling in the corner of the room. He had been ill that night, body racked with fever and nausea. His mother had set him near the flames to still the trembling, tingling pricks that seemed to come from the inside out, from somewhere deep within him. That fresh breeze on his sweating brow had been so welcome, until they heard the roar.

Get to the prince, his mother had demanded.

But his father had shaken his head, gaze darting to the orange glow growing stronger and stronger across the night sky. *I won't leave you. I won't leave our son.*

Go, you must.

It had been too late. Before she'd even finished the words,

35

a sea of flames swept across the balcony and into their room, then another, and another. Rafe could remember nothing more than pain and screams and that burning, acrid smell as his vision went dark and his body cried out in agony.

He'd heard the rest of the story from Xander. How the beast had breathed fire into all the lowest layers of the castle, then landed in the courtyard. How it had taken twenty soldiers to finally bring it down and countless more to douse the flames. How it had stolen more than fifty lives with its raging blaze and razor-sharp teeth. Xander had watched the battle from his rooms at the top of the castle, safe and guarded, before running down to the servant quarters to ensure Rafe was all right. Xander had found him buried beneath the charred bodies of his parents. Injured, but still breathing. Alive, somehow, even though everyone else in that section of the castle had perished.

The queen wanted to execute him. The people cried out that he was blessed by the fire god, a usurper who would one day try to steal the throne, a curse upon their people. But Xander stood before them, their crown prince, their future king, and ordered they step down. Their ruler was only five years old, but they recognized the authority in his tone, one he'd never used before. A child had grown into a man in a single second, his youth dying with his father.

Rafe was moved to the royal quarters after that, to a room beside Xander's. But those few seconds before the dragon's call —there in the servant quarters, nestled between his parents— were the last few seconds when he ever felt as though he belonged.

A dragon had once stolen everything from him.

And I'll be damned if I let it happen again.

He dove, zipping through the channel, plummeting beneath the sky bridge to meet the beast head-on. In the narrower space between the two floating isles, he'd have the best shot at slowing the creature down. Rafe's wings were nimble and swift, but the dragon's were wide and cumbersome in the tight space, made for gliding rather than agility.

The beast acted quickly.

Flames shot from its mouth, barreling toward Rafe, but he cut to the left, moving out of the way just in time. The heat blasted into his side, slightly painful as the fire flew past, but he ignored the sting, flattening his wings to build speed as he plummeted underneath the creature. He then flared his wings wide, letting them catch the wind and flip him in midair so he stopped beneath the belly of the dragon, the perfect place to strike.

He shoved his twin swords into the scales, but the steel barely pierced the tough hide. Before he had time to try again, a claw slashed at his vulnerable wing. Rafe pumped once, twice, narrowly escaping as he twisted around the creature's body, staying close despite the suffocating heat, because it was the safest place to be.

There was a reason the ravens had their own house, separate from the other songbirds. A reason theirs was called the House of Whispers. When they crooned to their patron god, Taetanos, god of death, he answered. Not to them, but to their foe. He sent shadows into their enemy's mind, a dark fog meant to distract and confuse, to disorient. Not every raven had the gift—only the greatest warriors did—but Rafe was one of the lucky few.

He wasn't sure it would work with a dragon.

But he had to try.

He took a deep, strangled breath and released his raven cry. The ethereal sound carried across the wind, otherworldly as it echoed through the narrow space, filling the channel with its undercurrent of power, a glittering of dark shadows.

A ripple coursed through the dragon's scales and a screech tore up its throat. Its head whipped back and forth, throwing its body off balance. The edge of a leathery wing caught on a channel wall, and before Rafe realized what was happening, the dragon slammed into the cliff, rolling with the speed of the collision, crashing into stone and sending bits of it flying.

Rafe dropped as quickly as he could, searching for cover, but even he couldn't outmaneuver the debris cascading around him. He dodged a boulder only to be hit by a pebble landing squarely on his forehead, causing a blinding flash of pain. Within moments, the confusion cleared, but it was too late. The dragon beat its vast wings, lifting its body swiftly through the channel and into the open air above the sky bridge. Then it looked down, red eyes even more enraged, as it released a blast of flames at Rafe's head.

He dove beneath an outcropping of rock, but wasn't fast enough. A hiss came unbidden to his lips as his primary feathers, coated with flame, got singed. Another river of fire rushed past him, bringing beads of sweat to his brow. Rafe ruffled his wings, trying to put out the fire, but the burning wouldn't stop. He kicked off the wall, gazing up, but all he saw was another blast of orange that drove him under the canopy once more.

How do I get out of this?

How do I get out of this?

Think, Rafe. Think.

He peeked around the edge. The dragon sat on the lip of the sky bridge, scanning for a sign of its enemy along the cliffs. Those massive wings were folded. Sharp claws gripped the crystal walls. A long, spiky tail slithered in the breeze.

Rafe turned his attention to the cliffs on either side of the channel. He was no more than fifty feet below the edge, a quick trip if he could steal a second of flight unnoticed. He'd only have one shot, one chance.

After taking a long, even breath, Rafe released his raven cry again.

Without looking, he flapped his wings, surging up and out of his hiding spot, into open air. The dragon growled, but Rafe didn't have time to look, to wonder, to question. The edge was thirty feet, now fifteen, now ten, now—

A wave of fire engulfed him.

All he could see was bright light.

All he could hear was the crackle of flames.

All he could feel was pain.

Then more pain as a claw reached through the fire, wrapping around his torso like a vise, squeezing tightly. One sharp talon sliced through his abdomen. The flames disappeared, but they were replaced with bright sparks as his head slammed down against a hard surface, once, twice. Rafe screamed as the bones in his wings were crunched. The dragon tossed him to the side, and he rolled, bouncing over stone, muscles lacking the strength to resist. He came to a stop with his cheek against the ground and blinked.

A fuzzy view of the cliffs slipped into and out of view.

He couldn't move. Not even as he heard the roar, the flapping of wings, the deep breath of the dragon in its final killing strike. Rafe remained facedown, gazing through the crystal stones of the sky bridge at the air and fog below, with only one thought in his mind. *I'm sorry I failed you, brother.*

His vision began to flicker and fade. For a moment, he thought he saw the flutter of ivory wings, then consciousness slipped through his fingers—gone.

5

LYANA

L yana felt the raven's scream all the way to her core, as though a fist had taken hold of her insides and yanked, ripping everything out of place.

She'd never heard such anguish, such pain.

She'd never seen such bravery.

Before her mind could catch up with her instincts, she spread her wings and jumped, diving through the mouth of the cave, leaving Cassi no chance to stop her.

"What are you doing?" her friend shouted, panic in her voice.

Lyana didn't know how to answer. She didn't know what she was doing—she just knew she had to do something, anything. After hiding in the shadows, hearing those cries, catching only glimpses of the battle raging outside, she couldn't sit still any longer. She soared through the channel, up and over the edge of the sky bridge, sneaking up behind the dragon before the beast even noticed she was there. It stood over the fallen raven with its neck pulled back, bubbling with unreleased fire, and its wings spread into a span probably five times her own.

Lyana gasped, trapping the sound within her lips as she stared in awe of the creature. Sure, she'd learned of them. She'd read the reports with her brother, sat in meetings with her father. She'd heard the sightings had become more frequent, heard that the fire god's strength appeared to be growing. Still, reading something and seeing it with her own eyes were two very different things.

Was this what waited beneath the Sea of Mist?

Was this what the world below had become?

Her hands trembled, not with fear but with indecision, as she gripped the daggers always clipped to her belt and pulled the two sharpest ones free. There was a beauty in the dragon's ferocity she couldn't deny—something glittering beneath all the terror.

Something that gave her pause.

No dragon had ever flown so high as to reach her homeland. The other isles were all arranged at different heights, some closer and some farther from the Sea of Mist, but her home was at the top—the apex of their floating world because the patron god of the House of Peace, Aethios, was the keystone holding everything in place. The god of the sun and the sky. The god who had lifted their lands into the air. The god who kept them aloft.

Aethios, she thought, blinking her wonder away. *Aethios is the god I worship. Not Vesevios. Not the god of fire. Not this creature's keeper.*

As though hearing her thoughts, the raven crumpled against the stone moaned—a soft, broken sound. Yet it was loud enough to pull her from her thoughts and jolt her into action.

There were only two options she could see for attack—the wings or the eyes. The raven had gone for the stomach, her first choice, but she'd seen his sword barely make a dent, which meant her daggers would be useless. And since she wanted to remain out of sight for as long as possible, Lyana decided to go for the wings first.

The dragon hitched its head, about to unleash its wrath.

Fully aware of how idiotic her actions were, and fully aware of the promise she'd made her brother, Lyana stretched her arm back and zeroed in on her target—the joint where the wing met the body. The spot was a vulnerable one for any flying creature, including her, and she'd seen how the dragon had skidded across the cliff face, scuffing its wings and scales. While there was no trace of blood, she was sure there had been damage done—damage she would use to her advantage.

Lyana released one of her daggers.

The blade landed true, as she'd been confident it would.

The beast roared in pain, head rearing as it shot a useless flame into the sky. Its neck whipped around, body following, and its wings flapped, one not quite as well as the other.

Maybe the eyes would have been better after all, Lyana

thought with a gulp as a single ruby iris focused in on her. Her fingers shifted on the second dagger, moving into position as she drew back her arm again. Before she released it, an arrow landed with a *thunk* in the middle of that furious pupil.

The dragon shook its head as though confused at what had happened. Lyana, on the other hand, wasn't surprised as Cassi soared into view, as lethal as she was silent, and shot a second arrow at the dragon's other eye. The beast bellowed as the arrow missed its mark and ricocheted off its impenetrable scales. But while its mouth was open, Lyana threw her poised dagger toward its open jaw. The blade disappeared in the cloud of flames erupting deep inside the creature's throat. It must have landed true, since the dragon took off into the sky, diving over the edge of the bridge and plummeting out of view before they had the chance to strike again.

Lyana's lungs emptied with one strong *whoosh* as her friend landed on the sky bridge with an ominous *thud*.

Cassi grabbed her by the forearm, spinning her around. "Do you have a death wish? What were you thinking?"

"I don't know," Lyana confessed, head itching to turn and locate the raven. "I just had to do something. I had to help."

"Help what? He's already in his god's arms, like we probably should be."

"You don't know that. Maybe there's something we could do. Something *I* could do."

Cassi's silvery eyes darkened to hard iron, and her grip on Lyana's arm tightened. "You can't be serious."

Lyana's lip twitched with humor. "Now where have I heard that before?"

"He's not worth the risk."

Lyana glanced over her shoulder, finding the deathly still body, noting how the pool of blood around the raven's torso expanded. "My brother said the same thing about you once."

Cassi sighed, loosening her fingers. A memory flickered in the corners of her eyes, one Lyana tried hard not to think about too often. She and Luka practicing swordplay in her room. The surprise of the door opening. The dagger slipping accidentally from her fingers. The blade sinking into Cassi's gut. The pleading look in her friend's eyes, as if she knew Lyana had the power to save her. The fear on her brother's face as she exposed her deepest secret to an owl who was still in many ways an outsider—but who, after that day, became a sister.

Glancing away, Cassi broke the moment. "It's not the same."

"Isn't it?" Lyana urged.

"We were already friends when you saved my life, and you were all I had in the world. He's nothing. A stranger. And we have to go before his companion gets back."

"No."

Lyana wrenched her arm free and spun, daring her friend to stop her as she flew to the fallen raven and dropped to her knees beside him. His face was charred beyond recognition, pale skin turned to raw and melted flesh. But that wasn't the biggest concern. A person could live with burns. Maybe not ones so severe, but it was possible. The gaping wound in his abdomen, however, was fatal—a fact confirmed by the blood spilling onto the crystal rocks beneath them.

Using another of her daggers to cut through his leathers, Lyana was careful not to slice his skin as she peeled back the soiled garments. She put her hands on his naked chest, took a deep breath, and reached for her magic. The space around her palms began to glow with a golden hue that reminded her of the sun. She pushed the light under the raven's skin, following it with her mind as she let her eyes fall closed so her thoughts could focus on the broken body sprawled next to her.

The wounds slowly began to heal.

Inch by inch.

Tear by tear.

Lyana worked methodically, focusing on the area that required her immediate attention, using her power to seal the gash in the raven's belly. But there was so much damage. The bones in his wings were crushed. Every inch of his exposed flesh had been burned, and most of his feathers, too. Some of his clothes had melded with his skin, impossible to remove.

Focus on the puncture wound, she reminded herself.

Focus on the bleeding.

Just focus.

The going was slow and required her full concentration. Her magic was awkward, an unexercised limb that fumbled and struggled, out of practice through no fault of her own. The people of all seven houses shared a common belief—that magic was a symbol of the evil which once enslaved them, and a power meant only for their gods. A person in possession of it, whether she be a princess or a pauper, would be sacrificed in order to save the faith.

Every house had a different method of execution. The

House of Prey was particularly brutal, she'd heard. They stripped magic-users of their wings and pushed them over the edge, sending them into Vesevios's arms. Most other houses used public beheadings. Her own, to maintain the image of peace they'd crafted so well, brought people discovered to have magic into the sacred nest, where only the king, the priests, and Aethios himself would witness the slaying.

Sitting on the sky bridge, saving a man from the edge of death, Lyana had no idea how anyone could ever think her magic a blight on their devotion to the gods. It was a gift from Aethios. Why else would it sparkle like the sun's rays on a clear day? But that didn't change the fact that if an outsider saw what she was doing, she'd be put to death. Even if that outsider happened to be the person whose life she'd saved.

"Ahh," a deep voice groaned.

Lyana snatched her hands away as her eyes flew open.

"Who?" The man spoke again. This time he blinked, cerulean irises flashing to life once, then twice, as his vision adjusted, finding her face—seeing it. Only when their eyes met did she realize he wasn't an old man. His gaze still held the vitality of youth, the stupidity of it. Hers must have reflected the same.

The unmistakable creaking of a bow pulled taut filtered into her ear. Lyana turned to Cassi, holding up her hand, ordering her to stop.

"He's seen your face," her friend murmured darkly.

"I didn't save him just to kill him."

Cassi widened her imploring eyes, the arrow steady in her hands, ready to strike. "He's seen your face."

"And in his delirium, he's noticed nothing else."

"Then we should go, now, before he does."

Lyana turned back to the raven, scanning the burns all over his body, thoughts returning to the shattered bones in his wings. He'd never heal on his own. He'd never fly again. He'd be as good as dead if they left now, or worse even—alive without access to the sky.

"What if we take him somewhere? What if we hide him?"

"And then what?" Cassi asked with relentless logic, when all Lyana wanted was to act on instinct and heart.

She knew this was risky, insane, dangerous. But with her knees soaked in his blood and her ears picking up on his every strained heartbeat, she couldn't find the will to do the smart thing—to leave. Deep in her chest, something bubbled and prickled, a warm sort of fizz. The thrill of adventure. The excitement of doing something for herself in these last few days before she was mated, shipped to some foreign land, and forced into the role she was born to play.

"We'll take him to the cave," Lyana said in a moment of pure clarity. "We'll come back tonight when it's dark and check in on him. With his wings so broken, he won't be able to escape unless I heal him. And before I do, we'll make him swear an oath of silence before the gods. I'll wear some sort of disguise, plain clothes, so he won't realize who I am. And we'll release him in a few days, after the courtship trials are over, so he'll never learn the truth. He'll live, and my secret will be safe."

"You really want to risk so much?" Cassi pressed. "For him?"

"It's not for him." Lyana turned, finding her friend's gaze. "It's for me."

Cassi blinked. By the time her eyelids slid open, all the iron ore was gone. Her irises were the soft silver of the moonlight, lit with the understanding of Lyana's true wish— one last chance to be herself before she belonged to someone else.

"I don't like it," Cassi said, determined to state her opinion one final time. Then her wings drooped as her shoulders caved in. "But I'll do it."

Lyana fought the knot in her throat. She hastily looked back toward the raven, watching as he slipped in and out of consciousness. "I'll grab his shoulders. You grab his feet. Let's go before anyone sees."

He struggled when they lifted him, eyes blinking fast, limbs twitching, unintelligible protests pouring from his lips. After a few seconds, his body went still, overwhelmed by the pain. Carefully, they carried him beneath the sky bridge, fighting the whipping winds as they made their way to the cave they'd occupied not too long before. This time, they didn't stay near the surface. They ventured back into the farthest reaches of the cavern, where the space was pitch black and the air slightly warmer. They placed him face down on the ground, fanning his onyx wings to cover him as he blended into the dark.

"We have to leave before the ravens return," Cassi urged, pulling Lyana away from the body. "We saw the one leave. He was probably going to get the others, to warn them about the dragon."

"I know, I know," Lyana answered, keeping her head turned toward the man, unable to see anything but the subtle sheen of his pale skin in the shadows of the cave. "But shouldn't we light a fire, or maybe one of us should stay to explain when he wakes up?"

"No," Cassi insisted. "News of the dragon will spread. We have to get back before your parents realize we're gone, especially if you want a chance to sneak out again tonight. If they're the least bit suspicious we have something planned, they'll double, no, triple your guards. He'll be fine for a few hours. We can bring more supplies when we return."

Lyana sighed. Of course, Cassi was right. She was always right. But that didn't mean Lyana had to like it.

"I'll give you a few minutes," Cassi continued, attention drifting to the bright light at the end of the narrow tunnel. "I'll wait at the entrance and keep watch while you finish up."

Lyana grabbed her friend's hand before she could leave, squeezing it once. "Thank you."

Cassi shrugged and released a heavy sigh, one Lyana sensed was filled with frustration, fear, and most of all, love. "What are friends for, right?"

She walked away, leaving Lyana alone with the raven. Brushing her fingers over his burned cheek, she winced at the slick blood and swollen boils marring his skin.

Later, Lyana thought.

She'd fix it later. For now, she sent her magic deeper, to his internal organs, fixing enough to ensure he'd still be alive by the time she came back. She removed the furs wrapped tightly around her neck and laid them across the exposed part of his back, right between his broken wings.

Later. She sighed, pausing there, taking a deep breath as the cool air provoked a shiver down her spine. *Later.*

Then she stood, leaving the raven in the dark as she turned to join Cassi in their hasty journey home.

6

XANDER

The world was eerily silent.

That was all Xander could focus on as he flew toward the sky bridge with his guards following him into battle. The air was too still. The wind was too hushed.

Rafe is fine.

Rafe is alive.

Xander repeated the phrases over and over in his mind. Throughout his young yet trying life, he'd learned one very important thing—positivity was a power all its own. He wouldn't panic. He wouldn't spiral out of control. He would remain determined, vigilant, and optimistic as he raced onward, wings beating as fast as they could, carrying him toward his brother.

A brother who was fine.

Who was alive.

Who was waiting.

That hope died when the sky bridge slipped into view and a pool of brilliant red filled his vision.

"Rafe!" he cried, landing at a sprint. "Rafe!"

But there was no response, just the echo of his own voice reverberating down the open channel and up into the vast sky —a sky that was clear of fire and smoke, filled only with endless blue.

He's alive.

He's alive.

Xander refused to believe otherwise—even as he stared at the blood, watching the puddle spread. It reached the edge of the sky bridge and started dripping over the side, drop after drop after drop falling into the unknown world below.

Then he noticed something else—a footprint.

"Hold," he shouted over his shoulder, raising his arm. Xander didn't turn to see whether the guards had stopped, because they were loyal to their crown prince, and he knew without a doubt they would obey. With his eyes glued to the red footprint, he stepped closer. Holding his boot above the spot, he sucked in a breath as hope formed like a bright star in his chest.

The print was small—smaller than his—which meant it was smaller than Rafe's.

"Someone was here," he whispered to himself, then shifted position again, using his wings to hover above the blood, careful not to disturb it.

"My prince," a voice called. Xander spun toward the sound, recognizing his captain of the guards, the woman he liked to consider his top advisor instead of the stuffy nobles his mother kept around her. Helen was a small raven, but her skills with a throwing dagger were astonishing, and her mind for politics was even sharper than the blades she wielded so well. "Your brother's weapons."

She gestured toward the two blades tossed haphazardly across the barren, frozen ground. Xander flew toward them and knelt to pick one up with his left hand. The sword was heavy, the hilt wrapped with black leather. He'd seen it enough times to know it was his brother's, and that the other was its twin. Yet the blade felt cumbersome in his hand. Xander had abandoned sword play a long time ago, preferring books and debate to the practice fields. But today was one of the times he wished he could move like his brother, with his strength and abilities. Had that been the case, he would have stayed. He would have fought. He would know what had happened.

Then you'd be dead too, Rafe's voice said, popping into his thoughts.

Xander dropped the sword and shook the comment away.

Because Rafe was alive.

He had to be.

And it was a good thing his brother wasn't the crown prince. Rafe would have leaped over the edge searching for vengeance, would have sped across the land after a body, would have screamed his frustration for all the gods to hear. He would have been angry and rash. He would have missed all the signs.

But Xander was patient and observant. He stood, eyes narrowed as he took in the scene, reining his emotions in, refusing to allow doubts and fears to get the best of him. They never had before, and they wouldn't today. Not when his brother needed him.

The evidence left behind was a puzzle he intended to solve. The swords. The scorch marks. The footprint. Xander's gaze darted around the open field, to the sky bridge, the edge, and the cliffs beyond. His soldiers waited patiently, hovering above his head, knowing how their prince worked. Slowly but surely, the pieces came together.

"The dragon must have caught him as he flew up and over the edge," Xander said, half to himself and half to Helen and the guards, eyes traveling along the scorch marks staining the frozen ground.

If he knew his brother, Rafe would have started the battle in the channel, a narrow space that might give him the upper hand. Clearly, something had gone wrong and he'd needed to flee. But the dragon had caught him.

"You see this?" Xander pointed at the black marks and the lines fanning out. "The flames were coming from the direction of the channel, shooting toward the land from above. They must have caught Rafe here, and…"

Xander followed the soot and ash, stepping through them until he spotted a mess of black, bloodied feathers on the ground. "The beast got him here. It's where the blood starts. Maybe the dragon nicked him with a fang or a claw, and then slammed Rafe's wings into the ground. Nothing else could have caused this mess. And in the middle of the beating, he dropped his swords, which is why you found them there."

He pointed again, pursing his lips as he noticed the

pattern in the blood trail leading toward the bridge. "The dragon tossed him, which is why there's a broken blood trail, from where he skidded across the ground. And then his body stopped here, where the concentration of the blood is the highest."

As far as Xander knew, dragons had never taken their kills as prizes or hostages. In all the stories, dragons came to wreak chaos for their god and either perished or fled. But they didn't collect bodies.

"This print, it's not Rafe's," he told Helen, glancing up at her as the others leaned forward with perked ears. "Someone must have come and stopped the dragon. I don't know who, or how, but there's no other explanation. Someone took him."

In any other house, the soldiers might have raised their brows, looked at their heir dubiously, questioned him. But the House of Whispers was loyal, perhaps to a fault. They'd kept Xander's disability a secret from the rest of the world out of love for him and his family. And they'd keep his hope alive until there was evidence to the contrary—they'd do whatever it took to prove him right, even if every one of their instincts insisted that he was wrong.

"Five of us will go left," Helen announced, taking the lead as she divided the guards into groups. "Five to the right, three to the other side of the bridge, and three under it. We'll search all day for any sign of your brother, and we'll report back to you at the House of Peace tonight."

"Good, go," Xander ordered. "I'll search for more clues here while I wait for my mother and the rest of our flock."

Not needing to hear more, the guards dispersed.

Xander hovered over the blood a few more seconds, and then landed on the other side of the pool, unable to look at it any longer. He walked slowly across the bridge, pausing in the center to lean his forearms against the rail, his attention drifting down the channel, beyond the cliffs to the Sea of Mist far, far below.

Where are you, Rafe?

Where'd you go?

I can't do this alone.

I need you.

A gust of wind struck Xander in the back, pressing against his wings forcefully, almost shifting him off balance. He clutched the stones for support, his head turning as though searching for a cause of the sudden blast, searching for a sign. But there was nothing, just empty air. The wind was just that —wind.

A flurry of feathers lifted into the sky, pulled aloft by the air. Xander watched them drift over the edge of the bridge and flutter this way and that as they fell in black ripples. Raven feathers. His brother's. Ripped and bloodied.

A bright spot caught his eye.

Xander leapt over the side of the bridge, diving headfirst into the channel, left hand outstretched for that bit of white that didn't belong. When his fingers closed around the item, he spread his wings to stop his fall and took a moment to look at what he'd snared.

A single ivory feather.

One that couldn't belong to a raven.

One that must have come from a dove—and he'd find out

who. His brother had survived dragon fire once before, and he would again.

Rafe was alive.

Xander knew it for a fact. And he had to find his brother before anyone else uncovered their secret.

7

LYANA

"Where have you been?" Luka seethed under his breath as Lyana came skidding into the royal chambers, off balance in her haste.

He was standing just inside the foyer with arms folded, wings uplifted, and deep wrinkles etched into his forehead. Clearly, he'd been waiting there, pacing, too worried for his own good.

"I was in Cassi's room," she whispered. *Washing the blood from my wings and changing into one of the dresses I keep stashed there…just in case.*

But he didn't need to know that.

"The first house arrived fifteen minutes ago," her brother announced.

"The ravens are here?" Lyana squealed.

Luka grabbed her by the arm, gaze darting around the

room in search of any eavesdroppers. Or perhaps in search of their parents, who were undoubtedly waiting for her somewhere. But the gilded doors to their private chambers were closed, and the guards were stationed outside. She and her brother were, for the moment, alone.

"You saw them?" he asked.

Lyana met his questioning gaze but remained silent—suspiciously silent.

Luka squinted, trying to read her expression. "What do you know?"

"I don't know." She shrugged, her features blank. "What do you know?"

"Ana."

"Luka."

They stared at each other, frowning.

Lyana relented. The more she revealed, the less he'd assume she was lying. "There was a dragon at the sky bridge, Luka. A dragon!" She tried to rein in the excitement leaking into her tone, but the feat proved impossible. Her voice trilled with awe. "Can you believe it?"

"You were there?" His eyes bulged, a reaction that was the opposite of hers. "I said to stay out of trouble, out of sight. What were you thinking? What—"

"No one saw us," she interrupted. *No one conscious, anyway…* Lyana focused on the cover story she and her best friend had put together. "Cassi and I were hiding in a cave we discovered along the cliffs. We saw the dragon. We saw the ravens fight it off. And when they left to report back to their queen, who was traveling a few miles behind, we snuck out of our hiding spot and raced home."

It was a good lie, a convincing one, and it rolled ever so smoothly from her lips.

Luka brought his palms to his forehead, rubbing his fingers over his short, black curls as he took a long, uneven breath. "Where's Cassi now?"

Gathering supplies, Lyana thought, a little twinge of guilt in her chest. She smothered it easily. "In her rooms."

"And she's all right?" Luka asked.

"She's fine," Lyana assured him, then grinned. "Though I'm sure she'll be overjoyed to hear how concerned you were for her wellbeing."

Luke rolled his eyes and shoved her playfully. "You two…"

"Us two what?"

Luka shook his head with a heavy sigh. But a moment later, a smile appeared at the edges of his lips—a reminder that the mischievous brother she remembered was still alive in there somewhere. The weight of being the heir hadn't smothered him entirely, at least not yet.

"So you really saw it?" he asked, eager curiosity in his tone.

"Luka…" His name came out in a delighted sigh, because she was unable to even find the words.

He stepped closer, widening his ashy wings and bending them like a protective cocoon, the way he used to do when they were children concocting a plot that would only get them into trouble. "What did it look like?"

"Fire and fury," she said, not sure how else to describe the dragon. "Like a star that had fallen from the sky and gained wings. When it roared, I swear the clouds trembled."

"How big?"

"Its wings were five times the size of mine, at least. And its mouth, the gods, it must have been as long as I am tall."

"Red eyes?"

"Just like the stories said."

"Ana…" He exhaled the word in a tone brimming with disbelief and wonder, then squeezed her shoulders, slightly crushing the silk sleeves of her gown. "I can't believe—"

"I know," she said, pitch high, hands balling into fists meant to contain the emotions rolling through her.

"What—"

"Surely these aren't my children standing in the foyer giggling like two fledglings?" a deep voice boomed, interrupting their private celebration. "Not on the dawn of their courtship trials."

Luka's wings snapped away from her, folding tightly against his back. Lyana jumped out of her brother's embrace, bowing her head as she turned to face the king.

"Surely the prince and princess of the House of Peace wouldn't be gossiping like common servants," the king continued, hands clasped behind his back, creamy wings wide and commanding as he scolded them, and not for the first time. "Not about something so incredibly disarming as a dragon invading our lands? As the fire god gaining strength? As Aethios being threatened on the eve of our most sacred ritual?"

"Of course not, Father," Lyana muttered.

"Oh? 'Of course not, Father'?" the king mocked, turning to his daughter.

Luka tossed her a sidelong glare. Talking back just made everything worse—for Luka, maybe. But if there was one person Lyana knew how to manipulate, it was her father. And she meant that in the most adoring way possible.

Swallowing a gulp, she took a step forward, then clutched one of the king's hands in both of hers and looked up at him as she shifted her wings a little higher and made her eyes as large as possible. "A dragon? Here? Father, you can't be serious. We had no idea. I heard the ravens arrived, and I came to find Luka to see if any other houses had come while I slept. We were talking about the trials. But a dragon? Today of all days?" Lyana paused, releasing a trembling breath as she pressed their clasped hands to her chest and glanced up at the ceiling as though it were the sky. "Bless Aethios."

Luka snorted.

Lyana stopped herself from wrinkling her nose at him. The delivery was a bit dramatic perhaps, but it worked.

Her father relaxed. "I pray the gods give you a mate with some backbone, daughter. May the skies help him if he doesn't have the wits to tell you no."

"Aw, that's not true." Lyana smiled at him as she stepped back, laughter bubbling in her throat. "You hope I find a mate just like you, so I can wrap him around my little finger."

The king tried to frown, but his lips disobeyed him and lifted into a grin as a deep laugh surged through his belly. "Maybe I do. Maybe I do."

"Maybe you do what, dear?"

The queen swept into the room in a sapphire gown the same color as her bluebird wings, bright as ever in a house with feathers made of neutral tans and grays. She'd been the Princess of the House of Song long before she became Lyana's mother and a queen. Her father claimed to have picked her from the flock during the first test of the courtship trials, when she'd shot three bull's-eyes in a row into her target from across the arena and landed the fourth arrow in the heart of his empty center ring. But they were happy, it seemed, political marriage or not. Lyana's family was close, a solid nest. Theirs was the sort of love she hoped for in her match, the one she'd make in only a few days.

"We were speaking of the trials, Mother," Luka said, ever the doting son.

The queen threw her daughter an unsurprised look. "Ah, that must be why your sister looks so sullen."

Lyana bit back a reply. Her mother was the only foe she was too afraid to face, with a sharp tongue and an even sharper ability to see right through her daughter's schemes.

"Are the advisors waiting?" the queen asked softly.

"They are." The king addressed his children, "Luka, Lyana, your mother and I want you to attend the meeting. We'd like your opinions on the matter."

"On the matter of what? The dragon?" Luka questioned. It wasn't so unusual for the two of them to be called into a meeting. After all, they were both learning how to rule. But something in the king's tone made this particular meeting seem different, more important somehow.

"On the matter of postponing the courtship trials," her father said.

Lyana's jaw dropped. "What?"

"How long?" Luka asked.

"The ravens have asked for time, a few days at most, to regroup after the attack and help tend to their wounded. Your mother and I believe the House of Peace should have a unified opinion before the other houses arrive and try to interject on the matter. We've never postponed the ceremony before, and now of all times, with the fire god gaining strength, the idea seems rash. Yet, I sympathize with their situation."

Luka nodded once, strong and sturdy, duty personified.

But Lyana chewed her cheek, thoughts racing a mile a minute. "The wounded? Did they say how many were wounded?"

"There's no tally yet."

"Are there any dead?" she asked, unable to help herself.

"Not that I'm aware of," the king replied. When she opened her mouth to say more, he stopped her with a look. "That's enough for now. We need to meet with the advisors before the next house arrives."

Lyana swallowed her questions, but that didn't stop them from swirling and churning in the back of her mind as she followed her family through the gilded door of the royal chambers, down to the meeting rooms on the level below.

Because she'd seen the fight.

She and Cassi were the only two people who truly knew what happened.

There were no wounded who needed to be tended to, no

soldiers to regroup, no battle from which to recover. There was one fallen soldier—a soldier the ravens must believe was dead. It was sad, yes, but hardly so dire as to require delaying the courtship trials.

So why were they lying? Why were they exaggerating the truth?

And more importantly to Lyana, what in the world were they hiding?

8

XANDER

Sphaira, the crystal city, was a magnificent sight to behold, yet Xander felt empty as he stared through the translucent wall of the guest accommodations. Every house had their own domed building, arranged around the center palace in the same way their islands were, which put his near the northeastern edge of the bustling metropolis. His view of the entrance to the palace, which faced east to welcome the sun, was clear. Small figures zipped in and out of those towering doors, and he scrutinized them all. Tan wings. Ash wings. Speckled feathers. Patterned feathers. On and on it went. Nearly every dove in the House of Peace had a few white plumes. It would be impossible to find the owner of the ivory feather crushed within his fist.

Impossible.

"Lysander?" a suave voice called.

He didn't move. "I've told you not to call me that a thousand times, Mother."

"Why?" Queen Mariam asked, wings carrying her swiftly across the room to land by his side, her ruby gown vivid against the snowy landscape before them. "It's your name. Lysander Taetanus, Crown Prince of the House of Whispers. And you'll be hearing it quite a lot over the course of the next few days."

Xander sighed. His wings drooped so low that his primaries dragged along the floor, but they sank further still when he turned to look into her brilliant violet eyes. "I'm not giving up on him."

"I'm not asking you to."

His laugh was a sad, dark sound. "Please, Mother. You think I didn't see the way your face lit with the briefest spark when I told you of the dragon's attack, when you saw the blood for yourself? You wanted Rafe gone the moment he was born, whether he was my brother, my best friend, or not. You've only ever seen him as a bastard."

"That's what he is," she said simply, but Xander heard the undercurrent of hatred in her tone—the undercurrent that was always present when she spoke about his brother. He understood why she spoke of his father in that tone, but not of Rafe, who had been nothing but an innocent child at the time and a loyal companion to her lonely son ever since.

"Well, if you're not here to tell me I'm on a fool's errand, what are you here for?"

"I'm here to tell you to believe in yourself."

Xander switched his attention to the world outside the

room, which suddenly had become suffocating. "To believe in myself? That's what I'm doing."

"No," she countered, her voice never rising, though it felt as if she were shouting all the same. "You are depending on him, relying on him, and you don't need to."

"We've already discussed this," he muttered through gritted teeth.

"No, you spoke to the advisors behind your queen's back and turned them all against her to get your way. The two of us have never spoken about this."

Xander rolled his shoulders, unable to deny that he'd gone around his mother in this one thing. She was queen, yes, but the courtship trials were about him, and for once he wanted to have the final say. The only say. "You're right, Mother. And I'm sorry for that. But I knew you wouldn't understand."

"Why don't we sit?" she asked, motioning toward the chairs on the other side of the room, away from the window, away from the view, away from thoughts of Rafe. "And discuss it as two sovereigns should."

Again, he didn't move. "You'll never understand, Mother, no matter how many times I try to explain. Rafe and I? We're two sides of the same coin. Where I'm patient, he's rash. When I plan, he acts. If I smile, he frowns. At home, I possess every trait of a king. Here, on the other side of the coin, in this foreign land, Rafe has everything I need for success. We balance each other. I can't do this without him."

"That's not true," she insisted, and lifted her wing, brushing her obsidian feathers against his, trying to soothe him. But he stepped out of reach.

69

In truth, his mother had given him every opportunity and every choice in life. She'd had special weapons made—shields that attached to his forearm, swords that strapped to his wrist, hooks, wooden hands, and metal fingers. Anything and everything that could be conceived, she'd ordered to be fashioned.

He'd hated them all.

The uncomfortable way they dug into his skin, the blisters that formed along his forearm, the way the sight of them made him feel somehow diminished, especially when his studies required no special tools or craftsmen. The books accepted him into their folds, their pages, and he in turn loved them. Mental exercise had always been his favorite thing. And even if he'd had ten fingers instead of five, Xander didn't think he would have been any different. If anything, his disability just made it easier to follow his passions by providing an excuse people were too afraid to challenge.

Rafe was the fighter, gifted with a raven cry.

Xander was the prince, the peacemaker, the scholar.

Unfortunately, the trials were a battle, and they required a warrior.

"Not all of the trials are about physical strength," his mother pressed, reading his thoughts.

Though he knew they weren't fair, he couldn't prevent the next words from spilling through his lips, because fair or not, true or not, he needed his mother, his sovereign, to understand. "The first trial is archery, correct? What would you have me do, Mother? Step to the line and pull a bowstring with my teeth?"

"That's only one of the tests," she said, but not fast enough —not before her gaze dropped to his right hand, or his lack thereof.

His phantom fingers were curled into a fist, holding all his anger, keeping it out of sight. Sometimes he liked to believe that was what had happened—not that he lacked a limb, but that all his hate and fury and pain were balled into a fist so tight, he couldn't undo it. That his fingers were wrapped so forcefully they'd molded into his skin, they'd trapped themselves, but trapped all those emotions there as well. For the most part, he was happy and positive and cheerful. Only at times like this, when he remembered the fist, did those dark thoughts creep out of hiding.

"What of the navigation trial? What of that?" the queen asked, trying to find his eyes. Xander faced forward, stubbornly refusing to look at her. "You'd be far superior to your brother at that. He may be a fighter, but he lacks the endurance of the hunt."

"He might not win all the trials," Xander conceded before he went for the kill, an argument his mother wouldn't know how to refute. "No one can. But there's a difference, Mother. A huge one. Rafe might not win all the trials, but when he loses, he will do so with dignity. He won't turn the ravens into the laughingstock of the seven houses. He won't be a joke."

"Lysander!" Queen Mariam snapped, no longer dancing around her son as she grabbed him by the shoulders, spinning him toward her. "Is that what you think? Don't for a second. You would never, never—"

"Stop it," he interrupted, pushing her away. "I'm not

saying it out of shame or vanity. I've come to terms with my strengths and my weaknesses. And our people have, too. But you cannot expect that from the rest of them, from the world outside our sheltered, secretive island. People can be cruel, as you yourself know." She bit her tongue at that, luminous eyes dimming with silent pain for them both. Xander softened his tone, "It's not about me, Mother. It's about our people. There will be five crown princes competing in the trials, but only four second daughters. One house will be left unmatched in the end, and it can't be us, not again. Our people need a good omen. They need to stop worrying we've lost favor with the gods, that we're being cast out. They need a win. And I'm not too proud to admit that I can't give them that. But Rafe can."

His mother lifted her slightly wrinkled palm to his cheek, rubbing her thumb along its ridge. As her hand fell away, her features hardened. "Not if he's dead."

Xander stepped back as though he'd been struck, off balance and off kilter even as he knew in his soul it couldn't be true.

The door to his room slammed open.

"My queen, my prince, pardon the intrusion," the guard stammered as Helen forced her way through the door, face grim.

Xander had never been more grateful for an interruption in his life. He nodded to the guard before addressing his captain, "Do you have news from the House of Peace, Helen?"

"They've given us a day," she said, spitting that last word as though it were a curse, not bothering with titles or pleasantries. "The king says it would be an affront to Aethios to postpone the courtship trials any further. They plan to squeeze the tests into smaller time increments so we can still hold the matching ceremony on the summer solstice, as is tradition." She collapsed into one of the chairs, grabbed an apple from the table, and turned to the queen. "I didn't realize you'd be in here, but it makes my life a little easier."

"I'm trying to convince my son that the delay isn't necessary," his mother said, raising her tone at the end in a silent question.

Helen's gaze moved to Xander.

When he had first raised the idea of switching places with Rafe for the courtship trials, she'd been his biggest supporter, helping to convince his mother's older, more rigid advisors to loosen their adherence to the rules. Helen never held her tongue. She didn't worry about hurting his feelings. Her focus was on the house. On keeping it safe. On keeping it strong. And it was the thing he appreciated most about her—it was the reason he'd appointed her as captain of the guards and unofficial advisor to the crown prince when his mother had told him to step in and start taking charge of the kingdom he would one day rule. They were of like minds and not afraid of making tough decisions.

But in this instance, Xander used the oldest technique in the book to save Helen from the unnecessary wrath of the queen. He changed the subject. "Are the patrols back yet? Did they find anything?"

"There's no sign of your brother, aside from what we found at the bridge," Helen said matter-of-factly, not even attempting to lessen the blow. "No more bloodstains, no more feathers, no body. Nothing. The teams came back completely empty-handed."

"What's our next move?"

She lifted the apple to her lips and sank her teeth into it, ripping out a bite. Xander narrowed his eyes as she chewed.

She's delaying.

Why is she delaying?

Before he had a chance to ask, Helen swallowed and sat up. "I think in this instance your mother might be right. You need to prepare for the trials."

Xander's invisible fist clenched so tightly, his right arm started trembling. "I refuse to believe that's the case."

And Helen refused to back down. "We searched the area—"

"Search it again. Someone was there. I saw the print in the blood. You did too."

Her eyes softened the slightest bit.

Xander hated to see it, hated the concession, because he saw it for what it really was—pity.

"Even if someone was there, even if someone recovered his body," Helen continued, voice forceful despite the subtle shift in her expression, "Rafe will be in no shape to compete in the courtship trials, which are being delayed only a single day. You saw the blood, same as I did. If he's alive somewhere, he's hanging on by a thread. He'll have no time to recover. I'll keep sending search parties day and night until you order me to stop, but that doesn't change the fact that you, my prince, will be representing the House of Whispers in the courtship trials, whether you want to or not."

Xander opened his mouth but shut it quickly, swallowing his counterargument. Revealing the truth would be even more dangerous than letting them believe his brother was dead. In fact, it would most likely kill him. And Xander knew in his heart that Rafe was alive somewhere out there on that frozen tundra, waiting for him.

"I'm going to join the search party tomorrow."

"You'll do no such thing," Helen said. "You have one day to prepare for tests we never thought you'd face. Leave your brother to me."

Holding his captain's gaze, Xander didn't blink or back down. "You were right. I am the Crown Prince of the House of Whispers. And I *will* be joining the search party tomorrow."

Helen folded her lips into a thin line but kept them shut.

Xander glanced to his mother. There was a mix of pride and frustration on her face, but mostly of love. She dipped her head, granting him permission to do what he would have done with or without the royal seal of approval.

I'm coming, Rafe, he thought, returning to the glistening city on the other side of the crystal wall. *Hold on. I'm coming.*

9

LYANA

Lyana was stuck with her family and the royal advisors for what felt like an eternity, but it made the hours after the meeting fly. Between gathering supplies with Cassi, avoiding another lecture from her brother, and straining to catch a glimpse of the remaining houses as they arrived, Lyana was caught by surprise when she glanced outside to find the burning glow of dusk upon them.

A thrill ran up her spine.

"We should go," she chirped, spinning toward Cassi, who was on the floor of her room, stuffing two packs with the odds and ends they'd managed to gather earlier that afternoon. Some food. A fire starter. Logs. Oil lanterns. A change of clothes, complete with warm boots and furs meant for this tundra the raven wasn't used to. "It's going to get really cold out there without the sun."

"He's in a cave," her friend drawled.

Lyana eyed her pointedly.

Cassi sighed. "Well, if you're going to be like that, let's just get this over with already."

Jumping from the edge of the bed, Lyana flew to her friend, crashing into Cassi with her arms thrown open for an enthusiastic hug. "Thank you for this. I mean it."

Cassi squeezed her tightly before pushing her off with a laugh. "You can take the heavier pack, *Princess*, since this was all your idea in the first place."

Lyana snorted, but the sound quickly changed to a groan of protest when she lifted the bundle from the ground, struggling to clip it around her wings. "What's in this?"

"All the firewood you demanded," Cassi said sweetly. "And the water."

"What do you have in yours?"

"Food…"

Lyana stared at her, frowning. "And?"

"The lanterns."

"The hollow lanterns?"

Cassi easily shifted her pack around her large speckled wings and fastened the straps in place. "They've got some oil inside." Lyana opened her mouth, but Cassi cut her off, "We could repack everything, but there isn't much time if you want to sneak out before they close the main doors."

Lyana flared her nostrils but sealed her lips shut.

Logic.

She hated when Cassi wielded logic like a weapon against her. It was frustratingly effective. But then she remembered the raven, the cave, and the adventure ahead, and a smile widened her lips. "Let's go."

Cassi left first, easing through the door and letting it close behind her. Those massive owl wings were too obvious, so whenever they traveled through the main entrance, they did so separately. Lyana waited the customary ten minutes, bouncing on her toes, before lifting the hood of her servant's jacket and opening the door. There was nothing Lyana could do to hide her ivory wings, rare even among the doves, but she could conceal her features and her status—a trick she and Cassi had used numerous times to sneak from the palace.

At this time of night, the atrium bustled with people. Servants were switching shifts. Dinners were being delivered. Guards were changing posts. With the unorthodox delay of the courtship trials, messengers were zipping back and forth between the palace advisors and the representatives from each of the houses. And though the daily market normally set up in the warm entrance hall was closed, preparations for tomorrow's festivities were underway, creating the perfect distraction.

Hidden in bland clothes and sticking to the edges of the room, Lyana went unnoticed as she followed a group through the towering east exit and into the massive hall leading to the outside. The exterior door was sectioned into several parts, so when they had formal celebrations such as the one that would take place the following evening, the thirty-foot entrance could be utilized. But usually, on a somewhat normal night like tonight, they kept one or two smaller sections opened, manned by a couple of guards.

Lyana tucked her chin into her chest, bowing her head to hide her features in the shadows of her hood. In all her years of life, there'd never been any malicious attacks on her family or her people, so she wasn't surprised when the guards failed to pay any close attention to who was coming and who was leaving. The House of Peace was just that—peaceful. Suspicion and distrust just weren't things they knew. Lucky for Lyana, rebellious princesses weren't either.

Cassi found her outside. They rounded a few buildings on foot before launching into the sky, racing for the sky bridge. When they got there, Lyana took Cassi's pack and left her friend standing watch at the entrance of the cave.

The cavern was impossibly dark. Even with an oil lantern lit, Lyana struggled to see beyond the dull halo of light immediately surrounding her. In the end, it was the soft chattering of teeth that led her through the shadows.

The raven lay right where she'd left him, curled on his stomach, onyx wings spread like a blanket over his body, though they didn't seem to help. His wheezing breaths echoed across the empty chamber, loud in the silence. And even in the dull glow she could see he was trembling, shivering against the cold stone, lips tinged blue as puffs of air billowed out of them. But that wasn't what made Lyana gasp, nearly dropping the lantern with surprise.

His skin was healed—not completely, not totally, but enough to make her catch her breath.

Lyana moved the lantern closer, so the golden glow illuminated his face. The burns that had marred his body only a few hours before, the ones she had lacked the time to heal, had all but disappeared. The raw, wet stretches of flesh were dried and unblemished. The bumps and flaps were smooth. Red bloodstains remained, but the open boils had vanished.

It's impossible, Lyana thought, shaking her head. *Impossible. Unless...*

Unless he was like her.

Unless, somehow, he had magic too.

Her heart leapt into her throat, excitement explosive as it coursed through her unchecked. Careful not to wake him, she tugged away the furs she had left draped over him, examining the planes of his back. The fabric that had melted onto his frame was still hardened and burnt, but no longer adhered to him like glue. She lifted the scraps away easily, eyes widening as unmarked pearly skin was revealed, practically shimmering against the dark depths of his obsidian feathers.

Lyana paused.

It wasn't *practically* shimmering—it was actually shimmering. Silver swirls glowed softly, twirling beneath his skin like the muted glitter of starlight through a gossamer curtain, subtle but undeniable.

Magic.

Lyana lifted her free hand and ran her finger down the center of his spine, mesmerized by the way his muscles and his magic rippled beneath her touch. The contours of his back were well defined, reminding her of the icy hills of her homeland as they sparkled in the sun. But unlike that barren land, he was warm, brimming with life and power. Her mind flashed back to his battle with the dragon—how deftly his onyx wings had soared, how lethal those twin blades had looked in his hands, the authority with which he'd wielded them.

The raven stirred.

Lyana snatched back her fingers, clutching her hand to her chest. But she couldn't look away as he shifted, groaning in pain twice before falling still once more.

A light flashed from the ground near his neck.

A reflection, she realized as she watched a flame blink on and off and on and off, oscillating. Lyana put down the lantern and reached for the spot, curious as to what had caused the sudden glow.

Shock stole her breath for a second time as she lifted a ring from the rocks, studying the smooth planes of midnight stone, recognizing it immediately—a royal seal. Her father's was similar, but it was carved from clear diamond, arched into a dome resembling their palace. This gem was so dark it seemed to devour the firelight, smothering the glow with shadow. And the cut was different, in the shape of a *V* with two tall lines extending from a point and a valley stretching between them. The seal of the House of Whispers.

He's a prince.

She dropped the ring and sat up, hardly registering as it clinked against the ground. Her mind raced, flashing to the many conversations with Luka and the advisors, when they discussed all the houses and all the royal families—all her possible mates. The House of Whispers only had one heir, a male raven.

He's the crown prince. Lyana's eyes widened. *The one who's supposed to be participating in the courtship trials.*

Suddenly, everything became clear—why the ravens had asked for a delay, why they had lied about the dragon fight, why they had needed more time.

A shiver ran across the sensitive spot at the base of her neck, making her hair stand on end. Her mind stilled. Her body paused. The sensation crawled over her shoulders, down her back, pulsing with undeniable anticipation, a sizzle firing to life beneath her skin.

Lyana looked away from the ring.

And stared directly into the raven's open cerulean eyes.

10

RAFE

He remembered her face as though it had come from a dream—those brilliant green eyes that seemed to sparkle like distant stars as they looked down at him in concern. In the memory, her face had been silhouetted by the sun, but he realized now that it was just her natural color, dark and rich, with golden highlights enhanced by the warm fire.

Who was she?

Where had she come from?

The longer they looked at each other, the more space the questions seemed to fill, spreading through his thoughts until he forgot who he was, where he was, aware of nothing but this mysterious beauty before him. His own eyes began to sting, yet he couldn't blink. He didn't want to break this moment, didn't want to end whatever was happening—the undercurrent throbbing in the air between them.

She smiled. Soft, nervous laughter spilled from her lips. Then she glanced away, her bashful gaze dropping to the ground as her shoulders bent forward and her wings curved around her arms as though she were trying to hide.

Rafe moved, attempting to lift his chest from the floor and turn.

Just like that, everything came rushing back.

He hissed with pain as his battered wings cried out, as his healing body shouted at him to lie still, as his heart thundered in his chest, all the worry and fear and panic returning.

"The dragon." He forced the words up his dry throat and through his shivering lips. "What happened to the dragon? What happened to my—" He stopped, catching himself in time. "To my people?"

What he really wanted to say was, *to my brother.*
Xander. Xander.

Was he all right? Had he gotten away? Was he safe?

Rafe's blood pounded through his veins, hot and painful. A groan left him as he pushed against the stones, trying to heave his body to a seated position—he had to get up, he had to go. There was no time to waste. Xander needed him. The ravens needed him. No amount of pain would stop him.

"Stay down," the girl instructed. Her warm palm pressed his shoulder back. "Be still before you make everything worse. The dragon is gone. There was no one there but you. And that happened hours ago."

"It's gone?" he asked, breath coming in short spurts as his tired body conquered his will. Rafe's muscles gave out and he collapsed on the floor, still trembling with cold. "How? When?"

A wider smile danced across the girl's face as she shrugged. "I scared it off."

Despite the injuries, the pain, and the dire situation, Rafe snorted, eying her skinny arms and small frame. "You?"

She drew herself up indignantly, arching a brow. "Yes, me. And you're lucky I was there, because a minute longer and you would have been the fire god's next victim."

A shudder coursed through him, the first provoked not by the cool air prickling his skin, but from the icy dread piercing his heart. Rafe remembered. The fire. The claw digging into his gut. His body slamming into the ground. The crunching of his bones echoed through his memory, only drowned by the sound of his screams as they ripped their way from his gut out into the world.

But then it had all stopped.

The pain had been there, but not the beast. He had seen her face, then heard her mutter words he couldn't make out over the ringing in his ears. After that, there had been nothing, blank space, until awakening now in a place saturated by shadow.

"Would you like some water?" she asked, interrupting his thoughts.

"Please."

Moving slowly this time, he pushed up again, easing his chest from the ground, wincing as his broken wings scraped against rock, every movement a new source of torment. Hands gripped his shoulders, helping him. A trickle of heat tingled down his arms and across his chest, flaring hot at the spot where his wings met his back and dulling some of the ache.

Rafe froze.

The girl swallowed audibly.

Glancing over his shoulder, he found her eyes through the soft golden glow of undeniable magic. They were wary of him, yet defiant. Cautious, yet unafraid. Bold in a way that was slightly unnerving.

"You..." He trailed off, blinking and shaking his head, trying to remember. His chin dipped as he looked at his abdomen, at the deep maroon stain on his leathers, the gaping puncture wound through the melted material, and the exposed sliver of intact flesh. "You... On the bridge..." He'd thought he was going to die. The wound was massive, undoubtedly fatal even with his magic. He'd lost a lot of blood. Vital organs had been slashed. Yet, here he was. Rafe stared into those dazzling eyes again. "You healed me."

The girl surveyed his frame, his cheeks, his arms, the bits of skin peeping through the scraps of fabric that clung to him —bits that he suddenly realized glimmered with the proof of his own power. Xander had never been able to see the glow of magic beneath his skin, but apparently, this mysterious stranger could.

"Looks to me like you healed yourself," she remarked.

He didn't deny it.

Then again, she didn't either.

The girl looked away and reached into a pack Rafe had just noticed, pulling out a water jug. She held it aloft like a peace offering, like a truce.

He accepted, taking it with a nod.

No one except Xander knew about his magic. In fact, Xander had been the one to point it out. After Rafe had been found underneath the charred bodies of his parents, Xander had ordered the castle guards to carry him up to his rooms. The left side of Rafe's body, the part his mother's thin frame had been unable to protect, had been badly burned. He remembered very little of what had happened, hardly anything except the pain. Xander had ordered the royal doctor to use every drop of salve from the House of Paradise on his wounds. They had wrapped his body in bandages, praying to Taetanos he would last the night. When they had returned the next day to repeat the process, his skin was nearly healed. The ravens had never looked at him the same way after that. They had said he belonged to the fire god. They had chanted for his death.

To the public, Xander had proclaimed Rafe's recovery a miracle wrought by Taetanos himself. In private, he had called it something else—magic.

Rafe hadn't believed him at first. After all, magic was a death sentence in their world. But they'd tested it out, as reckless young boys tended to do. And they saw it for themselves, how Rafe's skin sealed itself no matter how many ways they broke and battered his body. There was no other use for his magic—no other purpose. They made a blood pact never to speak of it again, so that no curious ears would ever hear the truth, and they let it go. Rafe let it go.

Until now.

Until her.

How many people knew her secret?

Why had she shared such a dangerous truth with him?

"Food?" she asked, ignoring the question in his eyes. Once again, she turned to one of her packs, this time pulling out a sack of dried fruits and nuts. She took a small handful for herself before giving the rest to him.

They ate in silence for a few minutes.

Rafe studied her movements. Her lips twitched every now and then, as though a grin was constantly threatening to burst forth. Her feet bounced. Her wings shifted. Her eyes darted to every spot within their small halo of light and into the darkness beyond, unable to remain still. Energy left her in waves strong enough to emphasize just how exhausted he felt in comparison. Between his wounds and the toll his magic had taken, he could already feel his lids growing heavy with sleep now that his stomach was full.

But he couldn't sleep. Not yet.

"Where are we?" he asked softly, still not quite able to find his full voice. "Where did you bring me?"

"Doesn't matter," she replied with a shrug, popping the last bits of food into her mouth before turning to the bags once more. This time she revealed flint and a few strips of wood.

"How long are you planning on keeping me here?" His tone was a little gruffer this time, a little more demanding.

She paid the change no mind, not bothering to answer as she carefully fluffed the kindling and stacked smaller bits of wood. Instead, she focused on striking the flint three times before getting a big enough spark to catch fire. There was a frustratingly superior air about her, one that reminded him of Xander.

"I said, how long are you planning on keeping me here?" he repeated.

Her eyes flicked toward him, then returned to the fire. "I heard you. Give me a moment, unless you wish to continue to freeze."

His nostrils flared. *Yes, she definitely reminds me of Xander. There's just something, something—*

"There," she said with a satisfied sigh, sitting up and staring at the growing flames. He was mildly impressed, but he wouldn't tell her that. Not until she gave him some answers.

Rafe opened his mouth to speak again.

As though anticipating the move, she cut in first, "Why are you in such a rush? If I'd just survived a dragon attack, I might be content to sit for a few days. Relax. Give myself time to recover."

She was baiting him. Her gaze dropped to the middle of his chest.

Rafe winced. He didn't need to look down to understand what she'd seen. He knew by the amused expression on her face what she was thinking—stranger or not.

That ring.

That stupid, goddamned ring.

"So, you know who I am," he said. Denial was futile. And if she believed he was the crown prince, he might get to Xander faster. "Are you going to help me? There isn't much time. The trials begin tonight. And—"

"No, they don't," she said. "The whole crystal city was

aflutter with the news. The House of Whispers requested a delay, and the House of Peace granted them a single day to regroup. Though I realize now, what they're actually trying to do is find you."

"You didn't answer my question," Rafe countered. "Are you going to help me?"

"Why don't you answer mine first," she volleyed right back. "Why do you need my help?"

A growl rumbled in the back of his throat. *This girl is infuriating.* He knew what she was asking, what she wanted to hear. But they'd danced around the issue of their magic—he wasn't sure if he was ready to come out with the full truth. "What do you want? A vow of silence? You have it. Coins? I can get them. Jewels? I have access to those too. But I need out of this…" He paused, glancing around at the rock and the impenetrable darkness. "Out of this hovel."

"Don't." Her voice was so sharp it startled him. Her eyes flashed with something he hadn't expected—lightning bolts of hurt. "Don't question my character. I saved you because you would have died if I hadn't. At least, I thought so at the time. And I'm asking for nothing in return, nothing but honesty."

Rafe bit back a retort as she tended to the fie unnecessarily, composing herself.

"I'm sorry," he whispered over the crackling of the flames, the only sound in their hidden world. "You're right, and I'm sorry. And…" He took a deep breath, gathering his strength as though preparing for battle. "And I need your help because flesh wounds are easy, but broken bones, broken wings? Those take time and energy to heal. Time and energy that I don't have."

Her features softened in understanding as her ivory wings dropped slightly, relaxing. "I'll help you." She furrowed her brow apologetically. "But not until tomorrow. I have to get home before they— Before it gets too late."

She stood, brilliant wings fanning out against the darkness, glowing in the orange firelight.

"What?" Rafe asked, disoriented by the sudden shift.

She backed away. "I have to go, I'm sorry. I've been gone too long already. But there's more wood, more water, more food. And, oh!" Her body jolted. "Clothes, there are warm clothes, clean clothes. And a rag to wash yourself with. But I have to go. I'm sorry, but I— I just have to."

"Wait," he called after her, stretching out his arm. Immediately, white-hot bolts of pain coursed through him, stealing his vision and his breath. Rafe collapsed to the floor, clenching his jaw against the agony, waiting for it to pass.

By the time he opened his eyes, she was gone.

And he was alone, very much trapped where she'd left him.

11

LYANA

Everything within Lyana screamed that she had to get out of there, away from him, away from those blue, blue eyes that seemed to yank the floor out from under her, sending her tumbling into a place she'd never been before.

His body had been covered in rags. His face hidden behind a sheen of gruesome blood. But those eyes, stark, confident, and unafraid to challenge her, those had pierced her, and she had to get away. To the sky. To the fresh air.

Lyana soared through the cavern, the subtle silver of moonlight her only guide through the darkness. The white patches of Cassi's wings became visible as she neared the exit, but Lyana didn't bother to stop for her friend. Instead, she burst through the narrow opening, practically tumbling into the channel between the cliffs, and pumped her wings to rise up, up, up and over the edge. She finally dropped to solid ground, leaned her head back, and took a deep, restorative breath of crisp air.

Staring up at the stars glittering in the night sky, she let her heart slow down and found balance. The stars seemed different somehow. Brighter. Just different. As though they'd shifted while she dwelt in the shadows of the cave and now were arranged in a more significant way, aligned in a pattern that had to mean something.

Cassi landed in front of Lyana, blurting, "Are you all right?"

"I'm fine." She kept her gaze on the sky.

"What happened? Did he... Are you..." Cassi shook her head as her feathers bristled. "Just tell me what happened."

Lyana dropped her chin, noticing that her friend's gray eyes seemed molten with concern and fear. Yet her own face was entirely different. A slow grin pulled at her cheeks as a wave of emotions bubbled beneath her skin—confusing and overwhelming but undeniably good. Her blood had turned to hummingbird nectar, making her light-headed and giddy with the fizz.

"He's the crown prince," Lyana murmured.

Cassi frowned. "What?"

"He's the crown prince," Lyana repeated, her voice between a whisper and a shriek. "I saw the royal seal hanging from a chain around his neck. I asked him, and he didn't deny it."

Actually, she'd teased him. She'd pushed and prodded, testing his limits, trying to see how far charm could take her.

He'd been gruff, and a bit of a grump, which was

understandable, of course, given the circumstances. But there had been a moment, right at the end, when he'd bit, and she'd bit right back. Something had flashed in his eyes, making them seem bottomless and tumultuous, just the way she always imagined the ocean beneath the Sea of Mist might be. Then he'd been sorry, and so kind. Honest and compassionate, vulnerable in a way she was too afraid to be.

And she'd fled.

Lyana sighed—an airy, breathy sound.

Cassi did too, but her sigh was frustrated and annoyed, laced with stress. "He's the crown prince? Are you serious?"

"Why are you always asking me that?"

"Why are you always saying things I can't believe are possibly true?"

"Don't you see how amazing this is?" Lyana asked, her head still in the stars.

Cassi gripped her shoulders, pulling her back down. "Don't you see how complicated this makes things? He's the Crown Prince of the House of Whispers. That changes everything. We'll need to let him go before the trials. We'll need to release him. And what if he recognizes you? What if he reveals your secret? What if—"

"He won't."

"Won't what?"

Lyana held Cassi's gaze, taking her hands and squeezing them. "He won't reveal my secret."

Cassi's wings drooped as strength abandoned her, her head falling slightly to the side as a warm yet pitying look took over her face. "How do you know that? You can't. You're too

trusting, Ana. Too sheltered by your station in life to understand how awful people can be."

Lyana held back her retort. She knew he wouldn't reveal her secret, because he had a secret of his own—one he would want kept at all costs as well. But that secret belonged to him. It wasn't hers to share, not even with her best friend.

"Maybe I'm naïve," she said instead, with a shrug. "Or maybe I'm too optimistic, but he promised, Cassi. He promised me, and I believe him."

Her friend remained unconvinced.

But Lyana's next words were sure to change her mind. "Besides, he wouldn't sentence his own mate to death."

"His own..." Cassi's eyes darted back and forth as she considered the meaning of that sentence. Then they widened almost comically. "Ana! You're going to pick a raven?" Her disbelief was acute. "You know what everyone whispers. That they're cursed. That the gods are turning their backs on them. They're notoriously secretive. Notoriously wary of outsiders. You haven't even met the princes of the other houses, haven't even seen them."

Lyana shrugged. "I don't care. I don't need to. He's going to be my mate, whether he wants to or not."

Cassi rolled her eyes, but Lyana was serious. The moment she had seen the silver glow of his unblemished skin, the second she had spotted the ring dangling from his neck, the instant she had met those impossibly deep eyes, she had known exactly what she was going to do. Because he already knew her grave secret, which meant she would have nothing to hide. She could be herself. And that was all she'd ever wanted in a mate—someone who saw the real girl beneath the princess and accepted her.

All the fear that had been coiling in her gut the past few weeks was gone. All the uncertainty. All the nerves. They'd vanished.

Instead, there was just stubborn anticipation, and a newfound eagerness to let the courtship trials begin.

"I'm going to be the Queen of the House of Whispers," Lyana told to her friend as a cold breeze brushed against her cheek, carrying an undeniable hum of joy. Was it Aethios, the god of the sky, quietly giving his approval? Or was it her new god, Taetanos, master of fate, murmuring that his plans were falling into place?

Cassi shook her head, as though aware that resistance would be futile when Lyana was in a mood like this. "How are you going to pick him, if he's not even there to participate in the tests?"

"He will be," Lyana said innocently, finally stepping out of Cassi's embrace. "Because we're coming back tomorrow afternoon so I can finish healing him."

"We're what?" Cassi cried.

But Lyana had already launched into the sky, leaving her friend in a cloud of snow. Cassi raced after her, catching up easily, but Lyana refused to stop. Instead, she flew in carefree circles, dipping and diving as they made their way home to the crystal spires of Sphaira, her mood a joyful bubble no prickly glance from her friend could burst.

The main doors of the palace were still open when they got back, though the traffic had died down. Lyana was sure one of the guards had recognized her, even as she dropped her hood low, almost to her nose. Perhaps they knew it was their princess sneaking into and out of the palace at all times of day and just kept quiet, a silent pact to give her some freedom while they could. Some of them were her friends, and the others had spent their lives watching her grow up. They were acquainted with the spirit that lived inside of her—the spirit with wild wings that time would slowly clip away, the spirit they could help keep alive a little while longer.

Lyana followed Cassi to her room, pausing just outside the door.

"Tell Luka I send my good night," she said, even as Cassi widened her eyes in silent protest. They didn't speak much about what went on between her friend and her brother, but it was there. And it would end tonight, that much Lyana knew. Come tomorrow evening, he would be on his way to finding his mate, just like her. And after their vows to the gods, there was nothing more important than the vows they would make to their mates, to honor and protect and love. To be faithful. "Tell him he doesn't have to worry about me and I'm not afraid of what tomorrow will bring, not anymore."

Something sad flickered in Cassi's eyes, but Lyana let it go. One thing she'd learned about her friend was that if she wanted to talk, she would. And if she didn't, no amount of pressure would make her.

"I will," Cassi whispered, then opened her door and slipped inside.

Lyana waited a moment before retreating to her rooms. When she laid her head on the pillow, her body was too abuzz with energy for rest. Her gaze drifted to the crystal walls on the far side of her room and the slightly fuzzy view of the night. She stared at the stars until they became so bright, so all-encompassing, that she could see nothing else. Eventually, she drifted off to sleep, mind empty of everything but the clear and open sky.

CASSI

Cassi stood from the bed and looked down at Luka, at his large ashy feathers, at her own body curled underneath his protective princely wing.

Dreamwalking was an odd magic.

She felt solid, but right now she was little more than spirit and air, a soft wind, a light caress, invisible to the naked eye. Her body was asleep, right there on the bed, with her speckled wings snug against her back as she lay on her side, face pressed against Luka's chest, using his heat to keep warm. But her spirit was here, wide awake and ready for the trip ahead, one she had made many times before. The only visible sign of her magic was the glow emanating from her heart, a silvery sheen that was currently hidden beneath the cotton fibers of her shirt.

Even if she weren't wearing anything, she wouldn't have worried about Luka noticing the glittery aura. He had no magic, which meant he couldn't see it either. If Lyana had been there instead of her brother, Cassi would have made sure to wear a second layer, one with long sleeves that covered her from wrist to throat—just in case.

As it was, she turned toward the crystal wall, unconcerned. In the daylight, the stones kept her in, but in these midnight hours, nothing could contain her. One flap of her spirit wings, and she jumped through the solid stone and into the dark sky.

Sometimes her soul had wings. Sometimes she flew without them.

Tonight, her imaginary owl feathers sliced through the cool air as she raced for the edge, moving faster than her body could, fueled by the power of her mind. When she reached the open channel between the inner and outer rings of the isle of the House of Peace, Cassi dove. Straight down. Not a bit of fear or hesitation as her spirit dropped, plummeting thousands of feet.

The Sea of Mist came upon her fast.

Within minutes, she was surrounded by a hazy fog, unable to see anything but clouds, unable to smell anything but the salty ocean churning below. The waves grew louder. Only when she felt the water in the air, heavy and dense, did she slow down.

At night, it was impossible to see anything in the darkness. She'd come a few times during an afternoon slumber, just to see what it was like in the day. But the sun couldn't penetrate the world beneath the mist. Everything was painted in shades of gray, dull and muted. The ocean had been dark and dangerous, a hidden world she had no interest in exploring.

The air had been thick and uncomfortable to fly through, even as nothing more than a spirit.

The extreme differences in the landscape made it easier for Cassi to separate what happened here, in the world below, and up where her body resided. As though one life was real and one pretend. As though maybe this truly was all just in her dreams.

In the world above, she was Cassi Sky, orphan girl, best friend of a princess, loyal, steadfast and protective, an outsider who had somehow been accepted into the highest fold. Her owl wings had never fit, but in a way, that was what had drawn Lyana to her. She had no magic. No secrets. No family. And no real purpose other than living a normal life, a good life, whatever that might be.

In the world below, Cassi was another person entirely. One she wasn't sure she liked. One she had no choice but to be.

Cassi pushed the thought from her mind as she always did, and instead thought of him, stretching out with her magic, letting it guide her to her king. Sometimes he was visiting one of the many floating cities of the world below. Sometimes he was on the few strips of land that had been left behind when the isles were lifted into the sky.

Tonight, he was on a ship in the middle of the sea. The window of the captain's quarters was open as though he'd known she would come, and he'd left it that way just in case. She could have drifted through the wooden planks, but he knew her spirit preferred the open air, as any bird's would. Yet when she visited him, her wings always disappeared. He'd never seen them, not even in a dream. Because in the world below, she always pretended she was just as human as he, as all of them.

Cassi hovered over his bed, pausing for a moment. People were at their most vulnerable in their sleep. Sometimes when she talked to him now, she forgot how young he was—only a few years older than she. But with his eyes closed and his face peaceful, free of the weight of leadership, Cassi remembered. Remembered too much. She pressed her phantom palm to his face, taking the barest moment to brush her fingers over his defined cheekbone, to shift them through the sandy hair that must feel so soft, if only she could touch it in reality...

Malek.

His name came unbidden to her mind, a forbidden whisper cutting through her thoughts, bringing long-buried memories to the surface. He'd been her best friend once upon a time. Long ago, back when her wings had been fresh, Lyana a stranger, and the House of Peace a foreign world, the boy king of the world below had been her lifeline.

They'd both been torn from their families as children. Handed over to the cause because of their uniquely opportune powers. Alone. Afraid. Unsure. Cassi used her dreamwalking as often as she could to visit him in the world below, and together they'd escape. To grassy plains and snowy hills. To make-believe lands where they painted the sky purple and the grass pink, where the moon was made of sugary confections and they plucked candy stars from the sky. Oh, how they'd laugh, for hours upon hours, their imagination knowing no bounds as he commanded she create more and more ridiculous things in the nighttime worlds they spun together.

And there had been quiet moments too, when she told him of her mother, when he confessed to fears he was too afraid to acknowledge in the daylight, and they shared visions of the future they were fighting to one day see.

A future free of the war the avians knew nothing about.

The war that had claimed their whole devotions.

The war that had once connected them, but slowly ripped them apart over time. Age and duty had stolen his sense of play, his sense of fun. He didn't dream anymore, not really. They met, they spoke, but not as Cassi and Malek. As Kasiandra and her king. A spy and her sovereign. Nothing more. Nothing less. No matter how much she hoped things could be different.

Cassi shook her head, burying the memories, burying his name, burying the boy and remembering the king.

With her thoughts clear, she dove into his dream.

Colors crashed and collided, explosions of rainbow dust as if every paint in the world had been thrown into a frozen sky, solidifying into powders that got caught in a mighty wind. Every sound she could imagine bellowed into her ears, and yet it felt almost as though there were an eerie silence—as though so many things had turned to nothing in the confusion, or into a vortex that had spun too fast and too far. The dreams always felt that way until Cassi reached with her magic, taking hold of the dreamer's mind, folding and warping the scene into one of her own making. With her king, it was always the same. A meeting room with a large wooden table and heavy wooden chairs. Walls of dark gray stone and a ceiling to match. The floor covered in thick woven rugs. A handful of windows allowing in the humid, misty air, with nothing outside of them but endless stretches of gray. And a chandelier made of iron and flaming candles, resembling the trap this room had become, the one she couldn't escape.

He appeared as he always did, standing alert at the window, hands folded behind his back, eyes on the horizon, always on the lookout for something dangerous, something deadly. As his mind registered where he'd been pulled, what room he was in, his body spun. There was no surprise in his gaze when it found hers. She hadn't seen his dark blue eyes sparkle with unspoken wonder in a very long time. Now they were always stormy and tumultuous, just like the ocean upon which his people lived.

"Kasiandra, you came," he said, his voice smooth and unwavering, confident in his authority. The sound brought a shiver to her skin. Kasiandra'd'Rokaro was her name in the world below. Her true name. The one her mother gave her. Though it sounded false, like a lie, every time she heard it.

"My liege," she murmured. "I have news."

"The trials have barely begun," he said, words pronounced like a question.

"They haven't yet begun. That's part of my news."

His dark-blond brows furrowed, but he kept his lips shut, nodding once.

Cassi continued, "A dragon reached the House of Peace."

His eyes widened a fraction, the only ounce of surprise he let show, and they remained that way, slightly surprised and slightly concerned as she reviewed the events of the past day. The fight with the dragon. Lyana and the raven. The delay of the trials. And lastly, the most important update of all: "Lyana said she's going to choose the raven prince as her mate. There was something else, something she wouldn't tell me though I could see the barest glimmer of a secret burning in the corners of her eyes, something about him, about what happened between them. I'm sure I'll figure it out eventually, but I wanted to come as soon as I heard, so you could prepare. At the end of the week, she'll be journeying to the House of Whispers. And that's where she'll be on the eve of her eighteenth birthday."

"You're sure?" he asked, dark ribbons of concern weaving through the words.

Cassi nodded, hating to bring an even greater burden. "I'm sure."

"I thought her father wanted her mated with the prince from the House of Flight."

"He did," Cassi agreed. "That's what I heard him tell his mate and his advisors, but I know Lyana. When she wants something, she gets it. And I've never seen her want anything more. The look in her eyes—it was the same one she gets when we go to the edge, when she looks out at the world. So much unspoken desire to see it all, to go everywhere, to explore."

For a moment his gaze became light and wistful, as though he understood the hopes of a princess he had never seen but knew intimately, as though he sympathized with them. The moment passed.

Cassi trudged on, ignoring the stinging in her chest, the needling prick of an emotion she didn't want to face. "Trust me. The raven prince will be her mate before the week is through."

"This changes things," he said under his breath, then remained quiet for a few seconds. When he looked back at her, endless calculations were spinning in his dark pupils. "You did good work. Excellent work. Come back when the trials are over to confirm, and I'll update you on the new plans. In the meantime, see if you can determine what this raven prince is hiding."

"Yes, my liege."

Cassi knew when she was being dismissed, and she released her hold on his mind, letting his dreams dissolve into chaos once more. By the time she'd pulled out of his spirit entirely, her king was awake, eyes blinking open as he lifted his hands to wipe away the sleep.

He stood and walked to the desk in the corner of the room, then shuffled a few papers before he paused, looking right at her. The hint of a smile fluttered over his lips as the slightest bit of warmth flooded his cool eyes.

"You can't spy on me, Kasiandra," he whispered, voice rich and full, the sort of sound only a true body and not a spirit could make—the sound she'd been waiting to hear. "Good night."

Cassi smiled, content.

She left her king with his worries, only taking one look back at the lonely ship surrounded by fog, something that might have almost been a dream, as she returned to her body and her life in the floating world above.

CASSI

When she woke the next morning, Luka was already alert, as though he'd been lying there just waiting for her to stir. She didn't need to look at his face to see the lines that would be carved into his umber skin, the shadows that would lurk in his warm eyes. Cassi knew they would be there just from the sound of his breathing—not the slow and smooth, carefree sounds of sleep, but the fast, broken, deep sighs that came with finally facing a moment that had been avoided for far too long.

Cassi blinked, opening her eyes and finding his immediately. He was still on his stomach with one smoky wing outstretched, draping over her back like a warm blanket, trapping all their body heat, keeping out the bright morning sun. She had rolled onto her side in the night, wings tucked back so she could sleep facing him.

There was nowhere to run or hide.

No more time to stall.

"You don't have to say anything, Luka," she murmured.

"Cassi…" He said her name as though it caused him pain, letting it trail off, unsure where else to go with his words.

"It's all right," she soothed, forcing a small smile to cross her lips. "I'm fine, really. We both knew this day would come. And now it's here."

She shrugged.

Luka's expression softened. That was one of the things she always appreciated about him—how caring and considerate he was. He thought she was trying to be strong, for him. He thought she was putting on a brave face. And maybe in a way she was. Or maybe she knew that she'd been using him just as much as he'd been using her, if not more.

"If I weren't who I am—" He broke off, his voice strained.

Cassi nodded. "I know."

"If there were any way—"

"I know."

"I think I might lo—"

Cassi reached out, covering his lips with her palm, trapping the word inside. "Don't."

He swallowed, appearing hurt. But she couldn't let him say it, even if it made him feel better. It was the sort of thing he could never unsay, the sort of moment she didn't want to steal from him, didn't want to take away, especially when she knew she would never say it back.

Cassi did love him in a way—loved his heart and his strength, his bond with his sister, his concern for his people, his honor and his loyalty, and just who he was. But deep down, that wasn't what had drawn her to him.

No.

That attraction, that spark, was only there because he reminded her of someone else. A person who lived a world away. A man she saw only in her dreams. They were both leaders. They were both boys she'd grown up with, boys she watched time tame, boys of mischief and fun who had become men of duty and action. But Luka was the only one she could touch with her real hands.

It wasn't a good enough reason to steal his first *I love you* from the woman who would become his mate and his queen, the mother of his children, his future. Cassi wanted to remain a passing memory, one that brought a nostalgic smile and not a regretful fold to his lips.

Which was why she kept her hand to his mouth and said, "You should go before your sister gets here."

With a heavy sigh, he drew his wings in and sat up, understanding the unspoken meaning in her words. Then he paused, glancing at her over his shoulder. "Why exactly is she coming here so early in the morning?"

Cassi arched a brow. "Do you really want to know?"

His tension eased as he shook in quiet laughter. "No, I guess I don't." His features sobered. "It's strange to think that in a few days, she'll be someone else's problem and I won't have to spend so much of my life worrying about her."

The edge of Cassi's lip twitched. "What are you going to do with all that free time on your hands?"

He stretched his wing back to nudge her playfully. "You're one to talk. What will you do?"

Something vulnerable hung at the end of his question. Would she move out of the palace? Would she find her own mate? Her own life? Would she forget him?

Oh, sweet Luka, I don't deserve you, she thought, fighting back a heavy sigh. He and his sister were far too trusting, far too naïve. But Cassi was a different sort, and almost nothing she did had the luxury of innocence.

"Actually, I thought I might ask to go with her," she said tentatively, as though unsure of what he would think. This scheme had in fact been set in motion a long time ago. An owl in a city of doves? An orphan? And now the ex-lover of the soon-to-be-mated crown prince? There was no place for her in the House of Peace. No place for her except by Lyana's side, just as she'd planned. "If she and her mate will have me, of course."

"If she'll...?" Luka shook his head, eyes wide with joy and the slightest bit of relief, perhaps because she'd be out of sight and therefore out of mind, or perhaps just because it meant she'd be happy. "Of course Ana will have you. I think it's brilliant, if that's what you want. Have you told her?"

Cassi shook her head. "I'm waiting for the perfect moment."

Luka wrapped his fingers around hers, squeezing once before letting go. "Trust me, she wouldn't dream of saying no. She loves you."

As I do.

The words were there, hanging between them—words he

wanted so badly to say. Cassi looked away, at the floor, at the bed, at the wall, at anywhere and everywhere except at him. Luka watched her for a few seconds, then stood up and left without another word.

She fell back against the pillow. Her black-and-white wings unfurled, spilling over the edges of the bed as all her muscles gave out and a throaty sigh coursed through every inch of her body.

Sometimes, she hated her life and the choices she had to make. But there was a bigger threat at play than anyone in the world above knew. Greater than the fire god they feared so much. Greater than they could imagine. And she had to do her part to stop it, no matter how difficult it would be, because as far as she knew, she was the only one who could.

"Oh, Cassi? My dearest, bestest friend in the whole wide world?"

She wasn't sure how long she'd been lying there, perfectly still, exhausted and worn out. But the sound of that singsong voice gave her new energy—not that she'd ever let Lyana know it.

Instead, she groaned, feigning pain. "You're here already?"

Exuberant as always, Lyana jumped onto the bed, making Cassi bounce with it. "I am. So it's time to get up, because we have a big day ahead."

Cassi couldn't help but grin. Her best friend's joy was infectious. And it was only in the time she spent with her that she could live in the moment, forgetting for a while that this was a role she'd been ordered to play.

"Let me guess?" Cassi drawled, eying Lyana, who was

leaning over her with a grin about as wide as she'd ever seen, green eyes sparkling like gemstones. "Does this big day include ensnaring a poor, unsuspecting raven prince who is just hoping his mysterious rescuer might come back to heal his aching wounds?"

"Indeed, my friend, it does."

1 4

RAFE

Rafe had no idea how long he waited for the girl to return. He'd lost all sense of time, surrounded by nothing but the dying glow of fire and the encroaching gloom. Sleep came and went in waves as pain woke him, and he used the little bits of energy he had left to heal whatever wounds he could, his magic acting almost subconsciously. But when she did arrive, she entered like a storm, blowing through the silence with an energy that crackled, palpable and overwhelming.

"How are you feeling?" she asked as she swept into the halo of firelight, wings flapping embers and ash into the air, sending a wave of glittering sparks into the darkness. "I'm sorry I couldn't come sooner. But, well, you know. Anyway, I brought some more food and water, a little more wood, though you should be out of here relatively soon, and... Wow." She stopped short when her eyes landed on his face, jaw falling open. It promptly closed as a smile tugged at her lips, one she visibly struggled to control. "You look...clean."

An amused grin widened his cheeks. "It's amazing what a difference water and a fresh rag can make."

"I'll say." She coughed, clearing her throat, but her gaze lingered on his features, slowly taking them in.

Why does she look so excited? So eager?

There was something calculating, maybe even mischievous, sparkling in those bright eyes he'd been unable to remove from his thoughts.

Rafe didn't like it. Not one bit.

"Food?" she asked.

"No, thank you. I'm not hungry."

"Water?"

"No, I'm good."

"Should I spruce up the fire?"

"I'm not cold."

"What about—"

"Please," Rafe interjected, quickly losing patience—which was easy, since he rarely had any. "Could we please just get on with the healing?"

She clicked her tongue against the roof of her mouth, as though considering his request. The tops of her white wings perked, lifting and spreading as her face struggled to remain neutral. "Yes, of course. Let's get on with the healing. If you could just take off your shirt and turn around?"

Rafe frowned. "Why do I have to take off my shirt?" The fire was warm, but he could still feel the bite of cool air through his layers and layers of clothes. "You did just fine on the bridge."

"On the bridge," she countered forcefully, clearly unused to being questioned, "you were near death and I didn't have time. But I'll work faster and better if I can see what I'm doing." He opened his mouth to protest, but she cut in quickly, "You do want to fly again, don't you?"

Rafe shut his mouth.

The girl sat waiting, a brow pointedly arched—the image of someone who usually got her way. Unfortunately for Rafe, he was in no position to argue. He was at her mercy. With a sigh, he began undoing the knots on the furs she'd given him, before moving on to the buttons on his jacket, then the clips at his sleeves. Piece by piece, his clothing was discarded, while she watched silently, eyes following his fingers, making him feel on display. The air seemed to thicken, as though the fire had flared without them noticing. His fingers turned cumbersome as his pulse beat just a little faster, and they slipped once or twice on the slick metal fasteners. As he eased his shirt around his wings, the cool air over his skin almost felt welcome, eliciting a sharp intake of breath—not just from him. A small gasp reached his ear, making him turn back to the girl. Her eyes were on his abdomen, drifting lower, and lower.

He cleared his throat.

She looked up.

"Should we...?" He trailed off, shoulders writhing despite the pain the small movement brought to his wing joints.

The girl jumped like a spring suddenly unleashed. "Yes,

let's. Why don't you, or I could, or we..." She paced back and forth for a moment, then stopped. "Can you just turn a little bit, so your back is to the light, and I'll sit right here, and, yes, this is perfect."

He moved while she spoke, listening to her clothes and feathers rustling as she got behind him. Rafe watched the flames flicker against the stone wall, following the orange glow as it danced across hard edges, making them appear soft. Beyond that halo, the darkness swallowed any other hint of light. The world outside their circle was nothing more than shadow, as though this little pocket of reality existed apart from everything else.

He started when her fingers touched his skin, the barest skim.

"Oh, I'm sorry, are my hands too cold?" she asked, her voice a little higher and sharper than before.

"Uh, no." Rafe's heartbeat became thunderous, so loud he was sure she could hear it too, though she said nothing.

Neither did he, as she pressed her palms again his shoulder blades once more. They were warm and soft, making his skin prickle. His spine straightened. Every nerve in his body turned alert as her fingers shifted, silk brushing against him as she ran them down the center of his back, feeling every muscle along the way and around the edges of his abdomen before sliding them up. Rafe clenched his teeth when she found the base of his wings, gently moving her hands along the edges of his feathers and over his broken bones, sending waves of soothing calm into the ache.

He was burning. Something molten had unleashed and

was coursing through his blood, setting his body alight. Rafe was almost surprised he wasn't giving off steam.

The world was too quiet—just the crackle of the fire and the soft, melodic lull of her breathing. He had nothing to focus on but her touch and what it stirred within him. Even the pain wasn't distraction enough. They were strangers. Complete and total strangers. Yet the moment felt more intimate than any he'd experienced in his life. And he had to stop it before he went mad.

"What's your name?" he asked suddenly, far too loudly to sound casual.

A giggle spilled from her lips, the sweetest sort of melody. "I'd rather it be a surprise."

He tried to turn around. "A surprise?"

"Stay still," she ordered, holding him firmly by the shoulders. Using a single finger, she drew a circle onto his back, then another, two loops that intertwined, repeating them on and on. "Are you excited to be mated?"

A surprised cough made its way up his throat. She drew her hands back.

"Sorry," he said quickly, not meaning to scare her away. "Sorry, I didn't mean... I guess I haven't thought about it much."

"Haven't thought about it?" she wondered with unabashed shock. "With the courtship trials so soon? It's all anyone my age has been able to talk about."

Oh, right, I'm supposed to be Xander, he remembered. *Crown prince. About to be auctioned off to the highest bidder. Well, any bidder really.*

I'm not Rafe, the bastard no raven girl would want.

Uncomfortable, he mumbled, "I'm just leaving it up to the gods, I guess."

"No specific princess in mind?" she pressed, amusement sneaking into her tone. "My princess is said to be quite charming, though I haven't met her myself. But I hear she's clever, maybe a bit mischievous."

Rafe snorted, unable to stop himself. "Sure, because a dove would surely pick a raven."

"Hmm." She paused. "Stranger things have happened."

"Even so, a pampered princess from the home of Aethios himself?"

Rafe shook his head, trying to imagine such a girl with Xander. She'd be too full of herself. Too spoiled to make it among his people. Too used to sticking her nose in the air to ever look down and understand how the House of Whispers worked. Most of all, she would never understand Xander. The House of Peace was too perfect, too virtuous. Even a *mischievous* dove princess was still a dove. She would never understand the trick he and his brother intended to play.

"I can't see that mating happening," he said.

She pinched his skin painfully, making him jump.

"Ow."

"Oh, sorry, my mistake," she commented offhandedly, clearly unconcerned. "Why don't we talk about something else? Can you tell me about your home?"

"The castle or the people?"

"Both." She practically breathed the word, wistfully sending it into the world. "I want to know everything."

"Everything?" He laughed. "That could take a long time."

"I'm not going anywhere," she whispered. Rafe felt there was some hidden meaning in those words, one he couldn't determine. The idea brought a shiver to his skin.

Or maybe the cold did that.

Yes, definitely the cold. The heat from the fire wasn't at all stifling. Not at all.

Neither was her magic.

Nor her hands.

Nor her touch.

"Um, there's not much to know, really," he began. "Pylaeon is the heart of the House of Whispers, the city of spirits as we like to call it, because, well, I'll get to that. The city itself is nestled in a valley between two mountains, and there's a river that runs straight through the center before splitting into a moat that flows around the castle and then cascades over the edge, into nothing but air. The water comes from a massive waterfall stretching across a wide cliff face at the other end of the valley. We call it Taetanos's Gate because it looks like an entrance to another world, especially at night, with the moonlight glistening off the water. We believe lost spirits travel to Pylaeon in search of rest, so we lead them through our city to the river, which in turn leads them to our god. Where he takes them, no one knows."

"That sounds magical," she said dreamily.

"Not magical," Rafe replied as the image of a powerful force even greater than nature came to the forefront of his mind. "Godly."

"And what about the castle?"

Rafe switched the painting his imagination had crafted, replacing certain colors and shapes for others as he spoke aloud, "The castle is terrifying at first, but then, somehow welcoming, like my god himself. It hangs at the edge of our isle, built on the rocks, teetering on the edge of life and death, as we do. Every room has a balcony, so that inside, with a fire lit, you're safe and warm—but just a few steps away, there's nothing but open air for thousands of miles above and below, a reminder that we're small players in a much bigger game."

"Game?" she asked. Her hands had stopped moving. They rested warmly in the hollow groove between his wings, palms half against his feathers and half against his back.

Rafe stole another glance over his shoulder. She was too entranced to see anything but the visions dancing through her head, the visions he'd spun. An almost childlike wonder was alive in her innocent, yearning gaze, igniting a spark in his own chest that he hadn't felt in a very long time. Not since his parents had died. Not since he'd grown up too soon.

"We like to think of Taetanos as the god of fate, not of death," Rafe said softly. The glaze in the girl's eyes disappeared as she looked into his. "We call life a game, because we each have our own wants, our own desires—but he sees everything, he knows everything, and he leads us down our destined path. We fight back sometimes, we make moves, and so does he. On and on it goes until, in the end, he wins, like he always does. But still, we keep playing. What other choice do we have?"

Again, her fingers brushed his feathers, but she didn't look away.

He couldn't, even if he'd wanted to.

"What do you think this is?" She paused to swallow. "His move or yours?"

His, he silently answered. *Definitely his.*

Because Rafe ached to fly, to soar, to get out of the darkness and back to his brother, back to the role he was comfortable playing, back to the sidelines. But there was a weight in his chest keeping him there, keeping him still, keeping him so lost in the fire reflected in her eyes that he couldn't find his way out even if he tried.

For a moment, he thought he could hear his god laughing.

Then he realized it wasn't laughter, but the soft whistle of a bird call—a signal he recognized. His move. His life. His brother calling him back.

Xander?

Rafe tensed.

His head whipped to the side, pulled by the noise growing louder, coming not from his imagination but from the other side of the darkness. He opened his mouth to call out in response, when a hand covered his lips and an arm slid around his throat, stronger and more ferocious than he'd expected. Rafe froze as the icy edge of a blade pressed into his skin, instantly recognizing the kiss of steel.

"Be silent," the girl ordered. "Don't say a word."

15

CASSI

From the outer edge of the darkness, Cassi cursed, torn between returning to her body and remaining the ethereal dreamwalker, torn between wanting to protect her friend and needing to learn the raven's secret for her king. They'd been together for an hour already, and she was no closer to finding out what he was hiding.

She was supposed to be standing guard at the entrance of the cave. She was supposed to be watching her best friend's back. If they were found, it would be her fault. If anything happened to Lyana, it would be her fault.

Yet standing there in her invisible body, a bit of pride burst from her as she watched her princess pull a knife on the prince, holding the blade so close the edge dug into the skin of his neck, nearly slashing it.

She doesn't need my protection.
Not anymore.

Although Lyana often preferred to live in the clouds, her feet were very much grounded on the isle. She knew when to push her limits and when to protect them at all costs. And Cassi liked to think she had a little hand in that.

Not sparing them another glance, confident in her friend, Cassi flew back toward her body by tugging on the line tied to her soul. But she didn't sink into her skin and end the dream. Instead, she burst through the entrance of the cave, still little more than air as she raced into the channel.

She saw no one.

Drifting with the wind, she rose higher and higher, until she was even with the sky bridge. And there, she spotted who had made the call.

A flock of ravens.

There were ten of them, maybe a dozen, and they were traveling fast—traveling straight toward her. At the front, she could see a man, strong grooves of determination carved into his stony face, eyes sharp as they swept over the frozen tundra.

It was only a matter of time before they reached the edge. Only a matter of time before they saw the cave, if they were looking hard enough.

Cassi dove, crashing back into her body so that she woke with a gasp, bolting upright, scrambling to separate reality from the magic. She blinked, once, twice, then reached for the quiver on the rocks and latched it to her back. She flattened her wings to the wall at the edge of the opening and drew back until her tan skin was even with the shadows. Taking a calming breath, she lifted her bow and notched an arrow.

Then she waited, arms steady, fingers itching to release, ready for the first raven who might pop into view.

16

LYANA

This is not going according to plan, Lyana thought as she held her dagger against the raven's throat, grip firm and steady, even as guilt coursed through her. *He'll forgive me. Right?*

The whistle came again, high and sharp, undeniably a call for someone. And as the prince tensed beneath her, Lyana had no doubt for whom it was meant.

"Please," he whispered.

She winced. This was not how the afternoon was supposed to go. Lyana was supposed to charm him with her feminine wiles, seduce him with the unnecessary skin-to-skin contact she'd been enjoying immensely, mesmerize him with her magic and her gaze, and be generally enchanting. She was supposed to learn about her new home and his whole life. She was supposed to talk herself up in preparation for the big reveal.

She was not supposed to hold a knife to his throat.

She was not supposed to threaten her future mate's life.

Lyana leaned close, pressing her lips to his ear. "I can't be seen."

He flinched.

"I can't be seen," she repeated. He swallowed, slowly enough that she felt the blade sway over his neck. "If you promise to be silent, I'll remove the knife. And then I'll finish healing you so you can be on your way. But you have to promise you'll be quiet. You have to promise I won't be seen."

"I promise," he swore, his tone rich and deep and earnest. "I promise, you won't be seen."

Lyana hesitated for a moment before she pulled the blade away, unsure of him in a way she hadn't been before, waiting for him to betray his word. For the first time since they'd met, he had the power—and she was trusting him not to abuse it.

The raven turned slowly, finding her eyes.

His own brimmed with understanding.

He recognized the panic in hers, the uncertainty, the hope. The clear blue of his eyes was like a mirror for her emotions, a sympathy born from shared experiences, shared fears even though they were little more than strangers. There was a connection there, born from their magic, bred from mutual secrets, solidified by a terror they both knew—the terror of persecution.

"No one will see you," he repeated. "No one will learn your secrets from me. You have my word. I swear it on the gods."

"Then turn around and let me finish," she replied, keeping her voice strong because he'd seen too many of her insecurities already, without even trying. And though he was the one without a shirt, Lyana felt exposed, seen in a way she wasn't used to. Not as a princess, or a friend, or a sister, but as a woman.

He heeded her command and presented her with his back once more. This time, Lyana didn't linger on his flesh. She pressed her palms to his wings, basking for one moment in the silken smoothness of his obsidian feathers, somehow made darker by the fire, before closing her eyes to focus on nothing but the magic. Glittering golden sparks spread through his bones and muscles as her power sank into his skin, healing where it found pain, sealing what it found broken, closing tears and mending wounds, working with her and apart from her, as though it had a life of its own and she were just the conduit it had chosen.

A gift, she thought as she worked. *It's a gift from the gods, not a curse.*

His magic rose to meet hers, coursing beneath his skin, a force of raw and potent might. Silver threads intertwined with gold, helping her work faster as his magic funneled strength and vigor into his newly mended bones, fortifying his body.

They worked well together—not speaking, but communicating in a much deeper way. A way she was positive neither of them had ever experienced before, because when he was healed, when his wings stretched to their full glory, like black ink rippling in the reflection of the flames, they both paused.

Neither of them moved for a breath. Her magic remained

wrapped up in his and they held on to each other in that secret place.

The call came again, slicing through the moment, sharper than a newly forged sword. Her raven prince stepped out of reach as he spun, wings shifting with new life.

"Ana," she said quickly, not really sure why. It just seemed unfair that she should know exactly who he was—Lysander Taetanus, born of the god Taetanos, Crown Prince of the House of Whispers—and he should have nothing of hers to remember.

Lyana Aethionus.
Born of the god Aethios.
Princess of the House of Peace.

That was what she wanted to say, to admit, but the titles stuck to her tongue, awkward and tentative. That wasn't how she thought of herself, not really. To those who knew her well, she was Ana. Just Ana. And she wanted him to see her that way too.

"Huh?" he asked, brows drawing together.

"Ana. You asked before, and my name is Ana."

"Ana," he repeated, as though testing how the syllables felt on his tongue. A smile widened his lips, making his cheekbones seem more defined and the edge of his jaw more chiseled. "Ana."

She held his gaze.

Then she turned, lifted the jug by her feet, and poured the remainder of the water over the fire. The flames came to a sizzling end. In the darkness, the barest hint of light glowed at the other end of the tunnel. Lyana took off, leading the way for her prince to follow. At the mouth of the cave, she crashed silently into her friend, placing her hand against the bow pulled tight, ready to be released. Cassi didn't break her focus for a moment. The arrow tip remained pointed at the unknown intruder.

"Trust me," Lyana whispered.

Cassi's impolite growl let her know exactly how the owl felt about her latest plan. She squeezed her friend's hand until she felt her body relax a smidge.

"Trust me."

The raven prince charged past them both, sparing a single glance back. His eyes met hers for too brief a moment, then dropped to the arrow in Cassi's hand. Without pausing, he dove through the tight opening just as the tips of another set of onyx wings slipped into view, hovering a few feet above the entrance to the cave.

XANDER

He couldn't get the image of the white feather cascading over the edge of the sky bridge out of his mind, a bright spot in the midst of shadow. The picture kept playing over and over, leading Xander back to the channel, back to the cliffs, back to this spot. Rafe was here, somewhere, hidden in the rocks, waiting for his brother to find him.

Xander took a deep breath.

Before he could release another call, he was startled by motion at the edge of his vision, as though his shadow had grown and solidified by his feet. He looked down. It wasn't his shadow, he realized as ebony wings tumbled into existence out of nowhere.

It was Rafe.

"Help," he sputtered, gasping for air.

Xander arched his wings to drop straight down and grab his brother by the shoulders, almost incredulous. "You're alive! You're all right. Where the gods did you come from?"

Rafe shook his head, his gaze shifting back to the cliff face before continuing to the open sky overhead. "My wings, they can't hold me. I need the ground. I need to land."

Xander squinted, searching for pain on his brother's face or for hitching in the movement of his wings. "What—"

"Now."

Those blue eyes seemed unusually harsh and demanding. That alone would have been enough to stop Xander's questioning, but the tone of his Rafe's voice was also laced with a panic that sounded unnatural.

"All right," he said, nodding as he shifted his hold, placing his forearms beneath Rafe's armpits to support some of his weight. "The others are waiting at the top. They won't believe — They thought I was mad to even— Well, they'll be surprised, to say the least."

His brother snorted, and they beat their wings, fighting the current of air as they made their way back up the channel and over the edge. They landed in a heap on the flatness of the isle as Rafe's remaining strength gave out.

"My prince," Helen began, stepping forward.

She stopped, gasping as Xander and Rafe rolled onto their backs, separating their tangled limbs. The other nine soldiers in their party took even sharper breaths, which didn't go unnoticed by their prince as he glanced around, noting the shocked, wary faces of his men.

"You…" Helen paused, frowning as she scrutinized Rafe's uninjured body. "You're alive."

But that wasn't what she meant, and Xander knew it.

You're healed.

That's what she was thinking. That's what they were all thinking. That yet again, Rafe had miraculously escaped a dragon and lived to tell the tale. And Xander could see the question in each of their gazes—could miracles really happen to the same person twice, or was something much darker was at play?

"Yes, and I can see you're all thrilled," Rafe drawled, his tone casual to the untrained listener but bearing the strain of a grievance familiar to Xander. He could practically see his brother's guard go up, as though it were a tangible suit of armor being draped over his shoulders to protect his heart. "Notify the queen immediately. I'm sure she's been waiting with bated breath for my return."

Helen wasn't buying the irony. Her eyes narrowed in a suspicious gleam, a caution Xander normally appreciated in his head advisor but at the moment silently cursed. She was too shrewd by half, and he didn't know how they'd be able to explain this miracle away.

"How exactly did you escape the beast?" she asked slowly.

Rafe opened his lips, but no sound came out.

Xander jumped in, stalling for time, subtly offering Rafe clues. "When we came back yesterday morning, there was no sign of you. We found your weapons on the ground, a handful of bloodied feathers on the bridge, scorch marks and a pool of blood. We thought the worst had happened."

"I did, too, for a second there," Rafe said, following his brother's cue. "When the dragon got close, I jumped into the channel to fight it, taking advantage of the narrow quarters. I got in one strike but couldn't pierce its fiery skin, so I released my raven cry and tried to flee. But when I crested the edge of the cliffs, the dragon spewed a wave of fire that singed my feathers, making me drop my weapons to slap away the flames."

"And did someone come to help?" Xander asked, offering up a little more missing information. Helen's expression was inscrutable as she studied his features. "We thought we saw a footstep in the blood."

Rafe's head jerked, his eyes widening with alarm as they found Xander's. A second later, the look was gone, replaced with concentration. But Xander couldn't unsee the fear on his brother's face—a fear he believed was for someone else.

"A dove," Rafe confessed softly. "A dove with black-and-gray wings came to help. The dragon caught him with its claw —hence all the blood on the bridge. I tried to help him, but the dragon hit me with its tail, square on the forehead. I fell off the side of the bridge before I could do anything. My head was fuzzy, and my burnt wings were barely working. I would have tumbled to my death if I hadn't seen the entrance to a cave within the rocks. It took everything I had to make my way inside, and then I lost consciousness. I don't remember anything else until waking up a few minutes ago to the sound of Xander's call."

A moment of silence passed.

Xander heard nothing but his own heart beating loudly.

"Hmm," Helen finally said. "It's strange the King of the House of Peace never mentioned losing one of his own. They seemed to know nothing of the dragon until we arrived, carrying the news."

"That's very strange indeed," Rafe allowed. "But they have a large population, and it was only one dove. It could have taken hours for someone to notice he was missing."

"I suppose," Helen mused, her tone completely at odds with the statement.

The nine soldiers around them shifted from foot to foot, skin itching, feathers writhing, but not because of the breeze —because of how eerily similar this story seemed to the one they'd heard more than a decade ago. That Rafe had been in the right place at the right time. That others had sacrificed their lives to save his. That he had managed to scrape by unscathed while all witnesses perished. That he had woken up with little memory of the event and the hours that followed.

Xander didn't need to read their minds to know what all of them were thinking. He remembered how they'd once demanded his brother's head. How they'd fought to destroy the bastard, the blight. He remembered the cries across the courtyard.

Fire cursed.

That's what they called Rafe under their breath, behind his back—a son of Vesevios, a son of flames, a bad omen, a curse born from the fire god's own lips. He had to remind them that Rafe was one of them, a raven, his brother and their kin. He was needed by their people.

"Thank Taetanos you survived," Xander said, his voice

strong with authority—the voice of their future king. "I don't know what we would have done without you. Are you well enough for the trials? After some food and some rest? Can you compete?"

The annoyance on Rafe's face gave way to gratitude as soon as he realized what Xander was doing. "I think I can."

Xander stood, shaking his feathers as he reached for Rafe's hand and pulled his brother to his feet. Their palms remained clasped as he asked, "Can you restore the favor of the gods to the House of Whispers? Can you win us a mate worthy of our home?"

Rafe lifted his other palm and placed it over their joined hands. Xander wasn't sure if his brother meant for the move to be a reminder that only one of them had the use of two hands —hands that would be essential to compete in the tests of the next few days. If he did, Xander was sure he meant it for the soldiers, whose bodies lost their stiffness as they watched the scene. He was sure Rafe hadn't meant for the gesture to sting, but he couldn't stop a little pang from echoing across the hollow cracks in his heart—cracks that acted as reminders that he couldn't be all he needed to be for his people.

"I will," Rafe murmured earnestly.

Those words, Xander knew, were meant for him. Not as a show for the crowd, but as a promise between brothers. "Then let's go."

If the soldiers wanted to say more, they held their tongues.

If Helen did, Xander was sure he would hear it soon enough.

For now, they were satisfied. Rafe was alive, which meant

the courtship trials would go on, and every other worry was secondary. Maybe when they returned home, the questions would bubble back to the surface, but he doubted it. His brother's performance was going to earn them a queen. Xander would have bet his life on that fact—in a way, he *was* betting his life on that fact. And in the face of such a victory, his people would forget this had ever happened. The dragon would be a thing of the past to a house yearning for nothing more than a brighter future.

But Xander wanted the truth.

Because for the first time in his life, he got the sense that Rafe had been lying to him, too. Not when he'd been spinning his story, but there in the channel, when he feigned a weakness that miraculously vanished during the long flight back to Sphaira as he kept pace with the group. There'd been a secret churning in his eyes, a closed door Xander could tell his brother had no intention of opening.

Yet Rafe's stubbornness had never stopped him before.

When they got back to the guest quarters, Xander followed his brother through halls he didn't know, smiling more and more the longer Rafe obstinately refused to turn around or ask for help.

"Not now, Xander," Rafe grunted.

"If you're trying to find your room," Xander said lightly, "it's one floor up and about three doors to your left."

Rafe paused, shoulders drooping, but still didn't turn around.

"If you'd like, I can look away first so you don't have to

136

meet my eyes. That way, you can continue to skulk for some unknown reason as you follow me to your door."

Rafe released a sound between a sigh, a groan, and a laugh. Then he finally spun, offering Xander a pointed glare. "Fine. Show me the way."

The corner of Xander's lips twitched as he tried to hide his amusement. But he knew when to press his brother and when not to. Instead of tossing an easy retort, a challenge Rafe would have never ignored, he quietly led Rafe to his room, followed him inside, and shut the door behind them.

"Tell me what happened. The truth."

"I did..." Rafe's gaze roved over the imposing city on the other side of the crystal walls.

"You expect me to believe an unknown dove jumped between you and a dragon? And that you got away without a mark on you? What do you take me for, Rafe? I assure you, my mind is fully intact even though my body may not be."

Rafe threw Xander a pleading look, silently suggesting the dig was unfair. And it was. His brother, of all people, knew how capable Xander was. But something about this secret nagged at him.

"What happened?" Xander pressed again.

Rafe pinched the bridge of his nose. "Can you just listen when I say that this one time it's better if you don't know?"

"No," Xander said, undeterred. He stepped closer, closing in on his sibling. "Do you have any idea how sick with worry I've been? The blood on the bridge, I know it was yours. There was so much of it, Rafe, so much. I really thought that this time you'd died. That you'd left me. There's no way you healed yourself so fast, not from a wound that large."

"Shh." Rafe covered Xander's mouth, even as his expression softened. "You have no idea if these walls have eyes and ears. We're in a foreign land, not home at the castle."

Xander bit his tongue, chest ablaze with the sudden fire of fear. Rafe was right. And they both knew what the penalty might be if someone overheard them. Yet, the magic was there, invisible, hanging between them as it always was, unspoken but present.

"You know I'm right," Xander whispered. From his pocket, he pulled the item he'd been carrying around all day—a single, crumpled ivory feather. "I found this on the bridge. I know someone was there. By the size of the footprint, I'd say it was a woman. Don't try to tell me she fought off a dragon all by herself. What's going on? Why won't you talk to me?"

Rafe released a long, slow breath, his body deflating as the air left his lungs. He took the feather from Xander and touched the bristles, the barest hint of a smile on his lips. Xander frowned, curious as he watched a tender feeling play over his brother's face—a feeling he'd never seen there before. When Rafe looked up, his eyes had a brightness that caught Xander off guard.

"You know what happened, Xander. Think about it and you'll know, without my needing to tell you. As you said, your mind is fully intact and far sharper than mine ever was." Rafe shoved the feather back into Xander's hand, jaw clenching for a long moment before he opened his lips to continue, "Besides, it doesn't matter anymore. We have bigger things to prepare for, like the trials. What's done is done. There's no going back."

Rafe stepped to the side. Xander stayed by the window, watching as his brother walked to the bed and collapsed in sheer exhaustion. He turned toward the crystal city, thinking over Rafe's words.

There had been a fight. There had been a wound. There had been a woman. Of that much he was sure. And the fact that Rafe wasn't speaking could only mean one thing—there had been magic as well. New magic. Magic that wasn't his to share. It was the only bond between strangers that could possibly be stronger than blood.

But who?

And what?

And why?

And—

Xander cleared the questions from his mind as his eyes landed on the crystal palace looming in the center of the city.

Rafe was right.

They had more important things to worry about, more important things to focus on.

"I'm going—" Xander stopped as he swiveled to find his brother fast asleep, a bit of drool dripping onto the wing he had folded like a pillow beneath his head.

I'm going to let it go, he finished silently. *I'm going to let you have this secret, because I know you wouldn't keep it from me if it wasn't important to you.* The obsidian ring still hung from Rafe's neck, the ring he hated to wear, the ring he was wearing solely because Xander had asked it of him. *And I know the sacrifices you are making for me.*

Xander walked to the edge of the bed and put the white feather on Rafe's nightstand. He left his questions behind him, looking instead toward the future.

The courtship trials were starting in only a few hours.

And there was much they needed to do to prepare.

LYANA

"A re you ready for this, Ana?" Luka whispered, leaning down as he squeezed her hand tightly.

They were standing before the entrance to the royal rooms, waiting for the signal to make their descent into the atrium at the center of the palace. Luka was garbed in a crisp white overcoat embroidered with silver-and-gold thread, the colors of the House of Peace. The royal seal, a sparkling domed diamond identical to the one their father wore, was pinned like a brooch to his chest, golden band gleaming. Lyana was by his side in a flowing ivory gown with sleeves made of translucent organza, two slits running down each arm, and a back that dipped low so her dark skin acted like a frame to her unblemished snowy wings. The fabrics of their outfits were similarly detailed and in matching colors, but hers had a bit more sparkle than Luka's, with diamonds, pearls, and gilded beads woven into the needlework.

A shiver darted up Lyana's spine, but it wasn't from the cold. It was the thrill of standing at the edge of the unknown, the ache of wondering what the future would bring, the anticipation of so many sleepless nights and vivid daydreams finally coming to fruition.

"I'm ready," Lyana replied, voice strong as she squeezed her brother's hand and turned to look into his honey eyes. "Are you?"

He shifted his gaze back to the wooden doors looming before them, the slightest hint of uncertainty on his face. "Ready as I'll ever be."

They let go of each other's hands and as one lifted the masks they were holding, securing them to the backs of their heads. Lyana glanced at Luka, smiling at the way his ashy feathers highlighted the richness of his skin and the warmth of his eyes, hoping her own did the same. The courtship trials were born of the more animalistic aspect of their nature, so during the tests, the heirs hid their faces behind their own molted feathers as a tribute to the gift the gods had given them—the gift of their wings—leaving only their eyes and mouths visible. The matches were supposed to be made based on strength and endurance, on intelligence and agility, on the instinctive belief between two souls that the gods had chosen them to be united—not on looks or the very human feeling of desire. The masks were only removed on the final day of the trials, when the mate selections were revealed.

"You look beautiful," Luka murmured, tone as unsteady as his nerves. Still, beneath the edge of his mask, a smile pulled at his lips. "Not at all like the scrawny little sister I know and love."

Lyana elbowed him in the ribs. "I'd say you look handsome, but I don't think you need the ego boost."

Her teasing did the trick. The grin on his lips widened and the tension in his shoulders lessened. Before he had a chance to respond, the doors in front of them swung open, turning whatever response had been rising in his throat into a gulp instead.

They'd practiced their entrance a dozen times in the past few weeks, so they didn't need to speak as they crossed the threshold, pausing at the rail for a few moments to let the crowd waiting below take in their full splendor. Then they beat their wings in unison as they rose over the edge and descended slowly to the mosaic floor.

No matter how hard Lyana had prepared for this moment, there was no getting ready for the almost physical weight of hundreds of eyes staring at her, judging her, scrutinizing her every move. Her heart thundered, but she refused to show her nervousness. A serene smile played on her lips. Her chin remained high and proud to keep her gaze straight. The outer layers of her skirt fluttered like a set of extra wings, while the inner layers remained tightly cinched around her ankles. Part of her voluminous hair was braided like a crown over the arch of her forehead, woven with diamonds and gold lace, while the rest was loose and wispy, an elegant black halo that flounced as she flew. She looked perfect. And she knew it. The only thing that remained was sticking the landing.

Though her knees wobbled, as soon as her feet grazed the

edge of the floor her legs did their job, muscles clenching to receive her weight. And Luka's did the same. He offered her his arm, and as the Prince and Princess of the House of Peace, they walked the remaining steps to the empty thrones waiting on either side of their parents. As soon as they sat, their father stood. And, simple as that, the courtship trials had begun.

"Welcome," the king proclaimed, voice loud and booming, reverberating through the hollow core of the palace and past the open doors of the entrance hall, so all their guests could hear.

Lyana's gaze jumped from wall to wall, taking everything in. She and her family sat at the helm, guarding the doors to the sacred nest, facing east so they had a clear, uninterrupted view through the atrium and down the stretch of the entrance hall, which was currently lined on either side with all the doves who had come to enjoy the show and, Lyana suspected, one owl, hidden somewhere within the folds.

The representatives from the other six houses sat on platforms fanning out on either side of her own, three to the left and three to the right, turning the domed atrium into a kaleidoscope of color, with each dais decorated to match its house. The red-and-gold banners of the House of Song. The yellow uniforms and bronze shields of the House of Prey. The deep black leathers of the House of Whispers. The bright purple-and-green silks of the House of Paradise. The liquid-blue garb and sunny orange flowers of the House of Flight. And finally, subdued yet still wondrous, the white clothes and amber accents of the House of Wisdom. The kings and queens of each house sat on thrones, just like her parents, surrounded by their guests, all dressed to represent their monarchs. And each royal dais had open seats ready to welcome the princes and princesses, who were currently waiting outside for the signal to present their gifts to Aethios on behalf of their patron god.

Every courtship trial began the same way—with the parade of offerings, which was truly just a way for each house to engage in little showing off. Each house except Lyana's, of course. She was there to humbly receive, though she wasn't quite sure she'd be able to keep her eyes from widening in wonder or her lips from opening with a thrilled little gasp. Nothing had even happened yet, and her heels already bounced with excitement beneath the many layers of her gown. She couldn't help but start as her father's voice boomed again, giving life to the story of their ancestors, as was tradition.

"A thousand years ago, we were little more than slaves and servants to unjust rulers who wielded their magic to keep us weak and small and submissive. But we had something they did not, something more powerful than all the magic and all the weapons in the world. We had faith. Faith in our gods, faith that they would one day come to save us, faith that they would set us free—and they did. They gave us wings. They lifted our lands into the air. They gave us the home we'd prayed for, a home of peace and safety and prosperity. So we gather here, on the eve of our most sacred ceremony, to give thanks to the gods who broke our chains and gifted us the open sky. I declare, on behalf of Aethios, to let the parade of offerings begin."

The parade always began with the isle to the east of Lyana's own, since it was the one Aethios first blessed with sunlight in the morning. And then the remaining houses presented in a path that followed a sundial's movements, circling around her home, until all the gifts were presented. Even though she knew who would be first, Lyana's breath still caught in her throat when the doors at the other end of the entrance hall slid open, sending a wave of cool air into the palace.

She heard them before she saw them—the gentle trill of a high-pitched whistle, followed by another, and another. Lower, then louder. Then higher, and louder still. Then soft but lingering, stretching on and on, until suddenly, the first bird slipped into view: a masked girl with a mix of brilliant red and dusty-brown feathers—the Crown Princess of the House of Song. Following her, also in a mask, the younger princess with wings of soft blue and orange. Both wore dresses in their colors, deep ruby with gold trim, and each held a log in one upturned palm to represent the gift their house had brought— wood, as was tradition. The bulk of their offering had already been stored in the warehouses on the outer isle, so this piece was just for show, as befitted the parade.

The two princesses flew slowly but with purpose. When they crossed the first third of the entry hall, the song that had announced their entrance burst forth again, with a rising and falling whistle, as the rest of their party soared into view in a flurry of bright colors and even brighter sounds. Red wings. Blue wings. Orange wings. Yellow wings. So many different feathers fluttered together, moving this way and that, a cacophony of color. The walls reverberated with their song, which filled the entire space as their voices echoed, colliding, chaotic yet controlled. High pitches and low tones followed in an arrangement Lyana couldn't recognize, yet instantly loved. The two princesses were perfectly poised, as if unaware of what was going on behind them. There was a pattern in the mess, an organization in the hurried movements and flowing notes, in the highs and lows, in the dance and the song.

Lyana's mother sighed, her lips moving ever so slightly as the softest chime sifted through them. Her wings were still, but Lyana recognized the itch ruffling through her feathers— the ache to rise and join and soar. These were her mother's people. This song was her song. And the bluebird inside her longed to get out, just for a few moments, to be with her flock once more.

But she was Queen of the House of Peace now. A dove, no matter what wings she possessed. And she remained on her throne—a sacrifice all the second-born royals in this gathering understood.

A sacrifice Lyana herself would soon know.

The princesses came to a stop before the dove thrones and landed gently on the floor, dropping into a low bow with their offerings held high. The song drew to an end as they rose, one single note holding steady until the princesses joined in and the rest of the voices faded away. The two girls sang proudly for what seemed like an impossibly long time before swiftly coming to a close and allowing a soft echo to linger.

The King of the House of Song stood from his throne, deep crimson cardinal wings stretching wide as he gestured toward his daughters. He was her mother's brother, and the two girls were Lyana's cousins, though they had never met. But she knew their names before he spoke them. She'd read about them in her mother's letters—something she wasn't supposed to do but, usually with Cassi's help, did anyway.

"May I present Corinne Erheanus, born of the god Erhea, Crown Princess of the House of Song. And her sister, Elodie Erheanus, born of the god Erhea, Princess of the House of Song."

As the king spoke, his daughters remained still, tall with wings wide, skin a soft peach like her mother's. Corinne proudly displayed a brilliant ruby ring on her finger, the royal seal of her house. But Lyana was drawn to her sister, unable to glance away from the brilliant green eyes sparkling in the shadows of Elodie's mask, eyes that reminded her of her own. It was almost strange in a way, to see a bit of herself in someone who was, for all intents and purposes, a stranger.

"May we gift our offering to the god Aethios in the name of Erhea, god of the love that exists between mates and kin," the songbird king continued. "Wood from our homeland to keep the House of Peace warm, and our gratitude for all that you sacrifice on our behalf in serving our god Aethios, the highest of them all."

The princesses quietly placed each of their logs in the long basket at the base of the dais where Lyana sat with her family and took their seats on the empty thrones to either side of their parents. The rest of their house followed.

In the silence, the anticipation of the next arrival grew, the buzz of whispers and wondering, as the door at the other end of the entrance hall swung open again.

Eight birds flew in—four with relatively simple brown-and-tan feathers, the females, and four with iridescent hues shimmering in the firelight of the hall, the males. It was, of course, the House of Paradise. They were the only house where extra feathers were common, either tail feathers jutting out from their backs just below their wings or a ring of pearlescent plumage around their necks. And all four males had them— one a simple curly white tendril, one a voluminous train of fluffy yellows and whites, one a ring of gleaming turquoise framing his face, and one a single long plume of deep black.

Lyana couldn't help but stare, which was the point of the natural display.

Her eyes widened when they started to dance. The four women in the center weaved a circle together, holding hands and releasing them, paying no attention to the men who danced around them. And the men, for their part, did their best to catch their mates' attention. They dove, twirled, and flared their wings, tossing their extra plumage this way and that. There was no music, but somehow, as they moved, Lyana almost heard the melody they created with their bodies. A mating song. A lover's dance. The women slowly turned their attention outwards, showing interest and retreating, leading the men to make even more dramatic displays of their brightly colored feathers. Lyana's heart beat faster as the men dove, then became light as air when they soared. By the time they reached the main atrium, she was enraptured, all attempts at a princessly pretense gone.

With the mating pairs set, the dancers descended to the ground as four groups of two, transitioning into duets. With a spin, the women transformed. Their dull tan garments unfurled to reveal brilliant emerald and amethyst silks that flurried like an extra set of wings as they moved. The men held them aloft as they kicked, brown wings synchronized with their limbs, gaining a beauty they hadn't had moments before. The pairs spun in each other's arms, nothing but moving swirls of color, twirling so fast Lyana wasn't sure how they didn't tangle into a knot and fall. The couples wove in and out, spinning and kicking and leaping and flying, shifting closer and closer, until they all collapsed—the males spreading their wings to cover the bodies of the females.

The hall grew still and the doors at the other end opened again.

Lyana leaned forward in her seat.

A girl with a mask of auburn feathers stepped through the entrance, her wings spread and all her weight balanced on the very tips of her toes. The top of her dress was a corset that seemed molded to her skin and made of liquid jade, and the skirt was short and broken into five sections, parting like violet petals as she glided forward. In a flash, she leapt and began to twirl, spinning and spinning, arching her arms as she raced in a straight line down the center of the floor. Two bare-chested, masked figures followed—a prince with sandy wings and a trail of emerald feathers down either side of his neck, and another with black wings attached by a patch of bright golden-and-sapphire feathers that looked nearly molten as he moved. They chased after their sister, flashing their bright colors, diving in circles around each other, forming a pattern in the air as the girl traced a path along the ground. All three came to an abrupt halt at the foot of the main dais, kneeling before Lyana had a moment to process their display of speed and skill. With bowed heads, each held a vial aloft—medicines, their traditional gift.

The Queen of the House of Paradise stood, her wings a speckled brown, and gestured toward her children. "May I present Milo Mnesmeus, born of the god Mnesme, Crown Prince of the House of Paradise. His sister, Iris Mnesmeus, born of the god Mnesme, Princess of the House of Paradise. And their youngest brother, Yuri Mnesmeus, born of the god Mnesme, Prince of the House of Paradise."

As the queen listed their names and titles, one of the boys looked up, eyes subtly searching Lyana's. His deep-green neck plumes perfectly set off the hazel of his irises as his gaze found hers and held it for a moment in evident curiosity. She understood why when her attention shifted to the jade ring dangling from a chain around his neck—the royal seal of his house, stark against the pale skin of his bare chest. He was the crown prince, and as such, he'd be one of her possible suitors.

Unfortunately for him, her mind was already made up.

Lyana blinked, glancing away, as his queen continued.

"May we gift our offering to the god Aethios in the name of Mnesme, god of the arts that preserve life and those that give us reasons to live. Medicines and salves from our homeland to keep the House of Peace strong, and our gratitude for all that you sacrifice on our behalf in serving our god Aethios, the highest of them all."

The princes and princess gently placed their vials in the offering basket and then swiftly fluttered to the empty seats beside their parents.

The hall grew quiet as hundreds of heads turned back toward the main door, waiting for the next house. Lyana, however, couldn't help but feel the heat of two sets of eyes studying her carefully controlled features—her father's, alight with anticipation, and her mother's, a bit sharper and more analytic. Luka, nervous and protective, tightened his hands on the arms of his throne.

Lyana's heart dropped yet rose at the same time, with a sense of dread and intrigue in an odd mixture that threw her off balance as the doors finally opened. The next house was the House of Flight. And she knew from all her snooping that its crown prince was the one her father had chosen for her. The mate she was supposed to select. The mate that was expected.

Lyana swallowed.

A flock of hummingbirds shot through the entrance, mirroring her nerves. Their wings beat so fast they were little more than blurs of blue silk darting around the hall. Each of them held a jug of what Lyana could only assume was nectar as they moved to their allotted positions, then hovered twenty feet in the air. There were now two lines of ten people along either side of the entry.

Two masked figures entered, walking slowly, wearing matching navy jackets and tan trousers, wings tucked so Lyana couldn't see them. By the feathers shrouding their faces, she could guess their coloring. One mask was a violet tanzanite that shifted into a rainbow of colors as the man walked, and the other had orange hues that reminded her of the setting sun. From this distance, she couldn't tell who was the crown prince, but she guessed the first, by his stature. His hands were clasped behind his back, and there was an aura of arrogance about him that reeked of a firstborn.

As the princes made their way, step by step, down the hall, a flurry of activity took place above their heads. The hummingbirds in formation threw the marigold liquid in their jugs over the princes until a glittering pattern filled the air as they darted around, catching, tossing, zipping, and zooming. They moved so fast their bodies seemed to disappear, as if the two princes were alone beneath a ceiling that moved with them. When they reached the main atrium, the hummingbirds soared higher and spread wider. Lyana winced, waiting for a splash to land on her head, but nothing did. The hummingbirds reached their final spots and hovered there, throwing the nectar back and forth so the pattern became clear —a lily.

Just as suddenly, it disappeared.

The hummingbirds turned their jugs upside down.

Lyana flinched.

Before a single drop hit the ground, an orange blur circled the room, catching every falling stream, then speeding to a halt before the offering basket with a bowed head. The other prince remained in the center of the room, and a moment later, the hovering birds produced flowers and tossed them into the air. The prince with the iridescent mask jumped into action, a figure of blurred glitter as he caught the falling buds, one by one.

He landed on one knee at Lyana's feet and offered her the bouquet, glancing up to meet her surprised smile with a charming lopsided grin of his own. A dimple dug into his right cheek. When she reached to accept the flowers, he brushed his fingers against hers, his olive skin warm and smooth. Before she knew whether to frown at his audacity or deepen her smile in approval, the prince disappeared, soaring to his brother's side with a flash and also lowering into a bow.

The king jumped in quickly, as though his son's display had been unexpected and unplanned, "May I present Damien Eurytheus, born of the god Eurythes, Crown Prince of the House of Flight. And Jayce Eurytheus, born of the god Eurythes, Prince of the House of Flight."

Neither prince looked up as they placed the jug of hummingbird nectar in the offering basket. When they were done, their father continued with the formal statement.

"May we gift our offering to the god Aethios in the name of Eurythes, god of water and the plentiful harvest it provides. Nectar and nourishment from our homeland to keep the House of Peace well-fed, and our gratitude for all that you sacrifice on our behalf in serving our god Aethios, the highest of them all."

The princes stood.

Damien, the crown prince, paused to glance at Lyana once more. His lips widened into a deep grin barely visible beneath the edge of his mask. When their eyes met, he tossed her a quick wink before zooming to his throne. He slouched in his seat, letting his chin rest against his fist as he settled to watch the show.

Lyana pulled her attention away, back to the door, but couldn't stop herself from lifting the petals to her nose and taking a quick whiff.

He's too confident by half, she thought as the scent of sweet honey filled her senses, so delicious she could almost taste the nectar the flowers produced. But when she closed her eyes, the smell shifted to one of burnt wood and dying embers, and the face she pictured wasn't masked, but open, honest, and vulnerable in a way that this crown prince could never be.

Two more houses to go before her big reveal.

Two more houses of excruciating anticipation.

Two more houses and then her mate would appear.

RAFE

Three houses down, Rafe thought, shivering in the cold as he huddled close to the bonfires they'd set up in the streets in an attempt to keep the wait a little warmer.

It wasn't working.

He needed to move. Needed to get his blood flowing. Needed to focus. Because the next few days would decide the future of his house and his brother's life, and he needed to be ready. As he stared at the doors towering a hundred feet away, however, all he could think about was who might be waiting on the other side with white wings that were just another pair in the crowd.

Was she in there?

Was she watching?

Would she see?

Not that it mattered. He'd be gone in a few days, home.

She'd stay here. They'd never see each other again. But even as he reminded himself of those simple facts, Rafe's mind wandered to her silken fingers as they shifted over his skin, running through his feathers, emanating a prickling heat only someone with magic could understand.

"Where are you going?" one of his raven guards asked. There were twelve waiting with him, uninterested in trying to pretend he was their prince. They stood by his side only because Xander had ordered them to be part of the show.

"Huh?" Rafe blinked away the vision of green eyes as he returned to the world, glancing down toward the voice. He was five feet in the air, wings pumping, and he hadn't even realized it. "Oh, um…"

The guard frowned at him. Without Xander, there was no need to keep up the pretense that they had any affection for him at all. But in an odd way, Rafe preferred this to the careful show they usually put on. He'd rather be honestly hated than dishonestly tolerated, especially when it meant he didn't have to pretend either.

"I'm going to take a peek," he said as he pushed hard with his wings, not giving the ravens any time to stop him as he soared into the air, rising over the entrance hall to look through the domed crystal roof and at the floor below, genuinely curious.

The House of Prey had shown up unlike any of the other houses—their crown princess and sole heir had come alone. No performers. No posse. No help. That alone had piqued Rafe's interest. Add the fact they were also the first house without an obvious act, and he was sold. The House of Song would, well, sing. The House of Paradise would, no doubt, flit and flaunt their extra plumes. And the House of Flight would... Well, whatever they performed, he was sure half the nectar they'd been carrying would end up in their stomachs by the end of the show.

But the House of Prey? They were notoriously isolated, even from each other. Aggressive in a way the other houses weren't. Their royal family lived alone in a castle at the center of their great hunting plains, while the rest of the families lived scattered through the woods. They'd be presenting furs as an offering, but the performance portion? That was a mystery.

When the doors opened, Rafe could see the blurred outline of the crown princess as she soared into the entrance hall, rich, brown eagle's wings larger than any he'd seen before. She kept them wide as she floated through the crowd, not even bothering to pump because, well, birds of prey didn't have to. The skinned carcass of a bear was draped over her shoulders, its head worn like a hood as she drifted, unbothered by the weight. Soon enough, she disappeared into the hollow of the atrium. Rafe caught a glimpse of her wings lazily flapping as she rose, no doubt circling the palace core, and then he saw her twice more at the very end of a death dive, rearing back seconds before her head splattered against the floor, not once losing hold of the fur on her back.

Rafe dropped back to the ground as he imagined the words being said inside by the King of the House of Prey, an eagle just like his daughter: *May I present Thea Pallieus, born of the god Pallius, Crown Princess of the House of Prey. May we gift our offering to the god Aethios in the name of Pallius, god of the hunt. A bear skin and other furs to keep you gentle doves nice and warm in this barren winter wasteland you've been forced to call home, all so someone is around to give the ever-demanding Aethios the endless amounts of love and attention he requires so that he doesn't drop all of our homes from the sky and let them vanish in the Sea of Mist.*

Or, well, something like that.

Rafe sighed as his feet touched gravel, shifting his weight from one side to the other, anxious to reach the end of the night. The more quickly the trials came to an end, the more quickly he could put the ring back around his brother's neck, go home, and forget this trip ever happened.

The towering front door of the crystal palace slid open, and the troop of owls that had been in line before him disappeared inside. He'd overheard their crown prince's name, Nico, as well as that of his sister, Coralee, and he already knew the House of Wisdom's offering would be a carafe of oil and a blank parchment where all the mate matches would be recorded at the end of the trials to be taken to their secret library for safekeeping. They were the guardians of history, the archivists and academics, serving Meteria, the god of intellect, which of course meant their performance would be a total snore—and something he had no interest in observing.

Instead, he turned back to the dozen ravens around him, trying to find the words for a rousing speech—the sort Xander might have made had he been where he should have been as the rightful crown prince.

All Rafe came up with was, "I know most of you don't like me, but this isn't about me. It's about our house, about giving

Taetanos the respect he deserves, so let's all try to remember that and get this thing over with. All right?"

Admittedly, not the best, but it would do.

Rafe sighed and shook his head as he turned, wishing Xander were there, wishing Xander were with him. But he was alone. And the only thing that kept him going was the anticipation of the queen's face when he brought a princess home for her son. He would be the savior of the ravens, an outcast no more.

The door swung open.

Rafe flew inside, not bothering to turn and see if the guards followed, trusting them to do exactly what he was doing—honoring the request of his crown prince.

The hall was nearly silent as he entered. There was only the gentle shifting of air as thirteen sets of wings flapped, not putting on a show—not yet. But still, he could feel the gaping stares, the curious eyes. By the time they had cleared the first half of the hall, a buzz of whispers started to follow them, growing into a soft hum to match the beat of his wings. Being gawked at didn't make him uncomfortable. He was used to it by now. But his throat went dry as he struggled to keep his gaze forward, fighting the yearning pull to search the crowd for a set of ivory wings that was sure to stand out from the pack.

Stay focused.

Stay on task.

He swallowed, resisting the urge as they crossed the remainder of the hall and entered the atrium. Rafe dropped to his feet and his guards followed, the *click* of their boots loud in the silence. An excited prickle in the air grew as he let the silence stretch, let their anticipation grow, let them wonder if that was all the ravens had to show, or if they were hiding something more—the god call these doves and other houses had heard so much about. He let the air thicken until it felt almost suffocating.

Then he released his raven cry.

The guards followed, each having been chosen for this ceremony specially because his ability to unleash the god call.

Gasps of shock and awe filled the silence. The gazes that had been curious turned confused and marveled as their eyes grew blank, unable to focus on the world, pulled somewhere else by the music in his call, a music his god had provided. As the high-pitched shriek bounced from wall to wall, echoing across the chamber, reverberating until it grew so loud even he found it deafening, Rafe got to work.

He had twelve onyx stones in his pocket, soft enough to crumble at his touch. One had a diamond hidden inside, but he had no idea which. That was part of the game. Taetanos was, after all, the god of fate, so he would decide.

While the raven cry lingered, Rafe made his way around the room. Lost in their trances, the other princes and princesses were completely unaware of him as he grabbed their palms, dropping a stone inside each. It was hard for Rafe to tell anything about the royal heirs as they sat behind their feather masks, their expressions emptied by his call. He could tell even less who would be the best match for his brother.

In the back of his mind, he heard Ana's voice, a sweet, melodious tune promising that the princess of her house would be a good match for him—fierce and charming. And though he'd scoffed at the idea, he couldn't get it out of his mind now as he circled the room, jumping from prince to princess, depositing his little gift. Drawn by a gut instinct he didn't quite understand, he found himself stopping at the princess of the House of Peace last, landing softly before her throne and reaching for the hand gently cradled in her lap. He lifted her slender fingers, brows drawing together at how familiar they seemed as he dropped the stone into her palm, and froze. Something in his chest plummeted as he stared at her dark skin, made somehow richer by the onyx rock he'd settled in her hand.

Don't look up.

Don't look up.

But he couldn't stop his gaze from rising. It skimmed the metallic fabric of her gown, the graceful arch of her neck, and traveled over the lush lips below her ivory mask to the emerald eyes open in eager wonder.

Rafe couldn't move a single muscle.

He remained there, kneeling before her, caught somewhere between horror and disbelief as she blinked a few times, her eyes clearing as the power of the raven cry faded. Soft voices filled the room, and still he remained, a bird who had flown right into a trap he'd never seen coming.

Her eyes began to sparkle with mischief and mirth. A smile curved her lips. With his hand still beneath hers, she formed a fist, crushing the stone he'd so carefully placed. When her fingers opened, a perfect, dazzling diamond sat in the center of the ashy dust.

Somewhere in the world, Taetanos was laughing, Rafe was sure. But when he finally stood, the only sound he heard was the soft giggle spilling from her lips, striking him like a knife to the gut. He stumbled back to the mosaic floor and knelt before the offering basket, holding a gilded dagger above his head like a gift to his own executioner.

2 0

LYANA

The reveal couldn't have gone more perfectly had she planned it herself. Well, she had played a part for sure. But Lyana couldn't help but think the gods must have had a hand in the rest, because the moment was just as divine as the diamond still sparkling in her palm.

Her prince retreated swiftly and knelt with his offering, but the sensation of his fingers lingered on her skin, as did the sight of those eyes growing wide with shock. She had hoped to get a smile out of him, or some sort of sign that he was glad to see her, that her surprise had been a welcome one, anything really, even the slightest wobble of his lips.

Oh well… She sighed softly, undeterred.

The Queen of the House of Whispers spoke loudly, and for some reason, Lyana thought she heard a hint of disapproval in the woman's tone, as though distaste made her tongue heavy and her voice sharp. "May I present Lysander Taetanus, born of the god Taetanos, Crown Prince of the House of Whispers."

Her eyes still on the prince, Lyana couldn't help but notice that he flinched as the queen said his name. In a beat, the grimace was gone. He spread his obsidian wings and dipped into a low bow as he placed the gilded dagger in the offering basket. The other twelve ravens stood in a line behind him, a wall of black, all of them garbed in ebony jackets, trousers, and boots, not a lick of color on them aside from the pale ivory or muted tan of their skin. The only thing that made the prince stand apart was the royal seal dangling from a chain around his neck and the mask on his face.

Lysander stood, but his eyes stared at the floor, obstinately refusing to glance up. Lyana pursed her lips but didn't look away as the queen continued.

"May we gift our offering to the god Aethios in the name of Taetanos, god of fate and fortune and all that comes in the life that follows. Metal ores and jewels from our homeland to keep the House of Peace prosperous, and our gratitude for all that you sacrifice on our behalf in serving our god Aethios, the highest of them all."

The prince flew swiftly to the empty throne by the queen's side, not sparing Lyana a second glance. Not sparing anyone a second glance, really. Even his own mother wasn't given so much as a smile as he took his place and kept his eyes down.

No need to be a grump, Lyana thought, fighting the desire to cross her arms and frown. Yes, she'd fibbed a little. Yes, she'd let him believe she was someone else. Yes, she'd wanted to shock him. But really, the least he could do was pretend to be thrilled, just a bit, just a smidge. Wasn't he happy to see her? Wasn't this a good surprise? Wasn't he relieved, like she had been when she'd discovered who he was?

Alas, even from across the room she could see the taut muscles in his neck as his jaw clenched. If he wasn't careful, she might be tempted to see what the hummingbird prince was all about after all.

At least he knows how to make a girl feel special, she huffed, snatching her gaze from the raven prince as her father stood, spreading his wings and his arms.

"The House of Peace thanks you and your gods for these kind offerings. We will present them to Aethios in the hope that he will show his favor with a gift of his own."

Lyana glanced at Luka. Together they stood, leaped from the dais in unison and landed on either side of the offering basket. This moment was the most important one of the night, and she wouldn't let any prince sour it for her. Instead, she fastened a smile on her lips and gripped the handle tightly, lifting the basket with her brother as they took to the air once more. They carried the offerings over the royal dais and through the doors behind, which had silently opened as her father spoke.

The sacred nest.

Lyana filled her lungs with the power that lingered in this hall. Behind them, the doors to the atrium slid shut with a *click.* Before them, the golden gate of the nest loomed. A priestess stood with a key, waiting until they landed before slipping the small door at the base of the gilded bars open to welcome them and their gifts inside.

No matter how many times Lyana walked into this room, she was still in awe. The towering crystal dome. The trees and vines and flowers draped over every surface. The chirps of hundreds of doves housed in the nest. And most of all, the orb floating in the center of the room, a few feet off the ground, alight with a glow nearly as bright as the sun, touching every spot around it, pulsing with an energy Lyana could feel in her core—the power of Aethios. His god stone thrummed with the same sparkling magic that ran through her veins. Some swore it was silver, others gold, others a mix of the two, but whichever the case, the orb thrummed with might. Every house had a stone, but his was the most powerful—his was the arch stone keeping their world high among the clouds and safely in his realm.

Lyana and Luka gently placed the basket on the ground and knelt, dipping their foreheads to the floor and spreading their wings as a show of devotion. Five more priests and priestesses appeared from the hidden depths of the grove, removing the offerings and placing them beneath the god stone. She knew she was supposed to keep her head down and her eyes closed. She knew she wasn't supposed to look. But she couldn't help it.

Lyana peeked.

Her gaze slid across the ground to Aethios's chosen. They hid their feet beneath layers of heavy, draping robes, so they almost appeared to float across the ground, although Lyana knew they couldn't fly. They were wingless. They were the mighty few Aethios himself had selected to live within his shrine and serve him in the holiest of roles—blessing everyone else with the gift they'd been denied.

It was hard to imagine that she, too, had once been completely human, a babe only a few hours old, not a feather to her name. But they were all born that way, and then they were brought here, to the sacred nest, where Aethios would select a bird from his collection to fuse with their body, giving them wings. The priests and priestesses were the conduits of his power—that was their gift. They'd never know the sky, but they were god-touched. If their gift felt anything like using her magic, Lyana imagined they were honored to have been chosen.

She kept watching as they arranged the presents in a circle around the god stone, each carefully situated where the isle that had offered it would be. The aura emanating from the stone pulsed, growing brighter, and the edges of the smooth crystal began to spark and sizzle. Aethios was pleased.

The priests and priestesses reached into their pockets and lifted a small polished crystal. They placed their free palms against the god stone, bodies jerking as the potent current of Aethios's might coursed through them, heads snapping toward the sky, pupils rolling into the backs of their heads, elated smiles passing over their lips. A golden halo began to shine from beneath their robes as the crystals in their palms lit with a hidden fire, clear centers turning murky and then brilliant as Aethios's power settled in. After a few moments, the priestesses snapped the connection, but the spark in the stones remained.

Lyana swiftly closed her eyes and returned her forehead to the floor, aware she'd moved slightly out of position as she'd watched. The priests and priestesses placed the six blessed stones in the basket. Five of them disappeared back into the forests of the nest, little more than spirits among the birds. One remained, pressing two fingers to the top of Luka's head and then Lyana's, the sign that it was time for them to go. Not saying a word, she led them back to the gate and opened it just long enough for the two of them to soar through.

They flew to the other end of the hall but didn't make eye contact until they stopped, hovering before the door into the main atrium. Luka lifted his hand to knock, but paused, finding Lyana's gaze.

"Did you look?" he whispered ever so softly, a certain gleam in his eye.

Lyana returned the gleeful expression, raising a brow even though he couldn't see it beneath her mask. "Didn't you?"

The softest laugh escaped his lips as he shook his head and drummed his knuckles against the door. By the time they reentered the atrium, he was the crown prince once more—lips folded in an inscrutable line, eyes focused, mood stoic. Lyana tried to copy him, but there was just too much joy tumbling through her, and she wanted to hold on to that little thrill of mischief, that vivacity of youth.

As she lifted her three stones from the basket, she didn't glance toward the grouch still frowning in the corner, even as her head longed to turn in his direction. Instead, she soared straight to the hummingbirds, presenting their crown prince with his god-touched stone, a sign of Aethios's blessing to his people, and met Prince Damien's grin with one of her own. She flitted to her next suitor, the puffed-up crown prince of the House of Paradise, whose emerald neck feathers ruffled with appreciation as she handed him his gift. And then she gave her final stone to the crown prince of the House of Wisdom, liking how his owl wings reminded her of her best friend, enjoying the shy gratitude in his dark brown eyes.

Lyana didn't spare a glance toward the House of Whispers, even as Lysander's burning gaze darted in her direction, almost like a touch she could sense without looking.

Two can play at that game, she thought, pointedly keeping her face turned forward. Princess Lyana Aethionus chased after no man. After all, why would she when it would be oh, so easy to get him to chase after her?

RAFE

R afe shook his head a little, trying to clear his mind as the princess before him spoke about something —what, he wasn't exactly sure, but something.

Focus.

Think about Xander.

This is for him.

Not for you.

For him.

Still, he couldn't stop his thoughts from shifting and his frown from deepening as his eyes landed on the ivory-draped princess on the other side of the ballroom, her clothes so bright in the firelight they may as well have been a beacon, her laughter so loud he could hardly hear the girl next to him. Three of the princes surrounded the dove as she held court, asking question after question, smile growing wider as she continued sipping on hummingbird nectar. His fingers balled into fists when he watched her reach out and squeeze the arms of the smug purple-winged jerk who kept flashing his dimples as though they were some sort of prized possession.

"Do you read much?"

"Huh?" Rafe mumbled, snapping his attention to the princess standing right by his side and away from the one on the other side of the room. His companion was one of the few princesses who had bothered trying to know him, the raven prince. For Xander's sake, he needed to get this right. All through dinner he'd been doing the math—there were five crown princes and four second daughters, which meant one crown prince would be left unmated. A simple numbers game. And he couldn't fail his people. He couldn't leave Xander without a queen. He couldn't fail his brother. "Oh, yes, I love to read."

At least, if he were truly Xander, that would be his response.

The princess lit up. "Oh, what sort of topics are your favorites?"

Coralee was her name. Coralee. He fought to keep that at the forefront of his thoughts, because a girl like this would be perfect for his brother. The Princess of the House of Wisdom was kind and sophisticated. Like all the owls, she'd spent her life tending to the books in the great libraries of legend, studying politics and history. She was someone Xander would speak to for hours on end. Yet here he was, sounding like a blithering idiot, unable to recall a single title of any of the books he'd been forced to read as a child.

Rafe gritted his teeth as the chiming laughter of another

princess filled the ballroom once more. Coralee waited patiently.

"Um," he grunted. "Everything. Anything. How about you?"

Before she could answer, a strain of music made the room fall silent. The next dance was about to begin. Coralee eyed him hopefully, but Rafe just wasn't sure he could bear another round. He'd danced with her once, and with the other two princesses he'd considered possible matches for his brother— Iris, the Princess of the House of Paradise, who had put his moves to shame as she twirled around him in graceful circles, turning his already grumpy mood even more sour; and Elodie, the Princess of the House of Song, about whom he could regrettably recall nothing, because Ana had been dancing with Damien, the arrogant hummingbird Rafe already loathed with a fiery passion. His mind had instead dwelt on the two of them for the entire time.

"Excuse me, I'm a bit thirsty," Rafe muttered quickly, watching Coralee's face fall slightly as he stepped away. Before he even moved a few feet, one of the other princes who had been by Ana's side swooped in with a bow, offering her his hand.

Not Ana, he chastised as he walked toward the banquet table at the back of the room and grabbed a drink. *Lyana. Princess Lyana. Princess Liar, more like it.*

"What are you doing?" Queen Mariam asked under her breath, making Rafe start.

His instinct to flee only grew as he turned to meet her

raging violet eyes. "What do you mean? I'm getting a drink, and I'm mingling."

"First the stunt with the dove, and now you're turning your back on a princess who clearly wanted to dance with you?" she whispered over the edge of her glass, her voice a silent arrow striking him right in the heart. A smile, sharp as ever, graced her lips. To the outside observer, it probably looked affectionate. "Need I remind you that you are representing my son right now? A true crown prince, who can evoke the respect and admiration that should go along with that title?"

"No, you don't," Rafe shot back with a grin to match hers. Xander had more charm in his pinky finger than Rafe had in his whole body, which was why Rafe had never wanted this job in the first place. But they couldn't risk Xander's handicap being discovered, not now that the ruse was set, so the queen was stuck with him, whether she liked it or not. Rafe rolled his shoulders, stretching neck muscles that had grown uncomfortably tight beneath her scrutiny. "I needed a quick break."

"Playing the heir means you don't have the privilege of a break," she seethed. "When this dance is done, go ask the Princess of the House of Peace to dance. You've been ignoring her all evening for no reason that I can understand when she is the best catch of them all. Do what you came here to do—"

"She wouldn't be a good mate for Xander," Rafe cut in, scanning the room to make sure they weren't receiving any unwarranted attention.

"I don't care what you think. She's the daughter of Aethios. Your opinion is irrelevant."

"The owl princess is sweet and scholarly. She—"

"You think I don't know that?" The queen reached out and took the drink from his hand, eyes harder than rocks as she glared at him. "I've studied all of my son's potential matches. I know who would suit him and who wouldn't. And I think as the queen of a loving people, I know better than you, a raven barely tolerated in his own house, how to play the game of politics. The doves will never pick us, their princess will never pick you, but if you can make the other houses believe it's a possibility, you will become far more desirable. Right now, we are the forgotten house, and if there's one crown prince left standing alone at the end of this, in their eyes that ought to be you. But we have to change that opinion, for Lysander. So be charming, for once in your godforsaken life. Be charming the way my son would have been if he weren't determined to use you like the crutch you are."

Biting back a response, Rafe turned on his heels and left Queen Mariam, clutching his hands behind his back as he retreated to the other side of the room, for once not aware of the princess but of his queen, of needing to stand as far away from her as possible—because she was right, and the truth of her words made her blows even harder to take.

Xander should have been there. He would have charmed the crowd, would have had them so wrapped up in his words they would have never even noticed his hand, never cared that he couldn't release an arrow from a bow or wield a sword well —not when he could make them laugh until they cried, when he could discuss theory until dawn, when he was intellectually and emotionally superior to every arrogant prince in this room.

Xander was using Rafe as a crutch.

And Rafe let him.

He didn't know how to say no to his brother—not when his brother was the only reason Rafe was alive, the only reason he had a place to call home.

This is for Xander.

For Xander.

Rafe repeated the words over and over as he scanned the room, searching for the source of that musical laughter, finding her in the center of the dance floor, gown fluttering in some unknown source of wind that seemed to be following her around as the hummingbird prince with the grating smile twirled with her.

For Xander, he thought again, taking a deep breath.

Then he stepped onto the dance floor and cut his way through the crowd, marching straight to her.

2 2

LYANA

At first, she'd admit, she had been playing up the laughter and the smiles for the benefit of the grouch in the corner who had yet to formally introduce himself to her or make polite conversation. But as proud, boastful Prince Damien continued to spin her around the dance floor, Lyana realized she was enjoying herself. Enjoying the attention, yes, but mostly enjoying the stories. For once in her life, Lyana could ask as many questions as she wanted about all the lands she yearned to visit, and someone was there to answer.

Milo, the boisterous and jovial Prince of the House of Paradise, had mesmerized her with tales of his rainforest home, an isle where the tree canopy was so thick it was sometimes difficult to see the sky, where flower petals could grow to be the size of her arm, where the air was so warm and heavy it stuck to the skin like a damp blanket. He was a far better dancer than she, but he never showed it. Instead, he used his skills to lead her in dizzying circles she could have never managed on her own, while describing the balls his family hosted and painting the most wonderful pictures with his words.

Nico, the more reserved but delightful Prince of the House of Wisdom, had eventually, after much pushing and prodding, overcome his evident shyness to tell her about his home, an isle similar to hers in that the air was cold and the ground uninviting. But unlike her home, his was so far north there were months when the sun never set, and months when it hardly seemed to rise. They didn't live in a city of crystal, but in the dark underground, in sweeping caves the size of her palace, connected by an elaborate system of hollowed passages, all of which led to the great library at the heart of his house.

And Damien, too charming by half, had spent their first dance enthralling her with the image of his homeland, the isle of the hummingbirds. A vast mountain range cut through the center of their lands. On the eastern side stood a dense rainforest with every fruit and plant imaginable, while the west held a sprawling desert with nothing but sand for miles, aside from a river that cut through the monotony. The palace rested on the riverbank, a location chosen as all the major cities were —by the god stone at their centers and the sacred nest they protected.

"Are the palace walls really made of towering gardens?" Lyana asked, continuing the conversation from their previous dance. Soft tendrils of music accompanied their movements. "I can't even picture it."

Damien laughed, a deep, rich sound that would make any girl's heart skip a beat. Lyana's was no different. "They are. My god, Eurythes, provides the water through a river he must have carved into the land himself. We take seeds from all different parts of the rainforest, cultivating our palace and the barren ground around it into the most beautiful garden you've ever seen, full of more color than a dove living in this snowy isle could ever imagine."

Lyana offered him a challenging smirk. "I have a very vivid imagination, you know. You wouldn't be building my hopes up, would you? Just to lure me with pretty words and even prettier places?"

He dropped his jaw in mock shock. "Of course not. I wouldn't dare mislead the Princess of the House of Peace, so beautiful and charming a meager hummingbird like myself would have no hope of wooing her."

The way he spoke made it evident he didn't believe a single word he said—well, about his meager station in life, at least. She hoped the part about her beauty and charm was true, though there was something unsettling in the fact that she couldn't know for certain.

Just as she was about to return the favor with a quip of her own, a determined voice interjected, "May I cut in?"

Lyana bit her lips to keep from smiling as she turned to face the raven blocking their path.

"No," Damien drawled, using the hand around Lyana's waist to try to spin her in the other direction.

But her feet were firm. A curious energy sizzled in the air, emanating from all the eyes that had followed Lysander as he crossed the floor. The crowd wondered what the raven prince could possibly be doing. Their shock at his interruption of her dance was palpable—she was the princess born of Aethios and so very far above him in their estimation. A false judgment, but that didn't make it any less real. To deny his offer would be a sign to all the other royal families that they should do the same, a blow from which the House of Whispers might not recover. And to accept? Well, Damien's ego probably needed to be brought down a peg or two, and most of the guests in the room would assume she was doing just that—trying not to humor the prince who was so clearly favored to win the role of her mate.

But that wasn't the thought that filled Lyana's mind as she nodded and slipped free of the hummingbird's grasp, opting to stare into a mask of deep obsidian feathers rather than pearlescent indigo.

There wasn't anything in her mind at all. Because as soon as the raven gripped her around the waist, her thoughts fled. His fingers brushed the exposed skin on her back, then moved away as though they had been scorched. He gently skimmed her flesh once more, tenderly enough to seem as if he were asking permission. Lyana placed one hand on his shoulder, using the other to take the arm still hanging by his side. As she moved, his grip tightened, boldly digging into her as he began to lead.

They didn't speak, not at first.

Lyana studied the buttons on his jacket, the gold band and black stone hanging from his chest, the leather panels beneath her fingers, smooth to the touch.

He studied her.

She could feel his gaze skim her bare throat, then dip along the edge of her dress, over to the slits in her sleeves where every so often her skin would show. And then his eyes lifted to her face, burning and brazen as they roved over her lips and the feathered edge of her mask, then settled on her eyes, staying there, not looking away.

She swallowed.

Her heartbeat thundered.

Her throat grew tight.

Beneath the layers of her gown, her temperature rose, bringing a flash of heat to her cheeks and a light sweat to her palms. The longer she avoided his gaze, the more demanding it became, until she was sure the whole room could see the steam that must have been rising from her skin.

I have to say something.

Anything.

But what?

She didn't want to apologize for surprising him because, well, she wasn't sorry. And in a place this crowded, with so many eyes focused on her, any mention of what had transpired between them would be dangerous. Even if she wanted to have a serious conversation, she shouldn't. And it wasn't really her style, anyway.

In the end, she settled on a provocation.

"I didn't think you were ever going to ask me to dance," she prodded, her tone airy. Yet her eyes remained on his chest, still too afraid to look up.

Lysander didn't answer.

"I was feeling rather rejected, to tell you the truth," she continued, noticing his jaw clench as her own lips twitched into a smile. She seemed to have a certain effect on him. "All the other princes came over as soon as supper was done, but not the grumpy raven prince, determined not to even glance in my direction. I was beginning to wonder if maybe I'd hurt your feelings somehow, though for the life of me, I can't imagine what I could have possibly done to earn your ire. Gratitude, maybe, but not anger."

His throat bobbed, and before she could continue, he released his hold on her waist, spinning her in a wide circle, putting some much-needed breathing room between them for a few moments before returning her to his arms.

Lyana didn't pause. As soon as his fingers settled on her back once more, she continued, unconcerned by his obvious desire to remain silent, "I'm starting to think you didn't even mean to give me that diamond, though it will make a beautiful necklace, and an even finer story, you know, to tell the children."

He groaned audibly. "Please stop talking."

"Now, why would I do that when you've finally responded?" Lyana grinned and looked up, meeting his penetrating eyes at long last, no longer frightened by the depth of the emotion churning in them. Had he been unaffected—now that would have been cause for concern. But furious? Annoyed? Stubborn? Those were all one little shove away from elated, and Lyana was determined to give her prince a push in the right direction. "I really thought you'd be happy to see me, you know. Excited, even. Or dare I say, thrilled."

He stumbled as she muttered those words, off balance enough to step on her toe. Lyana jumped back with a grimace, wings fluttering to lift the weight from her foot, drawing even more attention toward their spot in the center of the dance floor.

"You're not a very good dancer, are you?" she teased lightly, retreating from any real conversation. They could have one of those later…in the privacy of their own castle…after they were mated.

He refused to apologize, instead offering a shrug. "I'm perfectly adequate."

"Oh, yes, well," she mused, rolling her eyes. "Perfectly adequate is the dream, I guess."

Lysander frowned. "I'm much better without a chatty princess distracting me from the steps."

"I've heard that men aren't very good at performing several tasks at the same time, but I never really understood the statement until now."

He sighed, wings dropping from their tense position high above his back and fanning out to surround them in a black curtain—a brief reprieve from prying eyes. Not at all proper, but Lyana didn't care.

Her prince leaned in. "You want to talk?"

She nodded firmly.

"Then tell me why you lied."

"Because I wanted to surprise you."

His mouth opened, as if he hadn't expected such a simple answer. Or the truth. He sounded flabbergasted as he asked, "Why?"

Lyana spread her own wings, the tips of their feathers barely grazing as she completed the circle. The touch was somehow far more intimate than the joining of their palms. A shiver crept down her spine, but she told herself it was the cold air brushing against her exposed back, no longer covered by her wings. "Because I thought it would be fun."

"Fun?" he asked, amazed.

Her brows drew together and her heart contracted, a gentle ache spreading as her voice turned vulnerable in a way it hadn't been with him before, not really. "Call me crazy, but I thought maybe you'd be excited, like I was, when you discovered there'd be a princess at the trials who already knew your deepest secret, a person from whom you didn't have to hide. Call me crazy, but I thought you'd be relieved, just like I was when I saw that ring hanging from your neck and I realized who you were."

His face softened, as did his grip on her back. He closed his eyes for a long moment, taking a deep breath, releasing it slowly.

"Ana…" he whispered, shaking his head.

Coming from him, the sound of her name brought goose bumps to her skin, but his tone made her stomach drop. It was edged with a silent apology, strained and uncertain, the slightest bit pained. She decided she didn't want to hear what came next, because she knew it would be bad, knew it would mess up all the plans that had been running through her mind nonstop ever since she'd stuck him in that cave. He was going to say he didn't want her.

Yet he did.

She could see it in his eyes, feel it in his touch.

Whatever was holding him back, he'd get over it. She'd convince him to get over it. He was the only prince in the room who knew her secret, knew about her magic, and didn't care. And that was worth more to her than anything.

"Don't," she said, but she didn't need to.

The music had come to an abrupt stop. Lyana whipped back her wings, exposing them to the room, realizing they'd already stopped dancing a few seconds before the music had ended. People were staring. Lyana glanced around, pointedly ignoring her father's confused look, her mother's suspicious eyes, and her brother's overbearing gaze. Luckily Cassi wasn't there, because if she were, Lyana would have had to ignore her knowing expression as well.

She tried to step back, but the raven prince held her firmly. He paused with his mouth hardly an inch from her ear, the edges of their masks touching. His breath was warm as it brushed over her neck, making her skin tingle with awareness of him.

"I'm not who you think I am," he confessed softly.

Then he retreated, bowing deeply, sweeping his wings into an arch above his back. For a moment, she thought she'd imagined the words. But his eyes still burned beneath his hooded brows, full of an unspoken meaning she hadn't yet grasped. The raven prince shifted his hold so he could brush his lips against her fingers, pressing the customary kiss on her skin.

He turned, leaving Lyana rooted to her spot as she

watched him go—the outline of his lips seared into her hand like a brand, a mark she didn't want to erase.

What did he mean?

What was he trying to say?

What did he want?

Most of all, did it matter? Because Lyana knew what she wanted—the freedom to be honest with the person who would share the rest of her life. Happiness and hardship would come and go, she was sure, but the chance to be sincere? To live authentically with her mate?

This was it—her one shot.

And she wouldn't go down without a fight.

23

CASSI

Sleep was overrated.

At least, that's what Cassi told herself as she followed the raven prince around the ballroom. Her soul was weary, and she struggled to hold on to her power, fighting the lure of the pillow beneath her head where her body rested on the other end of the palace. The ballroom was bright enough to be blinding. The movement of so many fluttering wings and sashaying dresses was going to give her a headache. And her ears were ringing from the hum of so much conversation.

Yet Cassi fought to hold on to her power, fought to remain invisible, fought to remain there. Because the longer she'd hovered in the prince's periphery, the more intrigued she'd become.

At first, she'd only wanted to take a peek at all the finery, all the gifts, all the different houses. But then she'd seen the deep frown settle on his brow as he realized who Lyana was, and she'd been curious at the reaction. Dinner had been a bore and she was almost ready to leave, afraid her eyes would fall out of their sockets from rolling at her best friend's obvious ploy for his attention, when she overheard his conversation with the queen—a queen who had referred to someone else as her son. Then he'd danced with Lyana, if that was what you would call it, and their words had only confirmed her belief in the single thing that could have made her best friend so determined to call him her mate.

Magic.

Cassi didn't know what kind the prince possessed, but there was no doubt in her mind he had some sort of power. There was a hum in his blood, an electric sizzle that was undeniable, and she was surprised she hadn't noticed it before.

Blame it on sleep deprivation, she thought with a sigh as she continued to float behind him. The ball was drawing to an end, as was the first official night of the courtship trials. Tomorrow the real games would start, with two full days of tests before a day of deliberation. The following morning, the mate matches would be announced—and that was when Cassi's real work would begin.

She'd rest tomorrow.

Tonight, she was too intrigued.

As the flock of ravens left the crystal palace, Cassi followed, no more than a phantom in the wind as they traversed the city, making for the guest quarters belonging to the House of Whispers. As soon as the raven queen and her son walked through the door, another man emerged from the shadows, stopping Cassi in her tracks.

"What happened?" the second man asked, his voice carrying the sort of authority only high birth could provide. That alone would have hinted at his identity, but one glance into his lavender eyes, and she knew without a doubt this was the son the queen had mentioned—the true Lysander Taetanus. "Who did you meet? How did it go?"

The imposter grunted and pushed his way past, not bothering to stop. The true prince let him, smiling as he turned to the queen. "That well, Mother?"

She wrinkled her nose. "He was passable."

Lysander lifted the corner of his lip, in a good mood the queen couldn't spoil. Cassi instantly decided she liked him. "That's a better review than I'd even hoped from you."

She huffed. "I'm tired, Lysander. And you've already made it apparent you have no regard for my opinion, so I would assume it matters very little what I think. I'll be in my rooms if you need me, preparing for yet another day when I'll have to slap a smile on my lips as I make a mockery of our most sacred ceremony. Good night."

His head twitched as though he'd been slapped, and he stood slack-jawed for a moment as the queen swept from the room, her voluminous skirt rustling as she walked away. Cassi grinned as he shook the stunned expression from his features.

"Will no one tell me what in Taetanos's name happened?"

A petite woman stepped up to the prince, throwing her arm awkwardly over his shoulders. "Rafe caught the attention of the Princess of the House of Peace."

The prince showed his surprise. "The daughter of Aethios?"

"One and the same," the woman said, stepping back. She held out her hands as though to show they were empty of the answers to the questions in his eyes.

He clasped her arm, and that was when Cassi noticed his right hand—or, really, his lack thereof—and suddenly, everything became clear. They were using a fake prince to hide his deformity—something so innocuous it had taken her five minutes in his presence to even notice, but something so obstructive to the trials.

"My surly brother? You're sure?" the prince asked, leaning close to the woman as though the proximity could help him understand what she was saying.

Brother? Cassi frowned.

He wasn't a member of the royal family or he'd be in the trial, surely. She thought back to his stilted conversation with the queen, how the woman had made an effort to distance him from even the pretend role of playing her son.

A bastard, maybe, she wondered, *of the late king?*

"Lyana Aethionus might be my mate?" the prince muttered, voice clouded with disbelief.

The statement made Cassi freeze. Her curiosity turned into a sour, bitter taste on her tongue. The questions withered away, disappearing in an instant, as a painful knot curled in her gut at this new betrayal she'd be forced to endure. Because Lyana had no idea that the prince she thought she had met was a lie, and Cassi could never be the one to tell her—not without explaining the other secrets she'd been keeping all these years, which were far too important to expose before it was time, before her king was ready. Instead, she'd have to listen to her friend go on and on, plastering a smile on her face as her insides turned rotten, preparing to pick the pieces up when the truth came crashing down, as she was sure it eventually would.

But that was her role in life.

To lie.

To hurt.

To deceive.

Cassi drifted away from this trickster prince and his excited smile that had become sinister in her eyes, away from the imposter who had made her best friend believe he might be her salvation, away from the ravens and the conspiracy they had unintentionally roped her into. Her soul let go of the magic and she flew across the city, snapping back into her body. By the time she opened her eyes, there was a knock on her door, a chirping little *bum-bum-bum* that left no doubt as to who was on the other side.

Cassi winced.

She folded her wings to cover her face, as though hiding her shame might make it less real. But it didn't. And the churning nausea remained even as she rolled to a seated position, wiping the sleep from her eyes and the grimace from her lips, trying to muster the will to stand and unlock her door.

It doesn't matter, she told herself, closing her eyes and running her hands over her cheeks, through her hair, pushing loose strands from her face. *It doesn't matter who she picks as her mate, because she's the queen who was prophesized. My queen. The queen who will save us all. And her mate is fifteen thousand feet below, waiting for her on a foggy sea. What happens in these trials is inconsequential. Irrelevant. It doesn't matter.*

Cassi could have repeated the mantra a million times, and it still wouldn't have changed the way her heart dropped when she opened the door and stared into her friend's sparkling eyes. Nothing would have—nothing but finally speaking the truth.

A few more weeks.

A few more weeks and this will all be over.

A few more weeks and I'll be done.

A few more weeks—

"Cassi, you wouldn't believe everything that happened," Lyana gushed as she stepped into the room, not bothering with a hello as she flopped onto Cassi's bed and fell back, dramatic as ever, letting her wings drape over the edges as every muscle in her body relaxed.

Cassi eyed her friend, trying to shrug off the lies and the guilty mood to sink back into the life that took place outside of her dreaming hours. "I have no doubt you're going to tell me anyway."

24

LYANA

He was doing that infuriatingly adorable thing of pretending she didn't exist—heavy on the *infuriating*. Lyana tried to focus on the positive—Lysander seemed to be ignoring everyone else as well. The other princes. The other princesses. His own queen. Those brooding eyes of his were filled to the brim with resolve, focused only on the tests, on conquering each task one by one by one. And he was doing an impressive job.

He'd come first for the boys in the archery trial, bested only by the same person who had crushed them all—the Crown Princess of the House of Prey. Her aim had been so exact she'd pierced her first arrow with her second, so the wood fanned out like a flower around the bull's-eye. She then proceeded to land four more arrows in the center rings of four different moving targets, stepping back between each release to increase the difficulty of the shot.

To no one's surprise, the two hummingbird princes flew circles around the other boys in the speed races, but the raven hadn't been far behind. When they'd placed obstacles on the course, introducing the element of agility, Lysander had gained even more ground, wings shifting swiftly to dodge, dip, and dive as he flew, reminding her of his fight against the dragon and how deftly he'd moved.

While the rest of them had been breathing heavily during the endurance test, straining to hover in the air as weights were incrementally dropped into a bag between their hands, he seemed unbothered. Lyana secretly wondered if he was cheating a little bit, sending some healing magic into his sore muscles to keep them steady while everyone else's strength sapped away, but she kept her lips sealed. In fact, she smiled when the last holdout—the owl prince with his expansive wings and lifelong practice of shuffling heaps of books from room to room—dropped from the sky, proclaiming Lysander the male victor.

Some of the kings and queens frowned.

Some widened their eyes curiously.

The princesses glanced at him with a new sparkle of interest. A possessive knot formed at the pit of Lyana's stomach, coiling more and more tightly with each not-so-low whisper from the girls around her. She kept her gaze resolutely on the center of the arena as the guards prepared for the next trial, the one she'd been eagerly awaiting—dagger throwing.

The stands in the outskirts of the room grew quiet as large slingshots were wheeled around the ovular area, creaking slightly over the stone floor. There were eight daises—one for each royal family, decorated in their colors, and one for the committee, two elected officials from each house acting as impartial judges. Between the platforms there were rows of seats, filled with as many doves and visitors as could fit. The gentle hum of voices carried through the silence. In the background, the constant rustle of feathers could be heard as the people wriggled, searching for one more inch of space in the packed stadium, where none was to be found.

Lyana shifted her weight from one foot to the other, grip tightening on the dagger at her waist, itching to throw. But while all the heirs participated in each trial, they were separated into a boys' heat and a girls' heat, and the princes were going first. She watched, blood pumping, nerves tingling, body aching for action.

Her brother was most gifted with a sword, but he was still proficient with daggers, having been forced into practice because of her. He hit all but two of the wooden discs launched into the air. The two princes of the House of Paradise went next, hitting about half of the targets. Poor prince Nico from the House of Wisdom nearly missed them all, despite his sharp owl's vision. Lyana's favored mate, Damien, narrowly lost to her brother when his final dagger missed its target by less than an inch, leaving him with three targets unstruck. His younger brother performed in a similar way, though a few of his hits seemed to surprise even him. And finally, it was Lysander's turn. The raven prince tied for first place, missing only two targets, just like her brother.

Not bad, Lyana thought, watching him return to his dais. *But not enough to beat me.*

Because she was going to hit every target—every target but one. Oh, if she wanted to, she'd be able to hit them all. Of that, Lyana was positive. But she had something else up her sleeve. Something to force Lysander to finally take notice. Something she'd learned from her mother.

Luka eyed her through the holes of his mask, curious in a wary way. "What's that mischievous expression on your face?"

His own expression reminded her of Cassi's before they'd parted ways that morning—the look she was probably still wearing somewhere in the monstrous crowd. Only members of the royal family were permitted on the platforms, a fact for which she was grateful as she fought to ignore her brother and the nervous flurries his scrutiny brought to her stomach.

Just stick to the plan.

It'll work.

It'll be amazing.

With a deep breath, she reached for the belt of daggers presented by one of the guards. Twenty newly sharpened blades, same as all the other participants, were being offered to her. She tugged them free of the display and tucked them safely into her clothes—six into the belt already cinched around her waist, four into the holster across her chest, four on the back of her shoulders, one at each wrist strap, and two into each thigh band. Her hunting leathers had been specially designed to hold daggers, and Lyana had no problem letting everyone in the room guess her skill level while she prepared, taking her time, feeling the weight of each blade, not paying attention as the other princesses took their turns.

"Stop showing off," Luka murmured, but his tone was playful.

Lyana glanced at him as she snapped the last buckle into place. "Now, why would I do that?"

"Because the Princess of the House of Prey just hit every target but one," he whispered, nodding toward the center ring, where Thea had finished a steep landing. She snapped her eagle wings closed, a broad smile visible under her mask, and walked proudly back to her family.

Lyana frowned and shrugged, trying to play it cool. "There's winning, Luka. And then there's *winning*."

He narrowed his eyes. "What does that mean?"

"You'll see," she said vaguely, stepping forward as the focus of the room subtly shifted toward her—a thousand pairs of eyes, a thousand silent questions, a thousand people watching, but all she saw was one.

One man with his gaze on the ground.

One prince pointedly studying his toes.

One raven who would ignore her no longer.

Because there was winning a trial, and winning a heart.

Lyana knew exactly which victory she was after as she pumped her wings, rising from the family dais and floating casually to the center of the room, pulse not thunderous as she'd expected but eerily calm. Her feet softly found stone. She swallowed, wrapping her fingers around the first dagger she intended to throw, the one at the far-left side of her waist, and pulling it free. Then she waited. Blinking once. Twice. Bending her knees. Using her thumb to twirl the hilt, making sure the muscles in her hand didn't grow stiff.

A bell chimed.

Lyana launched into the air at the same moment the first wooden disc soared free, forgetting the room, forgetting the princes, forgetting everything but instinct. She released her dagger, not bothering to watch, smiling as a *thunk* made its way to her ear. But by then, the second disc had been thrown, the slight whistle hinting at its location over her shoulder. She dove toward the ground, flipping in midair and releasing her dagger as she rolled, before swerving to the opposite side where a third target raced by, then a fourth. Lyana reached with both hands, grabbing the daggers behind her shoulders and throwing at the same time.

Thunk.

Thunk.

She spared a glance at the raven prince, whose attention was still on the ground, and growled beneath her breath. But there was no time to be annoyed as the fifth, then sixth, then seventh targets danced through the air. She twirled, using her wings to propel her in a wide arc as she hit all three. A few of the doves in the crowd cheered. Lyana held her focus, finding an eighth and a ninth target, then hovered in midair as the arena seemed to pause.

All four slingshots were released at once, two targets shooting toward the center of the ring and two in opposite directions. Lyana hit the disc closest to her first, before racing through the center of the arena, turning for one, then the other. The final disc hit its peak and began dropping toward the floor, faster and faster. Her arm strength alone wouldn't be enough to reach it, so she snapped her wings, dropped to the floor, and landed in a roll before jumping to her feet, using the momentum and the muscles in her legs for the extra push needed to reach the target.

Thunk.

Lyana let out a breath and again flicked her gaze around the room. Luka watched her with a proud grin on his lips. The hummingbird prince had a hungry sort of expression in his eyes. The raven was still fascinated by his shoes.

A crack drew her attention as another disc was released. Then two more.

Thunk.

Thunk.

Thunk.

Lyana patted her clothes. Two daggers at her chest. One at her wrist. One more at her thigh. Four targets left, but she only planned to hit three.

Thunk.

Thunk.

Lyana tugged the final two blades free from her chest, weighing them in her hands, waiting in the center of the arena as the final two slingshots were quietly loaded. She breathed, in and out, in and out, and the room seemed to breathe with her, inhaling and exhaling at the same time she did, all doves hoping their princess would do what they knew she could— win the test.

The targets were released.

She hit the first one without hesitation and flapped her wings, rising higher and higher, above the crowd, above the remaining target, which was making a rapid descent for the floor, all the way to the apex of the dome. And only when she was as far away as possible did she stretch back her arm, not even facing the final disc, and let go.

Thunk.

A collective gasp filled the room.

Lysander didn't flinch as the blade landed squarely between his feet.

But he did, at long last, look up.

25

RAFE

He wished she hadn't done that.

He really, *really* wished she hadn't done that.

For starters, two inches to the left or right and he could be missing a toe right now. But that wasn't his main issue. No. While a self-satisfied spark lit her eyes, Rafe couldn't help but notice two other sets of eyes turn toward him, fueled by something far more dangerous—loathing.

He dropped his gaze to the floor, silently cursing that he'd given in to her tantrum when he promised himself not to pay attention to the princess. All that mattered were the tests, the games. All that mattered was proving his house's worth. All that mattered was winning, for Xander's sake. Because the heir with the most victories won first official pick of mate on the final day of the trials. Of course, the matches were truly made during backroom conversations and through secret messages passed from one house to the other, actions far more political than these tests of strength. But it was easy to say no in writing. Saying no out loud, surrounded by a crowd of a thousand people, that was something else entirely. And if Rafe won first pick for his brother, even if no princess was technically supposed to match with Xander, he was hoping that the pressure of the moment and the honor of being the first mate selected would make her a little less inclined to say no. It was rare for an heir to subvert whatever decision had been made behind closed doors—rare, but not unheard of. Which was why he had to win. There was no other option.

Three, Rafe thought. Tying with the dove prince marked his third top placement of the day for the male trials. First archery, then endurance, now daggers.

He ran through the calculations in his head. Damien, the hummingbird prince, had two victories. Luka, the dove prince, had one. Unfortunately for him, heading into the final test of the day, those just happened to be the two people attempting to burn holes through his skull—one provoked by protective fury, the other by jealous ire.

Rafe sighed. *I really wish she hadn't done that.*

He kicked at the dagger still lodged in the wood beneath his feet, but the damn thing wouldn't budge. He refused to kneel and pick it up. He refused to acknowledge its existence any longer. So instead, he took two steps forward. Out of sight, out of mind…

If only life were so easy.

Acting of their own volition, his eyes ever so slowly shifted up, up, up, finding the dove princess one more time.

Ana didn't look away.

Neither did Rafe.

They held gazes across the arena, not blinking, hardly breathing, as the center of the floor was cleared for the next test.

The bell chimed again.

Ana broke their stare, turning aside to accept the sword her brother offered, sliding the polished blade free of its sheath as she tested its weight in her hand and whipped it in a single wide arc, movements graceful and lethal. She looked to find him still watching and widened her smile.

Oh, she was dangerous.

In far more ways than one.

Rafe frowned as the princesses from each house stepped off their platforms and flew toward the center ring. New calculations occupied his mind—not of his victories, but of hers. Thea, the eagle, had won the archery trial for the girls and had tied for the lead with the daggers. She was at the head of the pack. The princess of the House of Paradise had won the speed race. The princess from the House of Wisdom had won the test of endurance. But Lyana had tied for the win with the daggers—the obvious victor if she hadn't pulled that stunt—and a worried knot was coiling at the pit of his stomach as he watched her land in a confident stride, sword far too comfortable in her hand, and begin the last assessment of the day—hand-to-hand combat.

Again, he returned his gaze to the floor, studying the wavy paths of woodgrain in the boards beneath his feet, counting the rings, each one a different story, a different age, a different year. No matter how he tried to distract himself, the sinking feeling just grew, as though the platform had begun to melt, sucking him down and down and down so deep that the air was stifling.

But he wouldn't look up.

Couldn't look up.

Refused—

The room erupted in a deafening roar of cheers.

Rafe's shoulders caved in, and he looked up.

Ana stood in the center ring, her sword at the Princess of the House of Prey's neck, wings pearlescent in the rays shining down the center of the arched dome. The winner. Tied for overall first place for the girls.

With that, he knew she was thinking the same thing as he —that, if put on the spot, her choice of mate wouldn't have the gall to say no, not to the daughter of Aethios, the most prized match he could ever hope to make.

And she was right.

Xander would never say no to the offer.

Xander, the Crown Prince of the House of Whispers, who would walk up to his new mate and slide off his mask to reveal his face on the final day of the courtship trials.

Xander, not Rafe.

A fist clenched his insides and tore everything out of place, leaving him off-kilter as he followed the other princes to the center of the floor. Rafe shook his head, trying to clear his brain as he slid his twin blades from the scabbards on his back. Nothing had ever felt more comfortable or more natural in his hands than those worn leather hilts, and yet his fingers were numb and his arms heavy as he waited for his first opponent.

An easy match.

Yuri, the second son of the House of Paradise.

Rafe lucked out, because if he'd started with anyone else, he wasn't sure his muddled instincts would have been up to the task. But by the end of that first fight, his focus had returned. Because this wasn't about a willful princess, it was about Xander. And that was whom Rafe kept at the forefront of his thoughts as he turned to face his next foe—the hummingbird prince.

Xander, who needed a mate.

Xander, who needed a win.

Xander, who deserved to be happy.

Xander, who was relying on him.

And, well, Damien, who needed to have that smug smirk cleanly wiped off his face.

Rafe spun the blades in his hands, loosening his wrists. Damien stretched his smaller wings, violet feathers glittering in the sun, far more lethal than they looked since they made him fast. Impossibly fast. Little more than a blur as the bell chimed, signaling the fight to begin.

Rafe dropped to his knees immediately—downward being the last direction most people would suspect a bird to go—and rolled, anticipating his opponent's charge. A whiff of air hit his cheek, the narrow miss of a blade's edge, as the hummingbird prince attempted to strike. Rafe shoved his weapon up, metal ringing as the sword found a shield. A string of vibrations coursed through his arm, but Rafe ignored the sting and launched into the air. Damien followed.

The gods, he's fast! Rafe silently cursed as he searched for the prince, blinking as a flash of purple caught the corner of his eye and spinning toward the blur. He held his swords in an *X*, stopping the prince's blade a moment before it struck true. This time, his entire body reverberated with the blow. The hummingbird wasn't playing. If Rafe hadn't realized it from the strength of his hit, he knew it from the seething light in Damien's eyes as the prince hovered for a beat before yanking his sword free.

This wasn't a game or a test.

It was a battle, through and through.

Rafe snapped his wings closed and dropped ten feet, escaping the swing of a shield, an attack the prince wouldn't neglect to attempt, obvious as it was. Before Rafe had time to balance his weight, the prince was there, dangerously swift, swinging his blade. Rafe kicked the center of the hummingbird's chest, using the momentum to soar out of the arc of his weapon.

Think.

Think.

Damien was fast, but Rafe could be faster. He could be better.

Then he heard it. A gentle buzzing sound filtered into his ear, growing louder, into a—

A hum.

A hum!

Rafe widened his eyes as the realization hit, twisting toward the sound just in time to lift his dual swords, catching the prince's blow with one arm and lashing out with the other, this time forcing his foe to retreat.

A hum.

Of course, a hum.

Rafe didn't need to be faster—he just needed to listen. Damien's speed was the very thing that gave him away. As with all hummingbirds, his wings flapped so fast they produced a light frequency, a gentle thrumming that was music to Rafe's ears.

He landed on his feet and closed his eyes. The room grew quiet as he pushed the noise of the crowd away, searching for that singular sound.

There.

Spinning on his heels, Rafe lashed out before Damien had a chance to attempt an attack. The prince retreated, rapidly shifting directions as Rafe charged, swinging his twin blades in sweeping arcs, high then low, left then right, kneeling and using his wing to knock the prince off balance before making for his thigh to draw first blood.

The hummingbird jumped, narrowly escaping.

Rafe remained on the ground, daring the prince to come back and face him.

The game took place three more times before the bell chimed once, the *ding* lingering as it stretched across the arena, signaling their time was almost up, signaling their fight would end in a tie.

But that couldn't happen—Rafe couldn't let it.

He needed to win. Xander needed to win. The ravens needed to win. So, he did the last thing he wanted to do, a cheap trick in such a setting, and took a deep breath before releasing his piercing shriek.

The hummingbird became visible immediately. His wingbeats slowed and his form turned solid. He blinked, confused for a second.

A second was all Rafe needed.

Before Damien's vision had time to clear, Rafe was there, sword pressed against the prince's throat, victorious. And while he wished he could say the urge to glance at Ana never crossed his mind, that was a lie—although he did stop himself from acting on the impulse, instead gluing his eyes to the ground as he waited for his next opponent to step forward.

Rafe fought four more times, won three and tied with the dove prince, refusing to use his raven cry again. Because he didn't need to. Everyone else had lost at least once except for him, and even with a tie, the committee declared him the winner. He had closed out the first day of tests at the head of the flock.

Tonight, he would sleep well.

Tomorrow, he would compete in games of strategy and intellect.

And then he would be done.

Whatever happened, he would be done, and he'd deal with the consequences as they came. For now, he kept his head down and his mind blank as he left the arena, and those dazzling emerald eyes, behind him.

26

LYANA

"I did it, Cassi. I won," Lyana exclaimed as she swept into her best's friend room the following night, weary from the tests, yet rejuvenated by the thrill of victory coursing through her veins, lighting her every nerve on fire. "I get first pick for the girls! I won!"

Cassi sat before the crystal wall to the outside, her back turned to Lyana, wings draped across the floor. At the sound of Lyana's voice, she drew herself up. "You won?"

Her tone was dubious at best.

"Yes, I won," Lyana confirmed indignantly, landing on Cassi's bed, still bouncing with energy. "Did you doubt me?"

Cassi glanced over her shoulder, one sharp brow raised over the rim of her reading glasses. "You didn't cheat, did you?"

Lyana glared at her friend. "No."

"Because the strength tests, I expected you to do well with those, but the mental examinations…?" Cassi trailed off, letting the implication hang for a few moments.

"Oh, stuff it." Lyana threw a pillow at her face. "I beat you at games of strategy all the time."

Her friend dodged the attack easily. By the time she turned around, the edges of her lips had started to twitch. "Yes, but that's because I let you."

"You do not." Lyana wrinkled her nose, then offered a wicked grin of her own. "You're too sore of a loser to let me beat you at anything."

Cassi looked at the ceiling as if weighing the truth of Lyana's statement, then shrugged before crossing over to the bed. After placing her book and glasses on the side table, she collapsed onto the mattress and Lyana dropped by her side. The two of them became a mess of feathers and limbs, a position familiar to them.

"What are you going to do?" Cassi asked, a heaviness Lyana didn't understand in her voice.

Letting her head fall to the side, Lyana studied her friend, but Cassi's eyes remained on the ceiling, clouded by thoughts. "My father is sending a note to the House of Flight, requesting a mate match with Damien."

Cassi's gaze sharpened as she turned toward Lyana. "You changed your mind?"

It was a hopeful question. One whose answer Cassi already knew, which was why no surprise lit her features as Lyana replied, "No."

Cassi continued to stare, waiting for an explanation.

Lyana's elation quickly seeped from her bones, leaving her weary and exhausted, ready to reach the end of the trials, ready to let her new adventure begin. "I told my mother and father I wanted to match with the raven prince. They forbade it. But tomorrow, when the time comes, no matter what deal my father made, the choice will be mine. And I plan to do as I wish."

"Ana…"

Words danced at the tip of Cassi's tongue. Lyana could practically see them, but she couldn't begin to guess what they were. Her friend had never held back before. Now certainly wasn't the time to begin.

"What? Tell me."

"It's just…" Cassi broke off and rose to a seated position, wrapping her wings close to her sides in a protective cocoon as though she couldn't look at Lyana. "I'm worried you're going to get hurt."

"Is that all?" Lyana asked lightly, reaching out to graze her friend's wings, unsure where her sudden sullenness had come from.

But Cassi wasn't joking. Again, she glanced over her shoulder, silver eyes as impenetrable as the mist of the foggy sea below. "You've turned the raven into a fairy-tale prince because of a few stolen hours together, and I'm worried that in the end, the truth will only disappoint you."

The truth? Lyana thought, frowning. It was an odd word to use, *truth*. Not in the end, the prince would only disappoint her. Not in the end, the House of Whispers would only disappoint her. Not in the end, her dreams would only disappoint her.

But the truth.

As if, somehow, Cassi saw a lie Lyana had not yet uncovered.

She shook her head, because the only truth was that in the end, it didn't matter.

"I know I can be too optimistic at times, too eager, too excited, but I'm not a fool, Cassi," Lyana said. "I know my courtship isn't one of love, but of political necessity. I know that no matter which prince I choose, a mutual respect and understanding might be all I can ever hope to receive. And I'm sure Damien would make a lovely mate. Beneath the arrogance, he seemed sweet, a good match. On paper, Lysander seems like the less obvious choice, more reserved, a little surly. But at least with him, I won't have to hide who I am—what I am."

Cassi held her eyes shut for a moment, before turning away. "I get it, Ana. I get it."

Lyana nudged her with the tip of her ivory wing. "Is this about Luka?"

Her friend's shoulders caved in. "Am I so obvious?"

Lyana released a breath. *Of course. I've been the worst friend. I haven't even asked how she's feeling. I've been far too preoccupied with myself.*

"Are you—?"

"Who is he going to be matched with?" Cassi interrupted.

"Iris," Lyana told her softly. "The princess of the House of Paradise."

"What's she like?"

"She seems…" Lyana chewed her lower lip for a moment, unsure of what to say or how to say it. "Well, she won the speed trials and she performed admirably during hand-to-hand combat. A little more practice, and she might have beat me. At the ball on the first night, she dazzled the crowd with her graceful dancing and obvious charm. I think—well, I hope at least—that they'll be happy together."

Lyana watched her friend nod silently, aware that the last thing Cassi would want to talk about was the only thing Lyana wanted to know—if she was all right. Cassi much preferred a witty retort to an honest answer, especially when it came to matters of the heart.

"Hey, Ana?" Cassi whispered quietly. "Can I ask you something?"

"Anything."

Cassi kept her speckled wings wrapped snugly around her shoulders. Lyana's arms itched to do the same, to hold her friend close, to protect her from an invisible wound they had seen coming. Cassi studied the crumpled bedsheets, not accepting the sympathy Lyana wanted to provide. Instead, she picked at her sleeping trousers, finding pills that didn't exist in the fabric.

"Do you think— I mean, I've been thinking, well, wondering if maybe— It's just, there's not really a place for me here, anymore, at least I don't feel there is, and I was hoping, that maybe you might, or I could, or we…" Cassi swallowed.

The uncertainty in her voice was something Lyana had never heard before. The friend she adored was confident, not full of jumbled words that tripped over themselves, spilling in all sorts of directions that didn't make sense.

Lyana grabbed Cassi's hands. "What? What are you trying to say?"

Cassi's eyes snapped up, clear in a way that didn't match the rest of her. "Can I go with you to the House of Whispers?"

Lyana blinked.

When her body caught up to her mind, she leaped onto Cassi's chest, crushing her friend's wings in an overly enthusiastic hug that threw them both off balance and sent them crashing into the pillows.

"Yes!" she shrieked. "Yes, you must!"

In truth, Lyana had secretly been hoping Cassi would make the suggestion for weeks, but she hadn't wanted to push. Their whole lives were here, in the House of Peace, and just because Lyana was forced to uproot her existence, Cassi didn't have to follow. But if her friend wanted to come along for the adventure, she certainly wouldn't say no.

"Do you think the ravens will allow it?" Cassi asked, voice somewhat suffocated by Lyana's weight.

Lyana hastily sat, giving her friend room to breathe, and shrugged, mind already whirling. "So what if they don't? Tomorrow their crown prince will whisk me away from the only home I've ever known so I can become the future queen of a foreign world." She paused as the weight of what the morning would bring settled on her shoulders—so many dreams, so many questions, so many unknowns. Straightening her back, she proudly lifted her chin. "I dare him to even attempt to tell me *no*."

They both knew what that *no* entailed.

Cassi closed her eyes and pretended to shudder. "I pity the man who tries to deny you."

Lyana grinned. "I do too, my friend. I do too."

27

XANDER

The crystal palace was even more magnificent upon closer inspection. The sweeping front doors. The entry hallway that must have spanned two hundred feet, all encased in clear rocks, so every inch of the mosaic floor glistened with sunlight, reflecting the majestic sky above. The central atrium, its dome towering impossibly high with a carved staircase spiraling up the outer edges, leading to more rooms and suites than he could begin to count. And that grand sight didn't even take into account the royal families from every house, their ornate garments, the vast array of feathers and jewels, the vibrant patches of color dotted around the room. Xander was trying his best not to gawk, but the task was proving difficult, especially for a raven from a house shrouded in nothing but black.

You've been participating in the trials for days, he silently reminded himself. *After the parade of offerings, the ball, the tests themselves, this sight should be old news. Close your mouth. Level your gaze. And stop smiling like a blithering fledgling. You're a crown prince, for Taetanos's sake—pretend that you belong.*

The flash in his mother's eyes seemed to say the same thing. *Pull it together.*

They'd considered allowing Rafe to close the trials too, unwilling to risk their deception being discovered during this final ceremony. But in the end, Xander knew he needed to reveal his own face, not Rafe's, to all the watching royals. Once the trials were over and the matches set, the heirs would finally be granted free rein to travel between houses, so he needed to be sure his face was the one remembered. His hand could always be explained away later as an accident, but the differences between his and Rafe's features, subtle as they were, could not.

Xander tightened his grip on the arm of the throne to keep his fingers from tapping. The scratching of woodgrain against his left palm kept him grounded even as his heart continued to pound.

Today, he was going to meet his mate.

Today, he would prove to the world that his people had not lost favor with the gods.

Today, he was going to give the House of Whispers a win.

Because he'd been matched.

Yesterday evening, Rafe had stormed into the raven guest quarters, grunting rather than speaking, eyes almost bleeding red, fists curled, all because he hadn't won. Going into the second day of tests, he'd had the clear lead, but the dove prince caught him during the strategy games, and they'd ended the trials with a tie. But someone had to have first pick, and a son of Aethios would win that privilege every time. The committee had given Rafe the second male and third overall pick of mate, which despite his temper tantrum, was more than the House of Whispers had even dreamed to attain. But that wasn't why Xander was smiling, why his heart thudded in his chest, why his eyes snapped toward the princess currently entering the room.

A letter had arrived late in the night—a message from the House of Wisdom.

Their princess had accepted his offer.

Rafe had looked relieved that all his efforts hadn't ended in failure. Xander had been too shaken to pay attention to the remaining anxiety in his brother's gaze. All his muscles had relaxed and he'd wobbled on unsteady feet until his mother gripped his shoulders, pride bright in her eyes. Her emotion spurred him back to life. A wave of energy coursed through him like a strong portion of hummingbird nectar, making him light and airy, more buoyant than he could ever remember feeling, as though even without wings he could have floated into the sky.

And now she was here.

Coralee, Xander thought, watching as she flew down the entrance hall with the House of Wisdom, wings the color of raw honey, glowing like the dawn as the sun shone through them. Her amber feathers against the white silk of her dress was a living embodiment of the two colors of her house.

He couldn't wait to show Coralee his library. It would be nothing, he assumed, compared to the wondrous place where she'd grown up, but perhaps it would provide her with a small sense of home, so his house wouldn't seem so strange, so foreign. And the maps, too. For a small island, they had a vast collection of maps—ones he used to study for days and days while Rafe practiced more physical pursuits. But Xander had always preferred the crisp shade of a reading room to swordplay under the hot summer sun, and the touch of rough parchment to a smooth leather hilt. The dusty smell of old books, though not always the most fragrant, was home, and he had a feeling Coralee would think the same.

He'd had a dream the night before, of the two of them sitting side by side next to a fire on a cold winter night, swapping a volume back and forth, each taking turns reading a chapter aloud, her voice a lullaby in the dark. And maybe that was all it would ever be, a dream, but he hoped not. He wanted more than just a match. He wanted a mate.

"Welcome," the King of the House of Peace boomed.

Xander started, pulled from his thoughts. Coralee was watching him too, a small smile on her lips as though she found him amusing. He dropped his gaze, embarrassed that she'd caught him in the act of staring. The king continued to speak, but Xander couldn't for the life of him listen, especially as his focus was drawn to his right hand by the questions swirling in the back of his mind.

Would the princess continue to be amused when she realized she'd been duped?

Or would she hate him for lying?

Would she understand the necessity of the trick he'd pulled?

Or would she turn from him forever?

Did she want Rafe, the warrior?

Or would she be satisfied with him instead?

As he examined his hand, for a moment even he thought it was real. They'd sewn a glove to the sleeve of his jacket and stuffed it with soft clay, so it had the weight and suppleness of a real hand, and the look of five fingers, though they couldn't bend. But if he rested it on the chair, no one would ever know the ruse. When he stood to remove his mask, the game would be a bit more difficult to play, but Rafe had used a special knot Xander could tug free with one hand. The only noticeable difference between them was the color of his eyes, lavender instead of Rafe's sky blue, but his brother assured him he'd kept his gaze on the ground most of the time, so hopefully no one would notice. If they did, perhaps they'd shrug it off as a trick of the light. Another hour, and the trials would be over. By morning, they'd be on their way home with a new princess in tow. He just had to get through this final ceremony. And then— And then— And then—

And then…what? Xander thought, shifting his weight in the seat, subtly moving his back muscles to stretch his wings. *And then my mate will magically forgive me for starting our new lives with a lie? Will the gods really restore their favor after this, or will we be doomed?*

The idea had been circulating in his brain ever since he'd conceived this plan, and it had been weighing more and more heavily these past few days. Watching Coralee now, Xander felt like a villain instead of the hero his people needed him to be.

We needed a win, he told himself.

We needed a match.

Taetanos needed a victory.

My god, my people, they needed this.

The excuses sounded emptier than they had been the day before. But maybe that was just because his eyes had found hers again, and for the first time he realized his future and his people's futures weren't the only ones that mattered.

A cheer filled the atrium.

Xander blinked, realizing the king had finished his speech. The matching ceremony had officially begun.

Pay attention now.

Don't embarrass yourself or your house.

Not so close to the end.

The matches had been set the night before, through notes and messages passed back and forth between the royal families, but nothing was final until it was stated before the gods. Even the slightest error could ruin everything. There was no rule forcing Coralee to agree to the offer he would bestow, and maybe that was why his heart had behaved like a wild, untamable beast in his chest all morning. Part of him didn't believe he was worthy, not when it was Rafe who had truly won her. Part of him expected her to say no.

Xander squeezed the wood beneath his left palm. In the folds of the clay hand on his right, his fingers curled tight, invisible but somehow so real he could feel them shake, so real his arm softly trembled.

The trial committee signaled to the dove prince, the male victor and winner of the first choice of mate. He stood from his throne and flew to the center of the atrium. After landing softly on the tile floor, he faced his people and bowed deeply, ashy wings fanning from side to side. Then he stood and lifted his hands to the back of his head to gently remove the mask, revealing his face to the crowd.

"I am Luka Aethionus, born of the god Aethios, Crown Prince of the House of Peace, and by my god's favor, I have picked my mate, chosen for her speed and her stealth, for her grace and her charm, for the shrewd mind she displayed and the strong heart we all witnessed."

The prince jumped, pumping his wings as he soared determinedly toward the House of Paradise, to no one's surprise. Xander had spent the night discussing the matches with his mother, and they'd guessed the mate the dove prince would pick. Still, relief trickled through him when Luka flew in the opposite direction of the House of Wisdom. Xander would be next for the men, and his princess would be waiting.

The dove knelt before his chosen mate. "Iris Mnesmeus, born of the god Mnesme, Princess of the House of Paradise, will you have me?"

The whole room grew still.

Hardly a moment passed before she stood and removed her mask, amethyst gown fluid in the sun as she took the hand he offered. "I will."

The princess turned, kissing her parents on the cheek and embracing her two brothers before she followed her mate back to his dais and settled onto the open throne by his side, no longer a member of the House of Paradise but now the future queen of the House of Peace. Their hands were tightly clasped.

Without masks, their faces displayed wide smiles full of hope and the slightest bit of fear. The doves cheered when he leaned down to press a soft kiss to the back of her hand. The sound was like a tiding of things to come, a promise that their house would continue to be a place of happiness, of light and air just like their god.

Again, the room grew quiet. The trial committee gestured to the female victor, who had won second choice of mate.

The princess of the House of Peace stood.

Xander had hardly noticed her before, but now he found he couldn't look away. There was something captivating about her, as though her energy were magnetic, forcing every gaze in the room to pay attention. And they did. The atrium was so silent he heard the scuffing of her silk slippers on the floor as she landed in the center of the room, heard the swish of fabric as the lace folds of her silvery dress settled around her. When she curtsied, her ivory wings ruffled in the sun, brighter than the diamonds woven into her tightly braided hair. As she stood, nimble fingers undid the knots of her mask, revealing her beauty to the room. Plump lips. Defined cheekbones. A rounded nose. And upturned eyes that were slightly big for her face, yet somehow only deepened her allure, especially with the impish way they sparkled, as though she were in on a joke no one else seemed to know.

The room hummed with the sound of a hundred people remembering to breathe, as if they had forgotten to do so at the sight of her. Xander's chest burned for lack of air and he drew in a surprised gulp.

"I am Lyana Aethionus, born of the god Aethios, Princess

of the House of Peace," she said, voice loud and confident, a woman perfectly assured in her person and her decisions, not at all afraid—not at all like Xander, who couldn't push the doubts from his mind. "And by my god's favor, I have picked my mate, chosen because we are all small players in a much bigger game, and this was the only move I wished to make."

Xander frowned. *That sounds just like something Rafe would say.*

He watched the princess rise into the air, a murmur of whispers growing to a dull roar as she turned toward her chosen mate—as she turned toward him.

Xander jolted, sitting up.

He looked to the left, where the hummingbird prince had already started to stand, gaping at his match in confusion before swiveling toward Xander, hatred simmering in the shadows of his mask.

Then Xander turned right, toward Coralee, his princess, his match, his mate. Her brown eyes were wide. Her mouth parted slightly beneath the feathers hiding the rest of her face. Those honey wings so alive just moments before were tucked close to her back, unsure.

Xander's gaze darted to the committee members who stood, staring in shocked silence. But no protests spilled from their lips. The princess was within her rights. They would not stop her. She'd won this choice. She'd earned it. And if it wasn't meant to be, the gods themselves would have to intervene.

They didn't.

Lyana soared closer, no doubt as to her destination. Then

she was there, landing on the dais a few feet in front of his throne and curtsying before him, seemingly unaware of the chaos left in her wake. Her attention remained on the floor, as though the confident person he had seen only moments before had been a ruse, and now she was laid bare, vulnerable, afraid that a raven of all people would say no to a dove.

Will I?

Xander swallowed. His gaze flicked to the owl princess again, mind spinning with dreams of parchment and firelight, and days of understanding that turned into nights of exploring that turned into years of love. He looked at the dove and the dream vanished. Their future was uncharted, a blank slate he couldn't read. She was beautiful, and she was bold. She was different from any match he'd ever imagined.

She's the daughter of Aethios, the crown prince in the back of his mind whispered, bringing Xander back to reality, reminding him that his heart wasn't what mattered in this equation. His people were. *She's the queen my god deserves.*

"Lysander Taetanus, born of the god Taetanos, Crown Prince of the House of Whispers," the dove princess murmured, words as smooth as velvet, as though she'd said his name many times before. "Will you have me?"

Xander reached back, arms moving as though the gods commanded them, since his mind was blank with shock and confusion. But his body acted with assurance, and his hand of clay pressed the mask to the side of his face, holding it in place as the fingers of his left hand fumbled with the special knot Rafe had tied, miraculously tugging it loose despite the way they trembled. That was where the miracle ended.

The mask dropped to the floor.

It smacked with an ugly *thud* against the wood base of the dais, landing on its side before spilling over the edge. A loud *clang* filled the silent atrium as it hit the tile floor ten feet below and shattered upon impact.

The princess watched it fall, then looked up—and froze. Her wide eyes widened even farther. Her luscious lips dropped open a centimeter. That sparkle in her eyes became one of panic. And he knew why.

Xander knew.

She'd expected Rafe.

She'd expected a warrior and got *this* instead.

But they'd come too far to turn back now, so Xander slipped from his throne and dropped to one knee as he lifted her hand to his lips. She flinched almost imperceptibly at his touch, but Xander felt the tremor pass beneath her skin.

"Lyana Aethionus," Xander stated, voice flat, the best he could manage when it felt as though the ground had opened and was swallowing him whole, "born of Aethios, but now Taetanos's queen. I will have you as my mate."

LYANA

What have I done?

What have I done?

The rest of the matching ceremony passed in the blink of an eye. She couldn't have described a single moment had her life depended on it. No, Lyana couldn't focus on anything except for her brother's concerned gaze, her mother's pointed stare, Damien's seething wrath, her own mate's chilling silence, and the question playing on a loop in the back of her mind.

What have I done?

Because the moment she looked at those lavender eyes, and at that face so strikingly similar to the one she'd expected yet so outrageously different, a chill had crept into her bones, deeper than anything she'd ever felt in her frozen tundra of a homeland.

Who was this imposter by her side?

Where was Lysander?

Where was her mate?

What have I done?

Lyana was numb as the courtship trials drew to a close. Her father spoke the traditional parting words, but her ears had stopped working, as though she'd dropped beneath the surface of her bath and all she could hear were muffled voices sifting through water, dull and far away. Everything was fuzzy. Everything was blurred. As she followed the ravens down the hall and out of the palace, a white speck in a mass of black, her thoughts were nothing but a silent buzzing, as though the panic were so overwhelming her body had simply shut down to avoid it.

The world came into sharp focus the second she stepped into their guest quarters. The second she saw him standing in the foyer, arms crossed, a foot resting against the wall, the picture of ease. The second her gaze landed on those clear eyes.

Lyana's vision turned red.

Before she knew what she was doing, she crossed the length of the room and slapped his cheek as hard as she could, leaving a brilliant rosy mark on his pale skin. He clenched his jaw, refusing to look away, taking the full brunt of her glare but giving nothing in return. His expression was a study in control, not revealing a single emotion, as though he were made of stone.

Lyana hit him again—just because.

"Why weren't you there?" she yelled, because her other option was a wailing that would sound far too vulnerable, far too hurt. Anger was much easier to manage. "Who are you? No, who are *you*?"

She flipped around, turning toward the man who had been at the ceremony. He was frozen in the doorway, crestfallen. A small woman nudged his shoulder, pushing him into the room. Then she closed the door behind them, locking the guards outside, leaving the five of them alone, including the queen.

"Someone tell me what's going on, now," Lyana commanded.

"*I* am Lysander Taetanus," the man by the doorway said, taking a step closer as his onyx wings drooped low to the ground and his shoulders seemed to follow, hunched and uncertain. "I'm the real Lysander Taetanus."

"But…" Lyana's voice trailed off as her eyes moved back and forth between the two Lysanders, nearly identical. Same jet-black hair. Same ivory skin. Same obsidian feathers. Same height. Similar builds, though one was clearly more muscular and one a little more slender. They were nearly twins.

Except for their eyes, she realized.

Her Lysander had slightly hooded eyes with irises the color of the sky on a perfect sunny day, daring her to explore the hidden depths beneath. But this new Lysander had slightly downturned eyes the color of lavender, honest and endearing, with no secrets lurking inside. And they matched the set on the queen's face, which were a darker color but the same oval shape, with the same arched brows, the only feature on either man's face that looked like her at all.

Lyana stepped back as the air left her. Her wings beat, keeping her upright as she swayed, off balance.

"I don't understand," she murmured, trying to find her voice but losing it just as quickly. Her fingers trembled as her heart began to pound. A dizzying swarm of nerves fluttered deep in her stomach, shooting down her legs and up her arms, invading her mind, until she was light-headed yet grounded by her confusion.

The real Lysander lifted his arm, drawing her attention away from the nameless young man who had yet to move from the spot where she'd found him. He tugged on the end of each finger on his left hand, pulling off a polished leather glove, revealing smooth skin. Then he lifted his right hand and paused for a moment before he said, "I'm the Crown Prince of the House of Whispers. The man you met during the trials is my half brother. He took my place because, well— Because I — Because when I got my wings— Because—"

The prince broke off abruptly. The muscles in his right arm trembled. He released a heavy breath and in the same moment, wrenched the glove from his hand. The sound of threads ripping filled the small room.

Lyana gasped and stepped back, the time involuntarily.

For a second, she thought he'd ripped his fingers clean off and a spike of terror shot through her. But then the shock cleared, and she realized there was no blood, no gore, no mess, just smooth skin where a hand should have been. A deformity that had been there long before he'd ever laid eyes on her or her homeland.

Lyana glanced up.

The pain was written clearly across his face, in every groove of his forehead, in the way the muscle of his cheek spasmed, in the way he'd squeezed his eyes shut and angled his head toward the floor as though that would make him feel less exposed.

Lyana lifted her own hand, stretching it toward him, letting her fingers hover in the air. A warm wave of sympathy coursed through her, not because of the injury, but because of the raw ache emanating from him. The healer in her yearned to comfort him. The princess in her instantly understood why he'd done what he'd done. But the woman in her still reeled from the wounds he'd inflicted on her with his deception.

"I'm sorry to have tricked you, Lyana Aethionus," the real Lysander whispered, voice raspy. "But I would still very much like to be your mate, if you'll have me."

At the word *mate*, her arm recoiled, dropping away from the prince. Her head turned, even as she tried to force it not to, and her attention landed on the stranger still leaning against the wall, the stranger who knew her darkest secret, the stranger in whose keeping she'd placed her wildest dreams—to live a life where she didn't have to hide, a life with a mate who understood a part of her that no one else in the world ever could. Deep in her chest, that golden spark flared to life and sprinkled down her arms. Her magic. And the memory of her fingertips pressed against his skin, aglow in the firelight as his power rose to meet it, flared in her mind—a moment more intimate than any she'd experienced before. A moment that now brought a rotten, sour taste to her lips.

Lyana glanced at the floor, then turned to her mate.

"I'll be in my rooms. No one is to enter except for my friend, who will be traveling with us to the House of Whispers come morning. Please, do not disturb me until my family arrives to bid their goodbyes. I would like to see them one more time before we leave."

Her voice was iron.

Sharp as a dagger.

She didn't wait to see if the tone struck true. She just snapped her wings and raced to the first rooms she could find, not caring whose they were, because now they were hers. The crystal wall gifted her with the perfect view of the palace she had until now called home. Lyana stared at it from the edge of the bed, unblinking. Her eyes burned, but the pain was a necessary distraction. She sat like that until the door opened and a familiar face slipped inside. Only then did she finally give in to the torrent of feeling crashing through her. Only then did she collapse and let the tears stream over her face. Because she knew Cassi's steadfast arms were there to catch her.

29

RAFE

The moment the princess disappeared, Xander threw the clay-filled glove at the wall as hard as he could. A loud *splat* echoed across the silence, then a *thud* as it dropped to the floor by his brother's feet.

Rafe stared at the mess, thinking, *How do I fix this? What do I do?* But the truth was he hadn't breathed since she stepped through the door, and all he felt was the briefest flash of relief now that she was out of sight once more.

He'd known this was going to happen.

The moment he realized she'd won second pick and he third, he'd known. He'd hoped and prayed to all the gods that it wouldn't. But fate was fickle, and the gods were cruel just as often as they were kind.

Destiny's dagger had struck him in the heart the second her eyes landed on his, so lost and hurt and confused, but it wasn't until she left that the dagger twisted, bringing a fresh round of pain now that he had nothing to distract him from his brother.

Xander was crushed.

Rafe set aside his own panic and kicked off the wall, trying to put a grin to his lips even as nausea continued to coil in his stomach. "That was a bit dramatic, don't you think?"

Head snapping up at this, Xander fumed. "She has every right to react however she pleases after what we did to her."

"I wasn't talking about her. I was talking about you," Rafe retorted before pointedly looking at the gnarled glove by his feet. "I think the poor girl thought you tore your own hand off. What happened to using your words?"

Xander frowned. "I— I'm not sure."

But Rafe knew. Everyone in that room knew. Even Xander, whether he would admit it to himself or not. The same insecurity had plagued him all his life—the idea that his disability made him somehow less of a man, less of a prince. Rafe wanted to grab his brother and shake him, but he didn't think that would help. Instead, he walked across the room and draped an arm over Xander's shoulder.

"Give her time," he said. "She's been lied to, she probably feels a bit betrayed, and more than anything, she probably feels scared—scared to be mated, scared to leave the only life she's ever known, scared to move to a foreign world she's never seen before. This isn't about you, not really. Give her time to adjust and then you'll see, she'll open her heart to you."

"Rafe is right," Helen added softly. "We knew this plan was risky from the start, but it doesn't sound like she plans to betray us to her king. We should look on the bright side. In two days, we'll be home. Our people's faith will be restored. And you'll have the rest of your life to make it up to your mate."

Xander grunted, his expression still haunted. After a moment, he slinked out of Rafe's embrace and pumped his wings, racing toward his room. Rafe moved to follow, but a hand on his arm stopped him cold.

"Leave us," Queen Mariam murmured darkly.

At first, Rafe thought she was talking to him, but then he saw Helen slip out, returning to the rest of the guards at her command, and he knew he wasn't so lucky.

"What—"

"Silence," she cut him off, voice as sharp as ever—as though she'd been forged in a smithy, not grown in a womb. Her eyes glinted like the polished iron of a blade about to strike. No matter how old he grew or how many dragons he faced, the queen would remain the most terrifying of sights. "I will not have my son fooled the way my mate fooled me."

Rafe swallowed, trying to clear his throat as a drop of dread slid through it. His voice was hoarse as he answered, "I don't know what you mean."

The queen laughed, a sound that was anything but amused. "I don't care what happened between you and the daughter of Aethios to make her defy the orders of her king and pick my son as a mate, but whatever it was, it ends now."

Rafe opened his mouth to speak, but no sound came out.

The silence said more than his words ever could.

Queen Mariam tightened her grip on his arm and leaned toward him. "You will not speak to her in the absence of my son. You will not visit her rooms. You will not try to ease her worries or her fears. You will not make her believe she is special. You will harden your heart to her, or I will do what I should have done years ago and remove you from my kingdom. Do I make myself clear?"

Rafe nodded slowly. "Crystal."

"Good."

The queen snatched her hand away, curling her lip as though touching him had left a distasteful smell in the air, and smoothed the folds of her dress before leaving. Rafe clenched his fists until his whole body began to shake. Only when the clicking of her heels faded did he release his tension to fall back against the nearest wall, painfully crushing his wings.

The queen was right.

This was Rafe's fault.

Rafe's mess.

And he had to fix it.

Xander thought the princess was upset because he was somehow less than she'd expected, but he was wrong. This had nothing to do with his hand. Nothing to do with him. Nothing even to do with Rafe. Ana—

Lyana, he corrected. Not Ana. Never Ana again.

Princess Lyana Aethionus.

His brother's mate.

His brother's queen.

What was it she'd said to him on the dance floor?

Call me crazy, she'd murmured as he twirled her inside the curtain of his wings, *but I thought maybe you'd be excited, like I was, when you discovered there'd be a princess at the trials who already knew your deepest secret, a person from whom you didn't have to hide.*

That was all she had wanted, all that had propelled her actions. Not a desire for Rafe, but a desire for what she thought he offered—freedom. Maybe he could show her that Xander offered the same thing. That Xander would accept her for who she was. That Xander was a better man than he could ever hope to be, a better man for her. Maybe then she'd forget about a few stolen moments in the dark. She'd forget about him.

The very idea stole the breath from his lungs.

But Rafe would do it.

He had to.

30

LYANA

With Cassi's help, Lyana successfully avoided the ravens for the rest of the evening, hiding in her room, getting her meal delivered, spending the night staring at the crystal palace that had never seemed so far away, and waking bleary-eyed and run down the next morning.

"You can't greet your parents looking like that," Cassi said after taking one glance at Lyana. "They'll know something's up."

Though she couldn't see herself, Lyana had no doubt her eyes were red and puffy, and that the normal cheer was gone from her face. She sighed. "I know."

"Well, come here. Let me see what I can do," Cassi grumbled, slipping on her glasses for the attention to detail required by the task. Lyana spun, granting her friend full rein. Immediately, nimble fingers began shifting through her head, folding and twisting her many braids into a perfectly royal crown of hair.

"This can't all be about a man," her friend said as she worked. "That's not the Ana I know."

"It's not. It's—" The words caught in Lyana's throat.

It's not about a man, she told herself. *It's not.*

But maybe it was…a little.

Watching him turn and face that dragon had been the bravest thing she'd ever seen. And their two magics dancing beneath his skin had felt deeper than any kiss she'd ever experienced. And when she'd dropped the edge of her knife from his neck, she'd given him more than her trust in his promise to keep her secret. She'd given him a piece of her heart as well.

A piece he'd crushed.

Now the two of them would be bound by a secret no one could ever know, not even her mate. Which meant this man, whose name she still didn't know, would have his claws in her forever.

"It's not about a man," Lyana repeated, more gruffly this time. Cassi yanked a little too hard on her hair, a silent protest that elicited a hiss of pain, but nothing else. "It's about my life."

Cassi sighed theatrically. "It's so tough being a princess."

Lyana planted an elbow in her friend's ribs. "I thought I was going to have a mate who knew my deepest secret, who knew and didn't care. And now all of that is gone. Can I not wallow in self-pity for a little while?"

"Nope," Cassi chirped, nudging Lyana to turn around.

Lyana met Cassi's raised eyebrows with a matching set. Cassi pinched her cheeks to bring some color back to her dark skin, then reached across the bed and dipped the corner of the sheet in a jug of water before pressing it to Lyana's eyelids to reduce their swelling.

"Everyone has secrets, Ana," she continued. "Everyone. The prince had a secret. The ravens had a secret. Your magic doesn't define you. So what if that imposter knows about it, as long as he keeps quiet? Maybe the prince will never know that one truth, but your mate will learn what's important. The things that are far more connected to who you are. You'll see."

The words did little to ease Lyana's mood. Needing to keep busy, she reached for one of the brushes on the side table and motioned for Cassi to switch places. Her own hair did better with fingers and a comb, but her friend's was different —wavy rather than coiled, flowing silk instead of fluffed tulle, slippery enough to never stay in one place for very long. A little unruly, Lyana thought, compared to her braids, which could last for a few weeks at a time. But she'd always enjoyed running her fingers through Cassi's hair and brushing out the knots. She'd always found it soothing.

They were quiet for a little while, Cassi lost in her thoughts, Lyana thankfully lost in the movement of her fingers, in looping and twisting the smooth strands. She divided her friend's hair into four sections, weaving four intricate braids that met at the crown of her head and then spun into a tightly cinched bun that would hopefully make it through at least the long flight to the edge of the House of

Peace, if not the long journey to the House of Whispers the next day. The design was far more ornate than the hasty updos her friend normally preferred, as though she'd sensed that Lyana had needed the distraction. But when it was finished, Cassi turned and took her hands, silvery eyes bright against her tawny cheeks.

"Why don't we try to remember what today is really about?"

Lyana frowned and tilted her head. "Huh?"

"Today isn't about a man, or secrets, or lies, or worries about what the future might bring. Today—" Cassi paused as an excited grin widened her lips and she squeezed Lyana's hands tightly as if trying to transfer some of her enthusiasm to her friend. "Today is the day our adventure begins, the one we've waited so long for, the one we've yearned for. Today, we travel to the edge of our isle, farther than we've ever been. And tomorrow? Even farther."

A smile tugged at the corner of Lyana's lips. "I guess..."

"You guess?" Cassi chided as she stood and pulled Lyana to her feet, toward the window and the city waiting outside. "Isn't that what you've always wanted? To see someplace new. Someplace exciting. To explore the world. Or was that all talk?"

Lyana's gaze skimmed the outskirts of Sphaira, past the crystal buildings to the tundra beyond, settling on that never-ending line where a snowy landscape stretched into a clear sky. But it did end. By nightfall, she'd be at the end, the spot where her isle gave way to air. After so many years of staring at a similar view, always wondering and questioning what lay beyond, she would finally have an answer. A bubble of joy spread across her chest, growing and growing, filled with light and hope and a sprinkle of something else, something that spilled out of her lips in the shape of quiet laughter.

"Fine." Lyana turned back to Cassi, ignoring the smug expression on the owl's face because her mood had finally lifted, and she didn't want anything to shoot it back down. For now, the adventure was enough. The worry, the fears, the hurt, she could deal with them later. "Yes, that's what I've always wanted. And you're right, that's what today should be about. You and me and the bridge that in these many years we've never dared cross. Well, the bridge you've never let me cross, because you were worried about the trouble I'd get into. Today, the sky bridge is ours, Cassi. We're crossing that bridge, together. We're going someplace new…" Lyana paused, but was unable to stop herself from playfully adding, "Whether you want to or not."

"I volunteered for this, remember?"

"I know." Lyana let her enthusiasm sweep her up like the winds of a great storm, ready to carry her away. "I must have finally rubbed off on you."

Cassi snorted. "Maybe I just knew you would need someone around who wasn't afraid to put you in your place, princess or not. From what I've seen so far of the ravens, they seem incapable of telling you no."

Before Lyana had a chance to retort, a knock sounded at the door.

Cassi fluttered over to answer, in case it was a raven, but Luka forced the door open. He paused in the doorway, looking at her for a moment before nodding awkwardly in greeting. Cassi stepped back and glanced away, giving him the opening to race across the room and crush his sister in an embrace—one which Lyana reciprocated wholeheartedly. Her mother and father followed, along with a handful of servants carrying breakfast.

Lyana ate with her family one final time, happy that for once there was no lecture, just mutual understanding. What was done was done, and they should enjoy these moments they had left. She learned that Damien had selected the owl princess as his mate when his turn came, and that the rest of the matches had followed as expected. Though she hadn't broken any rules, Lyana had been the only rebellious heir of the bunch. Her father had, of course, already forgiven her, despite the temporary strain her actions might have put on a few of his diplomatic relationships. But Lyana was stunned to find that when she cautiously met her mother's knowing gaze, she found no anger or disapproval. Instead, pride glistened in her eyes, reminding Lyana of the stories around her parents' courtship trials—of how her mother, bold and daring, had won her father's favor. Maybe she understood, after all.

So, they ate, and talked, and embraced, and kissed, until the sun rose high and the time for goodbyes came. There was no telling when her family would be together again, or when Lyana would next step foot in the House of Peace now that she was heir to another throne. But she didn't cry. Enough tears had been shed the night before, and over the wrong person. When a drop fell from Luka's eye, she brushed it from his cheek, telling him not to worry, that she would be fine, that she had Cassi and a mate and a new life waiting, that she had everything she could ever want.

For a moment, she even believed it.

She wanted so badly to believe it.

Lyana watched her family go, remaining strong until the door closed behind them. Cassi was there to catch her as she stumbled, the weight of so many changes ready to crush her. But with her best friend by her side, the wave passed. Lyana stood tall. And when the ravens came to collect her, she went with her head held high, following her new flock as they took to the sky and began the long journey to her new home. She did, however, allow herself one look back at Sphaira, at the city of her youth, full of so many dreams, at the crystal palace and the surrounding buildings glimmering like a diamond brooch in the sun.

They stopped before the sky bridge, landing at the edge of the inner isle.

She didn't look down toward the Sea of Mist.

She didn't glance at the cave nestled somewhere in the cliff below her.

She didn't pay attention to the red stain still on the rocks.

She looked ahead.

At the ravens as they walked across the bridge. At her mate when he turned around to find her, a glimmer of uncertainty flickering over his features as though he wasn't sure she would follow. And at the man by his side, whose hooded eyes still managed to pierce.

When Cassi stepped to her side, Lyana took the hand she offered.

Together, they walked into the unknown.

XANDER

"You should go talk to her," Rafe whispered, jolting Xander from his reverie.

"Huh? What?" He shook his head and pulled his gaze from where it had been lingering—on the princess. They'd arrived at the outpost an hour ago, a small set of crystal buildings right on the edge of the House of Peace, a place for a little rest before the long flight home tomorrow.

As soon as they'd landed, his mate had walked right up to the spot where land gave way to air and plopped on the cold stone, staring out at empty space. Her friend had been by her side for a while but must have gotten cold. All the ravens had come inside to escape the chill, but the princess remained outside, as though the ice of her home lived in her veins and didn't bother her in the slightest.

"You've been staring out the wall for ten minutes. Just go say hello," Rafe prodded.

"I don't think she wants to talk."

"I don't think she knows what she wants."

Xander snorted, gaping at Rafe in amazement. "Oh, and you do? You know what a princess who's been lied to, matched with a foreign prince, and practically tossed from her homeland wants? You know that?"

"Fine," Rafe relented, half growling the word. "Maybe I don't know what she wants, but I know she's your mate. And I know you need to start somewhere, Xander. The longer you two go without talking, the worse it will get. So..." He let the words trail off as his gaze darted around the sitting room, searching for inspiration. In a flash of motion, he grabbed a fur throw from a nearby chair. "Take this. Tell her you thought she might be cold. See what she says. If nothing else, she'll appreciate the gesture."

"I don't know, Rafe," Xander murmured, ignoring the blanket as he glanced at Lyana's solitary figure once more.

"Just go, Xander."

Rafe pushed him, but Xander held his ground, digging his feet in. If he was going to talk to his mate, it would be on his terms. He squared his shoulders, shook the tension from his wings, and turned toward the door of his own accord. Of course, he didn't take a step forward, because, well, his feet were frozen with fear, his heart thrummed wildly, and his tongue felt fat and idle, with nothing to say. Instead, he stood there for a minute, gathering his courage, trying to take deep, even breaths.

Finally, he gave in and turned around to snatch the

blanket—the gods if Rafe's idea wasn't a good one—but when he looked at his brother, he paused.

Rafe stared out the window, the muscles in his jaw clenched.

Something in his eyes took Xander back to a different time, years ago, when he'd found his brother in much the same position, standing in the rubble of a scorched room, staring at the sun burning in the morning sky. It had been the day of the king's funeral, but Rafe had been more interested in paying his respects to his mother, a woman no one else bothered to remember. He'd gone to her room to lay flowers on the balcony and had remained there during the royal funeral, until Xander had come to fetch him. There had been tears on his cheeks then, which had long since dried. For some reason, that same silent, haunted goodbye danced across his lips now as it had then. Though for the life of him, Xander couldn't imagine why.

"Rafe?"

His brother flinched and jerked his head toward Xander—too quickly. "What?"

"Nothing, just—" Xander knitted his brows, unsure why he felt like an intruder but unable to combat the sensation. "Thank you. Thank you for everything."

Rafe's face softened. "I'd do anything for you."

"I know," Xander replied, still torn without fully grasping why.

As though he sensed it, Rafe turned on his heels and crossed the common area, retreating to his room and leaving Xander with no more reason to delay.

I can do this, he thought, clutching the blanket, trying to bring his mind back to the task at hand. *She's a girl. Just a girl. I've talked to many before.*

But she wasn't just a girl.

She was his mate.

And somehow, that changed everything.

Xander shivered when he stepped outside, not just from the cold. He hastily tightened his jacket and flapped his wings, firing his muscles to warm his body as he flew the short distance and landed a few feet behind her, boots scuffing loudly against the snow. She glanced halfway over her shoulder, stopping when she realized who was there.

He cleared his throat. "I brought you a fur. I thought you might be cold."

The princess didn't respond. She just returned her gaze to the open sky, leaving Xander standing there like a fool.

I knew this was a stupid idea.

I knew she wanted to be left alone.

I knew—

"Well, are you going to give it to me? Or did you just come to gawk in the cold instead of behind the crystal? Speaking as someone who grew up in a palace made of the stuff, I can assure you, it's not the stealthiest of materials for spying."

"I— I'm—" Xander winced, and then sighed before stepping forward. "Here."

Lyana turned, accepting his offer, flicking her gaze briefly to his face before returning it to the blanket. She tossed the fur over her shoulders and crouched back down to perch on the rock, staring out at the world.

Xander was unsure whether she wanted him to go or to stay. But Rafe had been right—this was his mate, and sooner or later, they would have to talk to each other. Why not start now? He wasn't normally such a blithering fool. In fact, at home some people might have called him charming. Forgoing the practice grounds had given him plenty of opportunity to focus on other skills, and the art of communication was supposedly one of them, though his training was failing him at the moment.

He looked out, wondering what she could possibly have been staring at for the past hour. The sky was turning dark. Behind them, the sun was beginning to set. A white crescent hung low on the horizon, but there were no stars on which to make wishes. Just endless air spotted by clouds dropping into the misty void below, beneath which no one knew what lay.

"Thinking of making a run for it?" he teased as he knelt beside her.

The dove's tone was unnervingly even as she replied, "I haven't decided yet."

Xander gulped, but decided he would stay the course for them both, and that he would fight in the only way he knew how. "What do you think you'd find?"

"The place where the dragons come from, I suppose," she murmured, eyes flaring to life for the briefest instant. "I've heard the fire god walks the earth, the king of a barren wasteland."

"They say the ocean has turned to a sea of molten flame," he suggested. "To go near it would mean certain death."

"Certain?" She joined the fun. "I doubt it would be anything a little snow couldn't soothe. Worth a bit of pain, surely, to see beneath the mist, to know what waits there."

"You're not afraid?" he asked, surprised. "Of the fire god's wrath? Of his dragons?"

"Other things scare me more," she told him, voice so soft it was nearly drowned out by the wind whipping over the edge, pressing into their chests, making the blanket *snap* loudly, though she didn't seem to notice.

What?

What scares you more than that?

Xander ached to know what could make her afraid, this princess who had won the trials, who had bested all her peers, who had defied tradition, maybe even the gods, by her actions. What could she possibly fear?

"Why did you choose me?" he asked, instead. Because they were little more than strangers, and he didn't think he'd earned the answers to his other questions. Not yet, at least.

"I didn't, not exactly." The princess finally turned toward him, the barest hint of a smile on her lips.

He couldn't tell if she was teasing, but he thought maybe, for a moment, she was. Yet, despite being delivered in a light tone, the words stung. Xander tried not to cringe. "My brother, then. Why did you pick him?"

"I didn't pick him, trust me." A frown passed over her forehead, etched deep with frustration. "He's rude and somewhat of a grouch. And I just— I—"

The princess paused. Her words had released a knot in his chest, and Xander couldn't stop a small grin from flittering over his lips at her rather apt description of Rafe. But then she sighed as she unweaved whatever tangled mess was in her unreadable mind. "What would you have done? I had four princes to choose from, all of whom were little more than strangers. My father matched me with Damien, and I'm sure he would've made a good mate, but if I'd followed along, then my whole life would have been decided for me. And I wanted a say. Maybe that makes me the typical spoiled princess who doesn't realize how lucky she is. Maybe it just makes me human. I'm not really sure. All I know is that I chose the last mate anyone thought I would, and it gave me the slightest bit of pleasure to shock them all."

Xander nodded.

He understood the binds of royalty. He understood the weight, the restrictions, the sacrifices. But unlike her, he embraced them. All Xander wanted to be was a good prince, a great king for his people. Everything he'd ever done was for them—to erase the mistakes of the past, to ensure them a better future. In every decision he placed them first, over his honor, his desires, and even his pride.

"Why did you say yes?" Lyana asked.

"Because," he started, and then paused. He could lie and say it was her beauty or her brashness, that he'd been swept away in the moment. But it wasn't the truth. In his heart, he'd gone there expecting someone else, wanting someone else, mind full of a dream that would never come true—the silly dream of a boy, the sort of dream an heir wasn't allowed to follow. And his mate deserved honesty. "Because you're the daughter of Aethios."

Lyana nodded, a series of unsurprised rises and falls, before she let her lips spread into a wry smile. "Then I guess we both got what we wanted." She stood, ending the moment, whatever it was. "Thank you for the blanket, but the sun is nearly down, so we should probably go inside."

The princess held out the fur to him, and he took it. Their fingers brushed and they both hastily retreated, letting go at the same time. A gust of wind snatched the blanket, lifting it into the sky so it looked like a living thing as it wriggled in the air, then dropped beneath the edge, fluttering as though it had wings. Either one of them could have raced to retrieve it, but they didn't. They stayed there, watching it disappear.

"Lysander," she murmured. The word rolled from her lips, dipped in honey, tantalizing and smooth, as though his name were something precious, as though it held power. The sound sent a tingling down his spine.

He looked at her.

But she'd already turned around. Before he could ask why she'd said his name, her luminescent ivory wings flapped, leaving nothing but a plume of snow in her wake.

3 2

RAFE

Rafe must have paced the length of his room a hundred times in a row—walking to the door, pausing, shaking his head, returning to the bed, stopping just shy of lying down, turning, marching back to the door, over and over and over, until his mind was dizzy.

He had to talk to her one last time—but he shouldn't.

He wanted to explain—but what would he say?

It would be for Xander. At least, that was what he told himself. That he'd be going there for Xander, to praise his brother, to ease her fears, to give the two of them a better shot at getting to know each other.

For Xander, he thought, standing before the door, hand hovering over the knob but not quite touching it. *For Xander. For Xander. For—*

The door shot open.

Rafe recoiled, narrowly avoiding a plank of wood to the

face as he jumped away. The princess marched in, silently shut the door behind her, and whipped around to face him, features charged.

"Your name," she ordered, not a question. Her ivory wings were wide. Her arms were crossed. Her hip was cocked to the side. Everything about her oozed superiority and ire. Her haughty airs immediately set him on edge.

"No."

Her eyes flashed like lightning in a storm. "No?"

Rafe shrugged. "No."

"Tell me your name," she commanded, somewhere between disbelief and indignation.

He could have given in.

He should have given in—gotten it over quickly, told her what she wanted to know and then forced her to leave before any of the sleeping ravens around them woke up.

But he didn't.

And he really didn't care to linger on the reasoning.

"Why?" he asked instead, unable to stop the smile rising to his lips.

Hers curled. "Are you really refusing to tell me your name?"

"No," he said lightly. "If you tell me why you want to know so badly that you barged into my room in the middle of the night, I'll tell you what it is."

"I could just ask the prince," she countered, narrowing her eyes.

"You could."

"Or anyone else."

"So why didn't you?"

Her nose wrinkled in annoyance. Something about the gesture was undeniably endearing. He looked away from her, toward the curtains he'd drawn earlier that night, as though he'd somehow known something would happen that he didn't want the outside world to witness.

"Please. I only know you as Lysander, but now he's Lysander, and..." She trailed off as her wings dipped low enough for her primaries to slouch against the floor. Her features fell with them. And when she spoke again, her voice was hardly an echo of the vivacious girl he'd grown used to. "Just please."

He ached to cross the room, to press his hand to her cheek, to bring a smile back to her lips.

He curled his fingers into fists instead, because if he did any of those things, whatever had happened between them in that cave would become real—not a secret in the dark, but something tangible in the light, and he couldn't let that happen.

He had to bury those stolen hours in the shadows.

He had to snuff the fire out.

"Rafe," he answered gruffly.

"Huh?"

"My name is Rafe."

She frowned. "That's not a name."

"Well, it's the only one you're going to get." She stepped back at his rough tone. He stepped forward. "Is there anything else I can help you with, Princess?"

"I—" She shook her head as if to clear it. "Is that all? You're not going to apologize?"

"For what?"

Her mouth dropped open.

Rafe cut in before she could respond. The less she spoke, the better. The faster this was done, the faster she'd forget about him. "I never lied. You guessed at my identity in the cave, and I didn't deny it. On the first night of the trials, I told you I wasn't who you thought I was. Is it my fault a princess who is too used to getting her way didn't listen?"

"But...but..."

Rafe closed in, widening his wings, making his body as intimidating as possible. "You saved my life, and for that I thank you, but it didn't make us friends. I'm not your confidante. If you have a question, Xander will answer it. If you have a request, ask a servant. Don't come charging into my room in the middle of the night with demands. You're not my queen yet. I don't answer to you. And as far as I'm concerned, when I leave this isle tomorrow, I leave everything that happened these past few days behind me. Got it?"

She didn't give in to his ploy. The princess held her ground, widened her wings further, and met him head-on, not backing down. "Got it. Now you get this, you overbearing oaf. What happened in that cave happened, whether you want to remember it or not. We had a deal, and I intend to hold you to your promise. No one can know about me. Got it?"

Rafe held her stare. "Got it."

He expected her to turn and leave as quickly as she'd come,

but she didn't. She paused, not flinching, not looking away. Their faces were a mere foot apart, close enough for him to feel the soft brush of her breath on his neck, the heat simmering from her skin, the magic sparking just beneath the surface, daring his to come out and play. Her hands twitched, as though she wanted to push him or strike him, or maybe pull him close. Her plush lips were pursed. Her stare drilled into him like a physical weight.

Then she blinked.

It all vanished.

She leaned back, but not fast enough, because he saw the gleam of water pooling in her eyes. When she spun on her heels, a wad of feathers smacked him in the face. Rafe stumbled, his chest throbbing even though that wasn't what she had hit.

The princess quickly made for the door.

Good, let her go, he thought, clenching his teeth.

He'd done what he needed to do.

Then he remembered that look in her eyes, back in the cave, as he told her of his homeland. The childlike awe as visions danced across her irises, so naïve but so pure, a heart that hadn't yet been fractured. Those days were gone. His lie had carved a wound in her, and his actions tonight had made it bleed anew. But he didn't want her to hate his people or his home. He didn't want her to hate Xander. Only him.

Most of all, he didn't want to be the reason the bright spot of wonder should be gone from her eyes. She could still see her dreams come true. She could still live a life without hiding. Just not with him.

"Lyana," Rafe murmured.

She paused with her hand on the knob, not glancing back.

"My brother is the only other person in the world who knows about my magic," he whispered, barely able to hear his own voice over the wild pounding against his ribcage, as though something inside him were fighting to break free. "If you choose to, you can trust him with your secrets."

And your heart.

But he couldn't bring himself to finish the thought.

She didn't say anything. She just slipped out the door and back into the night.

Rafe stood in the middle of the room, fighting for control, forcing his feet to grow roots on the floor, forcing his wings to fall still, forcing his lips to close lest a shout tear its way out. His body began to tremble with the strain of keeping so many things inside—not just about Ana, but his wants and his fears and his dreams, all the things he never told Xander for worry they might hurt him. Sorrow over the loss of his parents. Pain that his own people had ostracized him for actions outside his control. Panic that his power would be discovered. Terror that one day his brother would see what everyone else saw, what Ana now saw—a nobody who never belonged.

The wounds were there.

Old and new.

Numb and throbbing.

So, he did the only thing he could think of to replace the pain—he slammed his fists into the glass table by his feet, slicing his hands with sharp shards, fighting the mental ache with something physical. Something real.

Rivulets of blood formed on his palms, sliding down the

contours of his hands before dripping to the floor. He stared at the red pool, watching the firelight from the lantern flicker on the surface of the liquid, another round of dragon flames that would this time swallow him whole. And he stayed there for a long time, seeing his fate dance across the butchery—long enough for the cuts on his hands to slide seamlessly shut before he retreated to the washstand to clean up the mess.

33

CASSI

She couldn't quite believe her eyes as the raven cleaned his hands, washing the blood away, revealing unblemished skin.

Cassi didn't know what exactly had compelled her to stick around so long after Lyana left. At first, it had been curiosity —his cruel words were such an obvious cover to the outside observer, though it seemed they'd hit home with her friend. And then it had been pity, as he knelt in a circle of his own blood, black wings draped against the floor as though to hide him from the world, or maybe to protect him from it. And even then, as the minutes flew by, she remained, bound by some gut instinct she didn't understand.

Now she knew why.

He's an invinci, she marveled, spirit hovering over his shoulder as deep red turned to muted pink, then to unmarked cream. His hand had been healed of its injuries.

It was something her king would want to know immediately.

Cassi retreated from the room as the raven began to gather the broken glass, using his hand to sweep it into a pile in the corner, unconcerned as new cuts formed along his palms, healing them just as fast as they appeared. As she seeped through the walls and out into the barren tundra, a different face came to the forefront of her mind. Sandy hair. Stormy eyes. Pallid skin that had never been warmed by the sun, though in her mind she always imagined it should be golden. She sensed his soul immediately, and instead of taking her time, Cassi yanked on the line between them, rushing through air and mist and sky and cloud, her soul shooting like a falling star, tumbling from the world above and plummeting into her life below.

He was stationed in one of the many floating cities—hundreds of boats that were tied together, connected by bridges and flat wooden platforms, some containing houses, some containing trading shops, some just open areas for conversation and a little bit of fun amid so much gray. This late at night, everyone was asleep. Golden orbs of lantern light permeated the mist, bobbing in the waves as the wood around her creaked and groaned. Water splashed over the edges. Every surface was damp and dreary.

Her king's ship was docked on the edge of the city, twice as tall as any other, painted with bits of gold to bring a little sense of sunshine into a world that did anything but dazzle. He'd left the window open, as always, a sign she was more than welcome inside.

He'd obviously been waiting, because when she put her phantom fingers to his brow and dipped inside his dream, it took hardly more than a thought to warp the chaos and take control of the scene. She painted the same gray stone walls, the same hulking table, the same tapestries and windows and overbearing chandelier, nothing new, nothing inventive, all duty and focus, the way he'd sadly come to like it.

"Kasiandra, what news?" he asked as he turned from the window, studied gaze landing on her before she'd even fully pulled the dream together.

"The trials are over. Lyana and I travel to the House of Whispers come morning."

He nodded as though he already knew.

Maybe he did. It wasn't her concern.

"My liege, I found out what the raven was hiding. I discovered his magic. He's—" Cassi paused, taking a deep breath as her anticipation flared. "He's an *invinci*."

Her king's eyes widened, blue flames coming to life as the information sank in. "That, Kasiandra, is a very intriguing development."

She smiled. "I had a feeling you'd think so."

He gripped his chin as calculations danced across his expression, new plans, new plots, each grander than the one before. Then he focused on her again. "How do you know? What did you see?"

"He punched his fists through glass and within minutes the cuts had vanished, deep gashes that had been dripping with blood and then suddenly were no more. I spotted a subtle silver sheen passing over his skin. There's only one power in the world that can do that."

The ghost of a grin crossed his lips before he smoothed them into an unreadable line. "Thank you for coming tonight. I'll meet with my council to adjust the plans accordingly. The raven might be the test subject we've been waiting for. Come back tomorrow and I'll let you know how to proceed. Things will move faster than you think now that the time is almost here."

Cassi was dismissed.

She knew it. Yet she held onto his dream, refusing to let go, even as she felt his spirit fighting to get away, to return to his desk and his lantern and the deep, dark night of planning ahead.

He paused, tilting his head at her. "Is there something else, Kasiandra?"

Funny how in the world above, Cassi never thought twice about questioning Lyana, the woman who would one day be her queen. Yet here, in the world below, surrounded by never-ending fog that only his eyes seemed to penetrate, questions died quick deaths before her king.

But he knew.

He sensed the tension in her soul. "What?"

He stepped closer. A flicker of concern passed over his features before he reached out and placed his hand on her arm. The touch felt real, though she knew it was as much a fabrication as the roof above their heads, the salty air sticking to their skin, the crashing waves five stories below that pounded more ferociously with each second she tarried.

"You can tell me," he said.

"It's just..." She broke off, but he continued staring, giving her time, waiting for her to speak.

That patient, curious look reminded her so much of the boy she used to know, so much of the Malek she remembered in her dreams. For a moment, she forgot the roles they'd come to play, the walls she'd built, and remembered the way they used to be with each other—free.

"It's Lyana," she finally said. "She's in so much pain. She's so confused. And I have all the answers on the tip of my tongue, but I can't say anything to ease the ache, to assure her that the bleak future she sees on the horizon isn't the destiny ahead. I don't understand why we have to wait. Why I can't—"

"You know why," he replied coldly, uninterested in her emotions, snapping Cassi back to the present. The vision of the boy in her head faded—she shoved it away, forcing it back into that small place where it always lingered. Now he was a king. A man who had no time for feelings. Not with the war he was waging—against a world that was broken down the middle, against an enemy that grew stronger with each passing day.

"But she's the queen that was prophesized," Cassi countered weakly, still hoping he might understand.

"We don't know that for certain. Not yet. Not until the day she turns eighteen. And until we know, I won't risk unveiling our presence. Not when surprise is the only weapon on our side."

Cassi shrugged out of his touch. "She'd come willingly. If I could only explain, she'd make the journey in a heartbeat."

"And what if she didn't?" her king asked, words edged with disbelief that of all people he had to make this point to her, his loyal servant, his darling spy. "Myth and legend are the only things that keep them from diving through the mist and destroying us all. And if they ever learned what we mean to do —what must be done to save the world? I don't even think our magic could save us."

"But—"

"I won't hear any more, Kasiandra," he interrupted, silencing her with a look that was sharper than any sword.

He swiveled his head to one side, as though he had heard something she couldn't. His muscles tensed. Before Cassi could fight, an invisible fist yanked on her soul, shattering the dream in an instant.

Cassi shot like an arrow, spirit ripped from his head and thrown back into the world. By the time she'd regained her focus, he was already leaping from his bed, unconcerned that he wore nothing more than loose trousers as he shoved his feet inside his boots and raced from the room. She followed, an invisible shadow as he ran through the ship and to the top deck, hastily making his way across the bridge before the first scream even erupted.

A moment later she knew why.

A burning ship blinked to life on the horizon. Angry, sweeping flames cut through the mist as the wind whipped into sails that were little more than tattered shreds. Yellow sparks of *aero'kine* magic were laced through the gusts. Two of her king's crew followed him, already lifting their hands, tugging at the elements. The yellow flares in the mist brightened as the air became a tight vacuum, sucking the ship in. Buckets of water rose over the hull, sparkling with sapphire *hydro'kine* magic, and splashed the fire to soak it. By the time charred wood banged against the dock, little more than smoke and embers remained, but the damage had already been done. One survivor leaned over the side, coughing to clear the smoke from his lungs, hardly able to breathe. No others were in sight.

"King Malek," the man wheezed, relief flooding his exhausted gaze.

"What happened?" the king called. A gangplank was hastily fashioned, and he climbed aboard. Cassi floated behind him, unseen by all except her king, who undoubtedly still sensed her presence.

"Dragons…" The survivor's voice trailed off into a fit of coughs. The side of his face was covered in rising blisters. She couldn't tell his clothes from his skin, as they had melted and fused beyond reckoning. His body trembled with something beyond pain—adrenaline was the only fuel he had left, and even that was quickly fading.

"Are there others?" her king asked as he pressed his palm to the man's chest. The air around his fingers sparkled with the golden force of his magic, the most powerful type of all— *aethi'kine*, the ability to bend, warp, and even heal spirits.

"I don't— I'm not—"

The man passed out before he could say any more.

Her king turned, still funneling his power into the

stranger's broken body as he yelled to his crew below, the lot of them pushing their way through the gathering crowd to get to their ruler. "Search for survivors. Bring them to me. And you," he said, turning to look up at the spot where Cassi lingered, "return to the princess and remember what it is we're all fighting for."

Cassi hovered above him for a few more seconds, watching as the man's burns began to smooth, as his breath became more even, as the ache across his features eased, as her king used his magic to restore him.

I don't care what he says. Lyana deserves the truth.

She's the queen.

She has to be.

But by the time Cassi returned to her body in the floating world above, all that had happened below felt like little more than a dream. When her eyes opened and she turned her head, her friend was curled on the other side of the mattress, one ivory wing cradling her head like a pillow and the other covering her body like a warm blanket. The words died on Cassi's lips. She'd lived in the lie for so long, she wasn't sure how to end it, what to say, how to explain.

So, she closed her eyes and went to sleep, wondering what the morning would bring.

34

LYANA

The Sea of Mist was endless. At least, that was how it seemed to Lyana.

For the first few hours of the long journey, the opaque mantle stretching beneath her had been mesmerizing. Every pocket of thinning fog made her breath catch. Every flash of orange made her heart race with excitement. She studied the thick mist as though it were a puzzle to solve. Was that flare of light a dragon? Was that spot of blue the ocean? Was there land or only fire? Did Vesevios wait somewhere in the swirling wisps of gray?

She ached to snap her wings and dive headfirst, plummeting through wind and air, but she didn't. Not out of fear, but out of duty—a concept that was far more frightening than the fire god would ever be. A concept that began to monopolize her attention as her adventure turned a little, well, tedious, if she were being honest.

The hours stretched.

The scene did too, on and on and on.

The questions of awe and wonder slipped away.

Her mind wandered, and wandered, and wandered...to places she really wished it wouldn't as her gaze darted to the front of the flock, where the prince and his brother flew side by side, so similar they could have been twins. So why did only one of them make her nostrils flare with barely contained fury? They'd both lied. They'd both deceived. But at least Xander had seemed apologetic, regretful, maybe even ashamed.

Rafe had been nothing more than an ass.

A complete and total ass.

Aethios help me, it's a good thing I'm not actually mated to such an arrogant prick. The nerve of him last night. The absolute nerve.

Oh, she could just scream with frustration.

Don't think about it.

Don't think about him.

She reminded herself, over and over, not to even consider him, taking a deep breath as she realized her wings had propelled her out of formation, fueled by the annoyance flaming across her limbs.

The feeling of eyes on her made Lyana turn. Cassi watched her with a concerned yet amused expression on her face, able to read every wayward thought in Lyana's head as though her misfortunes were somehow entertaining. She wrinkled her nose at her friend and shifted her eyes back to the mist. The Sea of Mist. The thing Lyana had been waiting an entire life to traverse. The thing that had filled her daydreams for as long as she could remember. A thing of myth. Of magic. Of...

Within minutes, her eyes were no longer on the thick carpet of gray, but on the prince, her mind wandering yet again. But she kept her focus acutely on Xander, studying the pumping of his obsidian wings, how they glistened in the sunlight, how he seemed stronger in the air than he'd seemed on land, more confident, more compelling. Her match. Her mate.

What would their life be like?

With her, he was nervous and unsure, hesitant to make an approach, but she'd watched him interact with his guards, with the small raven woman who seemed to be a captain of some sort, with his brother, with the queen. He smiled. He laughed, a loud sound pulled from the depths of his belly, pure and honest. It made her smile just to hear it. Who was the real prince? Was he docile or assured? Would he ever understand a princess like her?

Or would she always be a lone dove among ravens?

An outsider?

A stranger?

Lyana's gaze dropped again, this time finding solace in the blanket of fog stretching like a warm bed, soft and alluring, solid and steadfast. Would she regret not taking this chance to disappear into the mist and fly free?

A loud whistle pierced her thoughts.

All thoughts of escape vanished. They had arrived at The House of Whispers. It was little more than a black speck floating on the horizon, but a shot of energy pulsed through her, making her wings beat faster as her heart sped to match her excitement.

A new place.

A new land.

A new home.

Lyana shifted from her spot in the middle of the flock, swerving around bodies, fighting for the unobstructed view at the front of the group. Cassi had undoubtedly followed, but Lyana couldn't look to check. Her eyes were glued to the island growing larger and larger with each passing second, an island completely different from her home. Not made of flat expanses of endless white. Not frigid and frozen. Not barren, but brimming with life.

Everything was green—so green.

A lush forest extended all the way from the tops of mountain peaks, down, down, down, practically spilling over the edge, where dirt gave way to air. There were more shades of that single color than she'd ever thought possible—some deep and dark and full of secrets, others glimmering and glistening with the reflection of the sun. Lyana had been in the greenhouses of her home, where they grew food supplied by the other houses, but the plants in there had been arranged and organized, carefully trimmed and tended. Colorful and beautiful, yet controlled.

This was wild.

This was chaotic.

This was life.

And Lyana breathed it in as she ignored the flock and finally did the thing she'd been aching to do all day—she plunged into the unknown. Within seconds, she'd landed hard against the ground, dropping to a crouch so she could dig her hands into the leaves and dirt covering the forest floor, amazed that her fingers didn't freeze. The air here was thicker, richer, full of some invisible thing her sterile home had been unable to produce.

Lyana soared toward the nearest tree, and landed on a thick branch. Pressing her palms against the trunk, she marveled at the scratchy texture—moist and dirty, but so pure. Deep in her chest, Lyana's magic surged to life, as though the tree had a soul and was talking to hers, drawing out her power. The rustle of waxy leaves was a sweet melody to her ears. She darted to another tree, taller and narrower with needles that pricked her fingers and odd little things she knew were pinecones, which she'd never seen before. She plucked one, cupping it as if it might break at any moment, as if it were something precious, though there were probably thousands more hidden within the forest.

By the time her companions landed, Lyana was at a third tree, this one with bark the color of her wings, stark against the curtain of green but striped with brown.

"What is it?" she called without turning to see who waited on the ground beneath her.

The snark in the reply was familiar. "A tree."

Lyana met Cassi's gaze with a pointed one of her own. "I know that…"

She cut herself short when a flash of yellow caught her attention, the tree forgotten as she raced to a flower bed, reaching down to run her thumb along a smooth, bright petal.

Lyana breathed deeply, a smile passing over her lips as the scent of honey drifted to her nose. "What are these?"

Before anyone could answer, a spot of red berries also drew her eyes. "And these?"

Then a fallen tree, covered in patches of minty stains. "And this?

"And that?

"And those?

"And—"

"Ana!" Cassi finally interrupted, shouting across the forest. "You're making me dizzy. You're making *us* dizzy."

Lyana hovered in midair and spun, finally remembering she wasn't alone, and this wasn't a secret exploration back home. She had an audience—a group of patient guards, a queen who looked unimpressed, a prince who looked amused, and a sullen raven she refused to look at, even for a second. She was supposed to be a princess. Dignified. Controlled. A figurehead.

But—

But—

Oh, I don't care! Lyana thought as she dropped to the ground, leaves crunching beneath her feet, a sound she'd never heard before—and wasn't it marvelous? Princess or not, she threw her arms and wings to the side, resisting the urge to spin around, but just barely. "Oh, Cassi, come on. This is amazing!" Lyana shifted her gaze to her mate, brows drawing together. "Don't you think this is amazing?"

His smile deepened, but he didn't answer.

Queen Mariam stepped forward, instead. "While I

imagine this is quite different from what you're used to, daughter of Aethios, the sun is beginning to set, and we must be going."

Lyana kept her eyes on the prince, giving him the chance to defend her, to prove himself, to soar across the clearing, grab her hand, and whisk her on a grand tour of the isle, to surprise her. Thus far, her mate had been a man who had allowed someone else to fight his battles, who had run from a dragon and from the courtship trials, who hadn't had the nerve to stand up for himself, let alone for her.

She wanted more from him.

She needed more from him.

Especially when, hard as she tried not to, she was comparing him to someone else, someone she'd promised not to look at or think about or speak to ever again.

She ignored the pleading expression from her friend and quietly asked, "Lysander?"

His smile twitched as his focus jumped back and forth between his mother and his mate, the silence stretching. And then his shoulders dropped ever so slightly. "We really should be going, Princess."

Lyana fought the sensation that the wind had been stolen from her wings, a plummeting sort of feeling. But her sigh was audible, and she couldn't keep her face from drooping along with her feathers. "Yes, of course," she murmured, catching Cassi's eye for a moment before quickly sliding hers away. "Let's be on our way."

Lyana didn't miss the quick motion of an ebony wing stretching and shoving the prince forward an inch, but she refused to look at the source of the gesture. Her mind wandered where her eyes would not, drifting back to the night where her hands were pressed against his bare skin, in the muscular valley between his wings. Lyana blinked the vision away, focusing only on the words he'd spoken as he told her of his home—the mountains, the river, the city nestled in a valley, and the godly entrance to another world.

"Taetanos's Gate," Lyana exclaimed suddenly, some of her enthusiasm returning as she remembered the House of Whispers had much more to offer than the forest around her. "Oh, can we see it? Please? Even just from the air?"

"Who told you—" Lysander broke off abruptly, turning toward his half brother.

This time, Lyana couldn't help turning to the man she tried to remember was Rafe, and not Lysander. Rafe. Rafe.

What kind of name is that? she spat silently, clinging to every ounce of wrath she could muster, because anger was so much easier to deal with than all the other emotions swirling like a storm in her chest. *Rafe? More like rude, repugnant, repulsive, re-, re-, re-*

Real.

Rare.

Lyana shook her head to clear it, but her eyes remained glued to him. He'd turned away, presenting them with his profile as he stared into the woods. Lyana had a sneaking suspicion that if he'd dared to meet her gaze, she would have seen the same memory reflected in his eyes as was playing in hers. The two of them in their own world, a halo of light in a cave of darkness, something that now seemed little more than a dream—one that lingered in her waking hours, rather than fading blissfully into the realm of the forgotten.

Don't think about it.

Don't think about him.

Much as she'd loathed his delivery of sharp words the night before, Lyana couldn't deny they were true. He wasn't her friend, or her confidante, or her anything. A fact that had never been more evident than in this moment, standing in this clearing with the far-to-curious interest of the flock shifting between them. For the sake of her happiness, Rafe had to be nothing. For the sake of her mate, she had to bury him away.

The prince cleared his throat as the uncomfortable silence lengthened.

Lyana pulled her gaze from one raven and switched it to the other, remembering what Rafe had called the prince the night before. Xander. She liked it better than Lysander, because it was new and light, not full of foolish wishes that would never come true.

He was her future.

He was her mate.

She was determined to give their life a chance.

"Xander," she said, testing the name, enjoying how it rolled from her lips, a little hesitant and unsure, just like they were about each other. His eyes softened, losing their edge. "Will you show me?"

35

XANDER

He must have held his breath the rest of the way through the mountains. The sweeping forests of his homeland were mostly uninhabited, gliding up and down in sharp ridges and some barren cliffs, even a few snow-capped peaks that remained through summer. Most of his people chose to live in the valley, in the city of Pylaeon, where the castle was nestled. They were the least populated isle and the smallest, though the journey seemed endless as his eyes continued to drift to the princess time and time again. His chest felt tight, his mind unable to erase the disappointment flashing through her face—disappointment at him.

Please be impressed, he thought as the thundering of water made its way to his ear, signaling they were almost there.

Please be impressed.

By the view? By his home? By him?

Xander wasn't really sure.

All he knew was that when they crested the final peak, he heard her gasp, and it was one of the sweetest sounds he could ever remember. When he glanced in her direction, a warm feeling spread inside him as he saw her wide, dazzled eyes and the mouth that had opened in wonder. Her wings beat faster, led by her excitement, but the rest of her remained still as she took in the scene.

The waterfall seemed to appear from nowhere as the two mountain peaks framing the valley abruptly gave way to rock and cliff. The many small rivers hidden among the trees merged right before the lip, hardly blending for a moment before they crashed and cascaded down three different plateaus, finally plunging a hundred feet into the deep pool below. The mist caught the dying light, turning it into a thousand twinkling stars. Half the valley was hidden in the shadows cast by the mountains, but the far stretches were bathed in a soft golden glow. The river glistened, the shaft of a burning arrow leading to a sharp point—his city, his home. Pylaeon sparkled as the glass from various windows caught the blaze of the sun, stark against the open air beyond, which was already dark with the coming night.

Lyana dove over the edge, following the path of the water.

This time, Xander followed, ignoring the chiding noise from his mother as soft laughter spilled from his lips, coaxed by the echo of glee the princess had left in her wake. He landed by her side, blinking as cool droplets of water landed on his cheeks from the towering waterfall.

"This is Taetanos's Gate," he shouted over the roar. "The

water hides the entrance to a deep cave, and our god stone is housed within, as is our sacred nest."

Lyana didn't pull her gaze away from the view, but she did something else, something that made his heart lurch. She reached out and placed her hand on his arm, on his right arm, seemingly unaware that her fingers had found rounded flesh in place of a palm. She turned to him, finally finding his eyes as she said, "Show me."

He didn't actually hear the words, but he didn't have to.

And though he knew his mother would not approve, he didn't have the will to tell the princess no, not when she was looking at him like that, as though a little bit of her awe at his homeland belonged to him as well.

He gently slid his arm from her grasp and pumped his wings, flying over the pool of water toward the heart of his land, acutely aware that his mate followed. They were going to get soaked, not exactly the first impression he'd had in mind when he thought of introducing his new mate to his people, but he found he didn't mind the splashing over his wings as they rounded the side of the falls. Xander pointed to the semicircular hole near the base of the cliff, previously hidden by the water.

"The spirit door is there," he explained over the roar, and Lyana nodded as though she'd heard. "My people believe lost souls follow the river to the gate, and this is where they enter our god's realm. Our sacred nest lies at the end of the passage, though we use a separate entrance to access it, one that's a little less...wet."

Her smile grew even wider at his words. But her attention

had already shifted from the rock, turning instead to the water rushing past them and crashing into the pool below, spraying their clothes.

"Can I touch it?" she asked hesitantly as her hand extended toward the cascade.

Xander shrugged. A boyish sense of mischief bubbled in him, something he hadn't felt in a very long time. "Go ahead."

The princess paused as a hungry sort of gleam filled her eyes. Then she shoved both her arms into the fall, up to her elbows, releasing a yelp as the pressure of the water made her drop a solid ten feet before she was able to beat her wings and retreat. She spun to face him with a look of surprise. The front side of her body dripped wet—her leather jacket and trousers were drenched, and the fur around her neck had wilted with moisture. Just as quickly, she began to laugh, a loud, throaty sound that made her body shake.

"Did you know that would happen?" she asked.

His lips twitched. "Of course not."

The princess lifted a brow. Before he had a chance to back further away, her hands returned to the rushing liquid, this time to throw it in his direction. Xander darted sideways, but not before a splash hit his chest.

Part of him wanted to retaliate.

Part of him couldn't believe she'd done it.

And part of him remembered that he was a crown prince, she was a future queen, and this sort of frivolity was a luxury they didn't have.

Before he got a chance to figure out which part of him was the strongest, a cough sounded behind him, loud despite the thunder echoing around them. Xander turned to find Rafe hovering in the shadows at the edge of the water, hands clasped behind his back as his wings flapped, nearly hidden in the folds of the coming night.

"I know, I know." Xander spoke before Rafe had a chance to, because normally he was the one on the other side of this lecture. And if his brother's tight brows and thin lips were any indication, the mere thought of having to do the queen's bidding had left Rafe physically ill.

Xander turned back to the princess, noting that the grin was gone from her lips as she stared at the flowing water, the tips of her fingers grazing the stream, unwilling to be parted from it.

"I'm sorry," he told her with sincerity. "We really should get to the castle."

Lyana nodded.

By the time Xander swiveled, his brother was gone. And when he skirted the edge of the falls, the sun, too, had disappeared—taking all the wonder and awe and magic of the past few minutes with it. The sky was in limbo, too light for the stars, too dark for clarity—a muddled sort of indigo that only served to remind Xander that he was wet, a little cold, and looking not at all like the regal champion he ought to be upon his return.

You're going to be a king. Xander landed beside his mother, seeing the same rebuke flash through her eyes as they noticed the wet stain on his chest. *You must act like one.*

Yet he didn't regret it—this small moment of putting himself and his mate first, a luxury he could rarely ever afford.

Xander noted the wrinkled, wet clothes clinging to Lyana's body, the droplets of water spilling down her hair and onto her cheeks, the way her lips moved faster than a hummingbird's wings as she leaned over to whisper to her friend. The princess had a light all her own, vibrant and vivacious. The very sight of her brought a hopeful feeling that hadn't been there before. Lyana would never fit the mold he'd imagined his mate would, a quiet life companion, a figure of reserved strength, a ruler more like him. She was more than a princess.

She was a force.

If anyone could bring color to a house made of black, it was she. If anyone could return laughter to streets that had grown quiet from so much misfortune, it was she. If anyone could erase the past and restore the future, it was she.

As her bright wings took to the dark air, Xander couldn't help but wonder if, like the rushing waters of Taetanos's Gate, she would somehow slip right between his fingers—too much for this small island to contain.

CASSI

Cassi was exhausted. By the voyage, yes, but mostly by Lyana. All she'd wanted to do after the ravens led them through the claustrophobic stone walls of the castle to their rooms was collapse on the bed and sleep until she couldn't sleep any longer. Alas, Lyana had wanted to talk...and talk...and talk, until Cassi feared her ears might bleed listening to her friend.

First the trees, then the falls, then the river and the town and the castle. Just when Cassi had thought there was nothing else her friend could say, Lyana had swept aside the thick, heavy curtains blocking the balcony and charged outside, dragging Cassi with her so they could admire the view, which was, at least, magnificent.

The castle sat right on the edge of the isle, teetering on the precipice. Half of the scene glittered in the light of the oil lanterns scattered among the houses, while the other half sparkled under the stars. Lyana, of course, had wanted to take a flying leap over the rails to explore her new home, but Cassi grabbed her foot at the last second to keep her grounded—reminding her enthusiastic friend that perhaps the prince would want to introduce her to his people himself. Lyana had wilted, a flower ripped away from the sun, but had relented before Cassi's logic. Being reminded of the prince, however, had only given Lyana a new source of conversation. Cassi had obliged, fighting to keep her eyes open but eventually succumbed to fatigue.

She woke a few hours later to blissful silence.

Her back ached from falling asleep curled in a chair. Her wings were sore from draping over the arms at odd angles. But she was somewhat rested, relatively alert, and more importantly, Lyana was out cold in her bed, which meant Cassi's real work could begin.

She closed her eyes again, and awoke as the dreamwalker.

A twinge of guilt pinched her as she glided across the room, through the curtains, and into the open air above the castle, leaving Lyana behind. Had this morning been her first time in the House of Whispers, Cassi probably would have been just as enthused as her friend, just as talkative, just as amazed. Instead, she'd been guarding her tongue, worn out by the secrets as she tried her best to respond without revealing that she had seen these trees and these mountains and this city many times before. That the wonder had long since faded, replaced with grim determination, which was what stirred in her veins now.

Cassi dove through the mist, returning to the floating city

where her king had been stationed the night before. His ship was still there, majestic and towering, and she made her way quickly inside, too run down to linger. Within moments, she was in his dream, weaving the image to her will and meeting his stormy eyes.

"Thank you for coming back so soon, Kasiandra."

Cassi just nodded, mouth too dry for words, because she knew what was coming. It had been all she could think about during the long flight to the House of Whispers, with nothing to distract her but clear blue and dull gray, and a mind too imaginative for its own good.

The creases at the corners of her king's eyes deepened for a moment as he took note of her solemn mood, but as always, he moved past it and on to business. "I've decided on a course of action for the *invinci*."

She nodded again.

This time, her throat constricted. As her king continued to outline his plan, a flame in her chest stretched out to her fingers and down to her toes, making her numb and incandescent all at once. Protests stirred in her stomach, but none reached her lips. The longer they festered, the more nauseous she became. Sick and ill. Disgusted and ashamed. As though each order he gave chipped away at her, bit by bit, until she was worried that by the end of it, there would be nothing left—of Cassi, of Kasiandra, of either.

But she could do this one final thing.

Especially when it might help save them all.

"We're depending on you, Kasiandra," he concluded softly, placing his hand, heavy yet reassuring, on her shoulder—as though maybe, just maybe, he understood the weight of what he was asking. Her rubbed his thumb over the edge of her collarbone before dropping his arm. Her body leaned forward, chasing his touch.

Malek...

The word danced across her mind before she could stop it, control it, remember who he was. *My king. My king. My king.* Thinking of him as anything else was too painful.

Cassi straightened her back. "I won't let you down, my liege."

The dream dissolved.

Though normally she liked to linger in his rooms, her spirit couldn't wait to fly away—from his words, from his commands, from his all-too-knowing gaze. Cassi raced back into the fog, losing herself in the impenetrable mist, not pausing until the lights of the floating city had disappeared behind her and all she could hear was the thunder of the ocean instead of the thunder of her dreaming-heart, pounding and pounding with all the words she didn't have the strength to say. *No. No. No.* She pushed the king from her thoughts and focused on the one good thing he'd requested she do—make a quick stop to see her mother.

Cassi was three when her magic made itself known. In a world of endless ocean and fog, resources were scarce and magic scarcer still. Everyone who had the gift was handed over to the crown to provide whatever service needed, and in Cassi's case, with her very rare, very specialized magic, that service had been subterfuge. Within a month of discovering her dreamwalking, she'd been ripped from her mother's arms, smuggled to the floating isle above, and deposited in a frozen tundra to be discovered by a troop of doves on their daily patrol. She hadn't seen her mother since, not in flesh and blood, the way that truly counted. But she'd never forgotten the scent of her mother's soul—salty air mixed with sugary-sweet magic and the slightest smoky burn of time spent chasing dragons.

Cassi used that to find her through the mist.

The ship wasn't far, and she came upon it fast, slipping through the wooden boards, floating into the captain's room, where a woman slept. Her tawny skin was etched with wrinkles and her brown hair streaked with gray, though the colorful fabric twisted around her curls made it difficult to tell.

Captain Audezia'd'Rokaro.

Her mother.

She slept curled on her side in trousers and a loose shirt. A pair of worn leather boots stood by the bed. A black overcoat, roughly sewn yet warm and sturdy, hung from a post. But Cassi's eyes went straight to the singular deep-brown wing with spots of white folded against her mother's back. In the darkness of the cabin, it looked dull and muddy, but in the light of the sun, it was a dazzling copper. Once upon a time, in a different life, her mother had belonged to the House of Prey. But she'd been tossed over the edge when they discovered her magic, becoming one of the lucky few to survive the long fall to the world below.

Cassi pressed her palm to her mother's brow and dove into her dream, fighting the torrent as she warped the image to one of her own making. An endless grassy field. A cloudless blue sky. A sun shining brightly. And by her side, a hawk appeared with two perfect wings and frosty eyes that reminded her of the moon.

"Kasiandra."

"Mother."

They didn't embrace or gush or wilt at the sight of one another. Her mother had led a tough life, one that didn't lend itself to histrionic displays of affection. She was a hunter, not a lover. But the warmth in her tone was enough for Cassi. In fact, it was everything.

"The king has a job for you," Cassi said, getting straight to the point.

Her mother shifted her stance, feet spreading wide, hands clasping behind her back, gaze searching the horizon—a sailor through and through. "And?"

Cassi's words tumbled out in a cascade, faster than she could control, but it was the only way—one quick shot. As she spoke, her mother's eyes darkened a shade, flickering with old demons, and a muscle worked in her cheek as if she were biting back memories. Her lips, though, remained a thin, determined line. The fortitude in her gave Cassi hope, because if her mother could endure this, Cassi would too. For the sake of them all.

In the quiet following her words, her mother sighed, closing her eyes for a brief yet long moment. When she opened them, all the shadows were gone. She turned to her daughter, expression soft with sympathy. "Is that all?"

Cassi snorted. "Is it not enough?"

The captain reached across the space between them and

pressed her palm to Cassi's cheek, there and gone, a touch so swift it could have been imagined except for the warm tingle that lingered. "Leave your worries to your waking hours, Kasiandra. They will always be there, waiting. Dreams, especially your dreams, are made for so much more."

Cassi followed her mother's eyes as they moved to the sky and then returned to her, sparkling with streaks of silver. The corner of her lip lifted, as did a single brow in silent question as she nodded toward the blinding sun.

With that her mother turned, ran, and launched into the sky with the graceful speed of a predator, a hunting cry spilling from her throat. Cassi leapt after her, a set of matching hawk wings on her back. They dipped, dove, and sped in unison, drawing arches in the wind, two birds moving as one. The landscape changed to fit Cassi's mood, into canyons they could swerve through, mountains to scale, trees to dodge, or even crashing waves that splashed water on their skin. Whatever she wanted. Whatever she imagined. Her mother was right—her dreams were beautiful, and they were made for more than dark thoughts and draining ruminations.

In the real world, Cassi was an owl because that was the only bird they had been able to steal for the transformation at the time. Her fears and doubts were sometimes suffocating. Her double life hung around her neck like an ever-tightening noose, one that was becoming more and more difficult to ignore. Her mother was a sea captain because standing at the bow of her ship, a single wing wide to catch the wind, was the closest she could come to flying. She was lonely, though she'd never admit it, and always searching for something more in that distant, ever-deepening horizon.

But here, in Cassi's magic, they could be whatever they wanted. A mother and a daughter. Together. United. Just two hawks racing in the breeze, for a few short hours at least.

37

LYANA

A quiet knock on the door pulled Lyana from the last vestiges of sleep, forcing her to finally open her eyes and stretch muscles still recovering from the long flight the day before.

"I'm coming," she called, wondering who it could be.

Cassi was still asleep on the chair in the corner, and the sun had barely risen in the sky, if the lingering pink hues outside her window were anything to go by. When Lyana opened the door, an unfamiliar sight greeted her—a raven girl in simple clothes, whose head was lowered.

"Good morning, Princess," the girl whispered, voice on the edge of apologetic yet tinged with something else— curiosity, maybe. "The queen requests your presence at breakfast."

Lyana sighed.

Before she had time to respond, three other raven girls

appeared and shuffled into the room without a word. One quickly moved to the bed, tugging the sheets into place and fluffing the pillows. Another went to the closet, pulling the door open and shifting through a wardrobe. The third hurried to the vanity near the balcony, opening drawers and arranging bottles full of salves. The girl who had knocked walked to Lyana, removed her sleeping garments, and pushed her through a door she hadn't yet noticed. A bath had already been drawn for her.

"I'm—" Before Lyana could finish speaking, a bucket of warm water was poured over her head, drowning the words.

"I can—" Another bucket came.

"Please—" She started again, but the raven girl's lips were drawn with quiet determination, and Lyana knew better than to try to stop her. Clearly, the queen had ordered she be prepared, and prepared she would be. The only time she piped up was when they began attacking her hair with brushes that snagged and caught in her voluminous curls, eliciting a hiss of pain. Lyana used her fingers instead, yearning for the combs hidden somewhere in her travel trunks, and quickly twirled a large bun on the crown of her head to keep the strands out of her eyes if she flew.

Through it all, Cassi slept, still wearing her heavy flying leathers from the day before but looking cozier than Lyana.

She eyed her friend enviously as a violet dress was pulled over her waist, tied around her neck, and topped with a creamy overcoat to keep the exposed skin around her wings warm. The House of Whispers was much balmier than her home, but the morning air was still brisk as it fluttered in through curtains she'd forgotten to close the night before. The sliver of sky visible through that opening was more enticing than ever, but before she could get any ideas, the raven girl led her from the room.

The halls of the castle were wide and high, yet the dark, opaque stone made Lyana yearn for the crystal palace she called home. This was a maze of twists and turns and steps and doors, designed for walking instead of flying, nothing like the open atrium she'd grown up in. By the time she was deposited in the dining hall, Lyana was so confused she could hardly tell up from down, let alone how to return to her rooms.

Xander immediately stood when she walked in, offering her a bow. Queen Mariam merely looked up, taking a brief moment to inspect Lyana's attire before returning to the parchment in her hand. For her part, Lyana tried to smile, but her mood only soured further when her eyes landed on the piles and piles of books stacked between the plates of food. She spared a longing glance at the sky outside the windows flanking the hall before taking a seat beside the queen.

"I hope you slept well," Xander said cheerily.

"I did," Lyana replied with a forced smile, fighting her unease.

The silence stretched on, serving only to remind her how different her new life would be. Back home, breakfast was grabbing a bit of fruit on her way to Cassi's room, fluttering any which way she chose, exchanging teasing remarks with Luka, enduring the occasional lesson, all while being surrounded by the invisible presence of love, a tender sort of quality in the air she'd never even noticed until now—when it was nowhere to be found.

The air in this room was stuffy and cold, and it had nothing to do with the temperature.

Lyana cleared her throat.

"Would it be possible for my friend to join us tomorrow?" she asked lightly, trying not to betray how much more at ease Cassi's presence would make her feel.

"I'm afraid not," the queen responded, the authority in her voice almost reminding Lyana of her own mother—a woman who could see right through her. But while her mother often chided her, affection always lingered in the soft edges of her words. Here there were only sharp sentences, clipped, precise and not to be questioned. "In this castle, breakfast is shared only with family."

"She's like a sister to me," Lyana countered, turning toward Xander unintentionally, her thoughts going to a different raven, one she'd feared to find here. "A sibling, surely..."

Xander winced.

At the same time, the heat in the queen's glare pierced the periphery of Lyana's vision, striking like an arrow.

Lyana swallowed the rest of her words. She didn't really know her mate at all—they came from two different worlds, one of ravens, another of doves—and she was starting to understand that their differences ran much deeper than mere feathers. Who was this family she'd chosen to join? Where two brothers could switch identities for their most sacred ritual, but couldn't dine at the same table? With a mother who seemed colder than the tundra she'd left behind? Who lived in a place where smiles had to be forced, friends kept away, and trust earned instead of freely offered?

A plate of oats and berries was set before her. Lyana picked at it halfheartedly.

"If we can move on to more important topics," Queen Mariam suggested, rolling the parchment in her hand closed, her tone demanding obedience. "You turn eighteen in three weeks, correct?"

Lyana nodded, already anticipating where the conversation was going. Traditionally, no mates could be joined before the gods until they were both eighteen—the age at which magic either made itself known or didn't exist. Lyana's magic had, of course, already announced itself, but she'd hidden it for years, and she could hide it for a few more weeks until she and Xander were united before the gods. Maybe then, with enough trust and ties to bind them, she'd consider what Rafe had told her just before she'd left his room two nights ago, words barely more than a whisper, so soft they almost weren't real. That Xander knew his secret—knew of his magic and didn't mind.

A bit of her heart warmed at the thought, and Lyana glanced up from her plate to find Xander observing her and gauging her responses, the lavender in his eyes soft in a way the queen's deeper color was not.

"Since we'll have been waiting longer than most of the other matched couples," the queen continued, not bothering to wait for Lyana's response, "my advisors and I have decided to proceed with the mating ceremony on the same day as your birthday so the two celebrations can be combined."

Lyana nodded, although the queen had formulated no question, because she'd expected as much. Most of the matched couples were probably, at this very moment, standing in their sacred nests, performing the ritual before the gods, declaring their unending loyalty to someone who was little more than a stranger. Luka and his mate had probably celebrated their vows yesterday while Lyana had been flying farther and farther away, leaving him and the rest of her family behind. How strange to think they'd shared everything growing up, their deepest, darkest secrets, and yet one day after she left home she'd already missed the most important moment of his life.

They were already moving on without her.

And Lyana was here, sitting at a table, surrounded by books and a foreign new family, her eyes on the windows across the room, on the balcony and the fresh air and the rising sun. But the idea comforted her, because that, of all things, hadn't changed.

The endless blue sky had always called to her.

And her soul still ached to respond.

"Excellent," Queen Mariam said, regaining Lyana's attention as she slid a bit of parchment across the table. "I've arranged a schedule for your next few weeks if you'll take a look. There is much to learn about our people and our customs before you become their queen. This afternoon, the owners of our mines and our most affluent tradesmen will be coming to the castle so Lysander can introduce them to you. In preparation, this morning we will be reviewing their names and stations, talking points for you to remember, as well as the goods they sell to the other houses—raw materials from our mountains like metals and stones, obviously, but we also have a small array of crops and specialty crafts we exchange as well. All of this will be very important for you to understand in the future, when it is Lysander's time to rule."

Inwardly, Lyana groaned.

Outwardly, she took the paper and kept a smile glued to her face as Xander opened the first of many volumes, his face more animated than she ever recalled seeing as he began to tell her of his home.

RAFE

ome sweet home, Rafe thought with a grunt as he swung the blunt blade of his practice sword at the bag of beans he'd strung up as his opponent, satisfied as the blow vibrated up his arms. He pulled back, spun on his toes, and sliced the air, again and again, throwing all his weight into the movement, controlled yet savage, precise yet reckless with frustrated abandon.

He didn't know why he had thought anything would be different.

First morning back, and Xander was dining with his mother in the room where Rafe was not allowed. The servant who had left a meal outside his door had scurried off immediately as though Rafe were a monster lurking in the night. The guards who had helped him during the courtship trials now watched him with narrowed eyes from across the practice yards, not bothering to include him in their exercises.

Even Helen, who normally helped him train, had proceeded with caution, observing him with a calculating gaze, not even offering her usual morning greeting—something he'd always known she'd done for Xander's sake, anyway.

He'd thought maybe when he helped bring back a queen, the guards at least would alter their opinion of him, even if the common raven would never know what had happened at the House of Peace.

Clearly, he'd been wrong.

Rafe arched the sword over his head and whipped the bag with his blade, unconcerned as a bead of sweat dripped down his brow. He had to keep moving, keep fighting, keep smacking things around so he wouldn't wonder if his sour mood had to do with something else—something like the princess currently dining with Xander and the wonder in her eyes as she'd stuck her arms into the waterfall. It was the same expression she'd worn when he'd shown her his magic, as though it wasn't something to fear but to celebrate—as though he wasn't someone to fear but to celebrate.

Rafe dropped his sword, curled his palms into fists, and punched the damned bag instead. The scratch of burlap against his knuckles was a welcome distraction from the pain lingering in other places of his body. The field of his vision narrowed, so there were no guards, no ravens, no practice courtyard and no castle, just him and this undying opponent, and the sting of blood gathering on his skin as he beat the senseless thing even more senseless. When his body was within an inch of giving out, Rafe pumped his wings and used the extra force to place a kick right in the center of his target, fraying the rope. Just as he was about to land the final blow, the hiss of an arrow made him start. The point landed with a *thud* in the center of his bag, immediately sending a cascade of beans to the floor, the sound like the patter of rain during a summer storm.

"What—" Rafe spun, surprise nearly making him choke on his words.

The owl stood behind him, lowering her bow as she shrugged. "I thought you could use the help."

"How long have you been standing there?"

"Long enough," she answered elusively.

He frowned. "Long enough for what?"

A smile tugged at her lip, a haughty sort of thing, as though she could see right through his skull and read every thought in his mind. The very idea made him wary. But a moment later, it was gone.

She blinked and stepped forward, walking past him to kick at the now loose pile of dried beans on the floor, sending a sprinkling over the dirt. "Long enough to know you could use a partner, and as it happens, so could I."

"Look..." Rafe shuffled through his memories, trying to recall her name. "Cassi, right?"

The owl nodded, ruffling her wings proudly, the black-and-white speckles even more out of place than anything about him, though she didn't seem to mind. In fact, she spread her feathers, as though unconcerned to stand out. "Yes, Cassi."

"Well, Cassi, thanks for the offer, but I'm fine," he gruffly replied, bending to pick up his sword as she watched with an eyebrow slightly raised.

"You're fine?" she asked slowly, her attention dropping to the blood caked over his knuckles before returning to his face. A challenge glimmered in the depths of her gray eyes, like a storm daring him to dodge its lightning. "Sure you don't need any help with those cuts? I've tended to Lyana's before. I know how to treat a few shallow wounds."

Rafe resisted the urge to yank his hands away and hide them behind his back. He flexed his fingers instead, not breaking the owl's gaze. "They're nothing."

She shrugged, the knowing smile lingering over her lips, then disappearing in a blink—but it was enough to make him wonder.

Did she know?

Had the princess spilled his secret?

As the idea traveled across his head, the owl released a heavy sigh as her shoulders fell, taking her wings with them, turning her into a woman who looked just as lonely as he did.

"Look, Rafe, right?" She didn't wait for him to answer. "The only other person I know on this island was whisked away before I even woke up, and I haven't seen her since. I've been wandering the halls, looking for a familiar face for an hour. You're not my first choice either, but right now, you're the only one I've got. And I was in the crowd during the trials. You were pretty wonderful with a sword, so can you please help me pass the time and show me what to do? I'm a killer with a bow, but I'm useless with a blade. And a little exercise seems like a better option than spending another hour talking to myself, so won't you just, just…" She was almost huffing as she crossed her arms and waited for his response.

Rafe tightened his grip on the sword, shifting his gaze from the owl to the guards casting curious glances in their direction, to the castle walls where his brother and his brother's new mate would be cooped up for hours, and finally to the bag of beans spilled across the ground—the physical manifestation of the dejection coursing through him.

"Fine," Rafe mumbled, unable to believe the response even as it rolled out of his lips. But this girl, Cassi, was right. It was her or another hour of carting a bag of beans to the practice yards before systematically ripping it to shreds. A little human interaction would be good for him. The gods, it could even show the other ravens they had nothing to fear. He tossed the practice sword in the air and caught the blunt edge, offering her the hilt. "Have you ever used one of these before?"

The glee on her face as she wrapped her fingers around the worn leather handle almost made him regret his decision. But her voice was calm as she answered, "Maybe a few times."

"Show me your stance," he instructed reluctantly, fighting against his own judgment as he stepped around her, adjusting her feet and her hands, shifting her balance, and ordering she remain on the ground until further notice. Within minutes, Rafe was lost in the movement, time racing as he did something he rarely ever got to do—share a bit of himself with another person.

The hour flew.

Then another, and another, until they were sticky with sweat. Their clothes were stained with grass and dirt. Their limbs were caked in mud. Yet they were smiling, even as their breath came up short and exhaustion overtook them, slowing their thrusts and parries. Still, they didn't stop. Not until the sun was setting, and Cassi fell to the ground, grunting as her wings got crushed beneath her.

"Enough," she cried.

"You need to work on your stamina," Rafe goaded, even as he swayed on his feet. A moment later, he was surprised to land as heavy as a rock on the dirt. His mind was so slow that it took her laugh for him to realize she'd swiped his legs out from under him.

"You need to work on your comebacks," she said, easing back against the grass to stare up at the sky.

Rafe opened his mouth before noticing she was right, and he had no idea what to say. So, he sealed his lips and followed her lead, letting his head fall against the ground as he blinked at the vast sky—a sight that had always made him feel small in an almost comforting sort of way. As though his problems were small as well.

"I'm hungry," Cassi stated.

His stomach rumbled as soon as she spoke. "Me too. Come on."

Rafe led her from the practice fields to the kitchens, quietly noting how her steps resembled the confident march of a native far more than the confused hesitation of a newcomer. She turned when he turned, shoulder to shoulder, at his side and not behind. There was no pause in her movements. No question. As though she knew exactly where he was taking her. The very notion was impossible, and yet Rafe couldn't quite shake the sense that the owl had been there before.

Don't be a fool. She'd probably just wandered to the

kitchen that morning in search of breakfast after she'd woken alone.

Sure enough, when she asked him for the way to her rooms after they'd had their fill of fresh bread, her strides were different, more like he had expected. Shorter. Unsure. When they rounded the next corner, she stopped dead in her tracks. With his eyes still on her, he bumped into a body he hadn't seen coming.

"Sorry," he murmured, turning to find the smiling face of his brother. Rafe jumped back. "Xander!"

"Rafe."

"Cassi?"

"Ana!"

The four of them paused for a moment. A spike of heat shot through Rafe's chest, leaving a smoldering path in its wake, the undeniable sense that he'd been doing something wrong, but he didn't know what. He glanced at the owl, but she was smiling at her friend. And though he didn't want his eyes to follow, he couldn't help it—they were drawn like a moth to a flame, and what a bright spot she was. Lyana. Standing there in an amethyst dress embroidered with diamonds, her face framed by the golden trim of her cream overcoat, highlighting the natural warmth of her skin.

"What were you two doing?" Xander asked, mirth evident in his tone.

Rafe suddenly remembered the dirt and the sweat, how much a mess the two of them must have looked compared to the crown prince and his princess in matching finery, pristine as royals should be. "I was, uh, teaching Cassi some swordplay." He couldn't help noticing how Lyana tossed a confused glance at her friend, but he cleared his throat and straightened his spine, refocusing on his brother. "You?"

"The usual," Xander smoothly replied with a shrug. "Breakfast with my mother. Meetings with the advisors. Now supper with the traders."

His eyes were shining in a way that belied the casual tone of his words. As they flicked to the woman by his side, Rafe knew why. He was proud of his mate, proud to show her off to his people, proud to be standing with someone they would love instead of someone they had shunned.

Rafe gritted his teeth, nodding as words escaped him.

"Well, we should probably be going. We're running late," Xander said to his mate with a gently prodding expression. She started, forgetting where she was for a moment, but followed him as he maneuvered around Rafe, whose feet were rooted to the ground. Cassi walked on, either unconcerned or unaware that her guide had become motionless.

Rafe waited a moment longer, listening to his brother's footsteps, each fading sound like a premonition of things to come. His heart sank deeper and deeper into the hollows of his chest.

He'd always known that things would be different after the courtship trials.

He'd always known his brother having a mate would change things.

But he had never realized how much until now. This insignificant moment had somehow flipped his world. It was the beginning of the end.

For the first time, he began to realize that Xander didn't need him anymore. Not really. He had someone else by his side, someone better. A princess instead of a bastard—a trade up in anyone's eyes. And it was only a matter of time before his brother saw how much of a useless burden Rafe had become—with the rumors, the strange looks, and the whispers in the dark, which hadn't ended as he'd hoped, but had instead strengthened.

"Uh, Rafe?" Cassi called. She was standing at the end of the hall, her arms crossed once more. "You're supposed to be showing me where to go?"

"Right," he muttered, taking a deep breath. "Right."

Don't be a fool, he thought for the second time that day as he hurried toward the owl and turned the corner, leading her. *Xander isn't going to forget you. You're his brother. He loves you, no matter what. Of course he does.*

But as he dropped Cassi off at her room and returned to the hall alone, the idea had become harder to swallow. And before he could stop himself, he found he was racing to the nearest balcony and jumping over the edge, wings catching him as he fell, pumping against the wind that whipped around the edge of the isle.

Rafe floated below the castle, to the rooms underground—rooms for the servants and the guards, and then rooms no one mentioned anymore. He didn't stop until he reached the lowest level carved into the rock, now nothing more than a burnt-out crisp. A thick layer of ash stubbornly coated the surfaces even after more than a decade. He landed on the balcony outside the remnants of his mother's room, pausing in the same spot he always did, scuffing his boots over old footprints and forming new ones in the dust. Even after all these years, he couldn't step inside, not fully. Every time he tried, the memory of that snarl, the overwhelming heat, and the acrid scent of their burning flesh, still so strong in the stagnant air, stopped him.

Instead, he walked to the edge and sat so his feet dangled and his wings shrouded him like the curtains that used to hang there. When the corners of his eyes began to sting, he blamed it on the wind and closed them. And when his cheeks grew wet, he imagined there must have been a storm. And when the loneliness became a physical pain clawing at his gut, for a moment Rafe wondered if the dragon had come back to finish the job. But when he opened his eyes, no one was there.

He stood, wiped his cheeks, and flew back to his room at the top of the castle to do what he had done many times before—wait for Xander to return from a dinner he hadn't been invited to, and do his best to be needed.

LYANA

By the time Lyana returned to her rooms that night, she was numb. Numb from all the talking. Numb from the monotony. Numb from the sheer amount of information they'd tried to shove down her throat. Just numb.

"Long night?" Cassi crooned.

Lyana found her friend curled against some pillows by the balcony, an open book in her hands, tan cheeks rosy from the breeze.

"Long week." She sighed and collapsed into the nearest chair, dropping her head in her hands. "I'm not sure I'll ever be able to call this place home."

"Ana," Cassi reprimanded, "it's only been a day."

"I know, but everything is just so, so…so different. Everyone gawks at my wings. They stare at me like I'm some piece of art on display instead of a person. The queen is…

Well, she's just miserable. She won't even allow you to come to breakfast, though I plan on revisiting that later. And everyone is just stuffy, too focused on work, not making room for even the slightest bit of fun. And the prince, he seems to enjoy it! The work, I mean, not the fun. I'm not even being myself— not joking, not teasing, not playing, because I feel so uncomfortable, I don't even remember how to act."

Cassi threw her a keen look over the rim of her reading glasses. But Lyana didn't back down, and after a moment, her friend released an exaggerated sigh as she eased to her feet and left her book facedown against the floor so as not to lose her place.

"It can't be that bad," Cassi said.

"It is," Lyana insisted and dropped back her head to stare at the shadows the oil lanterns made on the ceiling. Even her room was drab—drab and sullen and sulky just like her. "I'm not comfortable in my own skin here. They forced me to have a bath this morning while you were sleeping, like the dead I might add, but didn't give me a second to grab my own soaps. Now even my skin feels dusty, like it's thirsty for some excitement. And whatever they put in my hair made it dry and itchy. I don't know where to find my combs to fix it."

"Hold on," Cassi muttered, changing direction midstride as she made for a trunk on the other side of the room that hadn't been there that morning. Before she opened the lid, Lyana raced to her side, releasing a shamefully pleased breath as she took in the contents.

"Help get me out of this thing, please?" she asked,

spinning so Cassi could untie the laces at her back while she worked on the buttons of her overcoat.

Within a few minutes, the formal gown was off, replaced with the silk sleeping trousers and shirt she pulled from the trunk, a set to match the ones her friend was already wearing. Immediately she could breathe again, and she did, inhaling for a long moment, trying to draw the air from the balcony until it was under her skin to keep it there, fresh and wild and full of life.

Lyana untied the messy bun she'd woven that morning, dipped her fingers into the salve her grandmother had given her before she'd gone to the gods, and rubbed it into her scalp. Lyana's bluebird mother had skin as pale as a raven's. Her hair was stick straight and easy to brush, more similar to Cassi's wavy locks than her daughter's coiling ones. Lyana, like Luka, had inherited her father's looks—strong traits that Aethios himself gifted to all the doves. At least that was what her grandmother used to say as she gently forced a comb through Lyana's tight curls. The memory brought a smile to her lips as she tried to do the same now.

"Let me." Taking the comb from Lyana's hand, Cassi perched on the edge of the bed and motioned to her friend to sit on the floor, as they had often done before. "Small braids this time? So they don't try to wash them?"

Lyana nodded and sighed as Cassi's fingers began to part her hair, moving meticulously around the crown of her head, weaving her curls into many small sets of braids that Lyana would be able to keep for a few weeks and style easily, without requiring aid from the servants who had tried to help, but had instead made her bitter.

Without anything to do, her mind began to wander.

To her mate.

To his mother.

To the lessons and the advisors.

To the people she'd met.

And finally, to the encounter she'd told herself to ignore, because she wasn't supposed to be thinking about him, or wondering about him, or asking about him. But she wasn't. Not technically. Not if she played her cards right.

"What did you do today?" Lyana asked lightly, a little too lightly.

Cassi snorted behind her. "Oh nothing, just another day like any other."

Lyana tried to glare over her shoulder without moving her head, which was a pretty difficult thing to do. "Nothing you want to talk about?"

"Not really," Cassi responded, but her tone was too playful by half. "Not unless there's something *you* want to talk about."

"Of course not," Lyana countered, while silently grumbling in her head.

"Because if there was something you wanted to talk about," Cassi continued, as methodically as she worked on Lyana's hair, "something maybe that you expressly forbade me to let you talk about, or someone rather, then we could talk about him. It's just that you have to tell me, because otherwise I'd be defying a direct order from my princess and, well, we both know what sort of trouble I could be in if I do that."

"No trouble you haven't been in before," Lyana muttered under her breath.

"What's that?"

"Nothing."

Her tone was sweet, but against the floor, her fingers curled into fists and she bit her lips to keep from talking. Cassi began to hum quietly, an annoyingly cheerful little tune that made Lyana's blood boil. An image gathered in her thoughts, the image of the raven as he'd rounded the corner, eyes glued to Cassi, so enthralled by her friend he'd smacked right into his own brother, the crown prince.

It shouldn't have bothered her.

It shouldn't have mattered.

She was supposed to forget everything about him.

But a sensation clawed at her gut, digging and digging and digging, until suddenly, the words burst up her throat as though freed from some deep, dark place and propelled themselves into the world.

"Fine, fine." She spat the admission and raced on to the rest, "Why was he training you? What were you doing together? Why were you covered in mud? What did he say? What did you say? Is he— Are you— What—"

"Relax, Ana," Cassi teased. "Contrary to the sordid thoughts I know are racing through your mind, the raven and I did not, in one afternoon, begin an illustrious affair behind your back."

Tension oozed from Lyana's body, making her wings droop—in relief, this time. "You didn't?"

"No!" Soft laughter escaped Cassi's lips, and Lyana could

envision the way she was shaking her head while the rest of her body trembled with quiet mirth.

"Then why was he teaching you swordplay?" Lyana asked. "You know, the thing you did with Luka when I wasn't around that eventually transitioned into, well, other kinds of swordplay, if you know what I mean?"

The hands against the top of her head fell still.

Lyana winced. She hadn't meant to bring up her brother. Not really. Not as a weapon against her friend, whose heart was fragile at the moment. The words had just slipped out.

"Cassi—" She tried to turn around.

"Don't move," her friend chided, tugging at the strands of hair gently, yet hard enough to keep Lyana from twisting. Her voice was more somber as she continued, "I wasn't—"

She broke off with a sad sound that made Lyana's soul hurt for her.

"When I woke up, you were gone, and no one seemed interested in me, so I got dressed and wandered the halls for a bit," Cassi said. "Before long, I found myself at the practice yards with my bow, itching for something to do. He was by himself at the opposite side of the grass, hurling a blunt sword into a bag of beans he'd strung up to a post. The other people there seemed wary of him, watching from a distance. And he seemed very lonely, and then sort of desperate as he flung his sword to the grass and started punching the thing with his bare hands. And I had nothing better to do, so I went over. You know I can use a sword. I know I can use a sword. But he didn't, and he seemed happy to show me, so I just went with it. Then we had a bite to eat, we ran into you, he dropped me off here, and I've been in the room ever since, reading one of the books I stole from the crystal palace before we left home. That was it. That was all. And I should've said so right when you walked into the room, but…" Cassi paused. "You know how much I love to watch you squirm."

Lyana gasped and drew back her elbow, searching for resistance. Cassi lunged to the side, wings flapping to keep her from rolling off the bed. Lyana spun, but the second she met her friend's eyes, all the indignant suspicions faded away, replaced with a bubble in her throat that came out as pure laughter.

"I don't know what I'd do without you, Cassi," Lyana whispered as she pulled her friend in for a tight embrace.

"You won't ever have to find out," Cassi replied, voice earnest and certain. "That's a promise."

40

XANDER

The princess was bored. It had been three days of lessons and meetings and dinners, and with each passing moment Xander saw the light seep away from her gaze, eyes no longer filled with wonder but with fatigue.

He was determined to do something about it.

"I'd like to take you somewhere," Xander said as he led her out of the dining room after the daily ritual of breakfast with his mother was over. They had an hour before the dressmaker was supposed to fit her for her mating gown, and there was a place he'd been waiting to show her.

Lyana immediately perked up. "Where?"

Xander shrugged, unwilling to betray his hope. "A surprise."

Her grip on his forearm tightened. "Let's go."

They kept the conversation light as he guided her through

the castle halls, up and around, closer to the royal quarters, the place she'd call home in just a few short weeks. He was only half focused on what he was saying. The other half of his mind concentrated on holding the enthusiasm for his dreams at bay. He knew, *he knew*, Lyana's personality didn't match that of the mate he'd always envisioned. She was a mover, a doer, not satisfied to sit still when the other option was to fly. But dreams had a bothersome way of ignoring the truth, and hope made the impossible seem within reach. So, as he neared the room, his heart thundered and his mind dared to wonder, *"What if?"*

Xander wrapped his hand around the knob and slowly twisted. He stopped to look at his mate with his complete attention, waiting for her reaction as the door slid open.

His private library was in the tallest spire of the castle, a narrow circle three stories high with bookshelves lining every open wall and the windows in between them. Still, the many volumes he'd collected spilled out of the shelves and onto the ground, into piles that teetered on the edge of collapsing. A long narrow table in the center of the room acted as his workstation. The only other pieces of furniture were two leather armchairs, one worn and one intact, that sat before the oversized hearth.

Lyana stared at the room, mouth dropping open as she inhaled excitedly. Her wings fluttered as she raced inside, eyes lifting and turning and circling. Xander felt a rush of pure gold, like the richest hummingbird nectar, sweep over him.

He waited for a moment before he followed her inside, trying to blink away all the dreams drifting to the surface. But the feat proved impossible. Xander glanced around the room more familiar to him than any other in the castle as though seeing it for the first time. Because when he looked at the chairs, he no longer saw just chairs, but he and Lyana sitting in them, a book on their laps, a fire blazing as the windows frosted with the winter chill. And when he glanced at his desk, it wasn't empty but covered in parchments as he and Lyana bent over scrolls and books scattered over the scratched wooden surface, debating the topic at hand. And when his gaze roamed the shelves towering thirty feet into the air, he saw Lyana flying up the narrow space, darting between the stacks, grabbing more volumes than her petite arms could carry.

Xander started, realizing that vision wasn't in his head. His princess had taken off and her ivory wings pumped as she raced around the room, darting and dropping and twisting as her attention jumped from one spot to another. At first, he didn't believe his eyes.

Then, with a sinking feeling, he did.

Because her arms weren't full of books, and her focus wasn't on the shelves but on the windows. The longer he watched, the more she began to remind him of the firebugs he and his brother used to catch as children—how they zipped and zoomed in the little glass jars, glowing like magic in the dark. Once he and Rafe had fallen asleep before they remembered to release them, and when they woke, the bugs were nothing more than motionless black pellets at the bottom of the glass. He had turned the jar over, trying to release them back into the air, but they'd simply fallen to the ground and disappeared between the blades of grass. It was only then that he realized all the buzzing in circles hadn't been a show for his benefit, but a desperate attempt by the bugs to get out of the jar. He never caught them again after that.

"The view is spectacular," Lyana marveled, nose against the glass as though if she pressed hard enough, she could be outside, too.

Xander cast another longing glance at the fireplace before straightening his shoulders and walking across the room to open one of the windows. The wind whistled as it rushed through the crack, ruffling the pages all around him. Lyana was by his side in a second. Xander gestured toward the landscape, pretending this was what he'd wanted to show her, trying to infuse his words with an enthusiasm he could no longer feel.

"From here, you can see the entire city of Pylaeon," he told her. Lyana was enraptured, unaware of the lack of luster in his tone. "Taetanos's Gate is that spot of white all the way over there between the mountains, and you can see the sun glinting off the river as it cuts through the center of the valley and into the city. The wooden homes along the outer edges are for the more modest ravens, while the stone ones closer to the castle and city center are home to some of the people you've been meeting. I don't know if you can see, but over by the river, most of the buildings are on stilts or columns because during spring, the snow melts and the river spills over its embankments, flooding the streets. And do you notice the black archways spotting the city? There's one to the left over there, and another over there, and there and there. Well, we call them spirit gates. They lead lost souls through the maze of our city and toward the river so they can follow the water to the entrance of Taetanos's world. At least, that's what we're told as children. And that over there is the main town square, though it's more of a rectangle really, since the river cuts between the two halves. The bridge connecting each side is the widest and flattest one in the city. And the fountains on either side siphon water from the river to make them shoot into the air like that. Every month there's a market that gets set up and everyone in the town goes just to gossip, even if they have nothing to sell and no money to buy things. This time of year, children sometimes swim in the shallows of the fountains. But in the winter, the water often freezes over, and they hold hands while they slip and slide across the ice. I used to watch them all the time as a child, wishing I could go out and join them, but I never did, because, well, you of all people must understand why. Anyway..."

He trailed off, unsure what else to say. But he didn't have to speak. Even without his words, her eyes widened, focusing on the smallest details as though trying to memorize everything she saw, as though trying to drink it all in.

After a few moments, she blinked, only then realizing he'd stopped talking, and turned to him with a curious groove on her brow. "You really love them, don't you?"

"Huh?" Xander asked. "Who?"

"Your people," she said, as though it were obvious.

"I'm sure no more than you loved yours," Xander offered, feeling a little uncomfortable. Surely his actions hadn't warranted such scrutiny.

But the warmth in her expression was still there, steady and strong as she shook her head with a half smile. "No, no, you really care for them, about them. I can tell from your voice, from the way you talk about your home. I loved my house and the doves, but I'm almost ashamed to admit, I loved myself more. But you don't. You love them first, and yourself second."

"Isn't that what a future king is supposed to do?" he asked offhandedly, overwhelmed by eyes that seemed to probe into his soul.

"Probably, though my guess is they rarely do," she murmured.

Xander slid his gaze back to the window, searching for a distraction or a shift in the conversation—anything to take the attention off him and how easily she saw through him, especially when she remained a mystery.

"Oh, look," he exclaimed a little too loudly as he found a familiar figure down below—the owner of a set of speckled wings that could never belong to a raven. "I think that must be your friend Cassi in the practice yards, and that's probably Rafe with her."

The princess tensed beside him.

Xander turned from the window, observing how she watched her friend and his brother with a slight curl of lips. He suddenly remembered her words on the last night at the House of Peace, when they were standing at the edge of the isle, having their first few moments of honesty. She'd called Rafe rude and a grouch as a sneer passed across her features.

"You don't like him very much, do you?" Xander asked

softly. "My brother, I mean."

The princess inhaled sharply as she spun toward him, eyes wide as though caught in some illicit act. Her wings dropped, and a small puff of air slipped through her lips. "Am I so obvious?"

A soft laugh escaped his lips. "A little."

"I'm sorry—" Lyana paused, folding her lips.

"What?"

"Nothing."

He was grinning now. "What?"

"Nothing, it's just, well..." Her face scrunched tightly for a moment. "He never apologized," she rushed to say, as though the confession were a flood she couldn't control now that it had started. "He never apologized for tricking me in the trials, for pretending to be you. He acted smug when we returned to your guest quarters, and arrogant, and not the least bit sorry for fooling me, and I'm not sure I could ever actually like someone who acts like that."

Xander's throat constricted as he shifted his weight, mirth vanishing in an instant, because the princess could just as easily have been talking about him and his actions. Rafe hadn't been the only one involved in that trickery.

As though she could read his thoughts, Lyana continued, voice smoother this time, no longer filled with ire, "I don't understand how two people who look so similar could be so completely different. You are so kind, Xander, so honest, and I knew at a glance how horrible you felt about the trials. I could read the shame across your face as soon as you confessed the truth. But him? He just— He just— He—"

Lyana broke off, and her feathers bristled, leaving her words at that.

"He's complicated."

Xander sighed, turning from the window to lean against the shelf, feeling grounded and supported by the spines of his books as he faced the princess. He wasn't surprised at her words. Lyana had grown up with a mother and father who perhaps loved one another. Her brother was her equal in the eyes of her people, a sibling they all cherished just as much as they did her. His childhood, Rafe's childhood—they were as foreign to her as his home. But he didn't want them to be. Lyana would never fully understand him until she understood his brother. His mate and his brother were the two most important people in his life. He wasn't sure what he would do if they couldn't find a way to get along.

"Rafe is good at putting on a front, at pushing people away," Xander continued. "He always has been. Because, well, it's a lot to explain."

Lyana remained silent, watching him, giving him the opening.

Feeling exposed, he worked through the discomfort. Lyana was his mate. His *mate*. She deserved to know even the darkest parts of his past. "My mother was the first princess in five generations to bring home a mate from the courtship trials. Before that, our house had been shunned, the last pick in a string of unlucky trials that left our princes and princesses outnumbered and unmatched. But when she returned with a falcon from the House of Prey, our people were ecstatic. They glorified her and my father as the saviors of Taetanos, the ones who would return the other gods' favor to our small island. The day my mother went into labor with me, she rushed to my father's rooms in her excitement, only to find him in bed with one of her chambermaids. She wanted to murder the girl, but my father begged for her life, telling my mother his lover was pregnant, too. And though she seems callous now, she wasn't always that way, especially not with me or my father. She relented."

"Rafe," Lyana whispered in shock.

Xander nodded. "That's how my brother, Rafe, was announced to the world. And for five years, he lived in the lowest level of the castle, hidden away with his mother but close enough for my father to visit them. When we were children, they both died, leaving Rafe an orphan. I ordered he be moved to the royal chambers, with rooms next to mine. And though he's been my best friend for as long as I can remember, my mother and my people have never forgiven him."

Lyana's gaze slipped toward the window. "Forgiven him for what?"

Xander's attention was pulled by an unseen force, falling to the courtyard below, where a raven and an owl sparred, swords arching, bodies fluid as though made for fighting. He had few memories of his father, but one had taken place in that very spot, as he was given his first sword. The weight had been awkward in his hand. He'd stumbled over the steps. But he'd made an effort, practicing the footwork again and again, so focused that he'd failed to notice when his father's voice faded. Dripping with sweat, smiling because he thought he'd improved a little, Xander had spun, searching for his father's approval. Instead, he'd been presented with his back. Those sleek brown wings were spread as the king knelt over his other son, the one who held a blade twice the size of Xander's in two sturdy hands.

He looked at Lyana, tearing himself away from the memory and the view that had sparked it. "They've never forgiven Rafe for being the son my father loved more than me, the strong son, the warrior. And he's never forgiven himself either, which is why he never lets anyone get close. He doesn't think he deserves it."

Lyana turned to him in sympathy. "I'm sure that can't be true, Xander. Your father must have loved you both, just in different ways. How could a parent ever do anything but love his child? How could anyone do anything but love you?"

"Maybe you're right," Xander said indifferently as he pushed away from the wall and closed the window. He didn't need pity, especially not from her. "Either way, it's all in the past. But that's why my brother is the way he is. And maybe now that you know, you might find it in your heart to forgive him for his rough edges." Xander sighed, turning toward the door, needing air and quiet. "We should go. There's probably a seamstress worried sick somewhere in the castle because the princess she's supposed to be fitting is nowhere to be found."

He offered her a wide smile, trying to make it as real as possible. Lyana did the same, questions flickering in her eyes as they both pretended everything was fine.

He was silent as he led her out of his library.

Not because there was nothing to say. No, there was

plenty. But he couldn't bring himself to explain the truth—how he knew his father had loved Rafe and not him. There were too many memories, too many examples, all too painful to dredge up from the pit he'd shoved them into. Even something as simple as their names was riddled with countless levels of hurt and confusion.

Before Xander was born, his mother had wanted to name him Aleksander to honor his father. For months, while he grew in her belly, she'd thought of him as little Xander, the endearing nickname his father had been given as a child. But discovering the affair changed all that and turned her loving heart into a bitter one. When he was born, she locked his father out of the room and named her son Lysander instead, a raven name through and through—her father's name. Four months later, when Rafe was born, the wound opened anew. Word traveled up from the servants' quarters that the king had been by his mistress's side and had proudly declared his bastard son his namesake, Aleksander Pallieus, gifting him the last name of a prince of the House of Prey. As soon as his mother found out, she shifted the paperwork, changing his surname to Ravenson, the one given to orphans and bastards in the House of Whispers.

Xander, of course, didn't remember any of that—he'd been nothing more than a baby. But he heard the rumors growing up. And he remembered, as a boy, thinking that the way his mother resolutely called him Xander seemed to originate in spite rather than affection, especially as her eyes sharply slid to his father with an aura of victory. It was only after his father died, when his mother switched to calling him by his full name, Lysander, that he understood she'd only used the nickname so that Rafe couldn't. They called him Alek back then, a time so long ago he hardly remembered it. As soon as Rafe had been old enough to understand the problematic history behind his true name, he forsook it, shortening Ravenson to Rafe, and he'd gone by that single defiant word ever since.

Even as a boy, Rafe had seen how his very existence had stolen something from Xander. And that was why he pushed everyone away—he didn't want to take any more. For that unnecessary sacrifice, Xander loved him, and always would.

"Thank you," Lyana murmured as he dropped her back at her chambers, pulling him from his thoughts. She stepped closer and leaned on the tips of her toes, pressing a soft kiss to his cheek, a mark that tingled even after she eased away. "Thank you for showing me your library, Xander, and thank you for sharing a bit more of your world."

A mystified grin settled on his lips. "Thank you for accepting it."

Her shy answering smile was visible only for an instant before she slipped into her rooms, but it left him buoyant.

Maybe she hadn't loved the books.

Maybe she had only loved the view.

But it was something.

Even if he went there to read and she went there to wonder, they might go together. It could still be their place—a place where they were honest and open with each other, a place where companionship and perchance love might grow.

41

CASSI

The waterfall was like a beacon on the horizon as the moonlight turned the cascade to flowing silver. Cassi made her way swiftly across the valley, caring little about the sleeping town below, mind on her mission— on the god stone. Truth be told, she could have closed her eyes and still found it. The power tugged on her soul, exerting a magnetic pull that would have been impossible to ignore. But this wasn't about shooting her dream-spirit through rock and air. It was about finding a path a solid body might traverse in the bright light of day. She used the information Lyana had so freely given and slipped beneath the falls, finding the entrance to the sacred nest almost immediately.

The cave was dark.

There were no lanterns, no sources of light, making it difficult for Cassi to distinguish any detail. She only knew she was following a hollow hall because of the lack of friction on her spirit, something that was always present when she forced her way through solid barriers. She moved slowly, trying to draw a map with her mind as she reached out, using the subtle resistance of stone as her only guide.

The thunder of water grew soft and distant after a while, a clue as to how far she'd traveled down the winding path, but that wasn't what made her smile. As she turned another bend, the buzzing current in the air strengthened, and a new sound echoed down the empty corridor. It was the somewhat grating chirp of ravens, though tonight, the guttural caws were music to her ears.

She was close.

A soft bluish light blinked to life at the far reaches of her vision, but it was enough. Cassi abandoned her careful trek and flew toward the source of the light. Golden bars blocked her path, a gate like the one before the sacred nest in the House of Peace, but Cassi slid right through.

The onyx orb hovering in the center of the room caught her attention immediately. It was surrounded by a layer of undulating shadow, so thick the moonlight shining through the open ceiling couldn't penetrate it. Not that Cassi expected it would.

God stone, she thought, snorting at the idea as she made her way closer, stretching out with her spirit, pressing her invisible hand against the smooth surface of the stone and letting the energy sizzle where it touched her soul. *If they only knew the truth.*

The avians worshipped these floating orbs, associating each with a different deity, believing they thrummed with divine power. According to their legends, the gods had sacrificed their immortal bodies to lift the isles into the air, caging themselves within these stones to give their faithful servants a free, peaceful life high in the sky where no enemies could ever find them. And they believed these myths so strongly, they were willing to kill for them, to murder anyone who showed any hint of magic for fear it was an affront to their almighty gods.

That irony hit Cassi particularly hard.

She would be dead if her *dormi'kine* magic, her dreamwalking, was ever discovered.

Lyana too—their own beloved princess.

Cassi's mother had been a victim of the persecution. At the age of five, her power had been discovered. They had stabbed her in the chest and sawed off one of her wings before hurling her over the edge to fall to her death. But she was an *aero'kine*. Wind was her power, and while her family abandoned her, the magic never did. It cradled her, held her, softened the fall, and a captain from the world below had seen her through the fog as she gently splashed into the ocean. He pulled her from the water and tended to her wounds, saving her life, giving her a better one where her magic was appreciated, even exalted, the way it deserved to be.

Because the truth was there were no gods.

The energy pulsing through the stone beneath her fingers wasn't Taetanos, god of death—it was shadow magic. Pure and simple. There was no Aethios, only spirit magic like Cassi's, like Lyana's, the strongest kind of all. And Erhea, the god of love, revered by the songbirds? That beating red stone wasn't a heart. It was the thing those of the world above feared most—fire magic.

There were seven elements, not seven gods, and each stone was one of those elements bottled up and sealed in an elaborate web that had been woven a thousand years ago through the sort of power that no longer existed. No one, not even her king, truly understood how the isles had come to rise into the air or why. The truth had faded into myth and legend in both the world above and the one below, but the past mattered very little.

The future, however, was still in flux.

The future was what Cassi fought to preserve.

Reluctantly, she pulled her spirit hands from the stone and blinked away the thrall of so much magic as she tried to focus on her surroundings. The sacred nest of the House of Whispers was, she quickly realized, a collapsed cavern. Impenetrable stone walls towered at least fifty feet high, curving in toward an open spot where the ground must have long ago given way. The stars glittered overhead, and the moon was bright as it filled the room, shining through the bars across the opening, keeping the squawking ravens inside. The area was thick with trees, as dense as the forest they'd flown across, though there were a few open passages leading from the orb toward the exterior sides of the nest—one led to the gate where Cassi had entered, and the others had to lead somewhere, too.

She had a hard time believing that any time the royal family wanted to visit the nest, they were first soaked by splashing water. There had to be another entrance, an easier one, even if only to deliver food and supplies to the priests and priestesses who were most likely asleep in their beds. The sacred nest at the House of Peace had an elaborate scheme of rooms and secret hallways used for the same purpose. This place would be no different.

Cassi just needed time—time and daylight, neither of which she'd find tonight. She put her hand to the orb one more time and breathed in the powerful aura, pausing for a beat to let it fill her, before reluctantly letting go.

Soon, she thought. Her new mantra.

Soon. Soon. Soon.

LYANA

He was so kind—so kind and caring and chivalrous —and he deserved more.

That was all Lyana thought as the rest of the week passed, and her feeling of suffocation grew, while his affectionate smile never wavered.

He deserves more than me, she thought, in his library for the third time that week. Xander leaned over a table, mind deep in the scrolls he'd unrolled, while she stood off to the side, staring out the window at the town below—a town that called out to her, whispering her name, urging she open the window, spread her wings, escape the castle, and join them in the streets below.

Or maybe not more, she corrected, idly rubbing the glass pane with her fingers. *Just different. A girl who will stand beside him, not across from him. A girl who is content with being safe and secure, not always dreaming of adventure. A girl who...* Her gaze drifted down, down, down to the raven all alone at the far side of the practice field, visible even from this distance. *A girl who isn't staring at his brother, remembering the way his magic sizzled beneath his skin, the way he watched her through firelight.*

Lyana jerked away from the glass as if it stung her and spun, squaring her shoulders and facing her mate, determined to find a common ground.

"What are you reading?" she asked casually, stepping to his desk and pressing her palms against the worn wood to keep grounded.

"Huh?" He glanced up, surprised. "Oh, um, nothing really. It's, well… I'm not actually reading per se, just reviewing some old maps of the isles."

"Maps?" Lyana leaned over to peek.

Xander tilted his head as if perplexed but turned the spine of his book so she could see. Lyana touched the smooth parchment, following the contours of the mountains, the lines marking where land gave way to sky. But all she could think was, *Why?* Why sit in a tower and stare at old maps, when everything on that page was waiting just outside the window?

"Hmm." Her murmur was half a sigh, half feigned interest.

Xander latched on to the latter. A rush of color flooded his cheeks and he leaned closer, their shoulders and wings brushing as he put his finger next to hers on the page. "You see this, here?" he asked in the animated voice of a scholar. "You see the edge, there, on the other side of the isle? Not where the castle is, but on the more uninhabited part. You see how it juts out? Now…"

He pushed the book a few inches away, grunting as he reached with his left hand to grab another heavy volume. Lyana moved to help, but he drew his breath in sharply, so she stopped, gaze darting to his right arm and the rounded end covered in black silk to match his coat. She dropped her hand gently back to the tabletop. As though nothing had happened, Xander hastily opened the cover and began sifting through the pages, searching for something, and there! He stopped with the book open on another map.

"Now," he said, breathing out before drawing her attention to the illustration. "Look here, that same spot as the previous map, except the edge of the isle is now concave. The two edges don't line up at all."

Lyana knitted her brows and looked up at him. "A mistake, surely?"

"I thought so too at first," he agreed, but pursed his lips, eyes sharp and focused. "Though that's not the only difference. The others are just subtler. I've compared maybe a dozen maps from different cartographers across all different ages, and no two perfectly match."

"What do you think it means?" she asked, genuinely confused about what he was suggesting.

Xander lifted his brows as a jovial smile widened his lips. "That's what I'm trying to figure out. But either our island has been getting smaller and smaller, slowly enough for no one to realize it, or we are in dire need of new mapmakers."

Lyana leaned back. "Are you teasing me?"

"No." An almost comical, horrified look passed over his face, sincere enough to make her trust his response. "No, not at all. I'm being serious. I noticed it before the courtship trials. I even put in a request with the House of Wisdom for access to their records, which should be far more accurate in size and scope than mine."

"The House of Wisdom?" Lyana's chest filled with a familiar sort of anticipation. "But they don't lend their archives."

"No, no, I'd have to make a trip, which shouldn't be a problem now that the courtship trials are over," he told her offhandedly, attention returning to his books.

Her reaction, however, was anything but casual. Lyana gasped and seized his forearm as her eyes popped, mind spinning with every sliver of information she'd ever heard about the great libraries of the owls and their underground maze of a home. "A trip! When? How soon? Have you been before? Oh, can we go, Xander? Can we?"

He started laughing before she'd even finished speaking. "Are you so eager to get out of here?"

Although his tone was playful, there was just enough honesty in that question to make her pause, and a dimming of his eyes made her wonder if her unenthusiastic attempts at being a proper princess had been shamefully transparent.

"Of course not," she hastily responded.

Xander reached across the table and took her hand in his, gently grazing the tops of her fingers with his thumb, a yearning sort of touch that made her lift her chin to look at him, but his eyes were cast down. Before she could say any more, he pulled his hand away and walked to the window. Lyana followed with her eyes but felt stuck to the spot as she cradled the fingers he'd just abandoned to her chest, unsure why they tingled.

"You've been very patient with me, with my family, our customs and our plans this past week," he said as he touched the window latch.

A wry grin appeared on her lips—patient was not a word that had ever been used to describe her—but she kept her mouth shut, almost afraid to interrupt as he turned the handle and slid the glass pane open. A gust of wind blew into the room. Invisible arms wrapped around Lyana's waist, tugging her outside. She stumbled closer, unable to stop herself as her skirt flared and her feathers ruffled.

"I think maybe it's time I return the favor," Xander said, glancing over his shoulder before taking a single step back and leaping through the large window.

Lyana ran to the opening and stopped at the edge, certain this was a trick.

Xander hovered, onyx wings slick in the sun, eyes sparkling in the bright daylight. "Aren't you coming?"

"Don't we—" Lyana broke off before she could finish the sentence, shaking her head with disbelief. They were supposed to be meeting with the queen in half an hour. But if he didn't mind being late, neither did she. "Yes!"

She dove out the window and snapped her wings wide, blood pumping as her body began to sing.

43

RAFE

If he hadn't been in the practice yards waiting for the ever-tardy Cassi to arrive, he might not have heard Helen whistle, a high-pitched slow-quick-quick-quick sound that could only mean one thing. Rafe looked up, covering his brow to deflect the glare as he made out two figures zipping down from the top of the castle, racing toward the city on the other side of the wall—Xander and his princess.

Rafe flew over the lawn, landing at a run as he pushed his way through the circle of guards waiting for a command. "I'm coming."

Helen glanced at him, not an ounce of surprise in her expression. "You, me, and…"

She pointed to two other guards but Rafe had returned his gaze to the two descending figures. It didn't matter, anyway.

Whoever else was coming would treat him just the same. And it wasn't about the guards. It was about his brother—who was, at this moment, acting very much not like his brother. Xander rarely went anywhere unless the proper arrangements were made first, and unless his mother and the guards knew. He was the sole heir, and even though the seven houses were peaceful, and the royal family had no enemies they knew of, he still wasn't supposed to travel alone—not when so many hopes and dreams and people relied on him.

"Come on," Helen said as she secured a throwing knife to her belt and pumped her wings. "We'll stick to the sky, give them a little privacy. But keep a watchful eye, just in case."

Rafe and the two guards nodded. He felt almost naked going out without his twin blades, but they were resting on a table in his room where he'd left them the night before, and there was no time to retrieve them. Instead, he swiped a single sword from the collection, making sure it was sharp, before he followed the others.

By the time they were over the wall, Xander and Lyana had disappeared into the city streets, but it didn't take long to find them. If the rising hum of conversation hadn't been enough, the rush of movement certainly was. People running. People flying. All moving closer and closer to one fixed point —the main town square where a pair of ivory wings stood apart from the crowd, yet also its center.

Helen and the two guards remained high above the city, maintaining the aerial view, but Rafe shifted closer. Maybe he was a glutton for punishment. Maybe he was just being a diligent brother. Maybe it was a bit of both. But he found he couldn't help but sink toward one of the rooftops circling the square, crouching out of sight as he searched for the best vantage point from which to watch the pair.

They were as happy as he'd ever seen them. Xander spun in circles, shaking people's hands, introducing them to his new mate, laughing so hard he threw his head back, his whole body racked with mirth. And Lyana was right by his side, kneeling to accept the hugs children offered and threading the flowers they brought her through her hair. The crowd continued to grow and grow, but true to the House of Whispers, no one pushed, and no one shoved. They respected their prince and kept a ring around him, allowing Xander to approach them instead of the other way around. Still, it was an unusual day when the prince made a surprise visit to the town, especially with his new mate, and some of the ravens on the outskirts began to beat their wings for a few futile seconds to steal a quick glance as the couple walked by.

The longer he watched, the deeper the pit in Rafe's stomach grew, though he couldn't pinpoint precisely why. He was used to the role of outsider looking in, and this was no different—perched on a rooftop, watching the revelry without taking part. And yet, as he watched his brother, for the first time uncertain of what was going on in his head, Rafe realized he wasn't accustomed to this feeling, not at all, not when it came to Xander. And as his eyes flicked to Lyana, the image of the alluring girl in the cave—the one who had looked at him as though he might be the start of something—was shriveling away, replaced by a princess he hardly knew.

It was good.

It was how it was supposed to be.

Nevertheless, the gaping hole in his chest that no one else could see ached. Rafe glanced at the guards circling overhead, but didn't move. He kept his wings against his back and gritted his teeth as he turned again to the square, forcing himself to watch no matter how much it hurt, because there was no other option but to suffer in silence, which he did, keeping his eyes glued to the happy couple. His diligence was the only reason he saw Lyana freeze.

A moment later, he understood why. The air prickled with magic. A static charge made the hairs on his arms stand tall and sent a tingle down his spine.

She looked up, searching the sky.

Her eyes found him instead, widening before quickly dropping back to the square and the people around her. He didn't miss the frown creasing her forehead or the way her feathers bristled. He looked away, trying to shut out the world, if only for an instant. And that was when he felt the ground beneath him tremble—a small, subtle thing.

Rafe jumped to his feet, alarmed. The shingles on the roof vibrated ever so slightly. The water in the twin fountains on either end of the square rippled, not from a splash, but from movement unseen. He found Xander in the crowd, noticing how his brother smiled at a jewelry vendor, admiring his wares, unconcerned. Rafe turned to Lyana, but the princess had been pulled into a nursery game with some children, holding their hands as they skipped in a circle. He'd experienced earthquakes before, but this felt different, bigger, yet no one else seemed to notice or care.

The fizz of magic dissipated.

Then everything happened all at once.

A rumble turned into a roar and the ground violently shook, sending half the crowd to their knees as the stones along the floor of the courtyard ruptured. The statue in the center of one fountain broke, and a torrent of water spewed like heavy rain. Parts of the river splashed over the barriers, sending waves across the already slick cobbles. Laughter turned to screams. Through the chaos, a deafening *crack* split the air.

Where?

Where?

Rafe searched for the source of the sound, gaze jumping to the bridge connecting the two sides of the square, to the black arches of the spirit gates, to the stone façades of the buildings around the perimeter.

Then he saw.

All the buildings close to the river were set on low columns, no more than four feet tall, to escape the flooding that happened each spring. And one of those columns was now splintered down the center, a spidery fissure that crept up into the building above. The crack spread, foot by foot, higher and wider, like a snap of lightning cutting through stone.

The world continued to shake.

The stones began to teeter.

The surface wobbled.

A flash of white caught Rafe's eye. Two ivory wings spread,

but didn't move, didn't launch into the air like many ravens had done in the confusion.

She was still, shocked.

With her head angled up, she stared in horror at the avalanche of rock ready to crush her.

44

LYANA

Lyana couldn't move as the building behind her started to crumble. All she could do was stare as the rocks spilled loose, slowly at first, one dropping and rattling across the street, then another and another, until all at once the entire façade toppled, dropping almost in slow motion as the wall of solid stone made for her head, falling, falling, falling—

Something slammed into her from the side.

Lyana rolled painfully across cobblestone. Arms wrapped around her, holding her to a hard chest and closing her wings. The world disappeared as onyx feathers arched overhead.

"I've got you."

The words were rough, raspy, and gone in a flash.

They reminded her of a dark cave back home.

They made her feel safe.

Two seconds later, they were replaced by a groan as the

stones fell. The *crunch* of bones and the *snap* of feathers filled her ears. Lyana closed her eyes as though she could make the sounds fade, but they didn't. The fact that it wasn't her pain that she heard made it worse. Rafe was crushed, but still, he kept his elbows bent so he held the weight of the debris away from her body, keeping her safe against the ground beneath them. He trembled with the exertion. Another scream tore up his throat.

It was her turn to whisper. "Hold on. Hold on."

Lyana managed to twist her palms and press them to his chest. The dark shadows receded as the area around her hands shone gold and she pushed her magic beneath his skin, trying to give him strength.

"Hold on."

He had no breath for words, but it didn't matter. His magic rose to meet hers, sizzling beneath his skin, so familiar, so forbidden, so frantic, a long-lost lover coming home. Their gazes met fiercely across the subtle shine of power, a moment that extended into infinity.

Then his eyes rolled into the back of his head, and he collapsed. The weight of a hundred men landed on her as his muscles gave out. Her chest burned beneath the pressure. Spots filled her vision. The last thing she saw was her magic extinguish before the world faded completely.

45

XANDER

An ear-piercing silence filled the square as he and the others watched the dust settle—the sort of quiet that made hairs stand on end, that made the heart stop, that made the world slow as though even the open sky were too small to contain the mounting terror.

Reality came back bit by bit.

The ground fell still. Droplets sprinkled across the stones, the *pitter-patter* repetitive and loud as water continued to splash in the shattered fountain. Sunlight pushed through the ashy cloud, dissipating it. A single stone broke loose and tumbled down the chaotic mound and across the floor, coming to a stop a few seconds later.

Then the first scream sounded.

It took Xander a second to realize it had come from his own throat.

"Lyana!" The word burned, as though claws had cut their

way up his neck. Lightning ran down his spine, a jolt so scorching he had no choice but to jump into action. "Lyana!"

Xander flew across the square. Others followed, screaming their own sets of names. Where only minutes before there had been so much light and life, now there was a pile of rubble ten feet high and no telling how many bodies were buried underneath, caught in the crashing tide before they'd had a chance to fly away. He knelt, grabbing a stone in his left hand, his right arm shaking in fury as he tried with no success to pull it rock away. His grip was tight, his muscles strained, but he couldn't get a good hold with only five fingers instead of ten. Another set of hands quickly came into view, helping him shift the stone. Xander looked up, about to give thanks, when he met the eyes of his captain.

"You should get to safety," Helen said, though not an ounce of her believed he would. And without prompting, they knelt together to heft another piece of debris.

"Did you send for help?" Xander asked as they worked.

"On their way."

"My mother?"

"Being notified."

"Where's Rafe?"

She didn't answer.

He looked at her, heart thudding in his chest. "Helen, where's Rafe?"

His captain's gaze just slid to the rubble.

Stupid idiot.

Stupid, selfless idiot.

In an instant, Xander understood exactly what his brother had done.

Thank you.

There was nothing to say to Helen after that, to say to anyone. Nothing left but heavy breath and almost silent tears as every able-bodied person in the town square worked to clear the wreckage. The guards arrived shortly, lending their hands to the cause. And then the healer soon after, scurrying to where the recovered bodies had been laid—some barely moving, most horrifyingly still.

Xander had lost count of the stones he'd moved, one after the other after the other, until finally, a shout stopped him.

"Your Highness! Your Highness!"

Xander turned toward the sound. The peddler who had been showing him simple metal bracelets before the earthquake was frantically pulling at stones and tossing panicked glances in his direction. He raced toward the spot, stomach dropping as he saw what the peddler had seen—two pairs of feet intertwined, one wearing rich leather boots and the other elegant lace slippers, the sort not found on the city streets.

Lyana and Rafe.

"Helen!" Xander shouted. "Guards!"

They sped to heed his command, helping to strip the mound, the sight turning more and more gruesome as each rock was pulled away. There was a deep gash in the princess's calf, but it was nothing compared to the injuries sustained by the raven on top of her. Rafe's black wings were bent and crooked, unnaturally slick in the sun. Snapped bones jutted through his crushed feathers. Water from the fountain splashed across their bodies, carrying streams of red through the cracks in the cobblestones. One of the guards lifted the tip of Rafe's wing, exposing the bodies underneath.

Xander stepped back with a gasp—not of fear, but of the sort an intruder might make if he'd accidentally stepped into the middle of something he wasn't supposed to see.

They could have been lovers.

Rafe's arms, now slack, cradled either side of Lyana's chest, although they must have once held her weight. Her palms were pressed against his abdomen, fingers still gripping the fibers of his shirt. His face was buried in her hair. Hers was nestled against his neck. Their legs were entwined. The entire scene was oddly intimate in a way Xander didn't quite understand. If not for the blood and the gore, they could have been in a bedroom, doing something else entirely.

The guard gripping Rafe's broken wing turned a questioning gaze on his prince. But the move was enough to bring them all back to reality as the raven on the ground began to scream—a wild, uncontrolled sound.

"Careful!" Xander snapped at the guards, deflecting his sudden anger to the easiest target as he rushed to his brother's side. "Rafe, Rafe."

Grunts and groans were his only response. But as difficult as they were to hear, it was far, far superior to silence. Because it meant Rafe was alive, and that was all Xander needed to know. Because if his brother was alive, he would recover. He always did.

"I want four of your best men to carry him back to his rooms," Xander said, turning to Helen.

She stepped forward, murmuring so only the closest guard could hear, "You mean to the healers, surely?"

Xander's face hardened. "To his rooms. And not a soul is to disturb him. Understood?"

Suspicion sharpened her eyes, suspicion and defiance, but she held her tongue and nodded, remaining loyal before a crowd, though there would be questions later. Questions about why and how his brother had managed to survive yet another event that had killed so many others.

Xander had no time for that now.

As soon as Rafe was peeled away from the debris and lifted into the sky, he fell to his knees beside the princess, who, unlike his brother, had yet to utter a word. Xander slid his arm beneath her neck, careful with her head as he raised her torso onto his lap and used his other hand to rub her cheek. Her dark skin was still warm. Her lush lips were parted. Her dress was wet and wrinkled, but there was no obvious injury aside from the gash in her leg.

"Lyana," he whispered.

Someone passed a wet cloth to him, which he gently pressed against her brow. No breath came in or out of her mouth. Her chest didn't stir. Her body remained limp.

"Lyana," he urged more loudly. "Lyana!"

The princess's eyes opened wide as she inhaled sharply, her body jerking as though returning from the dead. She began to convulse with coughs.

"It's all right. You're all right," Xander murmured as he rubbed her back.

Lyana shook her head, opening her mouth to emit only raspy air and shuddering breaths. "What?" she finally sputtered. "Where?"

"There's been an earthquake," Xander explained.

She shook her head, blinking rapidly as though trying to clear her senses. She coughed again, but the sound formed a word. "Rafe?"

"He's fine—"

"I know," she interrupted. "But where is he? What happened to him?"

Xander paused, taken aback by her first words. "You know?"

How could she possibly know?

Lyana cast him a quick glance before her lids fell, but not fast enough to hide the knowing glint in her eyes. "I mean, good. Good. I'm sorry, I'm so confused. I need Cassi. Where's Cassi?"

"She wasn't with us," Xander said slowly, unsure if Lyana was disoriented or acutely aware as she put her hand to her head and frowned, wincing as if in pain.

"She wasn't?" the princess asked, voice mystified. Then her eyes widened again. "Oh that's right. She wasn't. I'm all mixed up, Xander. Please forgive me…"

She trailed off, taking another deep breath, and tried to stand.

This time, he knew her yelp of pain was real. Xander jumped to his feet, throwing his arm around her waist as her leg gave out and she swayed on her feet, wings fighting to keep her upright.

"Helen," he called. His captain of the guards was there in a flash, hands clasped behind her back, waiting for orders. "Please take the princess back to the castle and see to it personally that our most skilled healer visits her rooms to check the wound on her leg. Tell my mother I'll be back soon."

"My pr—"

"Thank you, Helen," Xander said, cutting off her protest. "I'll be home soon."

She tossed him a tired look and shook her head, but an affectionate smile pulled at her lips because she knew him, and she knew why he was staying. She obeyed, quickly calling a guard who swept the princess off her feet despite her quiet protests and launched into the air.

Xander watched them fly away for a few seconds, unable to fight the knots forming in his gut. Then he did what he needed to do—what his people needed him to do. He pushed his personal turmoil away and returned to the task at hand.

Xander remained in the town square for hours—lifting stones until his fingers began to bleed, letting his people cry on his shoulder, leaning over the bodies piled on the ground, using a wet rag to clear the blood from pale brows, searching for signs of life, and directing the healers to those with the best chances of recovery.

He was a beacon of strength.

A fixed point in the midst of so much chaos.

They needed him, and he held on to that as he fought to

stay focused, fought to ignore the image of Rafe and Lyana entwined, the gleam of understanding in her eyes, the questions churning in the back of his mind—questions about what had really happened between these two people who claimed to hate each other, about what had really happened to make a dove pick a raven as her mate.

46

CASSI

Lyana fell asleep soon after the healers left, exhausted from the day and from the gash in her leg, which gave Cassi the chance to finally go looking for some answers. The golden streaks of sun had long since faded from the horizon, and the moon was already rising. Her favorite time of day was here—the time for dreaming.

Cassi pushed through the door connecting their rooms and collapsed in her own bed, body exhausted from the long days in the practice yards, even as her mind whirled with the night's adventure. She slipped into her spirit form before her eyes had fully closed and turned back immediately, floating through the wall to lean over Lyana, who was out cold. Reaching with her spirit magic, Cassi pushed against Lyana's soul, trying to sense a change, a new awakening, any sign.

There was nothing.

She frowned and pushed harder, latching on to the energy

of her friend's magic, searching for a new spark, a new strength. Lyana grumbled in her sleep and rolled over, as if she somehow sensed Cassi's prodding.

With a sigh, Cassi pulled away.

It had to be you, she thought, staring at her friend. *It had to.*

The earthquake that shook the island had been magic through and through. A pulse of power had blasted through the air, invisible to anyone except those with magic in their veins, and had rattled the spell that kept the isles floating. That happened from time to time, when someone with immense power was born or came into their magic.

It wasn't Lyana's birthday yet.

But it had to be her. It just had to.

With a frown, Cassi turned to the window and soared through the curtains into the open sky. There were no answers in Lyana's rooms, at least none she could find. Instead, she made her way to the royal quarters to check on the other magic-user she knew.

Rafe was lying face down on his bed, wings spread as wide as they could go, bent and bruised, but already looking better. His back rose and fell in a gentle rhythm as he breathed deeply. He faced the balcony, his arms acting as pillows to his head. Deep grooves were etched into his brow, in a scowl even sleep couldn't quite wipe away.

Cassi reached for his spirit.

It was strong and sturdy. The silvery sparkle of his magic was a warm caress against her soul, but much like Lyana's, it felt no different than it had every other time she'd touched it.

With a sigh, Cassi drifted back into the night, ready to find her king, when a whisper on the breeze made her pause.

"It wasn't the princess's fault. It wasn't either of their faults."

The voice was Xander's, annoyed and frustrated in a way the mostly jovial prince had never sounded—not that she knew him very well. Their interactions had been few, but still, the anger in his tone made her curious. As did Lyana's title on his lips.

"You weren't there, Mother. There was no time to think how it might look. Rafe risked his life to save my mate. Before I even knew what was happening, they were buried in rubble."

He was standing in Queen Mariam's room. Well, not standing so much as pacing. His face was covered in a fine layer of dirt, and blood stained his clothes. The tops of his wings were lowered in exhaustion, but his expression displayed a fiery strength his muscles did not.

"It doesn't matter how it was," she icily replied. "It matters how it looked."

The queen was seated at her vanity table, putting cream on her face, ebony wings perched so only her primary feathers slouched on the ground. Through the mirror, she watched her son as he walked behind her.

Xander paused to run a hand through his hair. "And how did it look? I was there, yet somehow you managed to see something I didn't from all the way up here."

"I have eyes and ears everywhere, Lysander," she murmured, tilting up her chin as she applied lotion to her neck, her movements so casual they didn't match the iron in her tone. "So will you one day, if you want to remain king. And while you were diligently tending to your people, they were talking behind your back, whispering about the fire-cursed bastard who was trying to seduce our new queen and lure her into Vesevios's arms—"

"Mother, that's ridiculous! Rafe would never—"

"They said he brought the earthquake just so he could have the chance to act a hero. They said he survived where countless others died because his god is giving him power. They said he has us tricked with his magic. They said his very existence in our house is making Taetanos weak."

"What would you have me do?" he asked. "We can't succumb to frightened gossip."

"Frightened gossip has the power to bring a kingdom to its knees," she told him, and turned in her chair, long skirt dragging as she moved. "Our family has been in power a long time, but it wasn't always that way. The ravens are loyal, but even loyalty has its limits. Perhaps you should consider that before you decide which side to choose."

Xander met his mother's gaze and held it for a minute. Then he released a heavy breath, somewhere between a sigh and a growl, and stalked from the room without another word. Cassi's focus slid to Queen Mariam, who waited for the door to close before catching her head in her hands, her frigid strength melting away. Her face moved back and forth as her fingers rubbed at her temples, until, with a hiss, she stood. The monarch flattened the wrinkles in her sleeping gown, then she straightened her back and pinched her cheeks, as though even in the privacy of her own chambers she couldn't afford to show any sign of weakness, or any hint of vulnerability.

Cassi left her to the loneliness of her room and slinked back into the night, not completely sure what to make of the encounter. She let it replay in her memory so she could recount every detail, then cleared her thoughts to concentrate on the only soul she needed to find that evening.

"Did you feel it?" she asked as soon as she finished spinning his dream, placing them back in the dreary gray room with walls that loomed.

"I did," her king replied, sapphire eyes filled with storm clouds, lips drawn in a grim line opposite to the smile spreading hers.

"It was a sign, the sign we've been waiting for," Cassi said, finally letting some of the excitement from the day leak into her tone. In the world above, surrounded by the corpses of ravens, both children and adult, there'd been no place for eagerness. But in this dream, standing wingless by her king's side, all Cassi could think was that everything they'd been waiting for, everything she'd been working so hard to achieve, was here. She was almost done, almost free from the cage her dual life had become.

"We both know it wasn't," he murmured, frowning.

Cassi scoffed, rolling her eyes. Her king lifted a single brow in response, making her pause, swallow, and remember which world she was in—which monarch stood beside her. "What else could it have been? Lyana's birthday is only a fortnight away, and if she is who we think she is, it would be no surprise if the power started responding earlier than we thought."

"It's possible," he said sternly as he crossed his arms and turned to the window, watching the clouds churn as though they were real, and as though they carried news. "But so are any number of other things. The magic binding the isles to the sky is not as strong as it once was, you and I both know that, and there's no telling for sure what disturbed it. Not yet."

Cassi bit her tongue.

"I received no word of a dragon responding to the call of the magic, and without that, there's no way to know where the surge came from," her king continued, just to press the point a little further. He studied her for a moment before taking a seat at the table. "Now, we have more important things to discuss. You have updates for me, I assume?"

"I do," Cassi responded, emptying her voice of personality as she tried to focus on the business at hand.

With a simple thought, the dream shifted. Two quills and sheets of paper appeared, some blank, some filled with the parts of the plan they'd already figured out. Cassi dipped her feather into a pot of ink and began to scrawl as she described what she'd learned on her many midnight adventures, but only half of her mind was paying attention.

The other half was in her own dreams, not his. Because the earthquake had to have been Lyana. Cassi's lonely heart couldn't accept the idea of it coming from anyone else. Her friend *was* the queen who was prophesized. And in two weeks, Cassi *was* bringing Lyana beneath the mist. There would be no more lies. No more secrets. No more half-lives. They would walk across the wet wooden planks of the floating cities together. Cassi would show Lyana her power, would show Lyana that magic was to be treasured, not despised. That it was beautiful. That the people who wielded it were beautiful too. And that the life her friend had always been aching for, of adventure and travel and choice, could be hers—could be theirs.

As she bid her king goodbye, other thoughts filtered in.

That she would meet him, see him, touch him.

That in two weeks, she would no longer be the figment of his imagination, the invisible spirit in the night, but a girl, flesh and blood, made of magic and wings. He would see the real her, no more hiding, and she would see the real him.

Malek.

Adult. And grown. And tangible.

By the time Cassi returned to her body, she was wide awake. No matter how hard she rolled from one side to the other to get some sleep—some real sleep—her eyes remained resolutely open. So, she slipped out of bed and went to the balcony to sit with her feet dangling over the edge as a cool breeze brushed against her cheeks and ruffled her feathers, wrapping her in a loving embrace. She leaned forward, resting her brow against the rail, hands gripping the spindles as her gaze landed on the moon, creamy, glowing, and so familiar.

It looked so much like her mother's eyes.

Two weeks, Cassi thought one final time.

Then she'd be home—wrapped in his arms, surrounded by the scent of salty air made sweet with magic, a thing she'd tried to recreate in the dreams but always failed to reproduce.

Because even magic had its limits, and there were some things that just weren't the same unless they were tangible and physical and real.

Cassi was so lost in the moon and her memories, she hardly even noticed the little white dart flashing across her vision, a shooting star passing through the night, there and gone in one fleeting moment. It was only much later that she realized it had been Lyana, getting herself into trouble once more.

47

LYANA

Lyana stood on the balcony, peeking through the curtains at the raven sprawled across his bed, repeating to herself, *This is a bad idea. This is a bad idea. This is a bad idea.* The last time they'd spoken, he'd yelled at her to leave his room, a room with crystal walls that was hundreds of miles away, and yet could have been this one. He'd said they weren't friends. He'd said he was leaving all memory of her behind. He'd said all those things, and yet today in the square, as the stones had fallen and his body was all that had kept her safe, he'd said something else.

I've got you.

Lyana stepped out of the shadows and into the soft light of the lantern by his bed, low on oil but still burning, bright enough for her to see the grooves of his face, relaxed in sleep but not peaceful. She wasn't sure she had ever seen him look truly at ease—it was as if he lived his whole life teetering on an edge—but tonight, she knew the cause of his distress, the broken bends in his hollow bones, the blood still caked across his feathers. And this? This at least she knew how to fix, whether he wanted her to or not.

Lyana knelt beside the mattress, leaning over his bare shoulders so she could gently graze the top sides of his feathers with her fingers, magic already prickling to life beneath her skin.

Rafe sighed.

For a moment, the wrinkles on the bridge of his nose disappeared, then he blinked. Lyana watched the sleep leave his eyes, and the contentment too, as his vision cleared and recognition sparked.

"What are—"

"Stay still," Lyana softly commanded, pressing her palms against a broken part of his wings, hearing him hiss. She didn't relent.

"I'm fine," he protested.

"Could've fooled me."

"You shouldn't have come," he grunted. One side of her lips tugged into the smallest smile at the words, because they were empty of everything except stubborn pride. His muscles were loose and he surrendered to her touch as her magic intensified. Even though his expression remained obstinate, his body relaxed as her power shot over his skin. "I don't need your help."

"Whether you need it or not is irrelevant. I'm giving it regardless," Lyana countered. "So be quiet and accept it, because unlike all the bodies I saw piled in the square, and all the children who were crushed, and all the people who went to sleep tonight not sure if they'd wake up, you—" She paused to compose herself, realizing the word had come out like snarl. "You, I can help."

He winced, closing his eyes. "Thank you."

The words were so quiet she almost didn't hear them. And though a snappy retort was always on the tip of her tongue whenever she was around him, Lyana sighed instead. "Thank *you*. I would've— I should've—" The memory flashed clear as day— an avalanche falling toward her, one split second from sending her to the grave. A shiver crept up her spine. "You saved my life."

"It was no big deal," he murmured lamely, eyes darting every which way before landing back on her face, deep and rich and full of much more feeling than his words.

Lyana held his gaze and pointedly lifted her brows.

"You're my brother's mate," he offered as an explanation, though it sounded more like a reminder—to her, to him, to both.

"Did you know you'd survive?" she asked.

Rafe paused for a long time before he answered, "No."

She looked at her hands, watching his wings heal inch by inch beneath her touch, and focused on the work instead of the unease coiling in her stomach. But the silence just made her nausea grow, as though her body and mind were at war— one aware that what she was doing was wrong in every sense, and the other heedless as it took pleasure in the sizzling heat of his skin, in the searing twinge of his magic rising to meet hers.

Rafe writhed his shoulder blades and turned his head so it

faced the wall instead of her. Then he cleared his throat and asked, "So, how are things going with Xander?"

Lyana kept her focus on the injuries healing beneath her glowing fingers, trying not to wonder why he kept bringing the conversation back to the one topic she didn't want to discuss with him. "Fine, I guess."

"The two of you seemed happy. In the square I mean, before everything happened…"

"I didn't know you were watching."

"I wasn't," he hastily replied, head twitching as if he had winced again. An amused smile played on her lips as he went on, "I mean, I was, obviously. But just for your protection— Xander's protection— Both of your protections." He managed to toss her a frustrated look. "Would you just answer the question?"

"Which was…?"

"Are you happy?" He paused again. "With Xander?"

"We're…" Lyana searched for the words, keeping her attention on his wing. The area beneath her hands had been healed for a few moments now. She shifted her weight, moving farther down his wing, far enough from his torso to breathe, far enough the air coming in from the balcony cooled the back of her neck—just enough of a shock to clear the turmoil from her mind.

"We're different people," she continued as she brushed her fingers down the outer edge of his wing, finding the breaks in what should have been smooth bone. A shiver rippled over his feathers, catching the light from the lamp, the way she imagined an ocean wave might reflect the moon at midnight. "But maybe we've found a happy medium."

Her eyes flicked up, finding his.

He dropped his gaze. "Good."

Lyana finished healing the rest of his left wing before standing and walking to the other side of the bed, sensing his attention as she knelt at the far side of his right wing, starting from the outside this time.

"Why are you limping?" he asked softly.

"I can't heal myself," Lyana said with a shrug. "It's nothing, just a scratch, gone in a few days."

He frowned. Lyana could feel it without having to look up, as though his dissatisfaction were a tangible thing pressing against her, a finger nudging her arm like a petulant child. Somehow, she found it endearing.

"I'm fine, really."

"I—" He released a heavy breath. "It's a little strange, isn't it?"

This time, Lyana looked at him. "What?"

"You've never met anyone else with magic, have you?"

She shook her head.

"Neither have I." The crease in his brow deepened. "What are the chances that when we finally do, the person we meet has the exact opposite power to ours? Strange, right?"

"Unless..." Lyana swallowed to ease the sudden dryness of her throat. Because she'd never spoken to anyone about her theories, not even to Cassi. Magic was forbidden. Even mentioning it was dangerous. But here, in the ever-shrinking firelight, her power touching his, an act more soul-baring than words could ever be, Lyana felt safe enough to wonder out loud. "What if it's not magic?" He cocked his head, confused, as she pursued, "What if it's a gift? From the gods?"

She waited for his instant denial, his joke or his rejection, but it never came.

Instead, he simply asked, "How do you mean?"

"Have you ever been to your sacred nest?" Her mind was already jumping ahead, her magic flaring with her excitement. Palms glowing more brightly, she funneled all her power into his bones, moving to a spot still unhealed.

"Not since I got my wings," he answered.

"Well, I've been to mine, plenty of times, and there's something about being so close to the god stones—" Lyana flicked her gaze to his face, finding him enraptured, then returned to her work, letting her thoughts race as her hands moved again and again, faster as the energy pulsed through her. "When I was there, my magic would light up, as though something within me recognized the power inside the stones, as though they were one and the same, as though Aethios himself had reached out and put a little piece of his spirit in me. I don't think what we have is magic, Rafe, at least not the kind our ancestors feared. I think we were chosen—by Aethios, by Taetanos, by all the gods even. We were chosen for something more."

"For what?" he whispered.

Lyana put her hand on his shoulder, realizing that in her frenzy she'd finished healing his other wing and was kneeling beside him. Her fingers traced the curve of his biceps, running along his skin. His eyes followed.

"I don't know. I only know I've always had this feeling," she said, mesmerized by the contrast of her dark skin against his. She was made for the golden glow of the sun, just like her magic, while he was made for the silvery sheen of the moon. Two opposites, yet the same. "This feeling that I was meant for something more. A yearning in my gut, a beating of my heart, a sense that my destiny is bigger than what's expected of me. And I've always been looking for it, searching the world for a sign, for a clue, for a map to the adventure I know is waiting. I haven't found it yet, but I found you, and maybe we were supposed to figure out the rest together."

Her fingers had stopped and rested in his, curled so they almost held hands but not quite. Silver-and-gold static filled the empty space, crackling and sizzling like stolen starlight.

"Ana…" Rafe said her name as though it caused him pain. He removed his hand and snapped his wings closed, rolling to the other side of the bed and jumping to his feet. His face was stone, carved into resolute blankness. "You should go."

"Rafe," she countered. Even as the word rolled out of her lips, she knew it wasn't enough, didn't pierce him the way her informal name, Ana—short and simple and steeped in so many unspoken implications—pierced her. Again, she was struck with the frustration of knowing *Rafe* wasn't the name she was supposed to use, but Lysander wasn't either, not anymore. He was someone else, something else, something she hadn't figured out yet.

And she wouldn't tonight.

Not when his wall was back up.

He walked to the curtain draped over his balcony and

pulled it aside, looking at everything and yet nothing, certainly not at her. "You should leave, now, before anyone sees you."

Lyana listened.

She crossed the room and stepped out into the shadows of night, breathing the fresh air, her chest tight. As she spread her wings, she looked over her shoulder, meeting the blue eyes watching her beneath hooded brows. "I'll be back."

With a beating of wings she was gone, not giving him the chance to tell her no.

48

XANDER

He'd woken before dawn, but it had still taken Xander the better part of the morning to find the courage to walk to Rafe's room. And now he was there. Standing outside the door. Knuckles lifted to knock. Hesitating.

After a few minutes, he finally twisted the knob and barged into his brother's room unannounced the way he usually did. Rafe was in bed, arms thrown over his head, staring at the ceiling with bloodshot eyes as though the clouds painted there held the key to the universe.

"You look like hell," Xander said, forcing a cheerful smile to his lips, fighting the wave of anxiety coursing through his veins and making him jittery.

The conversation with his mother played on repeat in his head.

As did the image of Rafe and Lyana, buried in the

wreckage and tangled like star-crossed lovers in the last scene of a tragic play.

But what to say?

And how to say it?

And—

Xander funneled all the anger and the questions into his invisible fist, storing them away to be dealt with later, because now he needed to remain calm. Everything would go so much smoother if he could pass it all off as a ridiculous joke.

Rafe threw him a brief glance. "I couldn't sleep."

"How are you feeling?" Xander asked, perching on the stool in the corner of the room, his feet on the rungs. Casual. Ordinary.

Rafe sat up and flared his wings as he ran his hands over his face, pushing sleep and exhaustion away before taking a deep breath. "Awful, but alive."

Xander studied the bends beneath his brother's feathers, all exactly where they were supposed to be, no longer broken and battered and jutting out at all ends. They didn't talk about Rafe's magic. Not really. It was like dust, to be swept under the rug, there but not there, out of sight and out of mind, until it was too obvious to ignore. Now was one of those times.

"That was..." Xander searched for the word, eyes continuing to rove over the injuries that were no longer there. "Fast."

Rafe knew what he meant.

He closed his wings as he stood, hiding them behind his back and joining Xander at the window. "It looked worse than it was."

"It looked bad, Rafe," Xander said quietly. "It looked fatal. It was fatal…to nearly everyone else."

The edge of Rafe's lip rose, though his eyes remained stormy. "Let me guess, the people are talking?"

"Can you blame them?"

"No." Rafe faced him, the wrinkles at the corners of his eyes softening. "What do you need me to do?"

"My mother wants me to send you away," Xander said in a lighthearted tone.

He expected Rafe to respond with a snort and, *Banishment again? How unoriginal.*

Or perhaps a roll of his eyes and a tired sigh.

Or maybe even a grin and, *A vacation? Lovely.*

Instead, Rafe held his gaze, features disturbingly still as he asked, "Should you?"

A nervous laugh spilled from Xander's lips. "Come on. It's just gossip."

"It's only gossip if it's not true."

"Rafe, you're not cursed."

His brother just shrugged.

"Rafe," Xander insisted, putting his hand on his brother's shoulder.

Shirking the hold, Rafe stepped back. "Maybe you should send me away, Xander. You don't need me anymore. You have a mate and a kingdom, and I'm just a liability."

"How can you say that?" Xander squinted, as if unable to recognize the man before him. Was this why Rafe had been spending hours upon hours in the practice field swinging a sword? Never coming to lunch or to dinner? Hardly coming to his room at night to talk? Because he was afraid of being replaced? "You're my brother. I'll always need you. And if you weren't the way you are, if you were anyone else, my mate would be dead and my kingdom lost, and that's the truth, no matter what anyone else believes. All right?"

Rafe raised his chin almost defiantly. "All right."

"Good." Xander said again and offered his brother a wry look. "Now really try to hold on to everything I just said, because you're not going to like what comes next."

Rafe scowled.

"I need you to stay in your rooms, out of sight, until after the mating ceremony."

The blue glare deepened, but it had a resigned edge.

"I know, I know." Xander held up his arms. "But people need to believe you're recovering on a normal timeline. Well, a plausible timeline anyway. A few weeks and hopefully this will seem like old news."

Xander didn't want to give voice to the ugly thought that shouldn't be in his head, the thought he tried to push down, down, down his right arm into the invisible fist where all the malicious, nasty parts of him lived—but he couldn't quite get rid of it.

And by then, Lyana will be mine, before the gods.

It was jealous, spiteful, and he hated himself for it.

But it was true.

He couldn't bring himself to ask Rafe about the courtship trials now, not with that horrible thought knocking all the rest out of place. He didn't want to accuse his brother or his mate. He didn't want to place blame where there was none to place.

373

Because it couldn't be true. There was no way. Rafe loved him. Rafe was loyal. Rafe would never betray him like that, never, not with the past they shared.

He turned the conversation to lighter topics and stayed for a while longer, smiling and laughing with his brother, purging the unclean feeling before he left. By the time he got to the princess's room, he was himself again, and the sight of her smile made his day all the brighter.

"How are you feeling?" he asked as he stopped just inside the threshold, unsure if he was welcome.

Lyana was resting in her bed, being primped by the servants, tossing one of them an annoyed look as her pillow was stripped away to be fluffed. Her calf was wrapped in a fresh bandage, which meant the healers had stopped by that morning.

Sensing his gaze, she wiggled her exposed toes and said, "I'm fine." But then she eyed him suspiciously, even as her grin widened. "Unless you mean to drag me to more lessons, in which case, I'm in excruciating pain and don't wish to be disturbed."

A laugh popped out before he could stop it. "No, no, I promise."

Her eyes sparkled.

She was happy today, invigorated in a way he hadn't expected, as though the encounter the day before had somehow freed her, made her comfortable enough in the castle and on the isle to finally let him in.

"Actually..." Xander coughed and cleared his throat as he took a few steps closer, so he could sit at the edge of her bed, their eyes at the same level. "I thought, if you were feeling healthy enough, you might want to come with me to visit the injured?"

Her expression turned somber.

"I just…" he continued, unwilling to ruin her mood. "I thought it would lift their spirits, to have their prince and new princess visit and offer Taetanos's blessing. I can teach you the words on the way, they're simple enough. I wish there was more to do, but the healers are doing their best. No matter how small, I want to do something."

Lyana grasped his hand. "I'd love to."

"Really?" he asked, not surprised so much as hopeful— hopeful this could be a turning point for them, maybe the start of something deeper.

Lyana squeezed his fingers. "There's nothing I'd love to do more."

49

RAFE

Rafe spent most of his day praying she wouldn't come, hoping she'd been nothing more than a dream, telling himself she hadn't meant her parting words, but he couldn't ignore the pang in his heart when he heard the *swish* of feathers brushing against his curtains in the late, late hours of the night.

"I know you're awake," she drawled softly as she stepped into the room, her boots scuffing over the wooden floorboards.

He knew they were boots because the silk slippers most women wore in the castle would have been silent, and the very idea that she was wearing shoes meant for outdoors provoked a sinking feeling in his gut. Still, he kept his back to the balcony, cheek resting on his hand as he breathed slowly and steadily, feigning sleep on the off chance she might turn around and fly away.

She didn't.

She sighed, and the wood stool in the corner, the one usually occupied by Xander, creaked softly as it took her weight.

"I had an idea today," she said conversationally, as though they were two people at a dinner table instead of an intruder and a man who clearly—well, he hoped clearly—wanted to be left alone. "Xander took me outside the castle walls, and we traveled to the houses of everyone who was injured in the earthquake, saying a blessing to Taetanos over their bodies. Some of them were awake but weak, and some of them had yet to open their eyes though their chests still rose and fell with breath. But their families were so grateful—they truly believed a simple prayer from their future king and queen would make all the difference. And I realized, as I said goodbye and they kissed my hand and looked at me through grateful eyes, that I could do much, much more to help."

Rafe sat up and spun in an instant. "No."

"I knew you were awake." Her grin was a triumphant thing that stretched from ear to ear.

"And I knew you were reckless," he countered, a frown tugging at his brow, "but I didn't take you for a fool."

"Is it so foolish to want to save lives?" she asked. "I would think it far more foolish to sit back and watch them die when I know in my heart I could save them."

He stood and made an imploring gesture with his hands. "It's dangerous."

"I didn't think a man who faced a dragon on his own would ever say something so cowardly."

The words struck him like a blow. "That was different."

The princess just shrugged. "Why?"

"Because"—he half growled, half spat the word as he took a step closer—"my life isn't important. Not the way yours is. Not the way Xander's is."

She looked away and back at him before she said, "Your life is important to me."

"And yet," Rafe said, seizing the upper hand and trying to ignore something her eyes stirred deep inside him, "you would risk it, and your own, on a—"

"Did you think about what I said?"

All I did the whole damn day was think about you, he thought as a sneer crossed his face, directed more at himself than at her. "No."

"Liar," Lyana muttered. "You just don't want to admit it, because maybe what I said was true. Maybe we were chosen by the gods for something more. Maybe we were chosen for this. To help people."

"Even if we were, what are you planning to do?" Rafe asked, pointedly eying her wings. "You don't exactly blend in as it is, and if anyone sees you, they won't care that you think your power is a gift from the gods. They'll label it magic and condemn you."

"I brought a large cloak," she said slowly.

Rafe noticed the black fabric in her hands, which she rung with her fingers, and he couldn't help it—he bent over at the waist as laughter erupted, heavy with disbelief. For a moment, he really thought he was losing his mind. "A cloak?"

Lyana crossed her arms and glared. One white wing

whipped around, shoving his shoulder and sending him off balance. "I wasn't finished," she practically snarled. "I brought a large cloak, so once we get on the other side of the castle wall, it'll cover my wings, and we can walk from house to house instead of flying. It'll take longer, but we have less of a chance of being seen. Xander told me the healers were giving all the injured sleeping tonics, so they shouldn't wake up if we sneak in, and either way, I'll keep the hood up so my face is covered in shadow. I noticed that nearly every house in Pylaeon has a balcony of some kind by all the windows, so it should be easy enough to slip in and out quickly."

The gods.

It actually wasn't a completely horrible plan.

"How are you planning to get out of the castle unseen?" he asked, not yet willing to agree. "You can't fly, not with those white feathers of yours."

Lyana smiled sweetly. "That's where I was hoping you might be able to help."

Rafe groaned and rubbed his face, his mind in turmoil. On the one hand, it was the most reckless idea he'd ever heard. On the other, he wasn't sure he'd be able to live with himself if ravens died when he could have helped save them—or if something happened to the princess. The gleam in her eye said she wouldn't take no for an answer, and he had the horrible feeling that even if he didn't accompany her, she'd go through with her plan anyway. Rafe knew what happened to ravens caught with magic—the sound sometimes haunted his dreams, that unmistakable whistle of the executioner's blade slicing through air before a dry thud announced the job was done. Beheadings were public affairs, though he could never bring himself to watch. Instead, he'd observe the crowd. Sometimes, that was worse. The cries of the loved ones. The cheers from everyone else. The haunting fear in Xander's eyes as he glanced at Rafe, wondering if he would be next.

No.

He couldn't let that happen.

Not to her.

"I know a way," he admitted. The words came out in the barest whisper, as though his throat had fought to keep them in. "There's a passage. My father once used it to sneak my mother into the castle, before he had rooms set up for her among the servants'. Xander and I used it as boys. It's old, as old as the castle itself. My brother and I used to wonder if it came from a time before the isles were lifted into the sky, when war was common and quick escapes more common still."

As he spoke, Lyana's eyes shone with intrigue. She clasped her hands to her chest, fingertips turning pink from being squeezed so tightly.

Rafe shook his head.

What had he gotten himself into?

"Let's go," Lyana blurted, taking a step toward the door.

"Hold on." Rafe grabbed her arm. "Let me see the cloak first."

Lyana obliged and threw the fabric over her shoulders. It was a deep-black velvet, expensive but not necessarily royal. There were no jewels or gems on it, no markings of any kind, and from a distance, it might pass for something cheaper.

Most importantly, when the hood was pulled up, it fell all the way to her nose, making him wonder if she could see. The back was voluminous enough to cover her wings and still trail on the floor.

"Where in all the houses did you find this?" he asked in wonder.

Lyana dropped the hood as she pulled the fabric close. "My grandmother was a, shall we say, large woman, and she used to complain that her wings would get cold when she ventured outside, so my grandfather had this made as a gift. When she passed, he gave it to me because I loved how much it still smelled like her."

The affection in her tone brought a warm feeling to his heart, a tender sensation he wasn't used to but liked. Though there was something else too, a subtle sort of yearning as he wondered what it must have been like to grow up with a family like that.

"Maybe I shouldn't have laughed when you said you brought a large cloak," he teased.

Lyana shook her head with a satisfied, "Hmph."

He eyed her hands. "Do you have gloves?"

She pushed the cloak aside to take two black gloves from a pocket in her jacket, pulling them over her fingers.

"What about something for your neck and chin?"

Again, Lyana produced a disguise in the shape of a deep ebony fur that would cover the exposed skin beneath her hood.

"Not the first time you've ever snuck out of a castle," he guessed, unable to fight the desire to smile at her antics.

Lyana studied him as he, too, donned gloves and a dark outfit meant to blend with the night, then pulled a hood over his eyes, shrouding his features. "Not yours either."

He nodded at her. "Come on, then, before I change my mind."

Leading the princess down the halls, he was careful to peek around each corner, searching for guards or servants on their nightly rounds. The passage was in the underbelly of the castle, not as deep underground as his mother's room had once been, but close. The path was dark and dank. Moisture from the soil seeped through the stones, leaving a layer of slick algae and moss. They moved carefully, and after a few stumbles, Lyana reached out to take his hand for balance. He tried not to think about how comforting her fingers felt, entwined through his, how soothing, how natural. When they reached the end of the passage, he broke hold to open the heavy iron gate, made to look like another sewage hole in the street.

From there, it was her turn to lead. They took a few wrong, circular routes before she finally found her bearings in a city that was still foreign to her, and they made it to the first of the injured. Lyana stared at the building, studying the windows and doors, fighting to remember.

"That one," she whispered, pointing to a balcony on the left of the second story. "That was his room."

Rafe nodded, taking to the air with a single pump of his wings to land softly on the platform. He pressed his nose to the window, trying to see through the shadows of the room, until he found a small body curled on the bed and turned, bending to offer Lyana his hand. Careful not to use her wings, she leaped. It took two tries before he caught her forearm firmly enough to drag her up. On the balcony, Lyana slid her knife through the narrow slit in the window, clicking the latch. They were in. She rushed to the child fast asleep beneath the covers, stripped off her gloves, and closed her eyes, focusing on the work.

Rafe, on the other hand, stood guard in the darkness, hardly able to blink as he watched her, mesmerized. The grimace on the child's lips disappeared. His raspy wheezing eased into long, smooth, flowing breaths. The tight little bundle of his body loosened, more comfortable as the pain seeped from his bones. And Lyana was a vision, lips slightly open, features relaxed. The golden light emanating from her hands glittered like the soft rays of the morning sun sifting through the clouds. And for a moment, he finally saw what she saw. That it wasn't magic. It was something more. Her god, Aethios, flowing through her, giving her the power to heal the world.

Rafe had spent most of his life resenting his magic. It had saved him, but not his parents. It had made him an outcast, something to be feared. It had made him a fugitive, someone filled with fear. It had turned his brother into a liar and his life into a lie. But standing there, watching her, for the first time Rafe understood his magic was a gift.

Because his magic had saved her.

His magic had created this moment.

And she, and this, were magnificent.

LYANA

Lyana woke bleary-eyed and exhausted, but feeling better than she had in weeks. Maybe even months. Maybe...ever.

Finally, she wasn't just sitting around, dreaming of something more, waiting for her life to find her. Finally, she was out doing something, something good, something with her magic. They'd only made it to four homes, but that was still four people who would wake up this morning miraculously healed, thanking their god, alive when they otherwise might not have been. And Lyana had made it happen.

Well, she and Rafe.

They'd made it happen together.

"What's got you grinning like a buffoon this morning?" Cassi asked as she slipped through the door between their rooms and collapsed on Lyana's bed, looking a little bleary-eyed and exhausted herself.

"Nothing," Lyana murmured, sighing. Try as she might to arrange her face into a more appropriate expression, her lips remained resolutely wide.

Cassi stared. "Nothing."

"It's a beautiful day," Lyana gushed, attributing her enthusiasm into something that might make a little more sense.

Leaving Cassi in bed, Lyana jumped to her feet and threw the curtains open as if her body had too much energy and could do nothing but explode with motion. The sun was high, higher than when she usually woke up, though she normally went to bed much earlier. And the sky was a clear, bright blue, reminding her of something else, someone else. She had the sense that she was exactly where she was supposed to be—a wonderfully foreign yet comforting feeling.

"Did they slip you some sort of herb for the pain? I've heard rumors that medicine isn't the only thing they brew in the House of Paradise..." Cassi frowned, watching her in confusion.

Lyana pranced back to the bed, hopping from foot to foot. "Nope, nothing. My leg feels fine."

Cassi watched her warily, nonetheless. "You're a little too happy, even for you."

"Honestly, Cassi," Lyana said, hands on hips. "Can't you just wipe the frown from your face and join me in this marvelous, wondrous, beautiful morning?"

Cassi watched her for another moment, then rolled off the

bed to take a step toward the tray in the corner of the room, which Lyana hadn't even noticed. She lifted the lid of the kettle, sniffing it. "What did they put in this?"

Lyana was prepared to argue with her friend some more, but her door crashed open, banging against the wall with a thunderous *boom*.

"Lyana!"

It was Xander.

An out-of-breath, smiling, excited Xander, as full of awe as she was. He paused, and his body jerked as though he suddenly remembered where he was. His eyes popping, he offered her a low bow before rising slowly. The sight made her feel even lighter.

"I mean, Princess, pardon my intrusion, I just— Have you — I thought you'd want to hear the news."

"What news?" Cassi asked, a wary edge still on her voice.

Xander spun in her direction, surprised by her presence. Then he shrugged, switching his attention between them. "It's all everyone has been talking about all morning. Four of the injured children we visited yesterday, a boy and three girls, they're all— Well, somehow, they're healed!"

Lyana didn't need to meet Cassi's glare to feel every suspicious, accusing prick in it. The left side of her body tingled with heat. She kept her eyes locked on Xander, feeding off his energy instead of her friend's because at the moment, his emotions matched hers. "Really? Xander, how? It's a miracle."

"No one knows," he explained with a shake of his head as words eluded him. "The people are saying it was a gift from the gods to thank us for our devotion. Someone claimed to have seen a cloaked figure pass beneath one of the spirit gates last night—they're saying it was Taetanos himself."

Lyana bit her lips to keep from squealing.

"Thank the gods," Cassi drawled.

Lyana ached to throw a pillow at her face, but she restrained herself…barely.

"Thank the gods, indeed," Xander said, not noticing the sarcastic undertone of Cassi's statement. He was pure of heart, and Cassi, well, wasn't. But that was one of the reasons Lyana loved her. "I'd like to think that maybe…" Xander mumbled with glowing eyes, reaching out to hold her fingers. "Thank you for coming with me to say the blessings yesterday. I think, maybe, it did something. Maybe, somehow, we helped."

"We did," Lyana said, squeezing back.

The words were true. If Xander hadn't taken her out into the city yesterday, she would have never even conceived the idea in the first place. Would have never known where to go or which steps to make. This was all because of him, because he'd taken the time to include her, and she was grateful. But not so grateful that she was ready to tell him the truth.

She released his hand.

He took a hasty step back and cleared his throat.

"Well, anyway, you missed breakfast, so I wanted to come and tell you the news myself." He paused to eye the leg which clearly caused her no pain or hardship, then looked up with a charming wink. "I'll tell my mother you require a day of rest to recover from your wounds. Shall I come back to escort you to dinner?"

"Please do," she murmured.

He left with another bow. Lyana winced when the door clicked closed.

Three, two, one—

"What were you thinking?" Cassi hissed, charging toward her the way Lyana imagined bears in the great plains of the House of Prey might charge toward a rabbit. But she was no rabbit.

"I wasn't thinking," Lyana countered, turning to meet her friend head-on. "I was acting, I was doing, and it was amazing, Cassi. If only you'd been there to see, you'd understand. But I didn't want to risk getting you into trouble."

"Since when?"

Lyana sighed. "Since we're in a foreign house and trouble here might have real consequences, unlike back home when I knew I could talk our way out of any punishment my father might have threatened."

Tension left Cassi's muscles. Her shoulders fell and her wings folded as all her edges softened. "You should have told me."

"I know," Lyana admitted. "I'm sorry."

"I'm sorry too," Cassi said, stepping close enough to put her hand on Lyana's arm. "I don't blame you for wanting to help. You're a healer—it's what you were born to do, to be. It's just—" She broke off.

"Just what?"

Cassi looked away, studying the rich fibers of the carpet instead of meeting Lyana's probing eyes. "You need to be careful."

"I was."

"So many people are counting on you, Ana…"

Lyana nodded along with her friend's words, because Cassi was right. The ravens. Xander. The queen. This entire house and all the houses, they were all counting on her to do her part, to be the princess she was supposed to be, the queen she was supposed to become. Not this. Not the person she was, magic and all.

"Just promise me," Cassi said. "Promise me you won't do anything else that might get you into trouble, at least for the next ten days."

Lyana frowned. "Ten days?"

Cassi didn't move for a moment, and then she gave a smile that didn't quite reach her eyes. "Yeah, ten days. Because after that, you'll officially be mated, and you won't be my problem anymore."

Lyana shoved her gently. "I'll always be your problem."

Cassi snorted. "Ain't that the truth. Now come on, I'm starving. Let's see if we can find some food, and you can tell me all about your little midnight expedition, all right?"

Lyana agreed, following Cassi out the door, but her mind was still stuck on those words.

Ten days.

You'll officially be mated.

You won't be my problem.

She'd tried not to think about the ceremony too much. About the fast-encroaching future. The vows she had to make —vows before the gods, vows she would never break, not once they were spoken.

Ten days was all she had left to be herself.

To be Ana.

A girl of magic and wonder—the girl she was with Rafe.

Not Lyana Taetanus, Crown Princess of the House of Whispers.

A woman bound by duty.

Ten days. It hardly seemed enough, so she planned to make each moment count, no matter what she'd promised Cassi. There was no time to be afraid. No time to be nervous. No time for anything at all.

RAFE

He spent the next few days in an upside-down sort of life, sleeping all day, awake all night, telling himself the sneaking around wasn't for him or for her. It was for Xander. For the ravens. To lift their spirits. To give them hope. To make them believe Taetanos was strong and mighty, not frail and failing. To restore their faith—a feat he'd certainly never been accused of before.

He was lying.

Sure, they'd healed the rest of the injured. Sure, the House of Whispers was celebrating. Sure, Pylaeon, the city of spirits, was more alive than he ever remembered. Sure, Xander was overjoyed by the display of Taetanos's strength.

But that wasn't why Rafe kept taking Lyana down the secret path and into the city each night. Those few minutes when she held his hand in the dark, those moments when her eyes were closed and he could finally watch her without worry, those seconds before they said goodbye, when they just stood and stared and enjoyed the magic simmering between them, that was why.

And it was why he jolted out of bed as soon as he heard the scuffing of boots on stone, heart hammering in his chest—a wild, caged thing—and rushed to yank open the curtains to his balcony. Before he even grasped the heavy fabric, the door behind him burst open.

"Going somewhere?" Xander asked, tone balanced between accusatory and amused.

Rafe jerked his hand away from the curtain and spun, hearing a gasp on the other side. His pulse pounded, quickened by a different emotion than a moment before—by terror and bitter, bitter guilt at his own treachery. "No."

"Calm down," Xander said, striding across the room to plop on his usual stool. "You're allowed to go outside. Just no flying, and no letting anyone see you, at least not for another week or two. But it's late enough now. I'd imagine the city has mostly fallen asleep, a feat that completely escaped me tonight. And you too, I see."

"Yeah," Rafe muttered and cleared his throat, trying to bring a smile to his lips. "I, uh, couldn't sleep. I'm going a little stir-crazy in here, I guess."

Xander nodded absently. His eyes moved around the room as he swiveled slightly on the stool, pushing with his legs as his wings flexed and relaxed.

Rafe's voice was soft. "Xander?"

The prince half turned toward him, but seemed to be in another place entirely.

"Is there something you wanted to talk about?" Rafe coaxed. He couldn't hear Lyana on the other side of the curtain anymore, but he supposed she was there, too curious by half to ever turn and fly away, and not nearly nervous enough to worry about being caught.

Xander sighed. "I just…"

He paused and turned to look out the window. If the princess was out there somewhere, she was in the shadows where neither of them could see.

"I was thinking tonight, while I couldn't sleep," Xander said. "I was wondering… What do you… Well, what do you suppose love feels like?"

Rafe froze.

But Xander kept rambling, unaware of how still his brother had become. "I mean, I know you've never felt that way yourself—me neither, of course—but I thought, maybe you might remember what it was between your parents? What it felt like to be around them?"

"I don't—" Rafe fell quiet when a knot in his throat cut off the words. "I don't know, Xander. I don't remember."

"You do," Xander countered, not accusingly. His tone was honest, maybe edged with the slightest bit of sadness. "It's fine, I understand. We don't talk about them, not really. I just thought this one time we could. Because I know what love looks like. I've seen it in the streets as I walk through them, between mated pairs, but never from so close a distance that I could recognize that light in someone's eye, that sparkle. My mother's faded long before I was old enough to notice it, and her parents were lost before I was born. But yours…"

He trailed off with a shrug.

Rafe found himself avoiding Xander's probing eyes. "Why? Why do you want to know?"

Xander scoffed, catching Rafe's attention as he gave half a smile. "I would think that's obvious, Rafe. I *am* to be mated in a week."

"That was true two weeks ago, too, and you didn't ask me then," Rafe argued, stubborn as always. But this was something more, a knife slowly digging into his gut, burning and painful. All he could think to do was grab the hilt and plunge it in more deeply, so at least the agonizing anticipation would end. Because he had to hear it—whatever it was, he had to.

"Something's changed," Xander said, almost mystified. He shook his head as the tips of his wings lifted. "I can't explain it, really, but Lyana's changed. The past few days she's seemed, I don't know, at peace in a way she hasn't been before, at least with me. There's something, a glow of some sort in her eyes, a smile always on her lips as though she just can't keep the corners down. And I'm, well, I'm trying to understand why."

The invisible blade twisted.

Rafe swayed on his feet before holding on to the wall to steady himself. He wondered if, outside, Lyana had done the same.

Xander didn't notice. He just kept talking as one of his legs bounced against the stool in a frantic sort of way. "And I'm different too, Rafe, when I'm around her, I think. Lighter somehow. She's, well, she's nothing like anyone I ever imagined being mated to—as you well know. We're different in so many ways, but I'm starting to think that doesn't matter. And I'd like to tell her all of this, instead of you—no offense, brother—but I spent the last hour trying to think about what to say, and for the life of me, I can't put this feeling into words. It's not love—it couldn't be, not in such a short amount of time. But if it's not that, I don't know what it is, or how to say it. I'm trying to understand, so that when I do talk to her, it goes better than this, because I can see I'm boring you, and never mind, I'll just go back to my room and you can forget I ever came."

The end of his ramblings only registered when Xander stood and began to shuffle toward the door.

"Wait," Rafe said, jumping into motion. He grabbed Xander's arm to detain him. "Wait. I—I remember."

Xander turned slowly, eying him expectantly.

Rafe closed his lids as the memories washed over him, a dam set free, a rushing torrent he didn't know how to control once it started. Oh, he thought of his mother often. The arms that used to wrap him up tightly. The voice that used to sing him to sleep. The laugh that was so infectious he would always laugh along with her, even in the middle of a tantrum. He thought of the two of them, alone in their room at the very bottom level of the castle, separate from the rest of the world, but it hadn't mattered, because they had everything they needed. The stories they'd create. The games they'd play. The love that had filled that room, so incredibly powerful it had stayed with him long after she'd passed—but that wasn't the love Xander was talking about.

No, the love she'd shared with his father had been different.

Rafe tried not to think about them—well, he tried not to think about his father—because whenever he did, he felt guilty. Guilty for those words that had been the king's last. *I won't leave you. I won't leave our son.* He'd died for loving Rafe more than Xander, for loving his mother more than the queen. And though he'd been little more than an innocent child, Rafe was exactly what the queen still called him—the bastard who had stolen so much from her son, who had stolen the meaning of love away and was now stealing something much greater.

"Love," Rafe murmured, remembering the way his parents would look at each other in that small room, how they would tease and sometimes fight, how they would dance like fools with him between them and then slow down as though he weren't there, how his mother would let her hair down and his father would remove his crown, and they'd be exactly who they were, for a little while at least. That feeling of freedom, of not having to hide, of being woven so closely nothing could ever undo them, that was love. And for a moment, Rafe pictured green eyes in the dark and two hands folded over one another, gold and silver sparking between them. But he blinked the picture away and turned to his brother, a hollow feeling growing cavernous in his gut. "Love is when you find a piece of yourself in someone else, a piece you never knew was missing, but without which you'd be broken. You feel whole, and complete, and accepted for exactly who you are. You can be your true self, because around this person, for the first time you have no desire to pretend to be anyone else."

Xander stared for a moment too long, brows quivering in the slightest frown, before he carefully cleared his features. "You sound like you're speaking from experience. Your own experience, I mean."

Rafe tensed.

His gaze flicked to the curtains, then slid along the carpet until it reached his brother's shoes. Drifting higher, he finally settled on the violet streaks of uncertainty in his brother's eyes. The air was thick and full and heavy, pressing on him from all angles, prickling his skin.

Two people were listening.

Two people who deserved the truth.

But it seemed that, lately, all Rafe knew how to do was lie.

He laughed, a hearty, throaty sound that traveled up his chest and spewed out into the world dripping with deceit. Then he slapped Xander's shoulder, giving him a light shove, as though he'd said the funniest, most ridiculous thing in the world. "In Taetanos's name, Xander, sleep deprivation is getting to your head. If you're going to talk nonsense, just leave me to my isolation. The only mate I spend my days longing for is the sky from which you've banished me."

Xander didn't move at first. He just maintained a contemplative stare. Finally, he released a breath and the barest hint of a smile rose to his lips.

"Then by all means, back to it," he said, nodding toward the balcony.

The words were strained. Rafe knew it. Just like Xander had known his laughter was fake. There was something unspoken hanging between them, invisible yet all too real.

An awkward silence permeated the air, even after Xander left. It was interrupted by the same scuffing of boots on stone, a swish of fabric, and a soft sigh in place of words. Because there was nothing left to say but—

"Go," Rafe ordered, his voice grave.

"Rafe—"

"Go." A little louder this time. A little more forceful. His body quivered with the desire to turn and face her, but he feared that if he did, all his resolve would wither away, burned to ash by the fire in her eyes.

"Please don't—"

"You're my brother's mate," he said, not recognizing himself in the tone—a flat, cold, unfeeling thing. "And whatever work we had is done. Go. Now. And don't ever, ever come back."

She didn't leave, not right away.

She stood there, staring at him.

And he stood, staring at the wall.

Just when he thought he might explode from the pressure, a rush of air pushed against his back, followed by a cold breeze blowing through the now-empty opening. He turned, rushed to the balcony, and crushed the curtains, closing them so tightly his fingers went numb.

LYANA

It took three days for Xander to finally approach her about the things she'd overheard. Three days of long meetings with the advisors, of appointments with the seamstress, of meals with the queen, of fleeting glances and nervous laughter and her heart leaping into her throat every time they had a second alone together.

In the end, they were in his study when he finally found the courage to look up from his books and say, "Lyana, could I talk to you about something? Just for a moment?"

She'd been standing by the window, looking down at the flurry of activity in the city below. The buildings that had crumbled were already being rebuilt. The street had been cleared. But what had caught her eye were the pockets of color at the base of each spirit gate. The flowers were made even brighter by the monotone backdrop of ebony arches and gray stone, and they were growing larger with each passing day. She'd spent the prior week healing everyone she could, and the people were rejoicing in what they believed was Taetanos's strength. But now the celebrations focused on something else—the upcoming mating ceremony of their god-blessed prince and princess.

His voice jolted her from her ruminations, and she spun. "Of course. What…"

The second she laid eyes on him, the words died upon her lips, because she knew. The moment was here. The one she'd been dreading for days. The one she knew she wouldn't be able to avoid. He was watching her with his head lowered, pale skin giving him away as his cheeks flushed pink. There was a box in his hand, though she could hardly see it, he held it so tightly between his fingers. And there was such a hopeful look in his eyes, hesitant yet hopeful.

Lyana swallowed.

She forced a relaxed smile to her lips even as her stomach muscles clenched. "What, Xander?"

"Nothing, I just—" He paused and took a few steps, crossing the room as he pushed the box into his pocket. Lyana remained motionless as he slipped his fingers between hers and stared deep into her eyes, searching for something she wished were there but knew wasn't. "The ceremony is only a few days away, and I just wanted to tell you— I mean, I hope you know by now that you're very special to me. And to my people."

"And you to me," Lyana replied. The words were true, but twisted, because she knew he would take them in a different way than she meant. He was special to her—so kind and caring and warm and charming, a wonderful friend and companion. But he was speaking of a different sort of special, a meaning she wasn't prepared to give.

"The vows we'll be saying," he continued, tenderly rubbing his thumb over her skin. "I'll hold them closer to my heart than any pledge to the gods I've ever made before. I've spent a lot of my life thinking about this day, wondering what it would hold, who I would share it with, and I want you to know, I'm happy it's you. And I'm happy we got this chance to get to know each other before the ceremony, so that when the vows are spoken, they won't just be empty words, but true and honest promises to each other."

Her throat was dry. Beneath her skin, her pulse pounded, a drumming she was sure he must have felt.

"I—" She licked her lips, trying to find the words, but there was a vise clamping down on her throat. The bookshelves in the room seemed to close in as the windows disappeared, and everything became very dark as her head swam.

Xander didn't seem to notice. He released her hand, cutting off her tether to the world, and reached into his pocket to retrieve the box. When he pressed a button, her vision started going blurry, but it was clear enough to discern the glittering emerald as the lid sprang open.

"I found this among the family heirlooms." He fumbled with the box. Using his leg as an anchor, he held it down with his right forearm and slid the ring free with his left hand. "It reminded me of you. And I'd like you to have it, because... love is giving a piece of yourself to someone else and trusting them not to break it, and I'd like this to be a symbol of the piece of my heart I've given to you."

The words were so like the ones she'd heard Rafe use the day before.

Similar, and yet so different.

From Xander's lips, with Xander's voice, they didn't pierce the way Rafe's had. They were just there, filling space, leaving a sick feeling in her gut as they lingered, growing larger and larger, cutting off air.

He slid the ring over her finger.

The band was slightly too big, and it wobbled unsteadily. Xander folded her fingers to keep it in place. He lifted her hand to his lips and kissed it softly, the way a true gentleman would, lavender eyes simmering so brightly she ached to turn away.

Her mouth fell open. Her lips parted and twitched. Pressure surged up her throat, words that wouldn't come.

He waited and watched.

Now would be the perfect time to give him a little bit of her, to open her heart, to maybe send a sprinkle of warm magic into his skin. Xander would keep her secret, just like he kept Rafe's—of that Lyana was certain. He was too good a person not to. There was even a chance he would still look at her the same way, as though she were the dawn of a new day, the beginning of something wonderful. If she told him the truth, if she gave him that chance, maybe his words wouldn't feel so empty, maybe their vows wouldn't seem so daunting, maybe the future wouldn't either.

But the sound wouldn't come.

The confession wouldn't come.

She'd already given that piece to someone else, and there was no more left to share.

"Thank you," she rasped instead.

Xander blinked for a moment, giving her time to continue, and then he drew himself up, trying to hide the disappointment that so obviously flashed over his features.

"It's beautiful," she offered lamely.

He smiled warmly. "I'm glad you think so."

"I do," she said, to fill the silence. "I really do."

"Anyway…" He cleared his throat. "That was all I wanted to talk to you about, so, um, yeah. I have a few more books I was meaning to review, but I was told by an unnamed informant that you'd been itching to get back into the practice fields and stretch your wings, so I told my mother you wouldn't be seeing her again today. Helen is wicked with knives. She's waiting for you, to give you a lesson, if you want one."

For the first time in minutes, Lyana felt as though she could breathe. And she did, sucking in a long, restorative breath, before letting a real, honest smile spread her lips. "Would this unnamed informant happen to have black-and-white speckled wings and a name that rhymes with *sassy*?"

He laughed softly. The mood between them eased. "A true prince never reveals his sources."

"And a true princess already knows them anyway," Lyana retorted. She stood on tiptoes and kissed his cheek, because it was the best she could do, and something he might not have expected. "Thank you, Xander."

With that small gesture, she turned and left, trying her best to walk casually and not run from the room. She glanced over her shoulder just as the door was closing to find a grimace on Xander's face as he shook his head and mumbled something that sounded awfully close to *idiot*. She kept walking. Once the door closed, she started running to the nearest window and then leapt into the sky.

Though she ached to pump her wings, soar into the horizon, and never stop, she arched gently down to the balcony outside her room instead. The ring was a heavy weight on her hand, so she slipped it off and placed it on the nightstand, trying to ignore the way the emerald seemed to watch her, judge her, as she practically tore the gown from her shoulders and dropped it to the floor, letting the cool air wash over her scorching, itchy skin. Unable to bear it, Lyana grabbed the ring and shut it inside a box, but the weight of watching eyes remained, following her from the room and to the practice yards and then to dinner that night, never relenting for the remainder of the day.

53

CASSI

Cassi was convinced the servants considered her the laziest person in the world, sleeping at all hours of the day, lounging like the queen she wasn't as they tried to work around her. But the truth was that, as the days passed and Lyana's birthday neared, it was just easier to slip into her spirit body and live vicariously through everyone else, rather than shoulder the heavy burden of her lies any longer.

Sometimes she watched Rafe, alone in his room, twirling his twin blades through empty air, a grim line on his lips and a hard look in his eyes. Sometimes she followed Lyana, noting her friend's longing glances outside, the forced smile on her face, the way she ruffled her wings like a caged bird aching to escape. Cassi discovered that her favorite place was a small room at the very top of the castle where the walls were made of books and a warm fire usually burned and a lonely prince often read to pass the time. She drifted along the shelves, reading the spines, hating that her invisible fingers slid right through the pages rather than gripping them, but relieved her spirit body didn't require glasses the way her physical body did. When Xander was there, she'd lean over his shoulder to read the open volume in his lap, though most recently he'd been scanning map after map after map, frustration pursing his lips.

You're not going crazy, she wanted to whisper in his ear like a guardian spirit. The isle was shrinking, slowly over a long period of time, but shrinking nonetheless. They all were, all seven houses. As the magic in the god stones weakened, chunks of rock fell away, no longer held in the air by the spell, falling back where they belonged—into the world below. It was only a matter of time before the damage grew worse, more noticeable, more fatal. Only a matter of time before someone aside from the crown prince of the least respected house took notice.

Cassi kept her lips sealed.

Because it was time her king direly needed.

She'd already found him that evening and gone over the plans a final time. Now it was a waiting game. Lyana's birthday was only one day away. They were throwing a celebration in her honor tomorrow, and the next day was the mating ceremony. More importantly, it was the day her friend turned eighteen. Cassi had no idea at what hour Lyana had been born, so as soon as midnight struck, she would be on alert, waiting for the sign, any sign, that Lyana was the person Cassi knew in her soul she was. Everyone was in position. Everyone was ready. There was only one more stop to make before morning broke.

It felt longer than three weeks since she'd last seen him, since she'd been the one sleeping underneath that ashen wing, since she'd been the one wrapped within those loving arms.

Luka.

Cassi floated over his bed, an odd sensation of both pleasure and pain swirling across her spirit as she watched him with his mate. The new princess of the House of Peace was beautiful, skin like porcelain, auburn wings that glowed amber in the soft candlelight. A small smile was barely visible over the curve of the shale-tinted feathers covering her in her sleep. Luka's face was relaxed, at ease. No creases. Dark skin perfectly smooth. They were curled toward each other like two sides of a heart, a moment she hated to interrupt, but nonetheless would.

Cassi pressed her wispy hand to his brow and dove into his dream. The chaos of his mind was like a calm stream compared to the rushing torrent of her king's, but that was to be expected. People with strong magic dreamed in brighter colors and louder sounds, in flashing sparks fueled by the power, a madness far more charged than that of a normal soul like Luka's. But Cassi didn't mind, in fact she liked it. She enjoyed slipping into the dream as though she were sliding into a cool lake on a hot day, rather than wrestling some beast to the ground.

The image was woven in an instant, maybe because she'd lived it so many times before. The two of them were in her room at the crystal palace, an hour before the sun was about to rise, when mauve dawn shone through the translucent wall, glittering across his ashy wings. His hand was beneath her cheek. Hers were huddled up against his chest. And though she knew it wasn't fair to make him dream this dream when he had a new mate and new life of his own, she couldn't stop herself. She wanted one more morning of waking up in his arms, of feeling like nothing more than a woman, simple and safe and secure, not the monster she knew she was about to become, the monster her deeds would turn her into.

"Cassi?" he murmured, eyes blinking open.

"Shh." She pressed her finger against his plush lips. They widened into a broad smile beneath her touch, but he remained quiet, watching her as though the entire world lived within her eyes.

Had he dreamed this dream before?

After she'd left?

Had he missed her?

It didn't matter. Cassi didn't have the luxury of missing him.

"Don't worry about Lyana."

Soft laughter escaped him. "How many times have you told me that before? What's she done this time? Did Mother catch her sneaking to the sky bridge again?"

He didn't understand.

It happened often when she visited the dreams of people who didn't know about her magic or the dreams of people who lacked magic altogether. Their minds fought to make sense of the impossible, fought to make her fit. Right now, his mind had sent him back into the past, before the trials, before the breakup, before she'd left.

"No," she said, and shifted her hand so her palm held the side of his strong jaw, her fingers brushing over his coarse, dark hair as her thumb stroked the curve of his cheek. "No, Luka. Please try to remember this. Lyana is fine. Lyana is safe. And you'll see her again, I promise. Don't worry about what you hear. Remember my words. Remember my voice. Lyana is going to save the world."

He raised his brows. "Cassi, what are you talking about?"

"Nothing." She sighed, not wanting to push him too far.

Luka would wake up imagining he'd had the strangest dream, but it could be nothing more than that, nothing that interfered with her king's plans. Cassi wasn't supposed to be there, but she couldn't help trying to give him a little hope to get him through the time to come. She owed him that much, at least.

He pulled her close. Cassi let her head glide toward the nook of his neck as her arms clutched his back to hold him as tightly as possible. He pressed a kiss to her forehead. She let him.

"Goodbye, Luka," she whispered against his warm skin. "Please remember."

Then she let the dream dissolve.

She retreated.

Luka's eyes opened when she slid from his mind. He blinked into the night, confused. His gaze darted around the room as though searching for her in the shadows, because that dream had been so vivid, so bizarre, so very real. But of course, it was only a dream. Nothing more. So, after a moment, he shook his head, dispelling whatever curiosities lingered in his mind, and settled back on his pillow. He tightened his grip on his mate and drew her a little closer, taking a moment to run his fingers over her smooth cheek and press a kiss to her brow. Then he went back to sleep.

Cassi fled to the sky and let the wind carry her back to her body for a few hours of true rest. She would need it. The real work was only just beginning.

XANDER

Lyana was quiet during dinner. Even from his seat at the other end of the banquet table, Xander could tell there was something off about her, something not quite right. Her focus drifted to the window. She fiddled with the emerald ring gleaming on her finger. Even chewing her food seemed like a taxing endeavor.

Though she'd met every guest at the table at least once, they were still little more than strangers to her, a fact painfully obvious as she smiled politely while they made conversation around her rather than with her. Cassi was her only true friend at the celebration, an invitation that had cause a mighty struggle with his mother, but it was the princess's birthday and she deserved to have her best friend by her side, even if that friend was a *poor orphaned owl* as the queen put it, instead of a wealthy trader or nobleperson from the town.

From where Xander sat, it was the saddest birthday celebration he'd ever attended. All he could think was, *Thank Taetanos*, when the dessert plates were cleared, because he had a surprise for Lyana, a surprise he was sure would finally put a true smile on her face.

"I'm sorry dinner was so dull," he said for her ears only as they walked away from the banquet hall.

She started and turned toward him. "No, no, it wasn't."

"She's being polite. It was a bore," Cassi chimed, making the corner of his lip twitch with amusement as Lyana tossed her friend a glare. "What? It's the truth."

"It is," Xander agreed and stepped between them, offering the women his arms, forgetting himself for a moment. But before he could drop his right arm away, Cassi took it, resting her hand on the crook of his elbow without an ounce of hesitation. They hadn't spent much time together, not nearly enough for her to understand how much that simple gesture meant. He swallowed quickly before continuing, "But I have a plan to cheer you up."

Lyana's eyes brightened. "A plan?"

"A surprise, really," he corrected.

Lyana stared at him with a narrowed gaze, as though trying to discern his secret. "A surprise…"

At his other side, Cassi scoffed, "You shouldn't have told her that. She's the most impatient person in the world."

"Don't worry." He laughed. "You won't have long to wait. It's just around the corner here, and—"

Xander stopped as light strains of music drifted through

an open window. Lyana drew a breath filled with wonder and dropped his arm, running to the sound, wings fluttering behind her as her feet skidded across the ground. She practically crashed into the railing.

"Oh, Xander!" A warm feeling blossomed as she turned around, eyes twinkling like bright stars as they found him, full of gratitude. "It's lovely."

And it was.

The sight before him.

The look in his mate's eyes, the look he had put there.

Cassi dropped his arm and slinked away, leaving the two of them alone. Yet not alone, really. Half the town was waiting in the open courtyard below, just as he'd planned. All the people they'd visited to give blessings, all the people she'd met who weren't *important* as his mother would say—though they were, at least to him, and to his princess too, he hoped. Oil lanterns were strung across the castle walls, glittering against the dark sky. An orchestra played in the corner. People were already dancing when a hush quickly spread and a whisper grew as they spotted their prince and princess at the window above. By the time Xander reached Lyana's side, she'd already grabbed the layers of her silk skirts in one hand, not minding if they got wrinkled. It was all he could do to take her other hand before she pumped her wings and rose into the sky. The crowd parted as the two of them gracefully made the twenty-foot drop to the floor below. Someone began to clap, followed by someone else, and before his feet touched the ground, a thunderous applause greeted them. His people, happier than he'd ever seen, cheering and hollering and whistling, alive and thriving, with hope of what tomorrow would bring. She wasn't yet their queen, but her presence had restored their faith. Lyana had captured their hearts. And his, too.

Music swelled.

Xander tugged on Lyana's hand, twisting her into a dance. There was a tear in her eye, teetering on the edge, and ready to drop. He lifted his fingers to wipe it away, grazing her cheek, then tracing the edge of her jaw before lifting her chin. Though her smile was wide, there was a shadow in her gaze, one he couldn't quite understand when the moisture in her eyes had to come from happiness. What else would make her cry?

"Lyana," he whispered.

"Thank you, Xander," she murmured, blinking fast as she took his hand and held it firmly. "You're a better mate than I deserve."

Before he could respond or refute her assertion, the tune shifted to something livelier. Lyana's wings stretched as she bounced on her feet, twirling in place, leaning her head back for a moment to look up at the sky. He followed her steps, pushing the questions and the doubts to the place where all his ugliness lay, forcing himself to ignore the subtle confession in her words, something he didn't understand—or maybe just didn't want to.

More dancers joined in the merriment. They formed lines and switched partners, and Xander lost himself in the movement, finding Lyana's eyes through the crowd, watching her bright smile shine against her dark skin, admiring the way her beaded gown glittered in the light. These were his people. That was his mate. And he refused to allow the sinking feeling in his stomach to ruin his good time.

RAFE

He watched from the shadows, leaning around the edge of the roofline. The celebration was happening so close and yet so very far away. Rafe couldn't make out their faces or hear the music or follow the dance, but he could feel the joy in the air, palpable, so rich he feared he might choke on it.

His eyes went straight to the white wings in a sea of black, but that wasn't what truly caught his attention. It was her gown, glimmering as the golden beads and gems sewn onto the tight bodice and trailing skirt reflected the flames.

She was magic come to life.

Her magic.

Yearning seared his insides. Rafe tore his eyes away and rolled over shingles, returning to the darkness where he belonged. No one noticed his presence, just as no one would notice his absence when he decided to disappear—no one except Xander. But his brother was the very reason he had to leave. Rafe was one breath away from making a mistake he could never take back, right on the brink of a line he knew he should never cross—a line he would cross if he stayed.

But when to leave?

And how?

Would it be a gift to simply leap from this roof and soar away without so much as a goodbye? No explanation he could give Xander would suffice, so maybe it would be best not to even try. To vanish into the night.

No.

He couldn't do that.

Xander would fear the worst. He'd worry. He'd go looking for him across all the isles. Rafe couldn't do that to him. Couldn't cause him more pain.

He would find his brother tomorrow, before the ceremony, and say he needed to chart his own course, forge a new path in a new place without the stigma of his past. He'd promise to return soon, promise to write. He'd do it fast and quick, before Xander had a chance to say no.

That was the only way.

The only plan.

Rafe dropped to his back and stared up at the sky, little more than a black blur as his mind whirled, swirling with all the *what ifs*. He rubbed his face and placed his arms over his head in an act of surrender. With his wings spread flat across the shingles, he bent his legs to keep from sliding down the roof. It was mindless movement.

Rafe was somewhere else.

He was the little boy sitting by the fire, playing with toys, as his mother hummed softly from the vanity in the corner of the room, brushing her long black hair, a soft smile on her lips. She'd always seemed happy, content with her life. But had that been the naïve musing of a boy who never realized, not until long after she'd died, that loving his father had destroyed her life? Her station had been stripped. She'd been shunned. Even her parents had turned their backs on her, so decisively Rafe didn't even know who they were. No one had ever stepped forward to claim him, the fire-cursed child who had brought the dragon to their home, though sometimes, when he passed older couples on the street, he searched for some glimmer of recognition in their eyes. Would she do it all again if she knew what her life would be reduced to? Three walls, a balcony so far underground no one would see her if she stepped into the light, and a cursed child who was doomed to repeat all her mistakes.

Given the chance, would she have run?

Would she have turned from his father's arms before it went too far?

Would she have left when she still had the chance?

Or had love really been worth it?

Rafe stayed on that roof, pondering that question, for he didn't know how long. But it wasn't long enough. Because when he eased to his feet and flew back to his room, someone was there waiting—a symbol of the answer he didn't want to believe, but knew in his broken heart was true.

56

LYANA

She was being stupid—so incredibly stupid.

He'd told her to go. To leave. To never come back.

Lyana didn't know why she had come, not really. She only knew that as soon as she got back to her room, the urge to fly had overwhelmed her, and her wings had brought her here. What made her stay were the drawers open and emptied in the corner, the twin blades polished and in their scabbards, and the sack of dried foods thrown at the foot of his bed. What made her stay was the understanding that if she left, she might never see him again.

The sound of boots made her heart stop.

Lyana turned, breath catching in her throat. He stood behind her in the shadows of the balcony, visible through the narrow slit in the curtains, his pale face glowing as it caught a sliver of light.

"I told you—"

"I know," Lyana interjected.

Neither of them moved, as though the line where the rug ended and the stone floor of the balcony began represented something else, something much more difficult to cross.

"You're leaving," she said, not a question.

He answered anyway, voice strained. "Yes."

Ask me to go.

Ask me to go.

Ask me to go.

The thoughts came swift, a strong desire tightening her gut. But she knew he wouldn't ask—and he didn't. She was grateful, because if he had, she would have had to find the courage to say no. She'd spent her lifetime staring at the sky, at the clouds above and the mist below, dreaming of disappearing into the adventure on the other end of the horizon. She'd had many chances to run from her responsibilities, with or without his help, but she'd never done it. Deep down, she knew, her dreams were just that—dreams. Ones that could never come true, not for a princess who would one day become a queen, a woman who had the weight of a thousand other lives on her shoulders.

Lyana took a step forward, then another, until her silk slippers silently crossed the threshold. She drew the curtain to the side and walked into the shadows of the balcony, the darkness of the night, the place where maybe they could live in a brief dream together. Her sleeves were long, but her shoulders were bare, and the cool kiss of evening brought a shiver to her skin. Lyana took a deep breath and looked up.

Rafe met her gaze.

The backs of his wings were already squeezed against the rail. He had nowhere else to go but the sky if he wanted to run.

He didn't.

He stayed, frozen in place, not breathing as she crossed the distance between them and took his hands in hers, letting her magic bubble to the surface so she could feel the spark of their power meeting one more time.

"Let's play a game, Rafe," she whispered.

He released a breath, chest caving in as he glanced to the side. "A game."

"Tomorrow, I take vows," she continued softly as their fingers danced, shifting together, magic sizzling between them, the gold of the sun and the silver of the moon, joined for this brief impossible moment. "Vows I will never, ever break. But that's tomorrow. Tonight, for a few more hours, I get to be free. So, let's play a game, Rafe. Let's pretend we're not in a castle, but a deep, dark cave. Let's pretend I'm a dove with no name and no title, and you're a raven with no past. Let's pretend we have one last night to do whatever we want before the sun rises and the world comes crashing in."

They lifted their hands, palms pressed together. Lyana stared through the glittering sparks, finding that her words had tempted him. He watched her through the starlight their magic created.

"What would you do, Rafe?"

Lyana stepped closer, the bottom of her skirt catching on the edge of his boots as their thighs pressed together. A bright flare passed over his eyes, like lightning in a storm.

"What would you do, Rafe?" she asked again, licking her lips, drawing his gaze to them for a quick, fiery moment. "I want to know, now, because this is your last chance to show me."

At first nothing happened.

He was still, so very still. And so was she, as though her heart had spilled from her chest and dropped to the floor, and any movement she made might crush it beyond repair.

Then a shudder passed through him—a surrender.

His hands slipped from her palms, sliding over the sleeves of her gown, following the path of her arms, until his fingers grazed her naked shoulders, making her inhale sharply at the heat of his touch. The searing path kept burning, slow, steady, until he came to a stop with one hand on either side of her neck, cradling her head. His thumb brushed the edge of her cheek, a gentle, coveting touch, as though he'd been waiting to do that for a while.

They moved as one.

Before Lyana had time to process anything, his fingers gripped her braids, her arms wrapped around his shoulders, and they crashed together like a storm against a shore, inevitable, electric, rough and frantic. His lips were on her lips, then her throat, then traveling across her shoulder as her head dropped back with a sigh. Her hands fell along his arms to his abdomen, feeling every muscle tense beneath his jacket, before sliding up his back. Rafe buried his face in her neck, stifling a groan as she ran her fingers over his feathers. Lyana found his lips again, moving fast then slow, sinking into the kiss because they had one night, one short, stolen night, but she intended to take her time, to make the hours stretch, to let every moment count.

Each one would be their last.

They staggered back into the room, tripping over the curtain, wings pumping to keep them balanced as their lips remained glued to each other. They stumbled over the obstacles on the floor, but not badly enough to break apart.

As they fell onto the bed, consumed by a fever spun by skin and magic, neither of them registered the quiet yet resounding *click* of the door sliding closed.

57

XANDER

He fell back against the wall, unable to believe his eyes.

Rafe and Lyana.

His brother and his mate.

He—

She—

They'd been acting strangely, but he never thought…

Not really.

Not in his heart.

Yet in the back of his mind he must have known, understood the signs, because why else would he have been lured awake by a whisper passing across his thoughts, the remnants of a vivid dream murmuring for him to come here?

Xander's arms began to tremble, true fist and invisible one shaking as something stirred within him, a wild, savage thing he'd never felt before, searing hot and threatening to erupt, a beast crawling from the spot where he'd shoved it, finally spurred to life. All the anger. All the hurt. All the pain. All the awful things he kept locked away kicked and screamed to be unleashed. Fire raged in the center of his chest, focusing his vision until he stared so hard he saw images flashing on the wall opposite him.

Lyana's surprised eyes as he'd slipped off his mask at the trials. The vehement way her palm had struck Rafe's cheek. That faraway, broken look in his brother's eyes. Their bodies entwined beneath the rubble. Her growing excitement. His growing denial. The happiness on his people's faces as they watched him with their queen, cheered for her, celebrated them both. All of it grew, and spun, and flexed, and settled, until Xander was stone, rigid and full of so many conflicting emotions they all cancelled each other out, leaving nothing but an eerie calm behind.

He pushed away from the wall, squared his shoulders, and returned to his room.

But he didn't sleep.

He stared at the ceiling for the rest of the night, wondering if this was how his mother had felt all those years ago, when betrayal had burrowed its way in her chest, carving its mark, and the weight of her duty crushed the pieces of her heart to dust, leaving her soul with an empty hole nothing would ever fill, not even her son. His body turned cold as if filled with ice, but it was better than the fire—easier to feel nothing at all. As the sun began to sift through his curtains,

Xander mumbled the words he'd been crafting all night and spoke his vows, practicing enough times that his voice no longer cracked and broke, but remained a steady, hollow, empty tone to match the numb feeling in his soul.

58

CASSI

Cassi couldn't sleep. Her legs bounced. Her fingers twiddled. Her heart pounded in a frenzied, uncontrollable way. She was acting more like Lyana than herself. Every sound made her jump. Every whiff of magic in the air made her pause. Every muscle in her body was tense and taut and ready to fly into action.

The sign would come.

She didn't know what or when or how, but it would come. Because Lyana was the one they'd all been waiting for. The queen that would save the world. The one who was prophesized.

She was.

Though, to be fair, she hardly looked like a woman of legend as she catapulted into Cassi's room in the soft light of dawn, flying through the curtains at a breakneck speed and stopping dead at the foot of the bed, wide-eyed and in a panic. No. She looked like absolute hell.

Cassi jumped to her feet immediately, reaching for her friend.

Lyana crumpled into her waiting arms. "Cassi, I— I— Please, just…help."

They tackled the easy things first—her messy hair, her puffy eyelids, her wrinkled gown. And though Cassi wanted to tell Lyana there was no reason to cry, no reason for all the hurt, that there would be no vows today, that bigger, better things awaited, she kept her mouth shut. She did as her king bid.

She waited, because the sign was coming.

Any second.

Any moment.

It was coming.

It had to.

59

RAFE

He woke alone, in crumpled sheets that still smelled like her. A single white feather sat on the pillow beside his head, mocking him. Rafe snatched it in a fist, and then paused. He sat up and opened his palm, looking at the now bent and wrinkled plume, and used his other fingers to smooth out the rough edges he'd created. In one swift, determined move, he rolled from his bed, gently tucked the feather into his already packed bag, and sealed it shut.

He was leaving.

There was no other option.

Not now.

Movements hasty, he threw on his leathers and shoved his feet into his boots. The only time he slowed down was as he strapped the blades to his back, sliding the scabbards around his shoulders and between his wings. It was the only part of that morning that had felt natural, had felt right. The rest was rushed and wrong, and the worst hadn't even come yet.

Facing Xander.

Saying goodbye.

Forcing a smile to his lips as he lied through his teeth.

That was the part he dreaded, the part that left his insides in knots.

One step at a time, he told himself. *Take it one step at a time. Walk across the room. Open the door. Go to Xander's suite. Don't think about what to say or how. Just focus on your feet, and on taking one step at a time.*

So he did.

He strode across the room, twisted the knob, opened the door, and—

He stopped dead.

Xander was there waiting, a vacant look in his eyes as they lifted to find Rafe's. Before he had time to gather his wits, Xander stepped past him and made his way inside, attention jumping from the bed to the bags to the balcony, quick, quick, quick, before settling on Rafe.

"Morning, brother."

The voice sounded unlike anything he'd ever heard from Xander before. A shadow with no color, no light, just dull shades of gray. No life. Just noise.

"Xander, I—" But his own throat choked him, tight and void of both words and breath.

A strange smile passed over Xander's lips, as though he

were laughing at something that wasn't funny at all. "Are you leaving?"

Rafe's gaze dropped to the bags on the floor. "I was going to find you first, to say goodbye."

"How thoughtful."

Though the sentiment expressed was meant to be pleasant, Rafe couldn't ignore the ominous undertone, as if on a hot summer day a cool lake hid some silent beast, luring one closer before the kill. He licked his lips as he frowned.

Something was wrong.

Something was terribly, terribly wrong.

"I— I'm not sure where I'm going yet, but as soon as I get there, I'll write…" He trailed off quietly as Xander knelt, black wings expanding to hide his torso from sight as he picked something up off the floor.

Rafe's heart dropped.

"Did you know our mothers were friends once?" Xander murmured, still crouching on the ground.

"No," he rasped.

"Your mother was my mother's chambermaid," Xander continued, motionless. "She knew all my mother's secrets, all her wishes, all her dreams, all her deepest, darkest fears. She was my mother's closest friend. One of the few people who saw her as just a girl, and not a princess. Not the future queen."

Rafe swallowed.

Revulsion curled his gut, self-loathing.

"It's funny," Xander whispered, tone quivering as though

he was struggling to keep it even and emotionless. "How fast things can change. How, in the blink of an eye, someone you thought was your best friend can become a person you hardly recognize, can't even stand to look at or talk to. How fragile unbreakable bonds can truly be."

Rafe's legs grew weak. He wobbled unsteadily as Xander stood, muscles rigid and strong and assured. It was all Rafe could do not to crumble to the ground as his brother spun slowly, holding his left palm open, an emerald ring flashing brightly against his pale skin.

"I'll return this to Lyana," he stated, words soft but perfectly clear. "I'm sure she's worried sick about where it might have gone."

Rafe's ears began to ring.

The world slowed.

The light was too bright and the shadows too dark.

He forgot to breathe.

Each step his brother took to the door made him flinch, but he couldn't move, couldn't speak, couldn't do anything. He was aware and yet not, drowning even as he tried to swim, falling even as he fought to fly, immobile even though every ounce of him wanted to move or shout or scream.

Xander stepped through the door and began to close it.

"Wait!"

Rafe lunged, gripped the edge of the door like a lifeline, and forced it open. Xander paused, glancing back over his shoulder as a violet pain flashed across his eyes.

I'm sorry, he thought.

The words were so insufficient they wouldn't come, too weak to even speak aloud.

There's so much you don't understand, Xander.

But only because Rafe had never bothered to explain, to give his brother honesty or any semblance of the truth.

She saved me.

From the dragon.

From loneliness.

From myself.

In so many ways, she saved me.

It was an excuse—an excuse for a betrayal so deep, Rafe knew in his heart there was no excusing it. The magic didn't matter. Nor did the fact that he'd fallen for her before he'd even realized who she was, and that as soon as he had, he'd tried to keep his distance, tried to stay away.

Because he'd failed. He'd known what he was doing last night, and all the nights before. He'd known, and he hadn't cared.

If he were to be honest, he would do it all again.

Rafe had his answer—love was worth any cost. Even when it was a brief star shooting across the night sky, gone before he could even hold it for a moment. It was worth it. The way she'd looked at him, as though every adventure and dream and desire lived within his gaze—he would never forget it. The memory would burn in his heart until the day he died, more powerful than any magic he'd ever known.

"Forgive her," Rafe whispered. He didn't deserve forgiveness, but he wanted them to find happiness together. "I won't— I won't be coming back."

Xander looked away and left without saying another word.

Rafe stared at the empty spot where his brother had just stood. He stared, and stared, and stared, until his eyes burned so badly, he thought they might bleed. Then he turned, picked up his bag, and left, needing to make one final stop before he said goodbye to his homeland for good.

60

LYANA

"I don't know where it is, Cassi," she shrieked, tossing the blankets from her bed, digging under the pillows, falling to her hands and knees to check the floor. "I have to find it. I have to!"

"It's all right," her friend soothed. "Stay calm."

Calm.

Calm!

Calm was not the word she would use to describe herself, not this morning. Panicked. Heartbroken. Disgusted. Nerves frayed beyond belief. Those were far more accurate descriptions. Ever since leaving Rafe's room, she'd felt off. There was a throbbing beneath her skin, a current making her stomach flutter and her insides whirl, confusing her thoughts and setting her body on edge. Her heart started pounding the instant she woke, and the drumming only continued, steadily inclining, a *thump, thump, thump* that she couldn't ignore.

A knock on the door snapped her back to the present.

Cassi put her hands on Lyana's shoulders, steadying her. "I'll keep looking for the ring. You just try to relax. We'll find it before he gets here, I promise."

But even as her friend said the words, Lyana knew the ring was gone. She'd had it during dinner, she'd had it during dancing, and that was where the certainty ended. Her night with Rafe was both perfectly clear and a dark shadowy mess, as though two different sides of her were at war, one remembering with flawless clarity and one trying to erase her undeniable betrayal. The emerald was in his room somewhere —it had to be. But she couldn't go back, not now. Not in the stark light of day, with the sun's accusing rays burning bright.

As the servants came rushing in, Lyana stood in the center of the room, detached from her body as if she were a ghost watching from the corner as her sleeping frock was removed, her hair carefully twisted, her cheeks rouged and her eyelids powdered. She stared at the mirror, unsure who the figure before her eyes was—the dove princess, the raven queen, a broken mix of the two that didn't seem to work?

Her mating gown was deep onyx at the bottom, shifting to charcoal, then pewter, then pure ivory around the bodice. Diamonds glittered across the wide skirt. Opals glimmered with a rainbow sheen. Pearls studded the top edge, bright against her skin. Her arms were bare. The back of her dress dipped low around her wings, which had been painted black at the edges as a symbol of her transformation. And finally, around her neck, they placed a wreath of her mate's stark obsidian feathers, snug and constricting, like hands around her throat, gripping so tightly she could hardly breathe. Though maybe that was in her head, because in her reflection, the effect was beautiful. Xander's feathers flared up around her chin, framing her face, and then fanned down, covering the bare skin of her shoulders, slightly longer along her back, as if becoming one with her wings. Just like that she was ready to be mated.

Her heart hammered at the thought, so forceful, so painful she feared she might faint.

"Lyana."

The sound of his voice caught her off guard, bringing a gasp to her lips as she turned. Xander stood in the doorway with his arms crossed, gently leaning against the frame. He was dressed in black, a mix of formal silks and smooth leathers, regal, the image of a future king, the image of Taetanos himself. A small bundle of her feathers was pinned to his chest with the royal seal hanging right beside them, a dark obsidian ring that somehow still managed to gleam against its midnight backdrop. His lavender eyes were cold, like flower petals frozen on a winter's day. The sight made her pause.

"Xander," she whispered, half breathing the word, unable to find her voice. Lyana flicked her gaze toward Cassi, lingering long enough for her friend to shake her head in a silent *no*, a grimace passing over her features as her focus shifted from one side of the room to the other, from one half of the royal couple to the other.

He pushed away from the frame and stepped into her

room. She had no idea how long he'd been standing there, watching her, before he'd decided to make his presence known. The servants scattered, doing their best to become invisible as Xander approached.

"I thought you might want an escort to the carriage," he said, his voice scratching like the sharpening of a blade, with something dangerous hidden in the tone. "So you don't lose your way."

A smile spread across his lips, but it was empty, devoid of all the warmth she'd grown used to. Lyana fought the nausea coiling in her stomach and swallowed. "Yes, thank you. That would be lovely."

He offered his arm.

She took it.

They left the room together, walking at an easy pace down the hall, unhurried, yet the air was so tense it urged Lyana's legs to run, her wings to push, her entire body to flee. Xander's steps, however, remained slow and steady—one, then another, then another, on a fixed beat.

"How was your morning?" she asked weakly.

"Enlightening," Xander replied smoothly. "Yours?"

Lyana offered him a smile, wanting to ease the tautness in her chest. "A little chaotic, but as you can see"—She motioned toward her gown—"I managed to get ready on time."

"Are you?" Xander countered. "Ready?"

"Hmm?" The strained sound was the only thing she could get through her lips.

"Are you ready?" he insisted, tone neither light nor heavy,

but with enough accents of both to make her uneasy. "Are you ready to make the vows? Ready to be a queen? Ready for all the sacrifices these promises entail? To think of your people's needs before your own? To do anything for them?"

A soft, uncomfortable laugh escaped her. "Of course, Xander. Isn't this what we've been preparing for our whole lives?"

They reached the door to the courtyard, but Xander stopped within the shadows of the castle. A few yards away, in the bright, gleaming light of the sun, their golden carriage waited, ready to be carted through the spirit gates in a parade that would lead them to the outskirts of the city and the sacred nest beyond.

"Can you promise me, Lyana?" Xander said, taking her hand in his. "Can you promise me that when you say those vows, you'll mean them? For the rest of our lives? That you won't break them?"

There was a deeper meaning to his words—one that made her stomach drop and her heart skip a beat.

"I promise," she said, meeting his gaze and holding it for a few seconds, so he could see the truth in her eyes. The past was in the past, no matter how broken the idea made her feel. There was no Ana. No Rafe. No dreams of different lives and different destinies. Once her vows were spoken, there would only be Lyana Taetanus. Somehow, some way, she'd make sure of it.

Xander dropped his gaze.

His wings and shoulders eased, no longer rigid and hard,

as if they bore less of a burden. He let go of her hand to dip his fingers into his pocket. Even in the shade, the emerald in his palm shone brilliantly. Lyana closed her eyes to fight the sting of guilt.

He slipped the ring over her knuckle.

There was nothing to say.

She knew where he'd found it.

He knew she understood.

Today, they'd be joined before the gods, mated for all eternity, so there was no choice but to move on, painful as it was for them both.

Xander strode into the light, his obsidian wings glistening in the sun, and Lyana followed. They climbed into the carriage together. After a few minutes, they were led into the street and greeted by the cheers of their people as their mating parade began. Petals and feathers fell onto their laps as they rode on a leisurely, circular route through every spirit gate in the city. Lyana smiled and waved. Xander did the same. But they didn't smile at each other. And when she slid her hand across the seat to touch his arm, he jerked away as if burned. The apology churned in the back of her throat, but with so many eyes watching and ears listening, it wasn't the time. Later, after the vows had been spoken, after promises had been made, maybe she would find the strength to explain, to tell him everything, the whole truth, about who and what she was, who Rafe had allowed her to be. Maybe he'd understand. Maybe he wouldn't. But he deserved to know.

When they reached the outskirts of Pylaeon, they

abandoned the carriage and took to the air, surrounded by guards and following the queen, as they traveled to the sacred nest. Lyana hadn't been there before, but she knew the way by instinct, something pulling her there, luring her. The feeling she'd had all day strengthened—the buzzing in her veins, the energy in her pulse, the roar in the back of her mind only growing stronger.

They landed by the base of a large tree. Queen Mariam pulled a hidden lever and a doorway appeared in the bark, an opening like the dark, hidden depths of a gaping mouth aching to swallow her whole. Lyana's body protested, but she followed Xander, mind so consumed by the growing thunder within she could hardly pay attention to the outside world. He led her into the tunnel, leaving the others in the woods to wait for their return.

Now was her time to speak, if she wanted to, but her tongue was heavy and her lips fat. Her mind was in such a whirlwind that no cohesive sentences, let alone thoughts, could be strung together. It was hard enough to focus on Xander and the steps as her legs shook and they walked in shadows for the gods knew how long. Suddenly, light appeared in the distance. A priest stood, holding open a golden gate. Lyana heard the chirping of birds, but her eyes immediately went to the god stone floating in the center of the room, barely visible through the trees, its power releasing a silent shriek that rattled her bones. A vibration shuddered through her, visible enough for Xander to notice as he turned toward her, curious, maybe even concerned.

Lyana blinked, trying to clear her vision.

The lights wouldn't disappear.

They came swiftly, emanating from the god stone, glittering and flickering across the air, shooting toward her skin. The stone was so black it swallowed the rays of the sun streaking through the trees, yet it sparked with every color of the spectrum in short bursts and long bands that reached for her like phantom hands. Her arms quivered. Her knees trembled. Her heart continued to drum faster and faster, more and more loudly, rhythm speeding and growing to match the one pulsing through the stone.

They reached the center of the sacred nest and knelt, preparing to speak the prayers, the first step in the long ceremony that would eventually end with the exchange of their vows. Lyana turned to Xander. He was oblivious to the beat drowning out every other noise in the world and the rainbow spiraling around her, making her dizzy, making the nest swim.

She turned to the priest and stopped cold.

He didn't look like any of the ravens she'd seen. His eyes were a midnight blue, clouded with angry storms yet bright with the piercing fire of lightning. His hair resembled flowing gold. His skin was sun-kissed, and a spatter of freckles covered his nose. No wings fanned from his back, and they weren't expected in a priest, but his robes didn't fit. The hem of silk was two inches from the ground, ruining the belief that those chosen by the gods floated on a different plane. Underneath the robe, she could see a pair of scuffed, muddy boots that didn't belong to the scene. The sight set her on edge, but it was the penetrating expression on his face that made her freeze, the knot in his brows, the tempest in his eyes, spinning as though attracted by all the lights around her, every spectacle of magic —as if he were waiting for an answer only she could supply.

Lyana opened her mouth.

Before she could think of what to say, her world exploded.

61

CASSI

Cassi stood in the dark corner of the room, watching the lone figure on the balcony, his onyx wings draped across the floor, his head hung low, two swords strapped to his back and two bags dropped by his side.

He'd been easy to find.

After so many weeks of watching and waiting, Cassi had known exactly where Rafe would go when his world fell apart. He was predictable, just like Lyana. The only one who had truly surprised her was the prince, with his steadfast loyalty and stubborn inability to see evil in the people he cared about. Manipulating him would leave a lasting scar in her. Exposing him to the harsh realities of the world would be the newest item on her long list of regrets. But there had been no other choice. Xander was the only person who would have missed Rafe when he left, who would have noticed his absence and maybe gone looking. But now, he knew who his brother truly was. And Rafe was alone, the way she needed him to be.

Because the end was near.

The sign would come.

The buzz of magic had been building beneath her skin all day, a current in the air that made her hair stand on end and chest thud. The sky sparkled with hidden static. Anyone with magic—well, anyone with magic who wasn't heartbroken and overcome with despair—would have been a fool to not recognize the signs that something was coming, something big.

And she was ready—ready to be done, ready to be with her king and her queen, ready to be with her mother. No more duplicity. No more lies. Free.

Rafe was her last job.

Her final task.

She stood in the shadows of the burnt-out room at the base of the castle where no one else would venture, deep beyond the line she knew the raven wouldn't cross, hidden from sight.

The bow in her hands was pulled taut.

Her arrow and eye were perfectly aligned.

Still she waited, as she had promised her king she would, for the inevitable.

62

XANDER

By his side, Lyana fainted. Her body twitched, back arching painfully as her spine bent, her arms curled, and her legs dragged along the ground. Invisible fingers lifted her into the air by her hips so her wings and toes skidded across soil and stone.

"Ly—"

Xander was cut off as a force slammed into his chest, knocking him back. He rolled on the ground and crashed into a tree, landing just in time to turn and realize with horror that Lyana's body had begun to glow. Fiery sparks lit her skin, filling the space around her with glitter, as though the air held diamond dust, as though she were a star that had fallen from the sky, as though she were a god stone in her own right, one made of gold instead of deep, deep shadow. He couldn't say how long he remained limp on the ground, eyes wide as he watched her, stilled by a strange mix of awe and terror, unable to look away or speak or move or act.

Then it stopped.

Her body fell, as though the string that had been holding it aloft had suddenly snapped.

Xander jumped to his feet.

The cries of a thousand ravens stopped him cold. Every bird in the sacred nest leapt from the trees at once, a black cloud flooding the cage, the flapping of their wings an ominous roar as they searched for a way to get through the bars that had held them for their entire lives. There was no way out, no escape for those ebony feathers casting shadows in the sun.

The ground lurched violently beneath him.

Xander joined his brethren in the sky as the nest shook, the swish of leaves and the groan of the earth joining the rustle of a thousand wings. Fissures snaked up tree trunks. Branches cracked and fell. Solid dirt crumbled, filling the air with dust, and the god stone quivered where it hung, suspended. At the center of it all, Lyana remained unaffected in an odd mix of peace and pain. The ground beneath her trembled, sending her body this way and that as her eyes remained closed and her wings limp.

When the ground fell still, the priest knelt beside her. A hand emerged from his robes to gently brush her cheek, and a victorious smile curved his lips, elation glowing in his eyes. That was when Xander noticed the muddy boots, the robes that were far too small, and the sun-kissed face.

He dove.

"What did you do to her?" Xander shouted as he crashed into the priest, grabbing a fistful of the man's clothes, pumping his wings and using his weight to keep him flat against the floor. "What did you do?"

The man offered a smile made of razor blades, sharp enough to cut. "I did nothing, raven prince. This is her destiny."

"Who are you?" Xander pressed his forearm to the man's throat, making him choke on a sound eerily close to laughter. "Where did you come from?"

"I hoped it wouldn't come to this, truly I did," the man said with a sigh, as though he were the one pinning Xander to the ground. "But I can't leave any witnesses."

Xander frowned, confused.

Then he gasped.

A sensation like nothing he'd ever felt in his life passed through him, as though a ghost had reached into his chest and latched on to his soul, closing a fist around his heart, stealing the breath from his lungs. A bond was severed, disconnecting his mind from his body. The priest pushed and Xander flew back, wings useless as a wave of pressure sent him stumbling over the ground, off balance, legs and arms no longer responding. His mind screamed to fight. He tried to beat his wings and kick with his legs, but it was useless, like running into a stone wall armed with nothing but the feeble hope of toppling it.

The priest stood, eyes focused and bursting with gold sparks of lightning, then took a step toward Xander.

When the man looked toward the ground, Xander

dropped to his knees. When he widened his eyes, Xander's spine curled and his arms snaked behind his back, as if tied with invisible string. His wings arched above his head, as if in the middle of a rapid descent. Phantom fingers lifted his chin. The white feathers pinned to his chest suddenly felt like a target on a practice field. His heart pounded, thumping against his ribs, because he knew without a doubt this stranger wasn't interested in playing games.

Another man stepped out from the shadows of the grove, then a woman. They stood to either side of the leader, paying him no attention, focusing on the princess by their feet, who was still lying lifeless against the ground.

Lyana!

No sound crossed Xander's lips, even as everything within him ached to fight, his voice trying to scratch and thrash and crawl its way out.

I'll save us! I'll figure this out!

But he couldn't.

And he wouldn't.

Because he didn't even know what this was, didn't even know what he was fighting. And for a brief moment, Xander wished Rafe were there—a desire so intense and so unwanted it burned across his thoughts with searing pain.

Rafe would have found a way to act.

He would have unleashed his raven cry.

He would have used his magic.

He would have done something.

But Xander wasn't his brother. He had no god-gifted cry. No illicit magic. No battle-hardened instincts. And there was nothing he could do but freeze in horror, bound by invisible hands, as the man ripped the priestly robes from his shoulders, revealing a coarsely woven jacket and an array of blades along his belt. A shiver ran through Xander as a small dagger was pulled free.

The man walked forward, grim determination on his face.

Xander switched his gaze to Lyana. Her chest rose and fell. Her mouth parted. One of her legs twitched, then her eyelids fluttered open. Those emerald irises, dazed and confused, found him across the room. A wrinkle appeared on her forehead as she pushed her palm against the stone, sitting up.

I'm sorry, Xander thought.

I'm sorry I wasn't enough.

The man drew back his arm, though Xander barely registered the way the sharp edge of the blade caught the light of the sun. Odd how the mind wandered in that last second of existence, stretching it into a whole lifetime of dreams. He and Lyana speaking their vows. The cheer of his people as they returned, a mated pair, the beginning of a new age for his house. The two of them at peace in their little haven of books and windows, a joining of two different sides. The sight of a smile finally returned to his mother's lips as she held her first grandchild in her arms. Teaching his son how to read while Lyana trained their daughter how to fight. The laughter that would have returned to his quiet streets. The light and warmth that would have filled the dark halls of the castle. And lastly, the two of them, side by side on matching thrones as they watched their heirs fight for their own mates, small smiles on their lips as their eyes met, remembering the pain and confusion and heartache of the early days, and how it had all given way to a life of so much more.

He saw all of that.

Then just as quickly it was gone.

The blade plunged into his chest and Xander fell back. He stared through the bars at the top of the sacred nest, finding trees and sun and open sky, distantly hearing Lyana's scream as his vision grew dim.

Then it faded.

He faded.

Entirely.

RAFE

s soon as the tremors stopped, Rafe jumped to his feet, heart in his throat.

Xander. Lyana.

Were they alive? Were they all right?

He had to go. He had to find them. He had to be sure.

Consumed by panic and fear, he didn't hear the whistle until it was too late. The arrow sank deep, slicing through the wing joint in his back, eliciting a hiss through clenched teeth as he tried to fight the blinding flash of pain.

Rafe spun.

Beneath his skin his magic flared, racing to heal the wound. His eyes were sharp as they scanned the back corner of the room. Was it a guard sent by the queen? He couldn't even articulate the idea that anyone had been sent by Xander.

When his gaze landed on his foe, he slackened, overcome.

"Cassi?" he asked, mouth falling open as the owl stepped from the shadows, bow already drawn with another arrow. All the warmth in his heart turned into a void. There was only one person who would have sent her to do this deed. One person, and he couldn't even think her name for fear it would cut too deep—for fear he would never recover from that dark truth.

Cassi didn't answer, anyway.

She just let another arrow fly free.

Rafe dove to one side, snapping his wings close to his back so he could roll across the floor, gritting his teeth as the wound hurt with the heat of molten iron. He stopped on his knees, crouching low, and reached to remove the arrow still lodged in his back. Again, Cassi stretched her arm, preparing another strike. Rafe whipped his twin blades from their scabbards and jumped to his feet. By the time the arrow was in the air, he was ready, using the edges of his swords to swat it from the sky.

He charged, focus acute and blades blazing.

But his heart wasn't in it.

Rafe stopped before crashing into Cassi, sure he could have used his size and skill to overwhelm her, but not trying. Because it was Cassi. His friend, he'd thought, after so many hours spent on the practice fields together.

"Why are you here? Why are you doing this?"

Cassi discarded the bow and reached for her sword, silver eyes as sharp as the blade in her hands. "It's not personal, Rafe."

He snorted and stepped closer.

She stepped back and to the side.

They circled, locking eyes as they sized each other up in the narrow space of the room. Rafe was used to fighting in open skies and large arenas, where he could fly and swing his arms without fear of obstacles. But this was different. His mother's rooms were modest. The floor was littered with furniture half-eaten by flames. The light was poor. The ceiling low. And already, the air had grown cloudy with the dust wafting up from their footsteps.

"We both know I'm better with a sword," he said, trying to give her a way out of the mess she'd started.

Cassi lifted a single brow, tilting her head. "Do we?"

She attacked.

Rafe jerked back, surprised at her speed. Cassi swung, the arc wide over her head. Rafe met her blow with both swords raised, taking the force of her assault easily. But he realized too late that the move was a distraction. As soon as his blades met hers, she dropped and spun, reaching for a dagger hidden at her back and cutting a deep slice into his thigh. A cloud of dust burned his eyes as she pumped her wings, retreating before he could counterattack. Magic flared, traveling down his body to the gash.

"You lied," he said simply, trying to gauge her reaction. As he spoke, Rafe took a few steps to the left, so his back was to the balcony. The tear in his wing was healed enough for him to fly, he hoped. Enough to get away. "About needing my help with a sword. You lied."

"I lie about a lot of things." Cassi shrugged. The words and the gesture were casual, but a tight gulp followed, revealing a different emotion.

"What other things?" He was buying time to take a deep breath, preparing to release his raven cry. Those few precious seconds of her confusion were all he would need to get away.

"There's a whole world you don't know about, Rafe," Cassi murmured, her gaze flicking over his shoulder. "But you will."

She threw the dagger in her hand.

He had no choice but to step to the side once more to avoid the blade, and now the balcony no longer presented as an easy dive behind him. Before he found his balance, she tugged another knife from her belt and sent it flying. The point landed in his abdomen, making him stumble back into the wall. Cassi swung her blade. He barely had time to lift his forearm and catch the blow with the hide of his jacket, laced with metal to act as a shield. He pushed her away with a kick to the chest and stood, ripping the dagger so his flesh could reseal, grunting as his magic flowed, bringing cool relief to the fire simmering beneath his skin.

But Cassi wasn't giving him time to heal or time to take the breath needed to release his godly cry. After so many hours of sparring with him, she knew exactly how he'd attack and how he'd retreat, exactly where he'd go, as though she'd catalogued every minute of their time on the practice fields, storing it for this very moment. She was fast, incredibly fast as she dealt different blows, fighting in a way he wasn't used to—not going for the kill, not going for the big, debilitating wound, but taking small jabs here and there whenever the opportunity provided, enough to make his magic slow and laborious, stealing half of his attention away.

And she had an advantage.

She fought with heart—with purpose. A fire lit her eyes. Energy reinforced her movements. Determination hardened her gut.

But Rafe was empty.

He was alone. He'd already lost everything. Did it matter if he lost his life, too?

No one would even realize. Xander thought he was leaving, never to return. Lyana had snuck from his room that morning without so much as a goodbye. The queen and everyone in the House of Whispers would rejoice to hear the fire-cursed bastard had finally fled their small isle, disappearing without a trace.

Maybe he was always meant to die in this room, surrounded by his parents' ashes—the spot where he'd first cheated the master of death. Taetanos always won in the end. If Rafe knew nothing else in his life, it was that there was no vanquishing the god of fate. There were only moves and countermoves, all leading to the same inevitable place.

A vicious sense of irony pierced his heart.

Rafe gasped and looked down, surprised to find the pointed end of a sword protruding from his chest. Cassi pressed a boot to his shoulder, crunching his wing as she pushed, sliding her weapon free. He fell face-first against the ground, crashing like a sack of beans whose string had snapped, nothing left but to lie there and blink as he watched his blood spill over the dusty tile floor, ready for the end. She pressed a knee to his spine, holding him down, and leaned close enough for him to feel her breath against his ear.

"I'm sorry, Rafe," she whispered. "Truly, I am. This is going to hurt. But you'll survive. I promise. You'll survive, like you always do. And I hope someday, maybe, you might find it possible to forgive me."

At first, the words didn't register.

Then she grasped the bones of his left wing and snapped. He bucked beneath her, trying to dislodge her as the terror of the truth hit, sending a cold wave through his veins.

This wasn't the end.

It's not personal, she'd said. *I lie about a lot of things. There's a whole world you don't know about, but you will. You'll survive.*

Cassi didn't mean to kill him. She had a plan—one that was bigger than him, bigger than Lyana, bigger than the ravens and the doves and this kingdom above the clouds—and he was the only one aware of her treachery. Xander wasn't safe. Lyana wasn't either. Cassi had been fooling them all and if he didn't escape now, they'd remain ignorant of her duplicity— vulnerable and in danger. He had to fight, if not for himself, then for them.

"No!" Rafe shouted with newfound vigor.

A raven cry hurtled up his throat and Cassi stilled behind him, disoriented by the godly call. With a pump of his right wing, he rolled just enough to grab her arm and throw her from his back. By the time her eyes cleared, he'd snatched a dagger from the floor and plunged it into her side. Cassi gasped. Rafe took the advantage, no longer seeing her as anything but foe, and scrambled to his feet. With his right wing limp, he had no choice but to take to the halls.

He made it two steps before a blade slashed his ankle, severing the tendon, and he fell, forehead hitting a bedpost on the way down. Mind swimming, he crawled toward the door. Cassi launched onto his back and wrapped her arms around his neck to cut off air. He jabbed his elbow into her wound. With a grunt, she released him and toppled to the side.

The exit was close, only a few feet away. If he could just get there, he might be able to lose her in the underground halls, a maze he knew like the back of his hand. If he could just—

A knife drove into his lower spine.

Rafe's vision flashed white, blinded by the agony, and his legs crumbled, useless. Cassi was on him in an instant. He was disoriented, weak, and paralyzed from the waist down. Magic flowed in his veins, but not enough. Though he arched and twisted with all his strength, Cassi held him down. A rope tightened around his wrists, securing them behind his back.

"I've been told this might help," she said as she grasped his hair and yanked his head from the floor to slide the hilt of a dagger between his teeth. Her face was grim, her lips thin, her eyes hard. Without another word, she gently set his chin back against the floor.

When the knife made the first cut into the joint of his wing, he bit down into the worn leather, fighting the pain with pressure, an inhuman sound escaping his lips. Then the second incision came. Then the third. On and on, until mercifully, the world gave way and he slipped into his dreams, going to a place where his mother laughed with him, holding his hands as they danced around her room, his brother and father by their sides, all four of them happy and united, then deeper still, to a small halo of light in an otherwise endless abyss where two palms created starlight in the dark and a soothing voice whispered, telling him to hold on, because this fight wasn't over.

The war was only just beginning.

LYANA

"No!" Lyana shouted.

The world came into perfect clarity as the dagger plunged into Xander's chest. She didn't know what happened, or how they'd gotten here, or why she didn't remember, but her blood sang with power and she knew she would do whatever it took to save him.

He fell back, still.

Too still.

Her head swam.

No.

No.

No.

Her gaze darted around the room, searching for something, anything, then landed on the stranger to her left and the dagger he was wearing on his belt. Without thinking, she tore the blade free and threw it, aim unflinching, focused on the man holding the bloody knife.

He spun.

The dagger stopped an inch from his heart. Just stopped cold, hovering in midair, subtly vibrating. He watched it, unconcerned. Lyana's jaw dropped. The blade did too, clanging uselessly against the ground. That was when she saw the mossy sparks glittering in the air to her left.

Lyana turned.

On her other side, a woman she hadn't even noticed held her palm forward, dark olive magic simmering at her fingertips.

"Don't be afraid," the man who had been disguised as a priest murmured, drawing Lyana's attention back toward him. Her gaze dropped to the body by his feet and the pool of blood already spilling onto the ground.

She was afraid of many things, but not of them.

"Get away from him," she growled, voice throaty, possessive, and beautiful in its ugliness, as though torn all the way from her gut.

Lyana stood, whipping the strangers around her with her feathers as she flew the few yards to Xander's body. Dropping beside him, she expanded her wings to hide them from sight.

"It's all right," she whispered into his ear, praying to all the gods that he would hear her. "It's all right, Xander. I'm here. I'll save you."

Golden sparks flared on her palms, and she pressed them to Xander's chest, sending all the magic and heat she possessed into the gaping hole above his heart. The power came fast, faster than she'd ever felt it before, a rushing torrent she struggled to control as it crashed into Xander. Lyana turned to glance over her shoulder, raising her eyes to their enemies as she kept her hands hidden behind her wings, half her mind on distracting them, the other half on healing him.

She addressed their leader. "Who are you?"

The man dropped his gaze to the curtain her feathers created, a knowing look in his eyes. "I'm afraid I can't let you do that."

Before she had time to respond with feigned ignorance, a violent wind whipped her wings, blowing her over with its force so she rolled across Xander's body. The gust shifted, spinning and spinning until she was caught in a vortex, mind growing dizzy. Through the leaves and the branches and the dust littering the air, pale yellow flashes caught her attention. Magic. Unabashed magic. The power called to her like a living, breathing thing. Lyana pumped her wings, fighting the torrent as she dove behind a tree, using the branches like a shield as she dropped back to the ground. The wind continued to whip her, but with her wings closed and her arms holding on to the bark, it was useless.

The man in charge remained standing over Xander, the look in his eyes daring her to come out of the shadows. The other two stepped to his side, magic flaring at their fingertips, ready and waiting to be used.

"Who are you?" she asked, unable to stop herself.

The smile on the man's lips reminded her of the curved sliver of the moon, hovering on the edge of total darkness. He lifted his hand. Lyana gasped as golden sparks dazzled to life above his open palm. "There is so much to teach you, Lyana Aethionus. So much you don't understand. But you will. In time, you will."

"Where did you come from?"

"You know, Princess," he said.

The gilded aura around his fingers lifted and pushed, crossing the distance between them to shower her in sunlight, a prickling brightness exactly like her own. Lyana found his gaze through the haze, realizing his deep blue eyes were now warm with subtle starlight. "In your heart, you've always known."

Beneath the mist.

As soon as the thought came, she knew it must be true. Where else could they hide? Where else could they live with magic and without wings?

"Why are you here?" she insisted.

"For you."

He stretched his hand like an offering—one she ached to accept. Because she wanted to go. Oh, she wanted to go. She'd never wanted anything more. Lyana had been waiting for this moment her entire life, all those days spent staring at the horizon, flying to the end of her isle, sure beyond a doubt that her destiny was somewhere else, something else. The promise in his words spoke to her soul. To embrace her magic. To leave this life and all its ties. To be free.

But she couldn't abandon Xander.

Not like this. Not dying a slow death in the place where they were supposed to make their vows, supposed to promise each other trust and loyalty and faith before the gods.

"Let me save him, and I'll come with you," Lyana begged, her eyes on the shuddering rise and fall of Xander's chest. If the cost of freedom was his life, she would spend the rest of hers in a cage.

"No."

He offered no reason, no explanation, as though his word was law, as though he was used to being obeyed.

Well, so am I.

"Then I'm not coming. And there's no magic in the world that will make me."

"You *are* coming." The man squared his shoulders as he faced her. "Of your own free will or mine. That's the only choice you have left."

The magic in the air intensified. Lyana watched it blaze, trying to understand. The man on the left had made a voracious wind strike her. If she stepped out from behind the tree, he would simply blow her over like he did before. The woman to the right had stopped a knife in midair. If Lyana lunged for one of the discarded blades on the floor, she would simply fling it out of reach. Lyana was a healer, a simple, pure power she would never trade for anything in the world, but it was a useless power in a situation like this.

Or was it?

The golden aura around her thickened. The man in the middle watched her intensely, his magic curling around her arms and legs like bindings. He tugged on the power and she felt something push against her back, almost as though he were there, behind her, giving her a little shove. Her will to fight was strong, yet her body obeyed the silent command—to go, to follow, to surrender. Her feet skidded over dirt and stone. She walked forward even as she struggled.

Lyana stared at the man's magic, unblinking, unyielding.

It was hers and yet different.

The longer she examined the shimmering tendrils, the more she saw not the rays of the sun, but the rainbow that came after the storm—wisps and specks of every color imaginable, twisting and circling together. A memory floated to the surface, of those same colors shooting from the god stone, wrapping her in its loving arms, and filling her spirit with a power that hadn't been there before, a power that was there now, aching, yearning to be used.

The potent magic stirred within her soul, vast and churning, a deep sea that had once been nothing more than a puddle of fallen rain.

Lyana closed her eyes and took a deep breath.

When she opened them, the world was changed, awash in bright, pulsating colors, a whole glowing spectrum that nearly burned her eyes. She gasped, arching her neck to gaze in wonder, even as her body continued to shift relentlessly forward. The trees were no longer just leaves and bark, but bright green strands that oozed with life. And the ravens hiding in the shadows suddenly glowed with a golden light edged in darkness that followed them as they flew. The sky overhead glittered with yellow and white sparks that crashed and whirled together. The god stone was a deep and endless black, yet shone with a thousand beautiful hues like the surface of an opal. And the three people before her were magic come to life, skin radiant with the power hiding beneath. In the center of each of their chests was a golden starburst, humming with a force she recognized.

Lyana lifted her palm and reached with her magic. These colors that minutes before had been invisible were now tangible. Her magic skimmed the edges of the glowing auras, a gentle graze, a testing, tenuous touch.

The strangers froze.

She flicked her gaze to the man in the center. His eyes were wide, yet hungry. The pressure on her back strengthened, urging her to move faster, to follow. Lyana flared her power and thought, *No.*

She stopped cold, digging her heels into the ground.

The corner of the man's lips twitched with unwilling delight even as his eyes hardened with resolve. His power built up, body glowing more brightly as he readied another attacked.

Lyana acted first.

Instinct took over. She didn't know what she was doing, all she wanted was to get to Xander, to heal him, to free him. To push them away, to give herself time, to shut the world out for a few minutes.

The beast within her broke free.

A wave of blinding, bright colors shot across the room, slammed into the group, and sent them all flying through branches and leaves, into the darkest shadows on the other side of the room so they disappeared from sight.

But it didn't stop.

The magic pulsed and pounded, shooting off her in waves she couldn't control.

She didn't try to.

She let the power flow as she ran to Xander and dropped to her knees, pressing her palms to his chest, trying to find the magic she knew, the magic she understood, somewhere within the mighty force she'd just unchained. Golden flecks simmered by her palms, bringing a smile to her lips, even as the rest of her body erupted in an explosion of color she didn't understand.

Breathe, she thought. *Breathe.*

Heal.

Breathe.

Open your eyes, Xander.

Please, please be all right.

Please, just live. Please.

The aura in the center of his chest was hardly an ember, the last vestiges of a dying flame, but at the touch of her magic it sparked and sputtered, burning with new life. With each passing second it grew brighter and brighter, and that was all she cared about, all she saw.

The earth beneath them trembled. Branches rustled and snapped. Bird cries pierced like bolts of lightning, the beating of wings a growing thunder. Distantly, Lyana knew she must be causing it all, but she didn't care, because Xander's lids fluttered open, a moment of calm in the eye of a swelling storm.

He blinked, finding her above him. "Lyana?"

"Xander," she cried and fell against his chest, clasping him. "You're alive. Thank the gods, you're alive."

"I'm fine, I—" He froze. "I...I was stabbed."

Lyana sat up.

"I was stabbed. By the priest. And you were, you...you..."

He trailed off, attention lingering on her wings for a few moments. He met her stare as silent questions raced across his eyes. But nothing else did. There were no reflections of the storm swirling around her, just a gentle glistening from the far-off sun. He couldn't see the magic raging. But the way he watched her made it seem as if he were in the midst of his own revelation. He sat up and paused, noticing the tremors on the ground for the first time.

With a gasp, he took her by the hand. "We have to go. We have to get out of here."

The rock walls of the sacred nest groaned. The metal bars stretching like mesh across the hollow ceiling screeched. The whole thing was going to topple and crush them.

"Lyana!" a deeper voice shouted across the roaring.

She spun to find the stranger walking toward her through the pulsing power, each step laborious as her magic tried to keep him away, tried to push everything away except Xander. But his own power swirled around him in waves, deflecting the force as he moved steadily closer.

The world dropped out from under her.

Everything plunged for a split second before the ground steadied.

Lyana was smacked hard against the floor. The god stone trembled precariously in the air. But her magic didn't pause—didn't flinch. It continued to come in waves that wouldn't cease, bigger than she knew how to control.

"Lyana!" the man called again, his tone commanding.

She didn't want to see the truth in his eyes, not yet—not until Xander was safe. Lyana spun, finding him among the chaos. He gaped in horror as his sacred nest ripped apart.

"Go!" she cried.

His eyes found hers. "Not without you. Come on!"

He reached for her arm and tugged, but she shirked his hold.

"No, Xander, go." Her voice was soft this time, but he heard every word. There was too much to explain. "Go!"

Lyana shoved her power into his chest. He soared backwards, flipping in the air and crashing through the gate they'd come through, tumbling into the shadows of the corridor.

"Go!" she cried again.

For a moment, he stood still, watching her.

Then he disappeared.

"Lyana," the stranger's voice soothed, as though he understood the turmoil churning inside her and spilling out into the world. He put a hand on her shoulder and she spun, trembling with the power that threatened to tear her in two, trying to keep her balance as the world fell apart around her.

"Help," she said. "Please, I can't— I don't— Help."

He cradled her cheeks. His palms were on fire, just like her skin, scorching with magic, but it was a comfort to know she wasn't alone in the middle of this inferno. He was with her, whoever he was, and his midnight eyes held the promise that he would save her.

"Listen to my voice. Listen to me. Calm down." He lulled her, rubbing his thumbs along her cheekbones, over and over, in a meditative rhythm. "Someday, you'll be able to control it." His gaze flicked away and then returned. "But today is not that day."

Something hard slammed into the back of her head.

She didn't feel anything after that.

65

CASSI

For a long time, Cassi could focus on nothing but the scraping of metal on bone, horrifying yet somehow soothing in its monotony. Back and forth and back and forth. She didn't see the blood spilling over her hands. Didn't feel her fingers begin to stick together. Didn't hear the moans that eventually grew silent. Just the endless *scrape, scrape, scrape* to keep her grounded, in an out-of-body trance, as numb as the knife wound in her side, as if this were nothing more than a dream.

Then the scraping ended.

She threw the knife so fast, so hard, that she didn't even register the motion until she heard it *thunk* into the wall at the other end of the room. Her arms were trembling. Her entire body shook. She blinked and sniffled, fighting for control as her stomach turned over and bile surged up her throat.

It had to be done.

There was no other way, not with an invinci.

He couldn't be allowed to heal. To escape.

There was—

The thought broke off, because she knew in her heart there was no rationalizing what she'd done here today, no making herself feel better. To be a bird without wings was a fate almost worse than death. She of all people understood that, understood the yearning in her mother's eyes to never wake from the dreams her daughter weaved. Cassi had stolen many things, secrets and plans and information, but this was something different, a black mark that would stain her soul forever. Because she'd stolen the sky, his sky, and she wasn't sure if Rafe would ever get it back.

There would be no forgiveness.

There would be no forgiving herself.

But she'd come too far to turn back now.

Hastily, she snatched the severed wings from the floor, unable to look at them any longer. The feathers oozed with blood as she folded them. The sound made her gag. She pulled a rope from her pocket and tied the bundle into a tight sack. Then she rolled Rafe over the floor and onto the balcony, grunting as the gash in her abdomen burned. Her king would heal it later. For now, there was still work to be done. Cassi tied a hasty bandage around her midsection and turned, surveying the scene.

The room was a gory disaster.

Blood splotches were everywhere. Their feet had left arcs across the dusty floor. Daggers and arrows lay like soldiers fallen on the field. There'd be no cleaning this, not in the time she had. Instead, she tugged at the broken bedframe, half-burnt wood groaning as she pulled the monstrous thing across the room to cover the largest puddle of Rafe's blood.

Carefully, she scattered the rest of the furniture pieces over the floor, covering the worst signs of battle, and tossed all the weapons over the balcony. She crouched by the fireplace, grabbed the soot, which made her wet, bloody hands pasty, and threw it about the room to cover her tracks. Finally, she ripped the shredded curtains from the window and dipped her fingers into her pocket, pulling out a small metal flint. A few quick slashes and the burnt fabric lit anew, flames bright as she tossed it onto the bed and watched the fire build. The blaze would wipe out any evidence she'd left behind, and any lingering belief the ravens still held in Rafe.

Cassi glanced at him one final time. "I'm sorry."

The words were more for her, though she knew she wouldn't feel the true weight of her actions until much later, like a bruise that starts to hurt long after the blow that caused it.

She grabbed him under his armpits to heave his torso over the banister. Their bones were hollow, but he was still heavy as she picked up his not-quite-dead weight from the floor. He hung there for a moment, teetering. Then she lifted his ankles, destroying the careful balance that kept him aloft, and released.

Cassi didn't watch Rafe fall.

She couldn't.

She grabbed the bundle of unrecognizable black feathers at her feet and pumped her wings, taking flight, every beat a harsh reminder of the curse she'd just laid upon someone she might have once called a friend.

Cassi tried to focus on the good as she flew—that it was finally over, that she was going home, that by the end of the day the world above would seem like a faraway memory as she showed Lyana the wonders of the world below. Her best friend would forgive her for her lies once she learned the truth, heard the prophecy, and realized who she was. Together they would use their magic to save the world. Lyana would help make Cassi the heroine she'd always wanted to be, instead of the monster she'd become.

From now on, she was done with duplicity.

She was free.

It was over.

Cassi stuck close to the cliff on the underside of the isle, hiding from sight as she maneuvered around the outer edge of the city, only rising above the surface once she was deep in the uninhabited trees and mountains beyond. Cassi arrived at the meeting point just in time to see a tip of white feathers disappear within the hull of a small metal boat. Her king stood outside, arms crossed and alone. The two warriors he'd brought with him, the metal mage and the wind worker, must have already gone inside with the princess, probably preparing to leave. They were all waiting for one thing—her.

Yet Cassi hovered out of sight, behind a layer of branches, as her stomach twisted and a knot jammed her throat, making it difficult to breathe.

Because she had waited for this moment for so long.

So impossibly long.

He would finally see her, the real her. Not the girl she made up in their shared dreams. Not Kasiandra, but Cassi. She looked down. Her trousers were ripped by a knife wound. Her jacket was stained a deep maroon. Her hands were covered in blood. Her face was probably splotched with it, too. She didn't even want to know how her hair looked—and the wings, the wings she'd hidden from him for so long, felt dirty after what she'd done, not wondrous or powerful or strong.

Her king spotted her before her feet grazed the grass. There was no hiding from his magic. She stepped into the light. His gaze darted over her frame, scrutinizing her. Hers did the same, roving over his features, which she normally saw only in the soft glow of moonlight and the forgiving replication of his dreams.

He looked harsher in the stark light of day. A bronze glow from his time above the mist stained his normally pallid skin, but it only served to make the angles of his face more severe. Sun-kissed strands were streaked across his hair, heightening the contrast. What she noticed the most was that the starlight in his eyes had disappeared. They were dark and cold and as impossible to read as the surface of the ocean clouded by a charcoal fog, as though his soul were still back home even if his body had lived a few days in the sun.

"Kasiandra," he murmured, voice exactly as she remembered, sending a quiver down her spine.

"My Liege." Cassi bowed her head in greeting and lifted the package in her hands, the bent and broken wings, trying to find her voice within the revulsion. "The job is done."

His features gave nothing away as he took the wings from her hands with no smile, no gratitude, no recognition. His lips were drawn in a thin line, hard and grim.

Her heart began to flutter, her throat to burn.

"There was an unfortunate hiccup in the plan today," he said, tone even.

Cassi swallowed, trying to calm her frantic nerves. Now that he spoke, she recalled the way the ground had quaked a second time, the way the isle had plummeted for a moment, though at the time, she hadn't stopped to think of it. She'd been too lost in the scraping of her knife to absorb anything else.

Her mouth was dry. The question came out like a raspy breath, "What?"

"The raven prince—he saw too much, and then he got away."

Her pulse took a painful leap. "No."

The word erupted before she could contain it. Because she could read the command hiding behind what he said, revealing what he wanted. She knew what he was asking.

Oh, she knew.

He frowned. "No?"

"I'm going home." She shook her head in thick denial. "I'm going home. Lyana will need me. She won't understand. I'm supposed to be there with her. To help her. I need to be there. I need to go home."

"Kasiandra." His voice could be so alluring when he wanted it to be, just like his magic. She wasn't sure whether she wanted to step forward or whether it was he who demanded it—but she did, closing the distance between them. He put a hand to her cheek. Magic smoldered beneath his skin, sinking into hers and healing her wounds. "He saw too much."

So had she.

She'd done too much—the blood proof was still on her skin.

She couldn't give any more.

"I'm done," she said, forceful this time, finally finding her voice.

The king raised his brows. "You're done when I say you're done."

"I'm not a killer," she snapped and stepped away from his touch, away from his magic, where she could breathe. "I'm not your assassin. I won't be."

"You're not an assassin, Kasiandra," he said evenly as golden flecks sputtered to life around his hands. A fist closed around her heart, one she couldn't see, but the viselike grip was more real than any touch she'd ever shared with him before. Her king stepped closer, so close he towered over her, his power pulsing through the air, making her feel small. "You are a weapon. My weapon. To be wielded any way I choose."

"I won't—"

He cut her off, "You will, because the cause we fight for is greater than you or me or any one person. Our lives don't matter. Our souls don't matter. We're the casualties of a war we have no choice but to win. You will do this last thing, and then finally, you'll come home." He paused—another silent challenge for her to refuse him. When nothing came, his posture eased. "You should wash in one of the rivers before you return to the castle. You look a fright."

Without another word, he left, disappearing in the depths of the metal boat.

But a piece of him remained.

His magic wrapped around her legs, binding them together, gluing the bottoms of her feet to the ground, creating roots so deep she had no hope to pull them free. Cassi beat her wings, pushed and flapped and fought with all her might, but there was nothing she could do.

Her king had stolen her sky.

No. Not my king. Malek. She shook her head, realization like the blow of the sharpest blade. King. Malek. They were one and the same. The boy she loved, the boy of magic and wonder, he was gone. Dead. Reborn into a man she didn't recognize. And she could no longer fool herself into believing anything else.

Malek has stolen my sky.

Something within her unraveled. A bitter, angry laugh seeped from her lips as the metal boat glowed with the olive spark of earth magic. A gust of yellow wind whipped through the forest, diving beneath the vessel and lifting it from the ground.

I won't, she thought, watching the magic gather. *I won't and from so far away there's no way you can make me. I won't. I won't.*

"I won't!" she screamed, refusal cutting its way out of her throat like the edge of a blade. "I won't, Malek! I won't!"

Again and again.

Each time more broken than the last.

Until his name held no more power.

Until the magic binding her to the dirt disappeared.

Until the ship blinked out of sight.

Cassi leapt into the sky, her wings defiant. And that was when she saw the orange glow at the edge of the horizon, growing larger—a dragon, lured to the world above by the irresistible scent of Lyana's magic.

THE CAPTAIN

The day was eerily silent, nothing but the slapping of waves on wood, the creaking groan of a ship long past its prime, the gentle flapping of loose canvas in the breeze. The crew sat alert but scattered across the main deck, attention on a thick fog so bright it burned the eyes. They were waiting, an ominous pastime for a group that had run to the seas to escape its enemies, some real, some imagined.

Then she felt him.

The mist was nearly opaque, but her magic stretched wide, flying with the breeze. His body was like a dagger cutting through the wind, heavy and piercing.

"He's here! Starboard side, raise the anchor, loosen the sails!"

They jumped into action immediately.

She closed her eyes, confident her crew would handle their

part, and pushed back her single wing, letting her muscles flex and feathers rustle as she tightened her hands on the wheel. The canvases snapped and a squall rushed across the deck, magic and air crashing in a wild torrent that brought a smile to her lips. She lived in that tornado, letting it whip her clothes and her hair, basking in that brief moment when the ground fell away and the sky held her in its arms and she almost, almost felt as though she were flying.

She opened her eyes and threw the breeze back across the sea.

The fog dispersed. White tendrils drew shapes in the air as the gusts swirled and twirled around a single falling figure. The blast formed a cyclone to slow the rapid descent, air turning into a cushion, a loving embrace that held him as he dropped gently through the haze. By the time they reached him, he was hovering in midair, a peaceful moment at the center of a storm.

"Ready?" she called.

The crew grunted.

She pulled the magic back beneath her skin. The wind died away. The boy dropped...and smacked against the moist wooden planks of the ship.

"Ten sailors and not a single one of you thought to catch him?" she shouted with a sneer, jumping over the rail of the quarterdeck and landing hard enough to make them flinch. *What a bunch of no-good sluggards!* "Look alive! Fresh water, bandages, and for the love of all the magic in the world, somebody fetch me a bottle of dragon's breath."

They scattered, which was good, because she didn't want

her crew to see the way her fingers trembled as she rolled the boy over and pressed her fingers against the bloody wounds on his back, silver magic flickering beneath his gnarled skin.

Her own scars burned.

The memory flashed like lightning, the sort of pain and terror no time would ever erase. The slash of the knife. The white-hot searing. The scream that couldn't possibly have come from her own throat. The echo of boots as her mother and father walked away without so much as a goodbye. The kick to her back that sent her teetering over the edge. And the never-ending fall, which still gave her the sweats in the dead of night.

Her shoulders writhed.

Her single wing folded around him, half-hiding them both from view. She brushed the hair from his cheek, revealing smooth ivory skin and a jawline that would make the handful of girls in her crew swoon, and hell, some of the men too. But she was sure of one more thing.

"This will not defeat you," she whispered. "It will not define you."

The curved edge of a glass bottle nudged her shoulder. She turned to meet the concerned gaze of her first mate. He'd been with her a long time, long enough to understand the turmoil churning in her icy eyes.

Captain Audezia d'Rokaro snatched the bottle and took a long sip, shaking her head as the fire poured down the back of her throat. It settled like a flame in her stomach, shocking her system back to life. *Dragon's breath, indeed.* She stood and stepped to the side, letting the crew take over. They cleaned the boy's wounds and wrapped him in bandages.

While they worked, her first mate leaned over, arms crossed, focus on the murky fog. "I got news of an attack on the floating city of Ga'bret. A whole district was burned, Zia. Could be the beast we've been tracking."

The edge of her lip perked. "Then by all means, old friend, take the wheel."

THE KING

He cut the necklace of onyx feathers from around her throat and tugged it gently away before running his gaze over the edge of her ivory wing. Unable to stop his fingers from inching forward, he ran them along the graceful curve, her plumes like living silk beneath his skin. Her eyes were closed. Her features relaxed, serene.

Like an angel from the myths of old, he thought, putting his hand to her cheek, holding her the way he did so often in the dreams that Kasiandra didn't spin.

He'd been alone with this burden for too long, hardened by it, molded by it, chipped away, bit by bit, day by day, until sometimes he didn't know what part of himself was left. The boy he used to be, a child of wonder and hope, was gone. Now he was a king—no, not just a king. *The* king. The King Born in Fire. He'd forgotten how to be anything else.

But finally, someone would understand.

He could share the weight.

The pain.

The fears.

The words of the prophecy were as ingrained in his soul as the blood in his veins, part of him, vital and sustaining, providing drive and focus and fuel whenever he needed it most.

The world will fracture, splinter in two,
One made of gray, the other of blue.
Beasts will emerge, filled with fury and scorn,
Fighting to recover what from their claws we have torn.
Two saviors will arise, one above, one below,
A king born in fire and a queen bred of snow.
Together they will heal that which we broke,
With magic and spirit, with mirrors and smoke.
But only on the day when the sky does fall,
Will be revealed the one who will save you all.

That was the burden he carried, the burden they would carry together.

A king born in fire and a queen bred of snow.

The pair foretold to save the world.

To heal the rift.

To defeat the dragons.

To fell the sky.

To force the chosen one forward.

He didn't remember his claim to the prophecy. He'd been nothing more than a babe. But he'd been told his mother gave birth in the middle of a sea of dragon fire, surrounded by the raging flames. They'd been called by his magic, lured to the spot by the power brimming beneath his skin. She wielded her power to keep the inferno at bay, pushing it back long enough to bring her son into the world. And then she tossed him out the window into the churning sea moments before the blaze devoured her. An *aero'kine* waited beneath the waves. He brought the air around them so they could breathe, and there they hid until the beasts flew away. Within days, he was delivered to the king and declared not only the heir, but the one foretold to save them all, a weapon forged from fire to do whatever needed to be done.

What of his queen bred of snow?

Did she have ice in her veins?

He gripped the shears next to him on the bed, steeling his resolve.

You'll need it.

He reached for her wing and gently spread it over his lap, so her primary feathers opened like a fan across his thighs. Then Malek cut, one by one by one, until he was satisfied that when she woke, she would have no hope of flying away.

68

XANDER

Xander emerged from the sacred nest to absolute silence. Eyes fell on the blood staining his chest and then darted to the gaping emptiness behind him, but no mouths moved. No one questioned as he took to the sky. Not his mother. Not Helen. Not the guards. As though something in his gaze had stolen the breath from their lungs, making them mute.

He was numb, still reeling, lost in the chaos of his own confusion.

How have I been so blind?

Everything was so obvious now—so painfully, achingly obvious.

The white feather he'd found on the bridge those many weeks ago? Lyana. The mysterious woman who helped heal Rafe from the dragon wounds? Lyana. The reason for the smile that had been lurking on his brother's lips during their stay in the House of Peace? Lyana. The reason it had disappeared the second they'd landed here? Lyana.

All Lyana.

And Rafe.

Two players in a game he hadn't even known was underway.

But that didn't explain what had happened to Lyana when they entered the sacred nest. Why had she fallen to the ground? Who was that man who had wielded such lethal power? Why had his isle rattled so precariously in the sky? And where was Lyana being taken? Because he had known without a doubt, as an invisible pressure shoved his chest and her shout rang in his ears, that she was going somewhere he wouldn't be able to follow. That she was gone.

Go.

Go.

Go.

The word played over and over in his mind as he soared over the forests of his homeland, back to the city of Pylaeon.

Fly.

Flee.

Go.

Go.

As he crested the ridge of Taetanos's Gate and the valley slipped into view, he stopped dead. Black smoke billowed in the sky. Gray dust formed a cloud over the city. Angry flames enveloped the castle. And now that he'd been pulled from his own mind, he could hear the anguished screams and cries of his people.

A roar shattered the air.

The dragon emerged from beneath the edge, a vision, a nightmare, so familiar Xander could do nothing but hope the beast disappeared, just a dark memory come back to haunt. Suddenly, he was back in his room, a boy, watching through the curtains as his city burned, too afraid to move, too afraid to fight, waiting for word from his mother that it was safe. A boy running through the charred halls of his castle. A boy finding his father too late and pulling his brother from the wreckage he'd had to face alone.

Go.

Go.

The word continued to ring, but he found the voice had changed, no longer Lyana's, but his own.

Go.

Go.

A million moments flashed through his eyes as the dragon landed on the castle wall and sent a blast of flame into the sky, so hot that a wave of heat struck his cheek. Xander letting his sword fall to the grass and walking from the practice yards, looking over his shoulder to realize his father hadn't even noticed he'd gone. Xander sitting alone in the tallest spire of the castle, no company but his books as he watched other children splash in the fountains so far below. Xander putting the royal seal around his brother's neck and disappearing at the first hint of danger. Xander anxiously waiting in the guest accommodations as his brother fought his battles for him. Xander afraid to approach his mate. Xander hesitant. And nervous. And running, always running from the things that scared him.

Go.

Fly.

Go.

Fight.

Go!

The voice grew into a shout that splintered his thoughts. All the anger that had been boiling beneath his skin exploded into a raging inferno. His mind went blank. His vision turned red. For the first time in his life, he let his invisible fist unfurl, releasing all the hate and the loathing and the bitterness he wasn't supposed to feel. He let the darkness take him. He let go.

Xander pumped his wings and raced for his home.

He didn't think.

He didn't question.

He just acted, plunging over the edge of the waterfall and following the path of the river. He had no weapon. No magic. No hope to best the type of beast it had once taken twenty of the finest guards to bring down. All he had was the unyielding sense that if he didn't do something, if he didn't for once in his life face his own demons, if he ran, he would die anyway. And he would rather die a hero than the coward he feared he'd always been.

Shouts for him to stop echoed. Shrieks begged for help. Cries of all kinds littered the air—of pain, of fear, of heartbreak, of hope. He heard them all, letting every piercing wail flood his blood, a fuel unlike any he'd ever known before.

With a beat of its leathery wings, the dragon launched into the air.

They flew toward each other, two enemies on a collision course only one would survive. Xander wasn't an idiot—he knew his odds. Yet he found he couldn't stop, even as the beast grew, doubling then tripling in size as it neared. Fire rippled across its skin. The blood-red eyes narrowed. Razor-sharp claws flexed. The dragon inhaled, chest expanding, preparing for the killing blow. Xander snapped his wings forward and stopped, hovering in the air.

Then he screamed.

It was no raven cry.

No god call.

There was nothing but raw human emotion, guttural and real, spewing from the volcanic pressure of being pent up for so long. But somehow, it worked.

The dragon reared, crying out in pain.

Xander blinked, first in confusion, then in victory. And then he noticed the arrow stuck through the beast's eye.

He spun.

Cassi floated behind him, covered in patches of blood, her bow pulled tight. Her silver gaze jumped to him, holding a deadly intent he'd never seen before. The point of her arrow was aimed directly at his heart. His heartbeat thundered. Her wings pumped. They watched each other across the distance as the world slowed for a moment, then two.

She released.

The arrow flew so close Xander heard the whistle as it sailed by, felt the shift in the air, then the beast behind them howled. A wave of fire slammed into his back. Xander crashed into the river below for protection. By the time he emerged from the water, his guards were there. Spears soared through the air toward the beast, along with more arrows, daggers, and blades. The dragon roared a final time before racing away and disappearing into the sky.

A deafening silence followed.

Water droplets slipped down his clothes, falling on the stone like soft rain. Cassi dropped to her hands and knees, an empty retching sound tearing up her throat. Xander stumbled to her side and pressed her shoulder. Her head snapped in his direction. He realized, for the first time, that her eyes were bloodshot with exhaustion and worry. There was only one thing he could think to say.

"She's gone."

Cassi looked away and swallowed, visibly choked up. Though she tried to hide it, a tear leaked from the corner of her eye and traveled over the contour of her cheek before dropping to the ground.

The sight was his undoing. Xander wrapped the owl in his arms, because he had so many questions and so few answers, but this one problem he knew how to solve. At first, she stiffened, so tense he almost pulled away. But after a moment, her arms closed around him, clasping tightly, as though he were the last bit of life she could hold on to.

"It's all right," he soothed. "Let it go. Let it out. I'm here. You're safe in my home. Always."

She didn't cry, or sob, or fall apart.

But she didn't let go either.

She clung to him as her body silently shook and a torrent of feeling was unleashed, something deeper than he understood, but he didn't have to understand. He just had to be there to hold her through it, to be strong as she clutched him for support—because in truth, the embrace was as much for him as it was for her. Her arms were a comfort he wasn't ready to lose. Not yet. Not when he'd never felt more alone.

No mate.

No brother.

As he watched the crowd around them gather, Xander couldn't help but notice the silent question in his people's eyes, the way their gazes darted to the sky searching for their future queen, then to the destruction caused by the dragon, then to their prince. The streets were still covered in a fine layer rose petals and feathers, but now they were also covered in splatters of blood and broken bits of stone. Whispers filled the quiet. He didn't need to hear them to know exactly what was being said.

Dragon.

Fire cursed.

Where's the princess?

Where's the bastard?

He took her.

He stole her.

Worst of all, there was a wary shadow as they looked at Xander, something he'd never seen before—dark and dangerous doubts wondering why he hadn't saved her. Wondering if the fire god had claimed him, too. Wondering if their crown prince was still their savior.

His mother's words came back to haunt. *Frightened gossip has the power to bring a kingdom to its knees.*

Xander shut his eyes.

He didn't want to see, didn't want to hear.

He buried his head in Cassi's neck.

"We'll get her back," he murmured as they clutched each other, the center of a growing audience, but for the moment in their own private world.

We'll get them back.

Rafe. Lyana.

He'd find them.

He'd make everything right.

He'd get the answers he needed.

Who that man was. Where he'd come from. What he wanted.

We'll get them back.

We'll get them back.

I promise.

~

ABOUT THE AUTHOR

Bestselling author Kaitlyn Davis writes young adult fantasy novels under the name Kaitlyn Davis and contemporary romance novels under the name Kay Marie.

Always blessed with an overactive imagination, Kaitlyn has been writing ever since she picked up her first crayon and is overjoyed to share her work with the world. When she's not daydreaming, typing stories, or getting lost in fictional worlds, Kaitlyn can be found indulging in some puppy videos, watching a little too much television, or spending time with her family.

Connect with the Author Online:

Website: KaitlynDavisBooks.com
Facebook: Facebook.com/KaitlynDavisBooks
Twitter: @DavisKaitlyn
Instagram: @KaitlynDavisBooks
Goodreads: Goodreads.com/Kaitlyn_Davis
Bookbub: @KaitlynDavis